"Fred Pohl is better than ninety percent of SF, a no-lose proposition."

—*Locus*

"There's been a rather surprising new development," said the deputy director. "We just received a new transmission from Starlab."

Pat caught her breath. "Do you think it's from the extraterrestrials?"

"Not this time," he said somberly, studying Dan. "It was from a human being. He said there were a bunch of people up there in orbit. He said they were going to come back to Earth in the orbiter's Assured Crew Return Vehicle, the emergency vehicle that's supposed to—"

"I know what it's supposed to do," Dan snapped.

"Yes. Well. Of course, we didn't believe him at first. So we checked his voice print, and by God he was right. The funny thing about it, Dannerman, is this guy on Starlab said he was you."

"Pohl writes a cozy, intimate prose, almost like someone we haven't seen for a few years showing up to sit in our living room and over coffee tell us what's been happening. Somehow, in this matter-of-fact approach, he gets across the vastness of his cosmological musings. And he leaves you thinking. Even after the last page is read, we are left mulling over the questions he asks and, like the best of any literature, they are not all comfortable questions. Some of them are outright disturbing."

—*Science Fiction Age* on *The Other End of Time*

BOOKS BY FREDERIK POHL

Bipohl
  The Age of the Pussyfoot
  Drunkard's Walk
  Black Star Rising
  The Cool War

The Heechee Saga
  Gateway
  *Beyond the Blue Event
    Horizon*
  Heechee Rendezvous
  *The Annals of the
    Heechee*
  The Gateway Trip

The Eschaton Sequence
  *The Other End of Time
  *The Siege of Eternity

Homegoing
Mining the Oort
Narabedla Ltd.
Pohlstars
Starburst
The Way the Future Was
  (memoir)
*The World at the End of
  Time*
Jem
Midas World
Merchant's War

*The Coming of the
  Quantum Cats*
The Space Merchants (with
  C. M. Kornbluth)
Man Plus
Chernobyl
*The Day the Martians
  Came*
Stopping at Slowyear
*The Voices of Heaven

With Jack Williamson:
  The Starchild Trilogy
  Undersea City
  Undersea Quest
  Undersea Fleet
  Wall Around a Star
  The Farthest Star
  *Land's End
  The Singers of Time

With Lester del Rey:
  Preferred Risk

The Best of Frederik Pohl
  (edited by Lester del Rey)
*The Best of C. M.
  Kornbluth*
  (editor)

*denotes a Tor Book

FREDERIK POHL

POHL

THE
SIEGE OF ETERNITY

With affection and gratitude this book is dedicated to my shipmates on the schooner *Rembrandt van Ryjn,* who know why.

THE SIEGE OF ETERNITY

Edited by James Frenkel

A Tor Book
Published by Tom Doherty Associates, Inc.
175 Fifth Avenue
New York, NY 10010

Tor Books on the World Wide Web:
http://www.tor.com

Tor® is a registered trademark of Tom Doherty Associates, Inc.

ISBN: 0-812-57766-3
Library of Congress Card Catalog Number: 97-15567

First edition: November 1997
First mass market edition: October 1998

Printed in the United States of America

0 9 8 7 6 5 4 3 2 1

BEFORE

The world was going about its everyday business when something happened that was quite strange.

For one part of the world, that everyday business it was going about amounted to nothing more than watching its television screens. Some of the world's people gazed at a prizefight in Kenya, some watched cop shows and soap operas in the Americas, a tiny fraction sat somnolent before the finals of the English National snooker matches. When those programs were interrupted for a news bulletin that part of the world was seriously annoyed.

The bulletin that interrupted their programs quickly made the viewers forgive the annoyance—at least, it did for that fraction of those viewers who believed it was real. The bulletin said that a genuine message from space had been received on a seldom-used radio frequency. Most of the message was indecipherable. A small portion was easier to decode and it turned out to be a crude form of video. Before long the simple animated drawing it displayed filled all the world's screens.

The animated sequence started with a dark screen, except for one tiny pinpoint of intense brilliance. Then that spot exploded. Smaller, less brilliant spots of light flew in all directions. That runaway expansion gradually slowed. Then it stopped entirely and reversed itself as all the spots, first slowly, then at increasing velocity, fell back to the center of the screen.

That was it. That was all there was.

As entertainment, it was pretty poor stuff. But, after

all, it did come from some off-Earth source. The people at the radio telescopes were sure of that; so the scientists and the newsmakers began to try to figure out what the cartoon meant. Their best guess was that it represented a condensed account of the life of the universe: beginning in the Big Bang, expanding as far as that original impetus would carry it, then recollapsing into the Big Crunch as everything fell back together again. So said the pundits. But not even they could think of any good reason why some extraterrestrials would want to tell the human world about it.

However, that wasn't the end of it. A few months later there was another of the same. This one was somewhat more interesting, too. It had people in it—well, sort of people, at least, though they were not in any way human ones.

This second message ran a little longer than the first. It started with that same old birth-and-death-of-the-universe bit, only this time a figure then appeared. The figure looked either comical or terrifying, depending on how seriously you took it. The creature depicted was as skinny as a scarecrow, and it had a head with a wide, toothed mouth that grinned like a Halloween pumpkin. Its "hands" were a forest of fingers, at least a dozen of them on each side; each digit ended in a menacingly sharp talon, and what the creature was doing with them was pitilessly crushing the bright coal that had been the universe. It wasn't alone, either. Around it appeared seven other, smaller figures, each one uglier than the next. One had a beard. One had a stupid smile. One had half-closed eyes. All were perfectly hideous, by the standards of any ethnic group on Earth.

That was it. A moment later the picture winked out. All that was left was the attempts of the world's savants (and some of the world's nonsavants, who played it for laughs) to figure out what it was all about.

Some people, especially the people who made their

living as the world's stand-up comics, took it to be a joke. It didn't take some of the comedians very long to identify the scarecrow as the one from Oz, and not much longer than that to give identities to the seven others. They mixed up their children's classics, to be sure. But the one with the beard they called Doc, the dumbly smiling one Dopey, the drowsy-eyed one Sleepy: why, they were the Seven Ugly Space Dwarfs, though there was no Snow White anywhere to be found.

Not everyone was amused. The world's terrorist crazies were getting particularly active around then, and some people thought the message might have something to do with that. Others took it to be a warning of some modern-day Armageddon about to happen, or perhaps an advance notice of the Second Coming of Christ.

It wasn't any of those things, though. As it turned out, it was a whole lot worse.

CHAPTER ONE

Uptown traffic was terrible and there was an abandoned vehicle on the Henry Hudson Elway at Sixty-first Street that everybody was afraid to approach until the bomb squad got there. Colonel Morrisey's driver had to detour all the way over to Broadway. It was snowing enough to slow everyone down, and the traffic went from terrible to worse.

---

10 A.M. Traffic Advisory

The New Jersey Turnpike is mined between Exits 14 and 15 southbound. One lane is open during mine-removal activities.

An abandoned car, presumed booby-trapped, is in the northbound Henry Hudson Elevated Highway at Sixty-first Street and traffic is diverted.

The Lenni-Lenape Ghost Dance Revengers have declared a free-fire zone within four hundred meters of the World Trade Center from 4:00 to 4:30 P.M. today.

No other warnings currently in effect.

Fortunately they wouldn't be coming back that way, because a plane would be waiting near the yacht basin on the river. But the woman who was on her way to arrest, or rearrest, her favorite agent was getting short-tempered. Her name was Hilda Jeanne Morrisey. She had kept that name unchanged all her life, even through her two marriages—both of them brief, ancient and (as she now thought) pretty damn stupid, since there were so many less troublesome ways of having sex. Hilda Morrisey stood a hundred and sixty centimeters tall and weighed fifty kilograms, give or take a kilo or so. That weight also had not changed since her long-ago days as a police cadet, although it was true that it seemed to take more and more effort to keep it so. Her rank in the National Bureau of Investigation was full colonel. It had taken a lot of work on her part to keep that unchanged, too. Colonel Morrisey was long overdue for the promotion that the Bureau's higher brass kept trying to force on her.

The thing about that promotion wasn't that Hilda Morrisey objected to either the higher pay or the higher rank. What she minded was the consequences. Being promoted one step higher would automatically move her to a desk in the NBI headquarters in Arlington, Virginia, and Hilda hated desk jobs.

The place where she felt at home was in a communications truck in, say, Nebraska, commanding a raid on their rad-right religious militias, or flying high over the Sea of Marmara to listen to the furtive, coded reports of the agent she had run into the Kurdish command post somewhere on the slopes of Mt. Ararat. Or, for that matter, her present assignment in New York, which was recruiting bilingual Japanese-Americans to penetrate the car factories in Osaka, who were apparently violating the trade agreements by using New Guinea–made parts in their allegedly all-Japanese cars.

Anywhere, in short, but in a desk job. A brigadier's star was hers by right of seniority, but accepting it would cost her all those fun jobs. True, Bureau policy was "Up or Out," but not for Hilda. She had been beating that rule for years. When the personnel people got too antsy about her status they always had to buck the question up to the director himself. Who always said, "Hilda won't take Up, and she's just too damn good for Out. Give the silly bitch another waiver." And they always did.

The other thing about Colonel Hilda was that, even

at never-mind-how-old, she was still a pretty neat-looking woman—which is to say one who had very little trouble in attracting any man who attracted her. Like, for instance, the man friend of the moment, Wilbur Carmichael, who—once this distasteful job was complete—she had every intention of giving a call that evening.

But the other thing about those jobs she liked so well was that every once in a while they had a bad spot. Like the present one, which required her to do something she really hated, namely to arrest—or rearrest—one of her own.

When they reached the corner of Jim Daniel Dannerman's block Sergeant McEvoy had to slam on the brakes to avoid hitting the overflow from a minor riot going on. Two sidewalk vendors were having an argument in the snow. It had gotten violent. Punches were being thrown, and one of them had overturned the other's tray of inflation-beating collectibles. Tarot cards and genuine guaranteed simulated Confederate currency were all over the sludgy, gray-black snow at the curb. The bystanders had joined in, and two street cops were doing their best to cool everybody down. When they caught sight of Master Sergeant McEvoy's uniform they hastily cleared a path for the Bureau van.

In front of Dannerman's apartment building Hilda unbuckled herself and looked over at the sergeant. "Target status?"

Sergeant McEvoy already had his head down over his instrument panel. "He's back in his room. He got himself one of those gyro sandwiches at the place on the corner and took it back to his room to eat."

"I hope he eats fast," Hilda said, stepping out into wet slush.

A little man was waddling hastily toward her. He wore a fleece jacket, a wool cap and an armband that said *Neighborhood Watch* and he was shaking, of all things, a golf club at her. A golf club! Obviously one of those nuts who had some sort of airy-fairy objection to carrying a gun like everybody else. He was belligerent enough for anybody, though. "Move it, lady!" he barked. "No double-parking today; you got to leave room for the plows to get through." Then, as he caught sight of the sergeant stepping out of the other side of the van—Sergeant Horace McEvoy, in full Federal Police Force uniform, big as a house and with his hand on the butt of his shotgun, the man added, "Oh." He didn't look impressed. He just looked surly, but he backed out of the way.

As Hilda got out of the elevator on Dannerman's floor she saw the landlady peeking at her out of one of the rooms. Clearly the woman recognized Hilda Morrisey. She didn't say anything, though she was looking surly, too.

The colonel let herself into Dannerman's room with her own key, and caught him in the act of taking off his wet socks. He was sober, if unshaved. He didn't look like the agent she had commanded through a dozen tough assignments, but then no one could look like an agent when he was wearing a house-arrest radio collar. "Oh, shit, Hilda," he said, wearily but unsurprised. "Don't you ever knock? I could've been doing something private."

"You don't have anything private anymore, Danno," she told him. "Did you sign that release yet?"

He touched his spy collar. "You know damn well that I didn't."

She nodded, since it was the truth, but only said, "Then put your socks back on. They want you in Arlington. You can eat your lunch on the plane."

Dannerman didn't ask any questions—not in his room, not in the car that took them to the VTOL pad by the river, not on the way to Arlington. He chewed away at his cold and congealing lamb sandwich with full attention. He didn't even ask for anything to drink with it. When the sandwich was all swallowed and its paper wrappings neatly stowed in the seat back, Dannerman closed his eyes. He kept them that way until the plane circled the Washington Monument, preparing to set down at the Bureau's pad across the Potomac. Colonel Morrisey approved. It was precisely the way she would have comported herself if, unimaginably, she had ever found herself in his position.

Hilda Morrisey was as fond of Dannerman as she ever let herself get of any of the field agents she was charged to run. She certainly didn't *spoil* them, but they were—well—family. As long as they remembered that she was the head of their family, with the power to punish or, occasionally, reward, Hilda gave them her unflinching support and even a little bit of as much as she had to give in the way of affection. Dannerman, now, had had quite a lot of both. The man was often a pain in the ass, and irritatingly likely to go off on tangents of his own, and at such times he needed to be brought back in line. But he generally got the job done.

Hilda's affection for Dan Dannerman wasn't sexual. At least it wasn't exactly sexual, though at rare times when she had nothing better to do she had let herself daydream a little about Danno as a stud. She certainly wasn't sexually jealous of him. She knew that he was currently banging some actress in that little theater group in Coney Island he played around with, plus God knew how many other previous women, now and then, when he was out in the field—well, God knew, but He wasn't the only one who knew. So did Hilda, because it was her business to know that sort of thing. She had sometimes even felt a little hostility toward the other women she knew Dannerman bedded, like that Kraut terrorist bimbo who had put him in the hospital. Hilda had to admit she'd enjoyed putting the cuffs on that one.

Federal Reserve Inflation Bulletin

The morning recommended price adjustment for inflation is set at 0.37%, reflecting an annualized rate of 266%. Federal Reserve Chairman Walter C. Boettger predicts continuing moderation in the inflation rate for the next sixty days.

But it didn't pay to think that way about Dan Dannerman. Not only could she not afford to get sexually involved with anyone in that much deep shit, but he was her property. The Bureau had strict rules about that. And so did she.

Dannerman opened his eyes at last when the sound of the plane's engines changed. They were switching to hover mode; they had arrived. While the plane was depositing itself on the landing pad by the three-story structure that was the visible part of the Bureau's headquarters, Hilda peered outside. Three people were waiting in the cold drizzle. It wasn't until they were out of the aircraft and Sergeant McEvoy and the two headquarters guards were hustling Dannerman away that Hilda realized that the third of the waiting men, his face obscured by the rain hood, was Deputy Director Marcus Pell himself.

Pell didn't offer to shake hands, and Colonel Morrisey didn't bother to salute. "Good to see you again, sir," she said, electing to be a little more deferential than usual. "Now, unless you've got something you need me here for, I guess I'll just catch the return flight."

He gave her the smile she specially disliked, the one that said he was about to give her an order she didn't want to hear. "Not today, Hilda. I want you to sit in on the Ananias team briefing before we interrogate your boy again."

"Sir! I've got this Japanese car-parts thing—"

"Screw the Japanese car parts. Don't look so unhappy; we've got some lunch for you, if you haven't eaten yet? Fine. Let's go."

There was no use arguing, but she hesitated. "What about Dannerman?"

"Well, what about Dannerman? He can sweat for a while. Do him good."

The Operation Ananias team had expanded since the last time Hilda visited Arlington. A dozen people waited in the deputy director's private briefing room, half of them strangers. As promised there was a small salad and a plate of sandwiches at each place on the blond-oak table, and big ceramic coffee jugs scattered handily about. Some people were eating, and that was good enough for her. As soon as she was seated she began to follow their example.

The deputy director, in no hurry to get started, was thoughtfully sipping at a cup of coffee while keying through his notepad. The men and women around the table were murmuring to each other or staring into space—except for the woman across the table, who was signaling for Hilda's attention. It was Pell's vice deputy, Daisy Fennell. She was pretending to scribble with one hand on the palm of the other, looking at Hilda with a questioningly raised eyebrow. Hilda got the message. She shook her head: no, Dannerman hadn't signed. Fennell pantomimed a sigh of resignation and went back to her own notepad.

Hilda chewed methodically (lettuce crisp, good; but whoever had had the idea of putting fruit-flavored dressing on it needed reeducation) as she sorted out the people on the team. The screen ID'd the civilians at the table for her and the Bureau personnel were mostly easy: Daisy Fennell, two of the staff psychologists, the elderly Asian woman who was in charge of electronic operations. That left one she couldn't quite place; a Bureau man, she was sure, but what was his specialty?

She got no help from Marcus Pell, either. As he refilled his coffee cup, he said, "Might as well get going. All you Bureau people know each other, of course, and I guess the rest of you have introduced yourselves around already. The colonel here is Hilda Morrisey, who has been Agent Dannerman's keeper. Hilda, this is Dr. Xiang-li Hou, from the Naval Observatory—" And he went around the table, repeating what the screen had already said. The stout black woman in the paisley dress turned out to be a cerebrospinal surgeon from Walter Reed; the two youngish women with the careworn looks were legislative liaison from, respectively, the Senate and the House, and one of them, surprisingly, had her senator sitting next to her: Alicia Piombero, the black woman from Georgia. (Not the worst of the senators, Hilda knew, but still the enemy: the damn Congress was always trying to mess around in Bureau business.) The aggressively trim-looking man with the obvious hair transplant was a brigadier general from the Pentagon; the one who looked like a prosperous corporation lawyer was. Was some kind of a lawyer, at least, though his specialty wasn't given. He wasn't a bad-looking man, though. He might almost have been a somewhat older edition of Wilbur Carmichael, whom—Hilda glanced at her watch—if this damn meeting ever got itself over with, she might still get a chance to see that evening.

She looked up at Pell as he finished. "So now we all knew each other, and I'd like to thank all of you from outside the Bureau for volunteering your time to—I beg your pardon, Dr. Evergood?"

Morning Report
To all National Bureau of Investigation units
Subject: Current terrorist alerts

Welsh Nationalist Dawid ap Llewellyn, sought in connection with the British Museum firebombing, has been reported in Mexico City, presumed en route to a United States destination. Scotland Yard requests Bureau assistance in apprehending this fugitive.

The Rocky Mountain Militia Command deadline for amnesty for convicted assassins in federal custody expired at midnight. The threatened release of anthrax agents in the Missoula, Montana, water supply has not occurred, but emergency measures are still in force.

All standing alerts remain in effect.

The surgeon had raised her hand. "I said, 'Who volunteered?' It was put to me as an order."

"Which makes us even more grateful to you, Dr. Evergood," the deputy director said, smiling tolerantly. "What we're here for is a matter that urgently affects the national interest. You probably know some of the background, but I'm going to ask Vice Deputy Fennell to fill in some of the details. Daisy?"

The vice deputy didn't miss a beat. "You all remember the messages from space that came in two years ago. Many people thought they were a hoax. A few did not. One of those was an astronomer named Dr. Patrice Adcock, head of the Dannerman Observatory in New

York City, who believed they came from an abandoned astronomical satellite called Starlab. Dr. Adcock, by the way, is on the premises and you will be seeing her later."

Hilda suppressed a grin as she translated for herself: what "on the premises" meant, of course, was "in one of our confinement cells." Daisy Fennell was as slick as the deputy director himself; she had come a long way since she was Hilda's own field manager, back when Hilda was a junior agent and the quarry of the moment was the man who had placed a bomb in the Smithsonian. And Daisy hadn't aged very much in the process. She hadn't gained a gram, and, Hilda observed, hadn't touched her sandwiches, either.

"Dr. Adcock," the V.D. was going on, "discovered some astronomical evidence that an unidentified object had entered our solar system and conjectured that it had dropped a probe which attached itself to the Starlab satellite." She glanced at the man from the Naval Observatory. "Dr. Hou?"

The astronomer stirred himself. "Yes. At Mr. Pell's request I made a study of that comet-like object. The data are sparse but consistent with what you just described, although I saw no probe being dropped."

"Neither did Dr. Adcock," Daisy agreed, "but she came to believe that one had been, and that there might be some sort of extraterrestrial technology on Starlab. So she asked the space agency to provide her with a spacecraft to visit the satellite, ostensibly with the purpose of repairing it and putting it back in service; she believed she had the right, under the original contract when Starlab was launched. The space agency was unable to grant her request—"

The translation of that, Hilda knew, was *we leaned on them* to slow her down until we found out what the hell she was up to.

"—because, among other reasons, no American

space pilots were available. However, Dr. Adcock recruited two other pilots: one was a Floridian, General Martín Delasquez, the other a Chinese national, Commander James Peng-tsu Lin. She obtained a court order requiring the agency to provide a Clipper spacecraft to carry out the mission. In addition to herself and the two pilots, she had obtained the services of a Ukrainian national, Dr. Rosaleen Artzybachova, an instrument specialist who had helped design Starlab in the first place; Dr. Artzybachova was to go along to study Starlab's present instrumentation."

The V.D. paused. "At this point," she said, "the Bureau had become aware that Dr. Adcock's purpose was not to repair the satellite, but to see if there was indeed some alien technology now present on it, which she conjectured might be worth a lot of money."

Marcus Pell held up his hand; now that they were coming to the good part he was taking over. "Which it damn well would be, of course. As well as being of great national interest to this country. So we took a hand. We arranged for one of our agents, James Daniel Dannerman, to go with her. This is not public information, and I caution you all not to discuss it with anyone outside this team. Go on, Daisy."

"So," she said, "the five of them—Adcock, the two pilots, Artzybachova and our agent—launched to the orbiter and came back. They reported that nothing had changed—no alien technology—and the satellite was not repairable. And that seemed to be the end of it."

She looked inquiringly at the deputy director, who nodded. "That's when it got hairy," he said. "Dr. Artzybachova was ill when they landed, I guess because of the stress of the trip—she was, actually, a very old lady. She returned to her home, near the city of Kiev, Ukraine, and died shortly thereafter."

He paused to look around the table. "I caution you again that what you are about to hear is highly classified, and not under any circumstances to be discussed except within this team.

Starlab, one of the largest and best of the world's astronomical satellites, was the property of the T. Cuthbert Dannerman Astrophysical Observatory. It was designed to house visiting astronomers for weeks or months at a time, in the days when passenger launches to Low Earth Orbit were merely very expensive, not preposterous. Then it was called the Dannerman Orbiting Astrolab—the DOA for short—until the last scientist to use the place, a condensed-matter physicist named Manfred Lefrik, had the bad judgment to die there. By the time the automatic monitors reported to Earth what had happened it was far too late to save his life and, in view of the declining interest in space exploration, not worth the trouble to send up a ship to rescue his body. What the Observatory did, however, was to rename the satellite "Starlab," because they thought "DOA" sounded too apt. Still, some people preferred to call it the Starcophagus.

"There is an organization of Ukrainian nationalists who think Ukraine should be ruling Russia, the way it used to like a thousand years ago, instead of the other way around, the way they claim it is now—I don't know enough about Russian-Ukrainian history to get the details straight. And don't want to, actually. Anyway, this group wants to take over Russia, and they're willing to use terrorist tactics to make it happen.

"Of course, that's a local matter. Normally the Bureau wouldn't consider it an American concern. But, like a lot of these cockamamie terrorist groups, they've got cells here and they get a lot of their financing from Ukrainian-Americans. So the Russians asked us to lend a hand. And one of our assets in place in the Chicago cell passed on a report that the Ukrainians had autopsied the old lady . . . and found something weird.

"Take a look at your screens."

It wasn't necessary to do anything to comply. The pop-up screens were rising again at every place, and what they displayed was a sort of X ray of a human skull. Where skull joined spine there was a fuzzy object the size of a hazelnut.

"This is a slice of a PET scan," Pell said. "It shows the thing the Ukrainians found in Dr. Artzybachova's head. And this other one"—*click*—"comes from the head of our agent, Dan Dannerman. There's one just like it in Dr. Patrice Adcock's head—and, we think, though we can't get at them to check, in the heads of Commander Lin and General Delasquez as well. Nothing like it has ever been found in the heads of anybody else we've examined, just in the people that went to Starlab and came back."

He paused there, gazing amiably around the table, until Senator Piombero couldn't contain herself any longer. "Well, what is it, Marcus? Some kind of a tumor?"

The D.D. shook his head. "No, it's not a tumor. We have a copy of the Ukrainian report on the object they took from Dr. Artzybachova's body. It's metal. It does not resemble any human artifact. It appears to have been implanted in them while they were on the orbiter." He paused, giving the group a sort of half smile—not so much a smile as the grimace of somebody who had bitten into something really foul. "Now we come to Operation Ananias. There seems to be a lot of lying going on. Both Dannerman and Dr. Adcock deny that anything of the sort happened. The Floridians haven't been very cooperative, but we've established that General Delasquez denies it, too; we haven't been able to get much out of the Chinese about Commander Lin.

"But what it is, definitely, is a piece of that extraterrestrial technology that Dr. Adcock went looking for. We want to find out why one of our senior agents is lying to us, not to mention that we damn well need to know exactly what the implant thing is." He glanced at his watch, seemed about to add something but changed his mind. "There's more, but let's leave it at that for the moment. Now we should go to the interrogation theater so you can get a look at Dannerman and Dr. Adcock yourselves."

CHAPTER TWO

With all twelve of them in it at once the elevator was pretty crowded. Conversation wasn't easy, but that didn't stop Senator Piombero. "What I'm wondering, Marcus," she said, leaning past the man Hilda couldn't quite remember to get the D.D.'s attention, "is, why don't you just take the thing out of your agent's head? I mean surgically? I certainly wouldn't want anything like that in my own head."

> According to the flow charts, the National Bureau of Investigation is part of the nation's federalized police force, but it keeps itself clear of the street cops. Those are the thin blue line—though noticeably thickened since the passage of the police draft laws—that does its best to keep the peace-loving citizen from the muggers and murderers. The street cops share a headquarters with the Department of Defense in the old Pentagon. The NBI's headquarters is a few kilometers away, in suburban Arlington, and it has a different mission. Its quarry is the transnational crooks and druggers and terrorists. It has inherited its ID files from the old FBI, and its habits from the old CIA. Although it chooses its agents from the police draftees, the ones it picks are the cream of the crop, and they know it.
> —*Inside the Beltway:* "The NBI."

"That is one option, yes," he agreed. "Unfortunately— Well, that's your department, Dr. Evergood."

"It's not that easy," the surgeon said obstinately. "I've

studied both subjects. Of course, the implants can be removed. But they are much more complex than they appear on your screens. Each of the implants has a large number of fine processes that do not show up well in those images but reach deeply into many areas of the brain. My opinion is that removing them might well kill the patients, and at the least would almost certainly cause severe loss of much brain function. I wouldn't like to take that kind of a risk if I didn't have to."

Watching Senator Piombero, Hilda suspected the woman wouldn't be satisfied with that. She wasn't. She gave the surgeon a narrow-eyed look, then turned to the deputy director. "Maybe we can get a second opinion," she suggested.

He looked surprised. "Of course, Senator. If that's what you wish. But Dr. Evergood is perhaps the best in the world at this kind of work. We've been grateful to her in the past for what she's been able to do for some of our own people. Truly amazing results."

Hilda repressed a shudder, because she'd seen some of those truly amazing results: mummified corpses in life-support capsules, looking at the world through electronic lenses and getting around in overgrown wheelchairs. She did not want to think of her Dan Dannerman like that.

"So you see," the deputy director said sunnily as the elevator door opened. "Now if you'll go to your right we'll go into the Pit of Pain."

The senator persisted. "Well, then, couldn't you, ah, secure the device the Ukrainians removed from the instrument person?"

Pell looked surprised. "Oh, didn't I say? They don't have it anymore. The silly buggers let somebody else steal it."

Hilda Morrisey knew the Pit of Pain well. She had watched many an interrogation from one of those seats, had often enough been the interrogator down in the pit herself, when the subjects were bombers, tax evaders, smugglers, all the kinds of nasties that the Bureau had to deal with. It had never been like this before, though. The problem had never concerned ridiculous alien creatures from Mars or some other preposterous place. More important still, the sweaty person being interrogated had never before been one of her own.

As the Ananias team took its seats in one corner of the stands Hilda saw that Senior Agent Dannerman was already sitting on one of the straight-backed chairs. He didn't seem to be doing much sweating. In fact, she noted with a faint, hidden grin of approval, he looked pretty much as though he were asleep.

Daisy Fennell said chattily, "It's all right to talk up here; they can't hear us. Now if you're all ready?" She looked at the D.D. He nodded; she spoke into the microphone at her place; down in the pit the door opened and the interrogator came in. Hilda didn't know the interrogator, who was female, young, good-looking in a severely no-nonsense kind of way—probably new to the Bureau headquarters. She placed a hand on Dannerman's shoulder and said, "Wake up. I need to ask you some questions."

If Dannerman had been asleep at all, he woke quickly and completely. He glanced knowingly toward the one-way mirror, yawning, before he said, "Is there any coffee around?"

"No," the interrogator said concisely, seating herself across the table from him. She plunged right in. "Agent Dannerman, you are accused of filing false reports to the Bureau."

"Yes, I know that; I didn't do it. By the way, I have to pee."

The interrogator ignored that. "When you returned from the Starlab orbiter you reported—"

"I know what I reported. Pee, remember? I have to do it."

For the first time the interrogator looked uncertain. "I think that can wait until we finish here. You reported—"

"Well, if you think it can wait," Dannerman said agreeably, "but it doesn't feel that way to me. I think it'd be better if you took me to the men's room. Or else I can just go in my pants."

The interrogator didn't scowl at him. Didn't look at the mirror, either, just got up, walked stiffly to the door and summoned a male guard to escort Dannerman to the toilet. The deputy director was frowning. Hilda wasn't; in fact, she was feeling a faint glow of pride; her agent, faithful to his training, was controlling the interrogation. He was a good boy. . . .

Except, she reminded herself glumly, that he wasn't.

When Dannerman was back in his chair he was more cooperative; he'd made his point. Yes, he'd gone to Starlab looking for traces of alien presence. No, there hadn't been any. Yes, he was sure of that; he'd said so about a hundred times now, hadn't he? Yes (as the interrogator activated the table's pop-up screen and he glanced at it), he had seen that X ray before. He was willing to take the Bureau's word that it was of his own head, but what that object was he had no idea.

"And you're aware that one just like it was found in Dr. Rosaleen Artzybachova's skull on autopsy, and that it is definitely a piece of alien technology."

"So you tell me," he agreed.

"Do you think the Bureau's lying to you?"

"I hope not, but you think I'm lying to you and I'm not. Hell, friend, you ought to know that by now; your shrinks have tested me a thousand times, and I always came up clean."

Agent Dannerman has one personal trait that comes in useful to the NBI. He was born rich, grew up among rich people and thus had entry to circles the average NBI agent couldn't penetrate. The late T. Cuthbert Dannerman, who was his uncle on his father's side, not only endowed the Dannerman Astrophysical Observatory but had enough left over to bequeath a tidy little fortune to his two surviving relatives, one of whom was Dan. Unfortunately for Dan, he was in deep cover abroad when the will was probated. By the time he got his hands on the money the world's rampant inflation had shrunk it to chump change.

In the spectator seats Hilda, and most of the others, looked at the pair of Bureau shrinks, who shrugged and nodded reluctantly.

"I don't know why that is," the interrogator agreed. "What it looks like is that you've found some way of beating the tests."

"Now, how could I do that?" Dannerman asked. "They shot me so full of drugs I was out of my head for weeks."

The interrogator paused. Then she said, "There is a way of settling this once and for all."

"Yes, I know what that is. You want to cut my head open so you can get a good look at that thing."

"That's right. There's a release form right in front of you, if you'll just sign it—"

"No, I can't do that," Dannerman said apologetically. "I wish I could help. But I hear that the operation could turn me into a vegetable."

"Maybe could. No one knows for sure. Not until they open you up and get a look."

"I'm sorry. That's not good enough. I'm not signing."

Dr. Patrice Dannerman Bly Metcalf Adcock attained her position as head of the Dannerman Astrophysical Observatory by virtue of her training as an astronomer, and also because she was the niece by marriage of the late T. Cuthbert Dannerman, whose money had funded the Observatory in the first place. Patrice Adcock was luckier in her inheritance than her cousin by marriage, Dan Dannerman; she was able to transfer her legacy to inflation-proof investments as soon as she received it. But two divorces depleted her cash . . . which was why she seized on the chance of riches from the Starlab orbiter.

"You don't have a choice," she said. "The deputy director is *ordering* you to sign the release."

"Well, that's different," Dannerman said cheerfully. "Let him give it to me in writing, and then let me give a copy of it to my lawyer . . . and then we'll see."

That was enough for the deputy director. "I think we've heard enough from Agent Dannerman," he said to the room in general, then spoke into his microphone.

As the interrogator, hearing, terminated the interrogation and took Dannerman out of the Pit, Dr. Marsha Evergood raised her hand. "Mr. Pell, you understand I can't undertake the operation without his consent."

Pell said heartily, "Naturally. No one in the Bureau would ask you to, Dr. Evergood."

"But if he won't sign—"

"I give you my word that you won't have to pick up a scalpel until you have his signature on the release form. Now they'll be bringing Dr. Adcock in."

Signature, signature, Hilda thought, cudgeling her memory. There was something about signatures. . . .

Down in the pit they were bringing the Adcock woman in, but Hilda wasn't looking at her. She was looking at the other Bureau man, tardily remembering where she had seen him before. He was the man who'd replaced old Willy Godden when he retired as Chief of Documents: the branch of the Bureau which was in the business of providing you with any papers, and any signatures, you might happen to want.

CHAPTER THREE

As Senior Agent Dan Dannerman, currently on administrative leave, left the Pit of Pain his interrogator cozily took his arm. "I'm sorry about all this, Agent Dannerman," she said, looking up at him with large eyes and an apologetic smile, "but I guess you know how it is. Still want that coffee? Why don't you wait in the conference room here and I'll get it for you."

"Fine," he said. But he was already talking to the door she had closed behind him, and when he tried it it was locked.

He had expected no less. The conference room—call it the "holding cell," because that was what it was—offered him a choice of two backless benches to sit on, both bolted to the floor. He chose neither. He perched on the edge of the table between them, idly examining its surface. The thing was undoubtedly packed with electronics. Lacking a pass card there was no easy way for him to get at them, though, and in any case what would be the use? This wasn't some crime gang that was holding him. It was his own Bureau—what had been his own Bureau, anyway, until all this preposterous crap hit the fan.

That was what was very wrong with the way things were going for Dan Dannerman. Under other circumstances he would have known what to do—what to try to do, anyway: maybe try to get into the table's electronic resources, maybe position himself by the door to coldcock this young woman when she came back with the coffee, maybe try to rid himself of the collar that made any escape attempt useless, maybe— Well, he'd been trained for almost everything that could happen to a Bureau agent in the field. But never for this.

Sooner than he expected the interrogator was back, juggling a little tray in one hand, carefully closing the door again behind her.

There were two cups on the tray. When Dannerman had taken his and seated himself she sat down on the bench across from him with the other and became conversational. "Like I say, I'm sorry to meet you this way, Agent Dannerman. I do know who you are, and I only wish I had your record. I'm Merla Tepp."

He nodded, slightly amused. She was being the good cop. She wasn't bad at the job, either. Although she dressed for no-nonsense business, she'd allowed herself a hint of perfume and the makeup, and all in all she was quite an attractive young woman. "So," he said sociably, "can I go home now?"

"You mean back to New York? I don't know. I'm waiting for orders. Was I rough on you in there?"

"You were doing your job."

"Thanks for taking it that way, Agent Dannerman. This is my first week in headquarters, and I get the jobs nobody else wants. You know how it is."

That was too obvious to require a response, so he didn't try to make one. The woman sipped her coffee, gazing at him over the rim of the cup. She wasn't being flirtatious, exactly. Confiding, maybe. She said, "Do you mind if I ask you a question? Why don't you want to sign that release?"

That was pretty obvious, too. He said it anyway. "Because it might kill me."

"Well, yes," she admitted. "I can't blame you for that. But don't you want to know what that thing is? What does it feel like, anyway?"

What did it feel like? It felt like nothing at all. He hadn't felt it being put in, hadn't known it was there at all until, without warning, the damn Bureau pickup squad had scooped him up and hustled him in for examination. And ever since then they'd asked him the same damn questions over and over again, just like this little jumped-up cadet—

Who was, after all, young, and rather pretty, and would have been more so if she'd let herself look girly instead of efficient. And it had been a long time since he'd seen his own girl. So all he said was, "I can't feel it. What's this, they've detailed you to soften me up?"

She looked at him quizzically over her coffee cup. "Do you think I could? When Colonel Morrisey and Deputy Director Pell couldn't? But we won't talk about it if you don't want to." She leaned back against the wall, trying to get comfortable. "Sorry about these benches. Do you want to talk at all, or should I just shut up? Like you could tell me about some of your missions."

"Or you could tell me about yours," he suggested, beginning to feel amusement.

"Mine aren't very interesting. They had me infiltrating some of the radical religious-militia groups in the Southwest. We cleaned up one little bomb factory, but it was taking a long time and that wasn't getting me any promotions. So I applied for a tour here."

"So you're a career agent."

"I guess so," she said, finishing the last of her coffee. "I was in protsy in college, and they called me up for active duty."

The Police Reserve Officers Training Corps; Dannerman grinned in spite of himself. "Me, too."

She said doubtfully, "Well, maybe it was a little different for me. See, my parents were very religious. I grew up in a fundamentalist group; and the Bureau needed somebody who could get inside some of them. So the machines kicked my name out. But I guess I'll stay in the Bureau. It isn't that bad—"

And so on, and so on. The woman seemed to like

talking about her life in the Bureau. Dannerman let her talk. It was a new and relaxing experience for him, these days, to be closeted with another agent when the other agent did all the talking. "—so here I am," she finished. "Want some more coffee?".

When human beings began to wonder if there were other intelligent races somewhere in the universe they began the SETI program—the "Search for Extraterrestrial Intelligence." That meant they listened for radio broadcasts from space, in the expectation that they might somehow establish peaceful communication with them. They did not take seriously the idea that some of those extraterrestrial intelligences might have similar programs of their own, with expectations a good deal less peaceful.

"Well, sure. And if you could find something to eat to go along with it?"

"I'll see what I can do," she promised, gathered up the cups and left, naturally locking him in again.

Dannerman yawned and stretched, wondering absently what the Bureau had in store for him next. Wondering what he would do if in fact the deputy director did give him a direct order, in writing, to sign the release. He didn't think that was likely. Marcus Pell was too sharp a bunny to put anything like that in writing, especially if he thought Dannerman would file it with his attorney.

Which, Dannerman reflected, wouldn't be all that easy, since he didn't really have an attorney. Unless you counted the old fart of a family lawyer who had screwed up his inheritance and helped him get the job with Cousin Pat's observatory that had led to his flight to the orbiting old Starlab and thus to all this other stuff. . . .

He turned as the door opened again, expecting Merla Tepp with the coffee refills.

It was Tepp, all right, but she wasn't alone. She had someone with her, and the someone was Dannerman's Cousin Pat. "I brought some company for you," Tepp said brightly, "and I've got to leave the two of you here for a bit. But I found something for you to snack on and the coffee's fresh."

Cousin Pat, aka Dr. Patrice Adcock, gave Dannerman a look that was part weary and mostly just hostile. As she took the bench across from him he ventured, "Hello, Pat."

Pat Adcock didn't answer. Dannerman hadn't really expected her to. She hadn't forgiven him, and in a way he didn't blame her. Nobody liked having a Bureau spook planted on them, especially when the spook was a cousin they had known since childhood.

He fingered his collar, studying her. It was the first time in many weeks that he had had a good look at his cousin. Apart from looking tired and cranky she looked smaller than usual, in her unornamented Bureau prison gown. Mostly she just looked mad.

He tried again. "So how've you been?" he asked sociably.

She gave him an eyes-narrowed look, but this time she answered. "Shitty," she said.

She didn't bounce the conversational ball back by asking how he was; she evidently didn't care. He sighed. "Pat, I know you're pissed at me, but what was I supposed to do? I work for the Bureau. The Bureau wanted to know what you were up to. If it hadn't been me, it would've been somebody else."

"Sure, Dan, but I wouldn't have trusted anybody else as much, would I?" She was silent for a moment, then said thoughtfully, "You just can't leave that thing alone, can you?"

He hadn't been aware that he was still fingering his

collar. He took his hand away. "At least they didn't make you wear one."

"Sure not. Why would they? I've been in solitary confinement in this dump." Moodily she picked up her coffee cup, which reminded Dannerman to inspect the "food" Agent Tepp had brought. It was an opened box of cheese-flavored crackers, but still pretty full.

Pat Adcock watched him chew for a moment, then asked, "Dan? Do you know what's going on?" He shook his head, his mouth full of stale crackers. "What was the point of that business in the interrogation theater? They just asked the same questions they've asked a million times before."

He shrugged, chewing. Of course they had; it was pure theater, designed for the benefit of whoever was on the other side of that one-way mirror, but for what reason he could not guess.

She fidgeted, unsatisfied. "Listen, do you think the whole thing with the implants could be some kind of trick? Maybe there isn't really anything in our heads at all?"

He swallowed the crackers. "I wish. No, we've got them, all right. I saw the images come up on the screen the first time they examined me." And most of the other times, too, through all the tests—the X rays and the PET scans, the ionic-resonance tests when they bounced some kind of radiation off the back of his neck and tried to identify the chemical composition of whatever the damn thing was that had somehow, unbelievably, turned up in his skull. "Anyway," he said, "they'd have to go to a lot of trouble to fake it, and what would be the point?"

"You're the spook. If you don't know, who would?"

"Well, I don't know. I don't remember it ever being stuck into my head, either."

"Same here." She sighed. "They say we've all got one, Jimmy Lin and General Delasquez, too. They want me to sign some kind of release so they can take it out. I—I told them I would sign if you did, and if you didn't I wouldn't."

Dannerman blinked at her. That was an indication of some kind of trust, after all, and he hadn't expected it from her. He didn't know how to react to it, either.

He didn't have to, because Pat had decided to be conversational now. "Well, anyway, what've you been doing since I saw you last—I mean before they started all this nonsense about implants? How's that girl of yours?" she asked sociably. "The actress?"

That was a downer, because he'd spent a lot of time wondering the same thing. He confessed, "I don't know. I haven't talked to her in a while."

She nodded, looking at him thoughtfully. "I, uh, I hear you weren't in real good condition to talk to her. I mean, they say you were drunk most of the time."

That touched Dannerman where he lived. "Just for the record," he said stiffly, "they shot me so full of their psychoactive chemicals that I was out of it. For weeks. I don't even remember what I was doing."

"I see. You're blaming somebody else for your behavior."

"I'm not blaming. I'm telling you what happened."

She didn't look convinced, but she didn't argue the point. He asked, "So, talking about love interest, have you got anybody special?"

"Now, how the hell could I? Anyway, I've got other things on my mind. Not just this crap here; I keep wondering what's happening at the Observatory. The way they came and took me away—God knows what they told the people."

Dannerman grinned. "They're very British about that. I imagine they told them you were 'assisting with inquiries.'"

"Yeah, well, they're not stupid there, you know. And I'm worried. You know I was having some money problems. I wish I knew what was going on with my funds—oh, what's this?"

What it was was Merla Tepp. Her face was as expressionless as she could make it, and what she said was, "Sorry to interrupt, people, but I've been ordered to take you for a little ride."

The ride wasn't that little. They were the better part of an hour speeding along the Beltway in one of the Bureau's unmarked electrovans, with two burly noncoms carrying stunsticks and riot guards sitting alertly behind them. At least they'd left the van windows transparent, so Dan and Pat could look out. He was a little surprised to see that it was dark; they'd spent the whole day stooging around. But the Beltway looked like the Beltway, wherever it was taking you, and Merla Tepp wasn't answering any questions. "Where are we heading?" No answer. "What's going on here?" No answer. "Who gave you the orders?" No real answer, but at least a kind of response: "Colonel Morrisey will meet us, and you can ask her when you see her."

But when the van at last turned into city streets one question answered itself. "Oh, shit," Dannerman said. "They're taking us to Walter Reed."

Pat blinked at him. "The hospital?

"Damn straight it's the hospital. Listen, Tepp! If you think—"

But he never got to finish, and she didn't have to answer; one of the noncoms leaned forward and placed a huge hand on Dannerman's shoulder, while the other casually unlimbered his stunstick. Dannerman saw the light and shut up.

Anyway, they were pulling up to a back entrance, and Dannerman saw Hilda Morrisey moodily waiting in the damp cold. She wasn't answering any questions, either, or at least not right away. "No talking; these people aren't cleared," she said, nodding to the non-coms. "Wait till we get you settled." And then, when they got out of the elevator and were herded into a small room that was a close copy of the Bureau's cell, she said:

"What about it, Danno? Change your mind yet?"

He didn't answer that, and she didn't wait for him to. "All right," she said, her expression frank and open—the expression she wore when she was being most duplicitous, "I understand your problem. I admit there are certain risks. But have you ever thought of the fact that if one of you volunteered for the operation, we wouldn't have to ask the other one?"

"Hilda," he said dangerously, "cut the crap. What've you got us here for? Neither one of us signed the consent paper!"

"No," she agreed, "and that's too bad, because it would simplify things just to go in and pull one of the gadgets out. But I've got good news for both of you. There's another kind of test, something the lab guys have just figured out."

Hero Astronaut Returns Home.

Major General Martín Delasquez has unexpectedly returned to Florida after a tour of duty in Kourou, assisting the Eurospace Agency in preparation for a mission to the abandoned Starlab satellite. On arrival, the general scoffed at reports in the Anglo media that his tour was cut short for security reasons. "There is no truth to them," General Delasquez told reporters. "My task was completed, so I came home. That's all there is to it."

—*El Diario*, Miami

"Hilda!"

"Agent Dannerman," she said frostily, elevating herself to the height of her rank, "don't give me a hard time. Do you understand me?"

"I understand there's something I don't like here. Neither Pat nor I agree to any kind of surgery."

"Of course you don't, you've made that clear. And Dr. Evergood certainly won't perform any without a signed consent, so this isn't like that. There won't be any cutting into your heads. They think there's a chance they can get more dope on that thing in your skulls with some new X-ray thing—don't ask me what it is, all I know is it takes a long exposure and you can't wiggle. Have you eaten anything since you were in the Pit?"

"A couple of crackers, but—"

"That's too bad. It might slow things down."

Alarm bells went off in Dannerman's head. "Does that mean we get put to sleep?"

"Now, how would I know that? Sounds plausible, though, doesn't it? Some sort of tranquilizer, I think. Nothing big, I'm sure of that."

"Now, really, Hilda—"

"Really, Danno," she began, her voice suddenly harsher, "there's no sense arguing about it. I'm not asking for your consent. I'm just telling you what's going to happen because you don't have any ch—"

Then she stopped in mid-breath. She didn't even finish the word "choice." Her eyes went unfocused for a moment. Then she blinked and looked at them again. "You two stay here," she barked, and hurried out of the room.

Pat turned wonderingly to Dannerman. "What the hell was that all about?"

He gave her an abstracted look. "What? Oh, she got a message. In her private phone," he explained. "The little button in her ear; you probably didn't even notice it."

"What kind of message?" Pat demanded. He shook his head. "Dan! Tell me what's happening here! Do you think they're going to operate on us anyway? They can't do it without our signatures, can they?"

Dannerman considered the question. "That's what the law says," he said. And didn't add that the Bureau had its ways of getting around laws. And decided that if the next person through that door was carrying anything that looked like a hypodermic, then that would be the time to get physical.

The next person who entered wasn't carrying a needle. He wasn't even hospital personnel. It was Deputy Director Marcus Pell himself. He nodded to Dannerman and spoke to Pat. "We haven't officially met, Dr. Adcock, but I've seen a good deal of you."

He was being courtly. Dannerman had no patience with that just at that moment. "What's going on?" he demanded.

The deputy director sighed. "I'm not sure I know," he said. "There's been a rather surprising new development. There has just been a new transmission from that satellite of yours, Dr. Adcock."

"But there's nobody there!" Dannerman said.

Pat had a different reaction. She caught her breath. "Do you think it's one of those funny-looking extraterrestrials?"

"Not this time," Pell said somberly, studying his agent. "It was from a human being, Dannerman. He said there were a bunch of people up there in orbit. He said they were going to come back to Earth in the orbiter's Assured Crew Return Vehicle, the emergency vehicle that's supposed to—"

"I know what it's supposed to do," Dannerman snapped.

"Yes. Well. The funny thing about it, Dannerman, is this guy on Starlab said he was you."

That took Dan Dannerman back as nothing else had. He goggled at the D.D. "He says he's *me?*"

"That's what the man claims. We didn't believe him, of course. So we checked his voiceprint, and by God he was right. He is."

CHAPTER FOUR

Colonel Hilda Morrisey liked orders that gave her some slack for interpretation, but this time she could have wished for a little less of it. The deputy director's parting order had been no more than, "Take care of those two and stick around." That was it. Nothing more specific. Especially nothing more informative, and then he was gone.

So when Dannerman demanded to know what was going on Hilda could only say, "I don't know any more than you do," wishing she did. She did turn on the screen in the van so he and Pat Adcock could hear the Bureau's recording of what the world had just heard. There was no secret about that! It had been a voice-only transmission, so the only picture on the screen was the legend *Transmission received from Starlab astronomical satellite, 2041 hours, 9 December.* Then the voice spoke, tinny, fuzzy, but definitely familiar:

"This is James Daniel Dannerman calling my associates in Arlington from orbit. Pat Adcock was right, except that it's a lot bigger than she thought. I'll try to bring some samples of the stuff we were talking about with me when I come back. That will be very soon, assuming Jimmy Lin can get this Assured Crew Return Vehicle thing working. And assuming that we can all fit in, because there are nine, ah"—the voice hesitated for a moment—"nine persons here, and we don't want to leave anybody aboard. Please acknowledge on this frequency."

That was it. Broadcast in *clear*, so every son of a bitch with a radio, all over the world, could have been listening in. And a lot of them had been. "Is that *me?*" Dannerman demanded, looking from Hilda to Pat; and, when they only shrugged, "Well, what does he—I— what do they mean, nine people? Only five of us went up there!"

"How would I know?" Hilda asked reasonably. "Maybe your friend Artzy-what's-her-name had quadruplets."

"Space Voice" May Belong to U.S. Intelligence Agent.

A retired member of the U.S. intelligence community has identified the "voice from space" as belonging to National Bureau of Investigation agent James Daniel Dannerman. Although the source declines to be identified, he states there "is no damn doubt at all" of the identification, adding that until recently Dannerman was reported to be under house arrest on unspecified charges. Officials of the NBI decline to comment on the report.

—The New York Times

He gave her a dangerous look, but all he said was, "Play it again!"

So they played it again, and again, and then they switched to a news channel to hear all the things everybody had to say about this astounding report. Hilda gave that five minutes. Then she squirmed ahead to the front seat, phoning ahead to make arrangements at the headquarters. Then she just sat there, the dead phone to her ear, because she had nothing to say to either Pat or Dan and didn't want to hear any more of their questions. There was one good thing, she thought. There was at least a temporary hold to the D.D.'s little plan to anesthetize Dannerman and Adcock and then blandly hand Dr. Evergood the impeccably best "signed" release the skilled forgers of Documents could produce. Maybe that hold would be permanent. Maybe even this baffling new development was going to confirm what Hilda had always known in her heart. Her own Dan Dannerman simply could not possibly have been turned or subverted. Oh, sure, the evidence had looked pretty bad, but that just meant the evidence had to be wrong. There had to be some other explanation.

Now it appeared that there was one—well, sort of an explanation, anyway—but who was going to explain this wholly incomprehensible explanation?

At the headquarters she wasted no time. She hustled the two of them into an elevator, down to the accommodations she had arranged for them. "You can watch the news," she said, "or you can go to bed or you can do anything you like—except leave here. I'll see you in the morning."

"Have a heart, Hilda!" Dannerman begged. "I want to know what's happening!"

"So do I. Get some sleep. I've got work to do."

The truth, though, was that she didn't. Everyone else did. Every other person she saw in the Bureau's underground fortress seemed not only to have something to do, but to be about thirty minutes late in getting it done and desperately trying to make up lost time, but not Hilda Morrisey. The last time she had seen the joint jumping like this had been when the President's press secretary got himself kidnapped and murdered—no, she corrected herself, not even then. That was just an ordinary kill; the only reason the Bureau got involved in it at all was because the President demanded it. What was going on now was—was—well, what was it, exactly? Weirdness, that's what it was. Unthinkably preposterous weirdness. But it happened to be real.

She couldn't find Marcus Pell or the director herself. She couldn't even find Daisy Fennell. They were certainly somewhere, on some level of the subterranean headquarters. No one seemed to know just where. More likely, Hilda thought bitterly, the ones who did know simply weren't telling. The topmost of the top brass were holed up somewhere, dealing with this new crisis as best they could, and they didn't want to be bothered with peons who would only get in the way.

Hilda Morrisey did not like being one of the peons.

The obvious place for them to be was the Communications Center. That was the first place Hilda looked, but when she had looked in every other place she could think of she went back there. At least there she could get some idea of what was happening, although what was happening seemed to be only that half the population of the planet Earth was asking questions that nobody here could answer. There were plaintive coded queries from the Bureau's field managers by the score. There were begging—or pleading, or sometimes demanding—transmissions from fifty or sixty of the friendlies, the other national intelligence agencies with which the Bureau maintained some sort of cooperative relationship. Then there were the heavy hitters, the question from the Senate and the House, from State and Defense, from the White House itself . . . not to mention the endless flurry of concerned citizens who somehow had learned the Bureau's least classified call codes and wanted to be informed. These last were the least bothersome. The only answers they got didn't come from a human being; they were computer-generated and all they said was, *Regret have no further information at this time. Please watch your local newscasts.* The other queries could not be brushed off so lightly. They took personal responses from some human being. Tending to them was what a large fraction of the Bureau personnel on duty were doing with their time, but though the responses were more elaborate, the information they contained was about the same.

But the little that was different about them was
interesting. Hilda gleaned a fact here and a hint there
and slowly pieced together a picture. Why had there
been no further transmissions from this other Dan
Dannerman? Because the Comm officer on duty had
been bright enough and quick enough to send an instant
narrow-beam order to this Dannerman on the satellite,
telling him to shut up, do nothing, just wait there for
further instructions. And a lucky thing that, for once,
this other Dannerman had done exactly what he was
told. . . .

There was a quick, breathy sound of surprise from
the group clustered around one screen. They had heard
something.

Half the Comm Center immediately dropped what
they were doing to see what it was they had heard. "It
was a blip," one of the technicians was saying excitedly. "No, nothing more. Just one quick pulse, but it
definitely came from Starlab. Direct? No, I guess
they're somewhere out of sight in their orbit; it was
relayed from Goldstone, but it was positively— Hey!
There's another one!"

It wasn't one. It was two. Everyone heard them this
time, and the screen showed them moving slowly
across the field, two brightly jagged spikes. So
Dannerman was communicating again, more or less.

That was enough for Hilda
Morrisey. She stood up, stretched, yawned and walked
out of the Communications Center.

She knew what had happened, because it was what
she would have done in the same case. What the closeted big brass had been doing was trying to figure some
way of arranging a two-way conversation that the rest
of the world couldn't hear. Apparently Starlab wasn't
rigged for narrowcasting—well, it wouldn't matter if it

were. Reporters weren't stupid, and they had resources of their own; undoubtedly there were forests of mobile antennae deployed all over Arlington, and probably all around Goldstone and the station on Wake and every other place where the Bureau might receive a signal. So they had worked out a simple code. The Bureau could ask a question, and Dannerman could answer by blipping his transmitter—something like one blip *yes* and two blips *no*—and maybe three blips for *How the hell do you expect me to do THAT?* But you had no hope of deciphering what the answers meant unless you knew what the questions had been.

She glanced at her watch. 0544. It would be daybreak in an hour or two, and she hadn't had sleep, a shower or a change of clothing since she got out of the bed in her New York City apartment nearly twenty-four hours ago. The lack of sleep wasn't a big problem; the Bureau's standard-issue wakeup pills took care of it. The problem was something else. Surreptitiously she bent her head for a quick sniff at her armpit, envious of the crisp cleanliness of everyone around her. She knew why that was. They had all been able to take enough time off to get cleaned and changed. That was the way it was when you were headquarters-based, you kept spares of everything on hand in case of emergency. If she were to give up the struggle and let them hand her that damned promotion—

But that was out of the question. Hilda Morrisey didn't belong in this place. She was a field manager. She could make herself at home wherever the job took her, San Diego or New York, Berlin or Karachi. In those places she was the boss, and as long as her teams produced results nobody got in her thinning but still bravely blond hair. Here she was just one of a mob of fifty or sixty people of equivalent rank, with the top-heavy Bureau executive staff over them all.

Here, as a matter of fact, if anything she was in the

way. But she couldn't leave. Not only was this whole
business a puzzle that Hilda Morrisey didn't trust anyone but herself to solve, but it was her own agent who
was at the core of it.

If she couldn't leave, sleep or bathe, the next best
thing was to eat. She sought out the field-grade mess,
sat at a table in a corner, swallowed another wakeup pill
and thought.

The mess was usually deserted this time of night—
or morning. Not this one. There were half a dozen others at the tables, and the graveyard mess shift, looking
aggrieved at their unusual workload, was clearing up
the tables that still others had left. While she was waiting for someone to take her order she popped up the
table's screen and coded for the news summaries.

When a waiter approached Hilda dumped the screen
and turned to give her order, but what he said was,
"Excuse me, Colonel, but there's a junior officer asking
to speak to you."

Hilda turned; the person waiting at the door was the
interrogator, the junior agent, Merla Tepp. "Send her
in," she said. And then, when the woman had come to
the table, "Sit down, Tepp. I didn't expect to see you
here for another couple of hours."

"I came in early, Colonel. Colonel? I'm sorry to
interrupt your meal but I wanted to apologize. I
wouldn't have given Agent Dannerman those crackers,
except I didn't know he was scheduled for surgery."

"No, you didn't," Hilda agreed. "In fact, you don't
know it now. You especially don't want to say anything
about it to Agent Dannerman."

"No, ma'am. Ma'am? I'm pretty sure he suspected
it."

Hilda surveyed the woman. "I'm damn sure he did;
Dannerman's a fine agent. Just don't confirm it for
him." She was silent for a moment, studying Junior
Agent Tepp while her fingers were absentmindedly

playing with the screen keys. After a moment, she said, "Actually, I would have done just what you did. Have you eaten?"

Tepp looked surprised. "No, but, Colonel, this dining room is for—"

Hilda overrode her. "What this dining room is for is for people like me and our guests. Waiter! We'll have a couple of sandwiches and salads—if it's that fruity dressing, put the dressing on the side." She waved him away and told the girl, "That stuff is too damn sweet. You might prefer to eat the salad plain. I forgot to ask if you had any special dietary needs?"

"No, ma'am."

"Because God knows what the sandwiches will be." She leaned back, studying the girl. Although she knew she had never seen Junior Agent Tepp before, there was something vaguely familiar about her. She couldn't place the thought and abandoned it. "Actually," she said, "apart from giving them the damn crackers, that wasn't a bad move, putting the two of them together."

Tepp looked rueful. "I was hoping that if they got to talking, they might say something useful."

"Did they?"

"Not really, Colonel. I have the recordings—"

Hilda waved away the notion of looking at the recordings. "I didn't think they would. Danno's too smart for that, but it was worth a try. Means you were using a little initiative. I see by your file that you've only been with the Bureau for a little over a year."

Merla Tepp did not show any surprise at finding that the colonel had called her file up on the table screen. "That's right, ma'am. Mostly in the field in New Mexico, after I finished training."

"Checking into the religious nut groups." Hilda nodded. "I get the impression that you've been pretty interested in religion all your life."

Tepp hesitated. "You could say I was a seeker,

Colonel. I was born Pentecostal, then when that didn't
seem to be giving me what I wanted I tried Catholic.
Then I went to shul for a year—I guess that's why you
asked about dietary requirements? Then I tried
Buddhism—"

> The American radical religious right came in five
> main flavors. There were the *fundamentalists,* who
> believe in the "verbal inerrancy" of the Christian
> Bible; the *born-agains,* who claim a personal expe-
> rience with Christ; the *evangelicals,* who are either
> of the above plus a drive to convert others; the *pen-
> tecostals,* who are any of the above plus public
> demonstrations of ecstasy; and the *charismatics,*
> who differ from the others only in that they retain
> communion in a conventional Protestant or Catholic
> denomination. Generally speaking, what the funda-
> mentalists thought the government ought to do about
> the possible space aliens who might have occupied
> Starlab was, if possible, to kill them, because they
> were probably the Antichrist. While most of the oth-
> ers thought they were probably angels of some kind
> and what the government should be doing was ar-
> ranging for them to be worshipped. What they all
> agreed on was that everything the government actu-
> ally was doing was wholly and unforgivably wrong.

She broke off as the sandwiches and salads arrived.
Colonel Hilda waved to her to eat, doing so herself. She
hadn't realized quite how hungry she was. With her
mouth full, she paused long enough to ask: "And now?"

The girl grinned. "I guess you'd say the Bureau's my
religion now, ma'am."

Hilda nodded. It was a good answer. It was the kind
of answer she might have given herself, and, as a matter of fact, she suddenly realized what that puzzling
familiarity was all about. Agent Tepp was just about her
height, just about her weight, just about her general

build; taken all in all, she was not far from a copy of what Colonel Morrisey had been, long before she became a colonel.

She had nothing more to talk about, so she switched the screen over to repeats of the news digests and watched them as she ate her meal. Another good thing about Agent Tepp was that she took the hint and didn't speak, either. When the waiter brought their coffee, she said, "Thanks for keeping me company, Agent Tepp, but I imagine you have duties here—"

Agent Tepp touched a napkin to her lips. "Yes, ma'am. Can I ask you something? If you're going to be on permanent duty here, you'll probably need an aide—"

Hilda didn't let her finish. "What's that about permanent duty? Have you been hearing latrine talk?"

"No, ma'am. It's just logical, I thought. But if I was wrong—"

"I hope to God you were wrong." Hilda thought for a moment. "Still," she said, "I wouldn't mind thinking about having you in my command if you wanted to come to New York."

Tepp looked disappointed. "Thank you, ma'am, but I'd really like to stay at HQ for a while."

"Fine. Now if you'll excuse— Wait a minute."

It was the deputy director on her screen. "Hilda, we need that Adcock woman. Get her down to the pit galleries."

So that was where he'd been holed up! Pell didn't wait for an answer. Hilda started to get up just as Agent Tepp was doing the same, saying regretfully, "Thank you for the meal, ma'am. It was a pleasure to talk to you."

Hilda put her hand on the woman's arm. "Maybe you can do me a favor. You look like you're about my size. Do you keep a change of clothes here? Fine, then lend me some clean underwear and find me a shower I can use."

CHAPTER FIVE

Dr. Patrice Adcock hadn't been taken back to her cell. Instead they put her in a quite comfortable bedroom in a little suite that apparently was kept for VIP visitors who couldn't, or didn't choose to, go home to sleep. It had a really comfortable bed, which was a nice change from the iron-hard cot in her old cell. For all the good it did her. First she lay awake, wondering just what the hell was going on *now?* Another Dannerman? Radioing to Earth from *Starlab?* When she did at last fall asleep it didn't last, because that Morrisey woman woke her to say the deputy director needed to talk to her. Right *now.*

So Pat climbed wearily back into her jail uniform. She let herself be conducted to where Marcus Pell and six or seven other people were huddled around screens and little tables littered with coffee cups and the remains of largely uneaten food, and then what was it he asked her? It was, Did Starlab have facilities for something called a 300-digit-prime coordinated-chaos encryption system? Of course she had no idea about that. Whatever it was. Well—less patiently—who would know the answer? Anyone at the Observatory? She thought about that, then shrugged. Maybe, but they would all be asleep now, for God's sake, and anyway the real expert was Rosaleen Artzybachova, who was dead.

And then, the funny thing, they all suddenly looked both surprised and relieved. The deputy director man— was his name Pell?—nodded to the Morrisey woman. That was the end of it. The woman took Pat back to her new home and left her to lie awake an hour or so longer, with all the old questions and a dozen new ones to keep her from sleep.

So when a uniform knocked at her door and opened it a crack she woke at once. "Good morning, ma'am," the woman said civilly. "It's oh-eight-hundred, and you might want to get ready to see the deputy director." Then she closed the door, without saying when the deputy director was likely to arrive. Or why.

But when Pat Adcock came out of her very own private bathroom—another touch of luxury, complete with a full array of toiletries in their original unopened wrappings—she made a pleasing discovery. The guard must have come back while she was in the shower. Pat's own clothes—the ones she had been arrested in—were draped over the foot of the bed, cleaned and ready to put on.

A few minutes later, dressed in something other than that jail uniform after all these long weeks and pleased about that much, anyway, she opened the door. It led into a little sitting room, with comfortable chairs and pictures on the wall and even a fireplace—fake, of course, but a nice touch. A moment later Dannerman came out of his own room to join her, just in time for the guard to roll in a cart loaded with breakfast.

Dannerman gave her an appreciative grin. "Hey, nice outfit. Did you have a good night's sleep?"

She didn't bother to answer that, and after an uncertain moment he turned his attention to their breakfast. Pat took a while longer to get to it, but when she tasted the fresh, ripe papaya and the cold, sweet juice she dug in as well. It was the best meal she'd had since the police had picked her up at her Observatory.

Her Observatory. She wondered if it was really still hers.

Well, probably the Observatory itself was still running,

more or less normally; Uncle Cubby's money was still available to finance its operations, and no doubt Pete Schneyman, or one of the other senior scientists, had taken over as acting director in her absence. Gwen Morisaki would be going right on with her Cepheid counts and Kit Papathanassiou with his cosmological studies and all the rest of it, whether she was present or not. Things might even be going better without her because, Pat had to admit, her last few months at the Observatory she'd been a lot more interested in Starlab than in doing science.

The other question that entered her mind was to wonder if she herself were in bankruptcy yet.

The economic fact was that she had hocked just about everything she owned to raise the money for her flight to the orbiter. Money shouldn't have been any problem at all. The government should have financed or provided the whole thing. But the government hadn't. So she'd had to find the money herself. It came to serious money, too, enough to bribe the Floridian authorities who controlled the launchpads at the Cape, to hire pilots, to fight the Feds' lawyers through the courts until, reluctantly, they did give in and provide a launch vehicle for her.

And then she had managed to get that Clipper launched with the five of them in it. And then—

And then it all went to hell. "Dan-Dan?" she said tentatively.

He looked up warily from his eggs Benedict. "Yeah?"

She said slowly, trying to think it through as she spoke, "You know what's funny, Dan? I can remember the flight up to orbit, I can remember the flight back. But all I can remember of what we saw in Starlab was that everything was just the way it was left when the satellite was abandoned. There wasn't anything there that wasn't on the specs. Nothing had changed."

How "United" Are the United Nations?

The current imbroglio in the United Nations General Assembly reminds us once more of the worser consequences of the infamous Resolution 1822. Under this, you may recall, the General Assembly decreed that each signatory nation was to elect one delegate to the Assembly by means of popular vote. This well-meaning "reform" was intended to ensure that the people at large, rather than some junta or clique, represented each country in its deliberations; the models for this were the European Community's Council and, more appositely, the United States Senate.

But what has been the effect? Rather than achieving unity, the delegates now represent parochial issues and, worse, political parties. In this "Parliament of Man," with its lamentable tendency toward passing sweeping resolutions that are meant to micromanage purely internal matters throughout the world, our own delegate, Mr. Hiram Singh—who, it will be remembered, was until recently First Lord of the Admiralty in the New Labor Party government—is not least at fault.

Do we really want to import the tawdry political practices of the Americans to govern our planet? We think not. We think it is time for a thoroughgoing reconsideration of this ill-advised measure.

—*Financial Times,* London

"Nothing had."

"Well, I know that. I remember *remembering* that, when we were on our way back. But I don't remember *seeing* it. Do you know what I mean?"

He frowned. "Well, that's the way it was for me, too. It's funny, now that you mention it."

"Do you think your Bureau people know why that is?"

But he was shaking his head. "Not those turkeys. They don't know any more than we do."

When the door opened again, the man who came in was the deputy director, Marcus Pell. He was followed by one of the uniformed cops. "Coffee for you, too, sir?" the cop suggested.

"Coffee my ass. It might be breakfast time for you, but for me it's just the tail end of a long, long night. Get us a bottle of Jim Beam and some glasses." He turned to Pat. "You were right, Dr. Adcock."

He caught her off-balance. "What was I right about?"

"Alien technology. The man said so himself. The orbiter's loaded with it . . . among other things. No"— he held up his hand—"I don't know exactly whose technology, or how it got there. We're having to be careful about communicating. You know all about that, Dr. Adcock; that's what we got you out of bed for."

"Was I actually any help?" she asked curiously. "It didn't look that way."

He gave her a judicious look, punctuated by a yawn "Sorry. Well, you were and you weren't. What you did was remind us of Dr. Artzybachova."

"But she's dead!"

He shook his head, looking amused. "Not anymore. She's alive and well on your Starlab. Or one of her is. There are a lot of duplicate people around, wouldn't you say? So we sent her a narrow-beam query. She didn't have anything that could make a really secure link, but we worked out a code."

Dannerman was asking the deputy director questions, but Pat hardly heard. She was trying to get used to the idea of Rosie Artzybachova alive again. Then she remembered to ask a question. "Why are you making such a big secret out of it?"

He grinned at her. "You're asking me that? The lady that bet the ranch on finding extraterrestrial technology? Because if any part of what this man is saying is true, then there's a lot of stuff there that we want, and maybe we want to keep it for ourselves—ah, about time," he finished, as the door opened, and two of the uniforms came in. Silently they set down the whiskey, some mixers, glasses, ice, even a tray of hastily slapped-together hors d'oeuvres, glanced at the deputy director for permission to leave again, and did.

Incoming dispatch.
Spanish Federal Police, Madrid.
To Director U.S. National Bureau of
   Investigation
Most secret.

Humint indicates probable major action by Catalan separatist forces in connection with the Iberian games, to be held in Barcelona this spring. Internal source states a large shipment of weaponry and explosive devices is expected from American sympathizers, probably channeled through Basque underground. Urgently request cooperation in dealing with this terrorist threat, in particular in identifying and embargoing arms shipment.

Pell poured himself two fingers of whiskey, disdaining the ice and the mixers. "Help yourselves," he invited.

Pat shook her head. "I didn't know prisoners were allowed to have liquor," she said.

He gave her a friendly smile—no, she thought, not really a smile of any kind of friendship; it was the kind of smile you manufactured to make somebody think you were being friendly when you wanted to soften them up. This was a complex and totally controlled man. "You're thinking about those federal charges against you. Bribery, filing false flight plans—all chickenshit, of course. You can forget them. They're dropped. And as for you, Dannerman"—he shrugged—"your suspension is lifted, too. You're back on duty, with full pay restored."

Dannerman looked wary, fingering his collar. "What about this?"

"Well," the deputy director said, "that's a whole other thing, isn't it? Are you sure you want it taken off?"

Dannerman's expression changed, now mostly puzzled. "Why wouldn't I?"

Pell's glass was empty; he refilled it, but this time with soda and ice and just enough whiskey to tint it lightly. "You know what you two have inside your skulls," he said. "Did it ever occur to you that some people might want to get their hands on those things? Even if they had to kill you in the process?"

Pat Adcock felt a sudden chill. "What people?"

"Why, Dr. Adcock," the man said cozily, "I would say just about anybody. Including some of our own people right here in the Bureau, I wouldn't be surprised. But don't worry about that; the President himself forbade any surgical attempts. So maybe you'd like to keep enjoying our hospitality for a while, don't you think? Or, if you'd rather go out into the world again, we'll supply you with as much protection as we can, same as we've done with Danno here, but there would certainly be a risk."

"Damn it," Dannerman said with feeling. "I knew I was being followed."

"Of course you did," Pell said, smiling that warm-hearted, empty smile again. "One way of looking at it, you were bait. If someone wanted to snatch you, we'd pick him up before he could get very far."

Dannerman was looking at him with distaste. "That's assuming they wanted to kidnap me alive. But if they were going to have to kill me anyhow—"

"You're not thinking it through," Pell said reprovingly. He reached out and tapped Dannerman's collar. "That thing is tough plastic and metal. As long as you had that on your neck nobody could whack your head off and hustle it away before we got to them. So what would be the point of killing you on the street? No, we figured you were pretty safe . . . and, of course, there were other reasons for having you wear the collar. There was always the possibility that you were dirty after all, wasn't there? Colonel Morrisey was pretty sure you weren't. But some people had other opinions, and we had to cover all the bases."

Dannerman said doggedly, "I want it off."

"Yes, I thought you would. Well, when Hilda comes back I'll have her take you down to the shop and they'll remove it. . . . Excuse me." There had been an inaudible signal; Pell lifted his phone to his ear. He listened for quite a long time, spoke briefly—Pat couldn't make out a word—and listened again. When he was through he looked up at them.

"Well," he said, sounding pleasantly surprised, "sometimes you get lucky when you least expect it. The Cape's socked in—thunderstorms, high winds; the weather's going to persist for a couple of days at least. So they can't land there. That's good; the last thing we want is to get the Floridians involved in this."

"So where will they land?"

"That's the question, isn't it? They're working on it. Meanwhile, the President has warned everybody, especially the damn Europeans, that Starlab is U.S. property and anyone who attempts to board it risks being shot at."

Pat stared at him blankly. "*Shot* at? What with?"

Pell said comfortably, "I always knew some of those old Star Wars orbiters might come in useful someday. There are two of them that still have some navigation capacity. They're in the wrong part of the orbit, but the guys in Houston are working on moving them into position even as we speak. Of course the Europeans and the Chinese and so on know that. So we can leave it alone for a while, and right now the first thing we're going to do is to get that party of nine down—and there are some surprises there. They're not all human, you see."

"Not all *human?*"

"That's what Dannerman says, yes. He said a lot of other stuff, too—until we told him to shut up, even in code, and report in full once he's landed." He hesitated. "One thing, though. You're an astronomer, Dr. Adcock. Have you ever heard of somebody named Frank Tipler?"

"Tipler?" She frowned. "I think I might've heard the name—"

"He was some kind of astronomer, too. Late twentieth century. We retrieved all we could find about him from the bank, but the only interesting thing was that he wrote a book once about how Heaven was astronomically real."

"Oh, right," Pat said, tracking down a faint recollection. "I remember hearing something about him—maybe in grad school? It sounded pretty silly to me. What does Tipler have to do with all this?"

"That's what I'd like to know. Dannerman—the other Dannerman, I mean—said we should look him up. If I get you access to the network, can you do the Bureau a favor and see what you can find?"

For Dr. Patrice Adcock the worst thing about jail was having nothing to do—this woman who had never before in her life found herself with nothing to do. Now things were looking up. She wasn't in jail anymore and, better still, she had a job to do that she was good at.

It took Pat an impatient half hour's waiting to get access to Bureau's databank—no, not the *classified* databank, of course, but to the one that accessed most of the country's libraries. Then it took a while longer to get used to the Bureau's procedures. She found the *American Men of Science* entry for Dr. Frank Tipler quickly and began sorting through some of the sources cited. She hardly noticed when Dannerman was back, collarless and occasionally touching his now bare neck to remind himself of the change. That Colonel Hilda Morrisey came in with him.

"New orders, Dr. Adcock," Morrisey said cheerfully. "We're all going for a little ride tonight. The people from Starlab are coming down, and we're going to meet them."

CHAPTER SIX

Dan Dannerman had never been in the deputy director's plane before. In spite of himself, he was impressed. It wasn't one of those custom-converted thousand-seat leviathans, like the President's Air Force One, but those few who had experienced both reported that it was just as luxurious. Dannerman and Pat Adcock were even given a private compartment of their own. Their little cubicle wasn't as fancy as the room Colonel Hilda had appropriated for her own use, and certainly it was nothing like the four-room private suite belonging to the D.D. himself, but it definitely was not shabby. It had full electronics. It had cut flowers floating in a sort of fishbowl, a pair of screens, a call button for one of the police-cadet flight attendants, even two pullout beds neatly made up in case they wanted to sleep on the way—on the way to wherever they were going, because neither Pat nor Dannerman had been given the word on where that might be.

Dannerman had lost his sense of time. Somehow a whole day had got away from him, all spent on waiting. After the long wait time while the deputy director got his ducks in order there was the waiting for the Bureau's sniffer squads to finish their routine inspections—you never knew where someone might sneak in a bomb. It was full dark again by the time they took off.

Dannerman saw Pat cast one yearning look at the beds, but then she resolutely turned her back on them. She had no time to sleep because she was busy at one of the screens, checking databases for information on the Tipler person for the deputy director. Dannerman wasn't sleeping, either, but the reason was different. The prospect of seeing this man who claimed to use his own name and spoke with his own voice had pumped him full of adrenaline. He used his screen on and off, sometimes to kill time by watching news summaries, sometimes to try to find answers to some of the questions that inflamed his thoughts. Perhaps some of the answers were there, but Dannerman didn't have enough clearance to penetrate these particular systems.

He was seriously considering trying out one of the beds after all when Pat made a small grunt of conditional satisfaction. She sat back, watching the printer squirt out hard copy.

"Did you find what you wanted?" Dannerman asked.

"I hope," she said, standing up, evidently getting ready to take the printout to Marcus Pell. "It's weird. You can read it for yourself on the screen."

"Weird how?"

But she was gone. He shifted to her seat and scrolled the screen, beginning to read.

Dr. Frank Tipler was a highly respected cosmologist until he published the book called *The Physics of Immortality*. In it Tipler predicted that the universe, currently expanding, sooner or later would fall back to what is called "the Big Crunch," reproducing the conditions of the Big Bang, but in reverse. At that time, Tipler said, everyone who had ever lived anywhere in the universe would be reborn to live again as an immortal. Most of Tipler's colleagues laughed at his idea, but there were two significant groups who shared his opinion, though Tipler had never heard of either.

"Weird" was the right word. This Frank Tipler had published a book, back in the closing years of the twentieth century. It was called *The Physics of Immortality*,

and what it was about was Tipler's theory—only he
didn't call it a theory; he claimed it was fact, and
offered a hundred pages of equations to prove it—that
the universe, after expanding as far as it could, would
contract again into what he called "the Omega Point"
. . . and then some very strange things would happen.

The first part of it wasn't surprising. That was what
the messages from space had described, years before:
the Big Bang and the universe's expansion, the recollapse into the Big Crunch. The surprising part was the
consequence that was predicted in Tipler's book.
According to Tipler, at that Omega Point or Big
Crunch, whichever you chose to call it, everybody who
had ever lived would inevitably be brought to life
again—in perfect health, at the peak of their powers—
and would go on living forever.

It was, Tipler said, the scientific reality that underlay
all the ancient human yearnings for a Heaven after
death.

Dannerman scrolled the report again, just to make
sure he hadn't missed something—like the reason why
this alleged other Dan Dannerman wanted the Bureau
to know about this Tipler person. He hadn't. That was
all there was.

That was typical of the way the Bureau was run.
Nobody told any inferior anything until they absolutely
had to. Dannerman had a cynical theory about that. It
was turf protection. The more information the higher-
ups hung on to for themselves, the harder it was for
some lower-down to leapfrog above them in the chain
of command. Of course, that kind of secrecy never
worked for long. Sooner or later some one person in the
know would see a tactical advantage for himself in
telling Dannerman what was up. . . .

Might, for instance, at least tell him where they were
going. When they boarded the plane Pell had said they
were going to meet the people from Starlab, and that

was all. Dannerman craned his neck to peer out the window, but that didn't help. It was starry dark out there, no Sun or Moon to give him at least a clue about their direction of travel. The only thing he could be sure of was that they had to be heading generally west or north. Had to be; because otherwise they'd be out over ocean by now, and they weren't. He could catch glimpses of lights on the ground far below.

Resigned, he decided to get a little sleep.

As it turned out, it was very little. He had hardly closed his eyes when Pat Adcock returned from Pell's private quarters forward in the plane. She was holding a partly full cup of coffee, trying not to spill any, and she looked annoyed. "Oh, listen," she said, setting the cup down, "I got this from one of the stews, but I didn't stop to think about whether you might want some."

Eschatology, which is the study of last things, is a fundamental part of nearly all of Earth's religions. Buddhism speaks of the eternal bliss called Nirvana, while the Biblical Book of Revelations describes the eschaton in more specific and concrete terms: "And death shall be no more, neither shall there be mourning nor crying nor pain any more." It is what some religions call "Heaven." As it turned out, there were other parties who didn't think of that state as religious. For them it was a strategic objective, and they were prepared to fight for it.

—NBI briefing document

"I'd rather sleep. What's all this Omega Point stuff?"

She gestured toward the screen, which still displayed her report. "All I know is what it says there. I think somebody once mentioned Tipler and his idea in one of my seminars, but nobody took it very seriously, and I don't remember anything else about it."

"And you gave the report to the D.D.? What'd he say?"

She grinned. "He was asleep. I woke him up when I came in and what he said was, 'Shit.' That was all. Then he waved at me to get out, but I didn't go."

"You didn't?"

"Well, I had some questions I wanted answered—like what I was doing on this plane. So I asked him. I said I knew they wanted you along to confront this other Dannerman, but what did they want from me?"

Dannerman, who had been wondering the same thing, asked, "So why did they?"

"He didn't exactly say. He just said he'd rather I saw for myself."

"Saw what?"

She shrugged. "He didn't say that, either. Then when I stopped for coffee on the way back the stew told me that we were going to start coming down for a landing pretty soon, so we better strap ourselves in. Oh," she added, fumbling for her seat belt, "there was one other thing. You want to know where we're going? It's Canada. They ordered the escape vehicle from Starlab to come down at someplace called Calgary."

Calgary turned out to be really cold, and when Dannerman left the warm plane for the freezing dark outside an unexpected memory struck him. He had been there before. It had been a summer when the girl he was involved with at the time had made up her mind to go off on a fossil dig in the Alberta bone beds. Somewhere or other among his scattered possessions—most likely in one of the Bureau's warehouses for storing the things an agent couldn't carry around with him—he probably still had a souvenir of her. It was a pair of neckbones of some terrier-sized hundred-million-year-old dinosaur. She had had them made into cuff links for him, just before she told him she was marrying her paleontology professor.

Dannerman didn't remember Calgary very well, but something he had been told about its airport had stuck in his mind. It possessed a hellish long runway, because at one time it had been designated as an alternate emergency landing site for the old Space Shuttle.

Which, of course, was just what was needed for Starlab's Assured Crew Return Vehicle.

Another plane was coming in, also a big one. It looked to Dannerman like a troop transport. He strolled over to where Colonel Morrisey was watching it land, close enough to the deputy director so he could find her if he had orders for her, far enough away not to intrude. "Okay, Hilda," Dannerman said, keeping his voice down, "explain something to me. I understand the return ship from Starlab probably needs a lot of landing strip, but why in Canada, for God's sake?"

She didn't look at him. "Security, what do you think? Everybody in the world is watching Starlab now, and they've seen the ACRV detach itself to come down. There'll be people waiting at every possible airport in the States." She gave him a sidelong glance, almost affectionate. "Don't worry. It's all worked out with the Canadians; the President himself flew to Ottawa to make a deal with the Prime Minister. Where's your cuz?"

"Pat went into the terminal to get warm." Actually Dannerman was thinking of doing the same thing. There was a freezing wind coming across the bare space of the airport; he'd been lucky enough to have the anorak he was taken to the headquarters in, but even so his face was hurting from the cold. Pat hadn't been that fortunate. When she was arrested they picked her up indoors and she hadn't been out in the open air ever since. At the last minute one of the stews had found her a spare jacket that belonged to one of the pilots, but it was meters too big and did nothing for her bare legs.

What kept Dannerman out in the cold was the spectacle overhead. There were more stars than he had seen in years, and what looked like a handsome aurora borealis display off toward the horizon. But when he pointed it out to Hilda she said mildly, "Asshole, that's the Sun getting ready to rise." She paused to listen to the button in her ear, and then said, "They've got through reentry all right. They say ETA in thirty-five minutes."

Dannerman felt a sudden chill of a different kind. He was that close to seeing this person who claimed to be himself. He tried not to speculate—some bizarre alien creature that had duplicated his voice as a disguise?— but it was a queasy, unpleasant feeling all the same.

Hilda was squinting at the horizon. "It ought to be broad daylight by then, and that's what they wanted— they didn't want to risk a night landing, but they wanted them to get down as fast as possible. But I dunno. I hope this Chinaman knows what he's doing. Isn't he going to be landing right into the Sun?"

"That's not how it works," Dannerman said, out of the superior experience of somebody who had actually once made a return flight from orbit. "They swing around to land from the east—it's to take advantage of Earth's rotation." He looked to see if she was impressed. She wasn't. "I think I'll go use the men's room while I can."

When he was inside the warmth of the terminal seduced him into lingering. He spotted Pat, wanly hunched over a cup of coffee by one of the vast glass windows with her junior-agent minder alertly sitting just behind. He located the place where the coffee was coming from and, supplied, sat down next to her; she glanced up at him, fretfully curious. "What are all the soldiers for?"

Looking out at the floodlit runway, he could see what she was talking about. The troop transport had nosed up to the hardstand next to the terminal. Its clamshell bow had opened and three personnel carriers, each filled with armed infantrymen, eased themselves down the ramp, followed by a company or more of commandos on foot. The newcomers were all in U.S. combat uniforms, but a pair of RCMPs were glumly watching the spectacle. "I guess the Mounties don't want anybody interfering," he said.

The minder cleared her throat to attract his attention. "Can I get you anything, Agent Dannerman?"

When he took a closer look at her he recognized the woman: Merla Tepp, the one who had interrogated him. "Since when are you a stewardess?"

"Since I volunteered for the flight, sir. You know how it is. You want to be promoted, you stay where the big brass can see you."

"You'll go a long way," Dannerman said absently, glancing toward the huge window. Something was moving. As it rushed past he identified it as another plane dropping toward the runway, and turned to the minder. "Hey, is that—"

She shook her head. "No, sir, it isn't the Starlab ACRV. That plane's from Ottawa; it's expected."

"Maybe I should get back outside."

Junior Agent Tepp touched her right ear, the one with the communications button. "They'll let me know when it's time," she offered. "If you want to stay in the warm, there'll be a while yet."

"Thanks," he said gratefully, and then realized that it wasn't all generosity on her part. As long as he and Pat stayed inside she could, too. He yawned and sat down, suddenly aware that the warmth had made him sleepy. Drowsily he watched as the new plane slowed, turned off the landing strip and trundled toward the terminal; it had a familiar look to Dannerman, though he couldn't see its markings. Airport crews were already rolling a flight of steps toward it, and the door was opening almost before the plane stopped. Three or four people got out and hustled toward the group with the deputy director. At least one of them also looked vaguely familiar to Dannerman, but he couldn't make out the face. He yawned and closed his eyes. . . .

He didn't realize he had fallen asleep until he felt Merla Tepp shaking his shoulder.

"Show time, sir," she was saying. "They want us out there now."

It was full daylight now, though not a whit less cold. But at least the bosses weren't standing out in the freezing winds anymore; someone had got smart enough to collect an airport bus, and they were all inside it, its heater going full blast, at the end of the runway. A squad of the commandos was deployed around it in full winter gear, all of them carrying weapons; but the soldiers waved them in when they saw the uniformed minder.

That was when Dannerman saw who it was who had just come from Ottawa. It was the Bureau director herself. The Cabinet officer. The woman whose pictures showed her always superbly coiffed, wearing what the latest fashion decreed, and perpetually busy on the highest of high-level affairs. Dannerman had not been physically in the director's presence since she addressed his graduating class.

He could hear only fragments of what the director and the D.D. were talking about. "Yes, Marcus," the director was saying to her deputy, now suddenly deferential, "the Prez squared it all. I wrote the Prime Minister's order to the Calgary people myself." An unheard question from Marcus Pell, then an answer from the director almost as hard to hear, because she looked around and lowered her voice. She seemed to be saying that they'd promised something to the Canadians. Probably a share of whatever they got out of Starlab, Dannerman speculated, and amused himself by thinking about how much the Canadians would ever collect on that promise. If he knew the director, not a great deal.

When the American Congress got tired of passing laws that instructed their successors of a few generations later—but not themselves—to balance the damn budget once and for all, they took a different tack. They simply decided not to bother anymore. It was simpler just to borrow more money. Of course, that led to the problem of paying the interest on the money they borrowed. That was a cost of government they could not escape, nor could they avoid paying for more and more police. So everything else had to be cut— notably the space program.

—*Ad Astra*

"Here it comes," somebody said.

Dannerman caught a glint of metal over the mountains to the west. As predicted, the ACVR sailed past them, far overhead but descending as it banked and turned. It grew larger, settling down toward the ground, wobbling slightly . . . and then it was touching down at the far end of the runway. Plumes of smoke erupted from its tires as they squealed against the runway. Then suddenly the thing was screeching past them, still going a hundred kilometers an hour or better on its stilty landing gear. Behind it ground vehicles began to give chase: two of the personnel carriers filled with troops, a fire truck, an ambulance. "Get this thing moving!" the deputy director roared, and the bus driver obeyed.

The spacecraft was well ahead of them, still speeding. For a moment Dannerman feared that even the

endless Calgary runway wasn't going to be long
enough for this job. But it was—barely. By the time
they reached the end of the runway the clumsy old
antique was sitting there, its ancient ceramic tiles
cracked and smoking, and two squads of riflemen had
surrounded it—to protect it from any of those expected
interlopers, Dannerman assumed, until he noticed that
the ring of soldiers was facing in.

As they all piled out of the bus he could hear crack-
ing sounds coming from it as it began to cool. "Get
those people out of that thing," the director snapped.

One of the men with him cleared his throat. "It's
risky," he said. "The lander's still too hot to touch; we
have to wait a minute—"

"So cool it off!"

The airport fire chief rubbed his chin. "We could
foam it, I guess," he said, "but I don't know if that
would make much difference. And of course we can't
use water."

"*Why* can't you use water?"

The fireman looked surprised. "It would crack the
tiles. It might ruin the vehicle permanently."

"Now, what difference do you think that would
make? Listen, half the radars in the world have followed that thing down. We're going to have visitors in
the next hour. *Ruin* the son of a bitch!"

When the pumpers started
to pour water on the spacecraft everybody jumped
back. Even so, they were splashed. The water from the
hoses flashed into steam as soon as it touched the skin
of the spaceship. Droplets of boiling hot water that
almost instantly turned into icy cold water flew in all
directions, and the ceramic tiles snapped and popped
loudly.

But it worked. Within no more than a minute or two

the pumpers stopped, and the airport crews trundled the wheeled steps up to the cabin door.

It opened.

The first person out of it was a real surprise to Dannerman and a far greater one to Pat Adcock. It was *another* Pat Adcock, grimy, worn, hunching one arm around her chest against the cold as she cautiously made her way down the steps.

The second person was a greater surprise still, because it was yet an additional Pat Adcock; with her arm around the frail and limping figure of a new Rosaleen Artzybachova. Who was alive! Dannerman had gone to Artzybachova's memorial service himself, after she died on the way back from their trip to Starlab. But here she was, suddenly possessing a new life.

The third figure was still another Pat Adcock. That made three of them to go with the fourth Pat Adcock who was standing beside Dannerman, who moaned to herself, "Oh, *Jesus!* What is happening here?"

Then a chunkier, male figure appeared. It had an unfamiliar skimpy beard, but it was definitely Jimmy Lin, the Chinese pilot, sulkily staring around him and shivering in the chill. He was almost immediately followed by someone who—though also bearded, and definitely somewhat beat-up and exhausted—looked exactly like Dan Dannerman.

It *was* Dan Dannerman. The watching Dannerman couldn't doubt it any longer. That was the face he had seen in his shaving mirror—less bearded then, of course—every morning of his life.

How that was possible he could not imagine; but that it was real was no longer in doubt. Those clear memories of what had happened in his trip to Starlab? They had somehow been falsified. His head had been implanted with that damn gadget the X rays showed, and his mind had been tampered with. And he hadn't been aware of a thing.

He shook himself and turned back to the gangplank. That had been six persons; but the Dannerman on the radio had spoken of a party of nine. Who were the other three? More Dannermans? A couple of Martín Delasquezes, the Floridian copilot on the expedition? Maybe even some more Pats?

It wasn't any of those. It was something a good deal more strange. The figure that appeared in the doorway was huge, pale, and not in any way human. It looked to Dannerman like a multiarmed golem, and it carried another creature stranger still—a dwarfish being that looked like a turkey with a cat's head, incongruously wearing a gold-mesh belly bag.

But he had seen those things before, Dannerman realized. Drawings of them, at least; they were two of the weird aliens whose pictures had appeared in the mysterious messages from space, long before.

As that first alien made his way down the steps a second of the same species appeared. By then the ring of soldiers had instinctively dropped to their knees, their rifles zeroed in on the aliens. "Don't shoot!" wailed a thin, high voice Dannerman had never heard before; and it was only one more surprise to realize that it came from the kitten-faced turkey that was cradled in the first golem's arms.

CHAPTER SEVEN

For once in her life Hilda Morrisey wasn't sorry to be in the presence of the Bureau's highest brass. There were decisions now to be made that had never come up in any field operation. The procession of improbables that had come out of the old spacecraft had simply paralyzed her decision-making faculties.

Fortunately for the people who had to make those decisions, some of the problems solved themselves. What to do about the old lady from Ukraine? The first medics to arrive took one look at her and didn't wait for orders. In half a minute they had her on a wheeled stretcher and one of the medics was pushing it toward the open ambulance door while the other two palped and poked her from alongside.

The other human beings were all lightly dressed and clearly freezing in the cutting Canadian prairie wind—like Hilda herself. The director and her D.D. were softly debating high policy considerations, frowning, pausing to make hurried calls on their coded carry-phones. They seemed impervious to cold. Hilda wasn't. She caught the eye of one of the Mounties, the one that looked to be the most senior officer around. "Any reason we can't get back in that bus?"

"Reckon not," he said, then took matters into his own hands. He hustled everyone into the bus—the Pat who had flown up from the Bureau's flight strip plus three (Hilda counted) additional Pat Adcocks, Dannerman and the bearded second Dannerman (apart from the beard quite indistinguishable to Hilda's eyes; if he was not the very Agent James Daniel Dannerman she had run in a dozen operations over the years, he was certainly so close that she couldn't tell the difference); the hired pilot from China named James Peng-tsu Lin, looking grouchy and, for some reason, upset. . . .

U.S. President Reported in Ottawa Airport.

Police sources confirm that the President of the United States arrived at the Ottawa airport early this morning for a top-secret meeting with the Prime Minister. The meeting is said to be related to the broadcast from the U.S. astronomical satellite, Starlab. No further information available at this time.

—*Toronto Star*

And three others.

It was the three others that made a peculiar situation totally bizarre. The little one that looked like a turkey didn't actually look that much like a turkey, after all. The face didn't belong to any kind of poultry. It was more like that of some ill-tempered tiger cub, Hilda thought. The plume that decorated its tail was almost peacock in its colorful splendor, but it wasn't made of feathers at all. It was a display of something more like fish scales that changed color from moment to moment as its owner gazed around in displeasure.

"Colonel Morrisey?" Hilda turned swiftly when she heard her name called, and wasn't surprised to find it was that ubiquitous junior agent, Tepp. The woman was pointing at the turkey, and her finger was shaking. "It's *Dopey!*"

And, Hilda saw, yes, it was. Its picture had been part of the zoo of weirdos that had been displayed in one of those unexplained—or now beginning to be explained—lunatic messages that had arrived from space a year or two before. This was the one they called

"Dopey," all right. It was not really comical in appearance, but it wasn't particularly scary, either . . . unlike the other two.

Those were definitely frightening to look at. They were *big*. The bus sagged perceptibly on its springs as they entered. And they were sure-hell ugly: fish-belly skin, multiple arms, with a white-fluff beard over the lower part of their faces that was more like foam plastic than hair. Hilda decided they were the ones called "Doc." The Dopey-creature seemed quite at ease at being carried by one of the pale monsters. Even the six humans who had come out of the spaceship seemed to pay them little attention. The Earthbound ones in the welcoming party, though, kept a wary distance. One of the Mounties had dutifully interposed himself between the Docs and the humans, presumably in case these space monsters suddenly began ravaging and murdering, but he did not seem happy about it. And when the Dopey hopped down from the arms of his bearer and began to investigate the interior of the bus the Mounty said sharply, "Scoot! Get back there, you!"

The man was waving his arms as though at an unfamiliar, but probably not really dangerous, stray animal. Dopey peered up at him.

"But why?" he asked reasonably, and, to Hilda's surprise, in impeccable English. "I am simply curious about this crude vehicle."

"Get back," the Mounty said, his tone still firm although his expression was distinctly uneasy. The little alien flicked its great spread of tail and sulkily obeyed.

All this Colonel Hilda Morrisey was observing and trying to remember in every detail. She wasn't pleased. There should have been recording devices in place to catch every word and every movement for analysis later on. Those first few minutes after you got a suspect in custody were the most important; that was when some unguarded remark might slip out that you could pounce on later. She fretted over wasting opportunities. The sooner they got these—people—into Bureau custody, the sooner interrogation could begin.

But she couldn't do it here. All she could do at this point was listen.

There wasn't much to listen to. The human arrivals were obviously on the ragged edge of exhaustion. Dannerman and Dr. Pat Adcock—the *real* Dannerman and Pat Adcock—were trying to engage the new ones in conversation, but they were too wasted to respond much.

Except for one of the new Pats, who was looking thoughtfully from one Dannerman to another. When she caught the "real" Dannerman's eye she smiled, got up and sat down again beside him and began a low-voiced conversation. Eavesdropping, Hilda was startled to hear the woman begin a cozy conversation— "They call me Patrice—saves confusion. Well, it saves a *little* of the confusion, anyway. Listen, I'm sorry about the way I look. . . ."

Hilda raised an eyebrow. That was pickup-bar talk! The woman was actually, incongruously, making a move on Dannerman! While the other Dannerman and one of the other Pats were already sound asleep in a shared seat, the man's arm lovingly around the woman.

Horny little devils, Hilda thought wonderingly, and looked outside. The firemen were slowly trundling their trucks away, no longer necessary and a bit disappointed, while a tractor was nuzzling up to the spacecraft to haul it somewhere. The director was standing by the little ship, talking to a man in the doorway with a Bureau tag hanging from his jacket. Not far away the three ambulances were parked, with all the medics clustered around the vehicle where the old lady had been taken. As Hilda watched, that one moved off, siren blasting. A pair of the other medics came trotting over to the bus and climbed in, asking, "Anyone here need medical attention?"

The other Dannerman, roused by the sound of the sirens, looked up. Yawning, he pointed to one of the other Pats. "Better check Pat Five over. She's pregnant."

The real Pat Adcock gasped. Hilda stared at the new Dannerman. "You dog," she said, half-admiringly.

He gave her a weary shake of the head. "It wasn't me that done it, Hilda," he said. "But that's a really long story."

CHAPTER EIGHT

The situation wasn't that Pat Adcock—the *real* Pat Adcock, or so she couldn't help thinking of herself—had nothing to say to these three new selves. It was the other way around. She had too much. She had so many questions to ask and so many things she needed to express that she didn't know where to begin.

The real shocker was that one of her was actually getting ready to have a *baby*. That took a lot of getting used to. Pat Adcock had never been pregnant, had never really wanted to be—oh, sure, maybe now and then there had been a fleeting wistful notion, quickly gone away. Who had the time for bringing up a child? So now she sat mute in the bus while they waited to be told what to do, then stood mute in the doorway of the deputy director's plane while the D.D. and five or six others wrangled over Jimmy Lin. *This* Jimmy Lin. The one who had just returned from somewhere in space. The one who now was adamantly refusing to go any-where at all until he had a chance to talk to the Chinese consul in Vancouver. The one, most amazingly of all, who turned out to be the father of this other Pat's child.

That was really hard to believe.

Down on the ground voices were raised in anger. The argument seemed to be between the deputy director and the RCMP officer, and the deputy director was los-ing. The Mountie was shaking his head firmly. Significantly, a dozen other Mounties were standing silently behind him.

Clearly the deputy director didn't want a major con-frontation. He turned and stormed up the steps.

"Canadian bastards," he was muttering. "First they take the old lady away from us, now it's the Chinese. Well, it isn't worth a war." More loudly, to the people in the doorway: "Get your asses on board. We're going home."

As soon as they were airborne it started. The agents unstrapped themselves, heedless of the fact that the "Fasten Seat Belts" lights were still on. Colonel Morrisey reseated herself at a little desk by a window and pulled out a keypad. She tapped swiftly, then nodded to the other spook. "Recording has commenced," she said.

"Right," said the other female spook. "I'm Vice Deputy Director Daisy Fennell. I don't think we met before, because I flew in on the director's plane, but now I need to ask you some questions. You first, Agent Dannerman—" turning to the Dannerman with the beard. "I want you to begin at the beginning, starting with your launch to the Starlab satellite—"

But the new Dannerman was shaking his head. "First we have to eat," he said.

The vice deputy raised her voice and lowered its temperature. "Agent Dannerman," she began frostily, "you will do as I—"

He stood his ground. "Have a heart! You don't know how it is with us. We've been eating crap for months and we are damn *starved*."

The vice deputy opened her mouth to speak again, but Colonel Morrisey stood up quickly. She murmured something to the other woman, then said, "I'll take care of that. But you start talking while you're waiting for the food, Danno."

"That'll be fine," he said, "if it's not too long." The look Hilda Morrisey gave him as she left was reproachful, but also amused, Pat thought.

"Begin," the older woman commanded. "You approached the satellite in orbit."

Dannerman nodded. "The first thing we saw was that there was some kind of blister on the side of the satellite that didn't belong there, and—"

Pat couldn't help herself. "But we *didn't!* I was looking for it; I'd seen it on the remote, and it just wasn't there."

"That'll do," Vice Deputy Fennell cut in. "You'll get your chance to talk later; now I'm taking Agent Dannerman's statement."

The new Dannerman looked at Pat quizzically, then went on. As soon as they entered Starlab, he said, they'd seen at once that it had been changed radically. New machines. Big ones. *Strange* ones. "The orbiter was full of them," he said, "and all the time we were there I had the feeling we were being watched. . . ."

It went on and on, Dannerman telling these incredible stories—these *untrue* stories, by Pat's own recollection!—while the three other Pats nodded agreement. But it hadn't happened that way!

Or had it? Had something gone really wrong with her own memory?

She hardly noticed when the food began to arrive, but all four of the returned people leaped at it.

And, as a matter of fact, when she absentmindedly took some for herself she discovered that it was an impressive meal, a tribute to the deputy director's airborne kitchen. There was a huge salad, the lettuce crisp enough to crackle, the cucumber slices neatly trimmed of skin, a few curls of a red onion and five different kinds of dressing in silver boats. It didn't go to waste. Before the steaks came—half-kilo steaks, beautifully marbled, still sizzling as the stew set them down—the three Pats and the recently arrived Dannerman (the other one had taken off for the deputy director's private office as soon as they were in the air) had finished the salad, every scrap, as well as the quarter-liter glasses of milk she kept refilling for them. The debriefing paused briefly for eating, and Pat took advantage of the chance. "Dan?" she asked. "I don't remember any of that!"

"No, of course not," he said kindly. "Dopey blanked out your memories."

"Who did *what?"*

Dannerman started to grin, but the Pat next to him tugged at his arm. He suppressed the smile. "It isn't your fault, Pat. They have all kinds of tricks—oh, what's this?"

What the stews were offering was fruit salad, and all four of the returnees cried a unanimous, "No!"

"Surprise us," one of them added. "Something that can't be freeze-dried or canned or irradiated, okay?" And then, looking at Pat, "We've been living on old stores from Starlab for months, so this is pure heaven—or would be, anyway, if this plane had a spare bathtub."

The Pat next to the real, or beardless, Dannerman apologized. "We've been a little short of that kind of thing for a long time, too. Especially poor Pat Five over there. At least Patrice and I managed to get a swim in a few days ago—oh, you want to know about the names? They were Rosaleen's idea. I'm Pat One. This is Patrice. Our pregnant one is Pat Five. What shall we call you?"

"Call me?" It was a problem Pat had not expected to face. What she was called was Pat or Dr. Adcock; that was an immutable given in her life, and there had never been a reason to think about it at all. Until now, when there were three others entitled to the same name.

"Anything but Patsy, please," said Patrice. "We had a Patsy, but—she died."

The Pat bit her lip; some interior struggle was going

on. "Oh, hell," she said unhappily, "we'll talk about
that later. Anyway, maybe I'll be big about this. You
stay with Pat. I'll be Pat One."

"Well, thanks," Pat said, a little bit grateful, still a lot
puzzled, just as a pair of stews made their entrance, carrying plates of hot apple pie with ice cream.

"Sorry we took so long," one of them apologized, "but
those weirdos are in the galley, trying to find something
they can eat. Christ but they take up a lot of room!"

"And they stink," said the other one, just as the *real*
Dannerman came in from the front of the plane.

He seemed cheerful. "Hey, I'll take a piece of that,
too. And some coffee. And then maybe a beer."

"A beer!" the other Dannerman said reverently.

The real one was grinning. "We're missing all the
fun," he said. "The whole world's arriving in Calgary
now. The Ukrainians are after Dr. Artzybachova, the
Chinese are taking Jimmy Lin off in a hell of a hurry.
Even the Floridians are complaining that you didn't
bring their General Delasquez back."

"Martín's dead," Dannerman-with-a-beard said
between bites. "We think he is, anyway."

"Yeah, well, I hate to second-guess the boss, but
maybe moving the landing site to Canada wasn't the
best idea he ever had."

Pat shushed him and turned to Pat One. "What do
you mean, Martín's dead?"

It was a short question, but
it had a long answer and not a cheery one. The
Floridian pilot Pat had hired for her mission, General
Martín Delasquez, had stayed behind to cover the rest
of them while they escaped. Escaped from what? Well,
there was a sort of a war going on. A *big* one. How big?
Well, as far as they could tell, it seemed to involve the
whole damn universe.

Backgrounder
NBI contacts file
LIN, James Peng-tsu, Cdr, PRC
   Spaceforce

Commander Lin has a somewhat shadowy background. A full commander in the People's Republic Spaceforce, he was dismissed from the service for reasons variously given as "political unreliability" and "sexual misconduct"; research has not definitively established which. If the misconduct was sexual, one account has it that Lin is given to reenacting the exploits of his remote ancestor, an ancient Chinese sage named Peng-tsu, who wrote a book extolling the necessity and varieties of frequent sexual experience. An alternative report, however, suggests that Lin is homosexual and the alleged heterosexual activity is a cover for what, in PRC eyes, is a serious crime.

Lin was hired as pilot by Dr. Patrice Adcock (see backgrounder file) in her mission to Starlab. There are now two of him, one who came back with the first batch of returnees from Starlab (this one bugged); the other with Agent J. D. Dannerman and the extraterrestrials. The second one is said to be the artificial-insemination father of the unborn child of the Dr. Adcock known as "Pat Five" (see backgrounder file.)

Vice Deputy Fennell sighed. "How weird is this going to get? Let's get back to the beginning, from where you all entered Starlab."

If what these people were saying was true—and Pat realized that she didn't have any choice anymore about believing them—they had been through a hell of an ordeal. Taken captive on Starlab by the creature they called Dopey and his Docs—by them, but not *for* them; they were only subject races, doing their masters' bidding.

And who were these masters? Why, all the newcomers agreed, the whole thing had been organized by that scarecrow creature from the space messages, a race of superbeings who chose to be called "Beloved Leaders," though why anyone should love them Pat could not imagine. Certainly their human captives had no reason to. They had been kept penned for weeks in a cell no larger than the airborne drawing room they were in, but without any of its amenities—without any amenities at all, even toilets!

That struck Pat as nasty. Then she heard a good deal nastier.

Backgrounder
NBI contacts file
DELASQUEZ, Martín, Maj. Gen. Florida Air Guard

General Delasquez qualified for astronaut training in the U.S. NASA program, but never went into space due to the defunding of the program. When the State of Florida declared itself sovereign in its own territory, Delasquez became part of its Air Guard, rising to the rank of major general. He was attached to the Florida mission to the United Nations, stationed in New York City, when Dr. Patrice Adcock (see backgrounder file) hired him as copilot on her mission to Starlab. He returned with the others and was subsequently found to be bugged.

He was then hired by Eurospace as a consultant on Starlab when they proposed to fly their own mission to the satellite, in which capacity he served for some months at the Eurospace facility in Kourou, Guyana.

Delasquez is said to be well connected politically in Florida's Cuban-American circles. A second Delasquez is said to have died while with the others in captivity by the Scarecrows.

At least the original band of captives had been allowed to live intact, as a sort of control group of humans to be studied. But the aliens had other studies in mind as well, and those had been far worse. The aliens had made additional copies of their captives for anatomical research. Nearly all of those unfortunates had died during the experimentation, generally, Pat Five said, in considerable pain. She herself had been lucky. She had been the one who was chosen, pretty much at random, to become pregnant so the aliens could discover how human beings produced their young. Romance was not involved, nor even actual sexual intercourse. She had been artificially inseminated with sperm—from, she thought, one of the Jimmy Lins, though she couldn't be positive even of that—and so she alone of that group had survived.

It did not seem to Pat that Pat Five had been all that lucky.

She tried to imagine what it might be like to be a laboratory specimen, with an unwanted new life growing inside her. Then she stopped trying to imagine it. It was more painful than she could bear.

CHAPTER NINE

Hilda Morrisey had a good imagination, too. She needed it in her work, but she also needed to be able to turn it off when it was troublesome. Which Vice Deputy Daisy Fennell evidently could not; the woman, listening with openmouthed horror, had completely lost control of the debriefing. Hilda quelled the uneasy stirrings in her own belly and spoke up. "Let's get back to business. One at a time, now. Go back to when you woke up in this place with the mirrors all around you. What happened next?"—pointing to the one who called herself Patrice.

Who shook her head. "I wasn't there. Patsy and I came along later—"

And then there was a whole confusing other story about this "Patsy"—still another copy of Dr. Adcock—and how she'd been electrocuted by some still other kind of alien monster that looked like a hippopotamus but delivered lethal electrical shocks. Only that didn't happen in the mirrored cell, it happened later on, after they'd all been taken out of the city—or the base, or the encampment or whatever you chose to call it—where they'd first arrived, and then been dumped out in the woods somewhere, because the other guys, the *other* variety of would-be universe-conquerors they called the "Horch," were fighting against the ones they called the Beloved Leaders—

Well, it went on like that. Hilda couldn't keep them from interrupting and correcting each other, not even with the help of the recovered Daisy Fennell. The two of them were trying to untangle the question of Horch *vs.* Beloved Leaders when the deputy director came in. He waved them to go on and listened for a moment, frowning silently. He didn't stay silent. That lasted only until one of the Pats said, "—so the Horch took over the helmets, you know, the things we could see things in, they showed us the Beloved Leaders destroying planets—"

"Hold it," the deputy director said. "Beloved what? Who loves them?"

"It's what the slave races call those scarecrow things," Daisy Fennell explained. "Remember? In the first transmission from space?"

"Beloved Leaders, my ass! Can't we just call them aliens?"

Hilda coughed. "There are a whole bunch of different aliens, sir."

He scowled and thought for a moment. "Scarecrows, then. That's what they look like, right? So who's fighting who in this war?"

"Basically it's those two, the Horch and the, ah, Scarecrows," Hilda said. "What they want is control of this eschaton thing."

"Which is what?"

Hilda gamely opened her mouth to try to respond, but one of the Pats saved her. "Remember what you asked us to look up, Mr. Pell? About this man Tipler? He wrote a book, back around 1995. It seems he thought at the end of the universe we'd all be born again and live forever."

The deputy director was staring at her. "You mean the Scarecrows got hold of the book by this guy Tipler?"

"Oh, no," one of the other Pats put in. "They thought it up by themselves. It wasn't until Dopey told us about it that we thought of Tipler."

"The little turkey told you?" Marcus Pell scratched his chin. "Well," he said, "maybe we should get it from the horse's mouth. Let's get them in here."

The first people in the room were a pair of armed guards. Not just armed, as everyone was these days—especially if they were in the Police Corps. These tough-looking individuals carried serious rapid-fire carbines. They took up stations beside the door just as the creatures they were guarding against came in.

**Astonishing Event!
Second Doktor-nauk R. V. Artzybachova
Arrives in Kiev.**

Hundreds of Ukrainians who mourned the death of the honored scientist of the Republic R. V. Artzybachova gathered outside Hospital No. 14 before dawn to welcome the return of their beloved technologist. The State Information Agency offered no explanation of how Dr. Artzybachova returned to life but stated, "There is no question. This is Dr. Artzybachova." Although the scientist was too weak to be interviewed, the Agency released a statement from her which said: "I am gratified to return to my beloved Ukraine. I wish to thank the president of the Republic and the leaders of the Democratic Duma, who have unfailingly striven to care for every citizen."

—*Vremya*, Kiev, Ukraine

Hilda smelled them before she saw them, but she wasn't prepared for what she saw. One of the big, pale creatures was carrying a selection of bowls and pitchers in various arms. The other was carrying the turkey-creature, Dopey. Who was spooning granulated sugar out of a bowl and complaining about the quality of it between mouthfuls. He was addressing the guards as they herded the golems into one corner of the salon. "Why do you treat the bearers as though they were dangerous animals?" he demanded, hopping down to the floor. "They are entirely obedient; it is their natures. Make them understand, please, Dr. Adcock, Agent Dannerman." He took one more spoonful of sugar, then handed the bowl to the Doc, dusting his hands on his belly bag. "Also make them understand that this simple sugar is not adequate for my diet. The bearer indicates it will not poison us, but why can we not have the proper food we brought from your Starlab?"

The deputy director looked at him with dislike, then turned to the Pats. "Please ask this, ah, person—"

"You may call me Dopey. I do not take offense."

"—Dopey, then. Ask him about this war that's going on."

The tiger-faced little turkey made a sound of protest. "Address me directly, please. Please answer my question about the food as well."

Hilda repressed a smile. She didn't mind seeing the damn Bureau bureaucrats embarrassed, and the expression on the face of the deputy director was enough to make a cat laugh—well, not the particular cat (or cat-faced turkey) who was telling him all this. Certainly not the Docs who were simply standing where they were put, holding on to chairbacks and swaying slightly in the motion of the plane. And it wasn't making anyone else laugh.

The deputy director collected himself. "All the artifacts that came from Starlab are under seal in the cargo hold. They can't be reached until we land, and then they'll go directly to the Bureau technicians for analysis. Now tell us about this goddam war."

Dopey flirted his bright-hued tail in irritation, but

complied. Hilda listened, doubting every word. Eternal life. Two great races, the Scarecrows and the Horch, each determined to rule it—forever. And willing to kill or enslave every other race in the universe to make sure they were the ones who won out. And not one word of it believable to as hardheaded a woman as Hilda Morrisey . . . if it hadn't been for the bizarre creature who was doing the talking

When Dopey ran dry Pell had a question. "So how did this man Tipler get onto it?"

"Yes," the little alien acknowledged, "it is interesting that even a primitive like yourselves had some suspicion of the eschaton. Most races do not."

The deputy director sighed. "And you expect us to believe this crap?"

Dopey looked surprised. "Expect? No. I do not care what you believe. However, it is so. We know this, because we have been told so by our Beloved Leaders."

"Beloved Leaders," the deputy director began, his tone derisory; but then his expression changed. As he broke off, all the others turned to look at what he was seeing. One of the golems had surprisingly moved from his statuelike stance. Startled, the guards turned toward him, weapons at the ready; but all the creature did was to squat suddenly.

There was a noise as of a fountain, and a stain seeped out across the rug around him. Hilda stared in revulsion. The damn thing had pulled a little cuplike thing off its surprisingly tiny genitals, and now it was urinating on the floor! And when it had finished it stood up again, looking at the puddle in surprise.

Patrice glanced up at Dannerman with a little laugh. "You'll have to forgive our friend, Dan-Dan. They've got better floors where he comes from. They just, uh, absorb waste. I guess he never heard of flush toilets."

The deputy director stood up in disgust. "Christ," he said. "I'm getting out of here. Corporal, clean that mess up." And then, as he turned to leave, he took another look at the pouch Dopey wore on his belly. "And we'll want that thing for analysis, so take it away from him."

"*No!*" cried one of the Pats—no, at least two of them, and Dan Dannerman shouting something as well; but the nearest guard did as he was ordered. Or tried to. The little alien did his best to scuttle away, but the guard reached out for the reddish metal muff. And screamed. And fell back, or was thrown back, and fell to the floor.

CHAPTER TEN

Whatever the little alien's belly bag had done to the guard, the man hadn't died of it. *More's the pity,* Hilda told herself. If the damn fool had been dead, that would have been the end of it. His corpse could have been off-loaded and transported at leisure to the Bureau's autopsy facilities, where something useful might have been learned. Alive, he was a lot more trouble. He had to be personally escorted to the nearest emergency room, with a senior officer going along to make sure he didn't blab anything he shouldn't, and who was the lucky senior officer to get the job? Why, naturally it was Colonel Hilda Morrisey.

Infuriatingly the man was wide-awake and apologetic long before Hilda got him to the emergency room. The duty doctors were annoyed. "There isn't anything seriously wrong with this man," one said to Hilda. "He could stand to lose a few kilos, and I'd watch that liver, but he doesn't belong here. You say he had some kind of electric shock? Has he had medical treatment already?"

"No. Well, yes," she added, remembering that one of the golems had forced his way over to fiddle with the unconscious guard for several minutes. For all the good that could have done. "I guess you could say he had some first aid. But our plane was just landing, so we brought him right here."

When the doctor said it would probably be best to keep him overnight Hilda agreed, but required the privilege of saying a word or two in the patient's ear. When she was confident that he understood the importance of keeping his mouth shut about anything that had happened on the plane she left him. She hurried to the headquarters and one of the suites for visiting VIPs, and the first real sleep she had had in more hours than she wanted to count.

Hilda slept dreamlessly and woke herself early. She didn't need an alarm; it was a matter of will, and as soon as her eyes were open she knew where she was and what she had to do. First thing was to peek out into the suite's living room to make sure her uniform was back, cleaned and pressed overnight. It was. She retrieved it and headed for the bathroom, scooping up the underwear she'd washed and left to dry on the little line. While she was pulling her stockings on she called the Bureau's New York office on the secure line, voice only, and got the night duty officer. "Colonel Morrisey here," she told him. "I'm going to be stuck at HQ for a while. Any problems your end?" There weren't. All the ongoing operations were proceeding smoothly without her, the man said, and accepted her instructions to turn all her Studebaker files over to Major Geltmann. Then she made herself a cup of coffee from the little machine in the bathroom while she checked the situation reports.

As she expected, all four of the Pat Adcocks and both Dannermans had been stowed away in a safe house, with plenty of Bureau security surrounding them. What was more surprising was that the aliens were squirreled away with them. That couldn't be permanent, if only, Hilda reflected, because the woman agent who ostensibly lived there would have a lot to say about the damage to her carpets.

The only other item that concerned her was that a meeting of the Ananias team was scheduled for 0900. Vice Deputy Director Daisy Fennell was to be in the chair, and Hilda herself was listed as one of the participants. But Marcus Pell was not, and when Hilda checked a little farther it turned out that he, too, was logged as remaining overnight in the safe house.

Well, that made sense. If there was anything important for the National Bureau of Investigation to investigate, the place to do it was where the Starlab people
were. Hilda felt a brief sense of resentment. She should
have been there herself. Would have been, if she hadn't
been stuck with that damn guard.

But she wasn't there, and meanwhile she had time
for some errands of her own. She checked her makeup,
swallowed the last of the coffee and took the elevator
up to the motor pool, because she did not intend to
sleep another night in that borrowed T-shirt from the
Bureau's women's bowling team.

Twenty minutes later she was parking at one of
Arlington's shopping malls. She did not miss the fact that
the valet who took her two-seater gave her one of those
oh-you're-a-cop looks—not hostile exactly, and certainly
not deferential, just wary. She got the same look from
the half dozen sidewalk vendors who were peddling
inflation-hedge knickknacks just outside the mall entrance. Even the two city cops who were interrogating a
young woman against a wall—shoplifter? someone with
a cause who had, perhaps, tried to plant a stink bomb in
the food department?—paused to salute her, but their
expressions were as stony as the perpetrator's herself.

It was the uniform, of course.

Yanqui Bureaucrats Refuse to Release Delasquez Alleged Death Data.

Once again the Anglo politicians in Washington
have denied the official demands of the sovereign State
of Florida for a full and complete account of the so-
called "death" of the "other" General Martín Delasquez.

—*El Diario,* Miami

Hilda Morrisey was proud of the uniform. It marked

her, and everyone who wore it, as part of that group that was charged with protecting all these people—from themselves, often enough. But there were times when she didn't want to advertise what she did for a living. If she were going to stay in this area for a few days, away from the closets of her little New York City flat. . . .

So once she had picked up the necessities she spent another half hour picking out things she could wear off duty. Some of them *nice* things. The sorts of things that made her look like the kind of woman a man, some man, might want to know better. Some man to replace Wilbur, who evidently wasn't going to be handy for a while.

On her way back with her acquisitions Hilda allowed herself a pleasant little reverie about that some man she had not yet met, idly switching on the news, half-listening to the garbled stories and wild speculations over the amazing reports from Calgary.

The message light flashed on the car screen.

She hit the display button. What turned up was an extract from the orders of the day. It said: *Col. MORRISEY, Hilda J. Reassigned Arlington HQ. Promoted brigadier.*

That took care of news, Wilbur and idle speculations. "You *bastard*," she said to the air, switched over to manual drive and whipped the car around in the direction of the safe house and Deputy Director Marcus Pell.

The safe house had sixteen rooms and seven baths, not counting the Jacuzzi and the pool in the backyard. It needed them all. It was crowded, with four Pats, two Dannermans, two Docs, the Dopey, the deputy director and a couple of his interrogators—and eleven, count 'em, eleven guards in and outside the house, plus about half a dozen maids, cooks and cleaners. Who were, of course, also guards, even if they didn't flaunt their weapons quite as conspicuously as the ones in uniform.

The guard at the gate wasn't uniformed; he was dressed in overalls, and he held what looked like a leaf blower. (Bad cover, Hilda noted. The thing wasn't a real leaf blower, of course; it was something a lot more effective against any possible trespasser—but a *leaf blower?* In *December,* with patchy snow still on the ground?) He looked briefly at Hilda's uniform and the ID she flashed at him, then waved her on to the next guard. Or, actually, guards. There were two of them here, this time in uniform and standing at a checkpoint with stop-'em-dead spikes in the driveway just past their post. Hilda's rank wasn't enough to get her past them. She had to sit in the car, fuming, until the deputy director himself came strolling down from the safe house. He gave the guards a nod of the head, and waited until they had taken themselves out of earshot before he spoke. "Morning, Hilda," he said pleasantly. "I bet I know why you're here."

"I bet you damn well do, Marcus," she snarled. "I'm here to tell you that I'm quitting, and as soon as I get to a secure terminal you'll have it in writing."

He shook his head patiently. "No," he said, "I won't. Calm down, Hilda. You know this business is too big for you to sit out. Jesus!" he went on, his expression changing. "You wouldn't *believe* what kind of technology these people have! I was up half the night with that Dopey creature, and he talked straight through. My God, how he talked! Matter transmitters. Jail walls the keepers can walk through but the inmates can't pass. Weapons—oh, Hilda, the weapons they've got! You're not going to want to miss all this—"

"The hell I'm not!"

"—but," he finished, not missing a beat, "even if you did, you don't have the choice. The President has declared a national emergency, so no resignations are going to be accepted." He gave her a tolerant pat on the shoulder. "So you'll be with us for the duration, Hilda, and as long as you're here you might as well come in and get in on the fun. And by the way—congratulations on your promotion!"

Colonel—now Brigadier— Hilda Morrisey never allowed herself to waste time on resentment. That didn't mean she wasn't capable of carrying a grudge; sooner or later, she thought darkly, she would find a way to pay Marcus Pell back for all this. But that could wait.

Meanwhile, she had to admit that, yes, she really did want to be in on this bizarre affair. Pell led the way to a large room where most of the people from Starlab were gathered, the human ones, anyway. The room appeared to be the mansion's library, since the walls were lined solidly with cases of books, but no one was reading. A screen was displaying the Dopey creature, sulkily describing some other weird creatures who were involved with his "Beloved Leaders" in one way or another, but no one in the library was paying much attention to that, either. They were mostly eating. The room smelled of recent bacon and eggs, and there were pitchers of coffee and juice and remnants of toast and fresh fruits on the low tables. It looked to Hilda like the sort of breakfast pigout you might find the morning after a high-school-girl sleepover.

There was a Bureau interrogator sitting alertly in a straight-backed chair, but he wasn't interrogating. Sensibly enough, Hilda thought, he was simply listening as they talked among themselves, while his recorders were capturing everything that was said.

They all looked a lot cleaner than they had on the aircraft, and the ones from Starlab were wearing fresh clothes from the safe house's stores. They looked as though they'd had some sleep, too—not necessarily alone, Hilda thought, noting the way the Dannerman with the beard and the Pat who seemed to be affixed to him were cozily sharing a bowl of strawberries in one corner of the room.

> Tipler's thesis was that when the expansion of the universe finally ran out of steam and the whole thing fell back into that bizarre point in space that had exploded into the Big Bang—the "Big Crunch," as they called that ultimate collapse—everybody who had ever lived would live again. Tipler called it "the Omega Point." That even more bizarre creature, Dopey, called it "the eschaton." But it was the same basic idea.

When she checked around they seemed to be one Pat short. "A couple of doctors are checking Pat Five over," the one called Patrice explained. "Want some coffee? There are clean cups over there."

She took some. So did the deputy director, looking pleased with the way things were going. Dopey, who was in the next room, had been telling his interrogators all kinds of things about the mass of high-tech matériel on Starlab. Pell nodded. "We're going to have to go back up there to get it. The director's getting that set up now."

Hilda looked skeptical. "How are you going to know how to make it work?"

But that wasn't a problem, Patrice explained. Dopey himself didn't know how to operate most of it—he had admitted as much, evidently somewhat amused at the thought—but he didn't have to. One of the creatures Dopey called his "bearers" was a specialist in that sort of thing. He could operate any of it, and show the Bureau's people how.

Hilda looked incredulous. "The golem can do that?"

"One of them can. The other's a kind of biological-medical handyman; he's the one who fixed up the guard last night."

"And he fixed Rosaleen up, too," Dannerman-beard called from across the room. "Between the two of them they can do all kinds of things, if Dopey tells them to."

They sounded like pretty handy gadgets to Hilda. She opened her mouth to say as much to the deputy director, but he wasn't paying any attention to the conversation. He was scowling at the screen, on which Dopey was complaining one more time to his interrogators about how desperately they needed their real food. It clearly was not what Pell wanted to hear from the alien; he got up and headed for the door to the other room.

But as he opened it Dopey caught sight of Hilda just behind Marcus Pell. "Stop now," Dopey said peremptorily, waggling his plumed tail in reproof. "I do not require much rest, but I must have *some*. I will answer no further questions for the next—" he twiddled his little paws in his belly bag—"twenty-five minutes." He didn't wait for a reply but hopped off his perch on a coffee table and brushed past the deputy director as he entered the library room.

He advanced on Hilda. "My dear Brigadier Morrisey, I appeal to you as a woman. Please relieve our distress! See that the foodstuffs are delivered to us at once!"

Hilda Morrisey was not used to being appealed to as a woman. Actually, she thought it rather quaint, but she shook her head. "I have nothing to say about that, Dopey."

The little alien sighed. "In that event I will sleep for the remainder of the twenty-five minutes." And he squatted down on the floor, under a dictionary stand. As he closed his eyes the great fan of his tail bent forward, covering him from the light, and he was still.

The deputy director glared around the room, looking for someone to blame. Then he shrugged. "You're in charge," he snapped at Hilda, and hurried out of the room—on his way, Hilda supposed, to find a secure screen so he could check in with headquarters.

Being in charge was nice, Hilda thought, but it would have been even nicer if she knew what she was supposed to do. For starters she nodded at the guards and interrogators. "You can all take ten," she said. As they left gratefully she peered at Dopey. "Is that the way the thing sleeps?"

Patrice answered for all of them. "I don't know. We never saw him sleep before."

"Um," Hilda said, and then got down to business. "All right. Tell me what you've found out so far," she ordered, looking at her own Dannerman.

He looked rebellious. "Christ, Hilda! They've been talking for hours! It's all on the tapes, anyway."

It was a reasonable answer, so she tried a different tack. "Then let's get to something they *haven't* talked about. Don't you have any questions that haven't been answered yet?"

Pat spoke up for him. "Well, I do," she said, sounding tentative, turning to the other Pats. "You said something about another one of us who died?"

The two other Pats looked at each other. Patrice sighed. "Yes, that was Patsy. We were swimming and these other creatures—they looked sort of like seals—"

"More like a hippopotamus," Pat One corrected.

"Anyway, they had some kind of electric shockers. Like electric eels, I guess. And they lived in the water and— Well, things went sour, and one of them killed Patsy. Do we have to talk about this now? It was bad."

"I'm afraid you do," Hilda informed her—not cruelly, but not particularly sympathetically, either. Making people talk about things they didn't want to talk about was basic to her job description. "You have to talk about everything. Now, these animals with the electric shockers—"

"They weren't animals," Dannerman-beard corrected her. "They were fellow prisoners, just like us."

"Anyway, all that's on the tapes already," Patrice said. "There were lots of different kinds of—people—from different planets there and— Oh, hi!" she said, turning to greet Pat Five as she entered.

"Hi," Pat Five said, looking belligerent. She spotted the table with the coffee cups and headed toward it.

"Come on," Pat One coaxed. "Don't keep us in suspense. What did the doctors find out?"

"They found out I was pregnant," Pat Five said, pouring a cup and adding four or five spoonfuls of sugar. "They wanted me to go into a hospital here for observation. I told them screw that. There are plenty of hospitals in New York and I want to go home. And then I want to get back to work."

"So do I," said Patrice eagerly. "I was thinking about it all the time we were in that damn cell. . . ." Then her face fell. "Oh, hell," she said. "I didn't think. How in the world are we ever going to sort that out?"

"Sort what out?" Hilda demanded.

Canada's Rights in "Starlab" Technology Unquestionable.

We must not forget that Canada has a special interest in the Starlab venture, since it was on Canadian soil that the first returnees from Scarecrow captivity reached the Earth.

—*Globe and Mail*, Toronto

Pat—the real Pat—answered for them all. "Sort out which of us is going to run the Observatory, of course." They were all silent for a moment, then she added gloomily, "I don't think it'll be me, anyway."

Patrice gave her a curious look. "Why not you?"

She glanced bitterly at Hilda. "Because these people tell me I'm goddam *prey,* that's why. I've got this damn lump of something in my head, and according to them somebody's likely to grab me and saw my head off to get at it."

"Oh," Patrice said, nodding, "you mean the bug. I've got one, too."

Hilda snapped to attention. "You do?"

"Sure. So did Patsy—the one of us who died. And, of course, all the ones who went back to Earth—you two"—nodding at the Earthly Pat and Dannerman— "and Jimmy Lin, and Martín, and Rosie. It's a spy thing."

Dannerman, frowning, opened his mouth, but Hilda was in command. "Tell me exactly what you mean, 'spy thing,' " she demanded.

And was astonished to hear the answer. The bugs in the head were little transmitters—well, no surprise there; everyone had guessed that much. But these weren't simple sound-only bugs. You put on a kind of helmet that acted as a receiver, Patrice said, "And then you *were* the other person. The other you. I saw that jail cell you were in, Pat. Through your eyes. Just like I was there."

The bearded Dannerman confirmed what she said. "I was in your head once when you were waking up with a hangover, Dan. And Martín said he was at Kourou, and Jimmy Lin was back in the Chinese space center; in fact I think one time when our Jimmy was listening in the one of him that was in China was getting laid. He said it was just like being there. You could see, hear, taste, smell, feel—it was virtual-reality stuff, only better than anything I've ever seen."

Then they were all talking at once, waking Dopey. "You people are very noisy," he complained, peering out from under his great plume, but no one paid attention to him.

"You mean," Pat said shakily, "you could feel and see everything I did? *Everything?*"

"Well, just when we had the helmet on," Pat One said consolingly. "And we could only receive ourselves—Patrice and Patsy and I could tune in on you, Dan-Dan on the other Dan and so on. Dopey had a way of tuning in on everybody—that's why they put the bugs in your heads in the first place. But he never let us do that."

Pat was shaking her head. "Thank God I wasn't doing anything very interesting," she said. "But now I really do want to get this damn thing out."

"Even if it kills you?" Dannerman asked.

Dopey yawned a little cat yawn. "You people concern yourselves over such trivial things," he complained. "Why should that procedure kill you? The device no longer serves any useful purpose, since you have destroyed the relay channel on your Starlab. My medically trained bearer can remove it without harm to you."

Pat sat up, openmouthed. "You're sure?"

"Of course I am sure. Was it not he who installed the devices in the first place?"

CHAPTER ELEVEN

Dannerman knew what going to hospital was all about, because he'd done it. More than once. You went to hospitals when, for instance, the knee-breakers of the Mad King Ludwigs or the Scuzzhawk enforcers had found out you were a narc, and consequently had beaten the pee out of you. Then, when you got to the hospital, the basic thing you felt was just gratitude that you'd made it there. All you hoped for was that maybe these people could make everything stop hurting.

This time was different. Dannerman had never before gone into a hospital when there was actually nothing wrong with him at all, and when the reason he was there was to let somebody chop holes into parts of his head where neurosurgeons hesitated to cut. Where, if they made one little slip, *pow!*, your brain was tapioca.

What made it worse—not that Dannerman required that it be made worse—was that the somebody who was about to stab him in the spinal cord wasn't even a human being. It was a two-meter-tall golem, with a lot more arms than seemed reasonable, from some preposterous part of outer space. The damn thing wasn't even looking at Dannerman as it stood impassive in the lurching Bureau van. It wasn't looking at anything. It seemed to be in a standing-up coma. And it smelled terrible.

The party had waited until after dark to make the trip to Walter Reed. Darkness wasn't perfect security. It wouldn't stop any professional snoop from switching on his IR scanner that turned any scene into broad, full-color daylight. But it might save them from being observed by some chance-met news reporter or simple civilian gawker who might just happen to be passing by the freight entrance when their little procession of cars slid through the door to the loading dock, and the door descended behind them.

> Walter Reed was meant as a veterans' hospital, but it happened to be really handy to the nation's capital. Presidents and congressmen noticed that right away, and so it became the sort of general all-purpose low-cost medical facility for the nation's top brass. What it didn't have many of anymore was military veterans, because there hadn't been that many wars lately. Now it was mainly the Federal Police Corps which supplied the bodies to fill those ready beds. The Bureau's casualties didn't mingle with shot-up street cops. The Bureau had its own little section, where security was easy to maintain.

Dr. Marsha Evergood was waiting for them on the dock. She glanced at the pair of aliens, the Doc and the Dopey, with a mixture of skepticism and dislike but said nothing as she led them into an elevator. They made a considerable procession, with the aliens, the three bugged humans and Colonel Hilda Morrisey. The Bureau's advance party had done its job. No one else was in sight. Not in the halls behind the freight dock, not in the elevator, which was manually operated by a uniformed Bureau cadet, not in the short stretch of hallway that led them to an operating theater.

It was a real operating theater this time, Dannerman saw. The difference between it and the Bureau's Pit of Pain were that this one had actual surgical machinery, some of the pieces faintly whispering and chuckling to themselves, and the glass wall to the gallery was ordinary glass. There was nobody watching in those seats, either.

Dr. Evergood planted herself at the head of the operating table and peered at the Doc. "How do you want to do this?" she asked the room in general.

The Doc didn't answer. It simply stood impassively, while Dopey methodically picked up surgical instruments and put them down again in disdain. "So very primitive." He sighed. "Still, we will do the best we can."

The best we can. That didn't really sound good enough to Dannerman. Involuntary little choking sounds that came from Patrice and Pat showed that they felt the same way.

There were four or five operating-room attendants in the room, meticulously scrubbed and masked. Though all Dannerman could see of them was their eyes, he was pretty sure that what he saw in those eyes was horror, as the weird little being from space touched their sterile racks with his unwashed fingers. What had become of asepsis? Why, for that matter, were Dannerman and Hilda and the two Pats allowed to enter in their inevitably germ-laden clothes, exhaling their germ-laden breaths, maskless, into the pure air of the operating room?

Dr. Evergood and Dopey talked for a moment in low tones. Then Dopey raised his voice. "Anesthesia?" he said. "No, of course not, we will have no need for your anesthesia."

"Hey," Pat said faintly.

Dopey turned to peer at her. "Have I alarmed you? But there is no reason to fear, this bearer is quite competent. You will experience little or no pain." He paused for a moment for some of that silent communion with the Doc. Then, "He is prepared to commence. Who wishes to be first?"

Dannerman glanced at Pat and Patrice. Both of them were gazing at him. "Me?" he said.

Dopey took it as an offer. "Then very well," he said. "If you will simply lie on that structure over there, Agent Dannerman? Facedown, if you please. Yes, that is fine. Do you Dr. Adcocks wish to watch? If not, you may wait outside, but I think you will find it interesting—oh, what are you doing to Agent Dannerman now?"

Dannerman felt something being draped over the back of his head as the nurses sprang to action. "They're masking the area," Dr. Evergood said.

"No, no, that is not necessary. One other thing, Agent Dannerman. Do you wish your actual memories restored in place of the simulations we imposed on you? That would take a bit longer, but if you wish—no? Very well. Then we can begin."

And they did. Or Dannerman supposed that they did, though all he experienced was the Doc's light touch at the base of his skull, then a sharp sting in the same place. . . .

And then Dopey was saying, "You may get up now, Agent Dannerman. Which of you Dr. Adcocks wishes to be next?" And next to the operating table Dr. Evergood was incredulously holding some coppery thing in the folds of a surgical cloth, and the two Pats were looking astonished and—well, yes, there was no other word for it—looking *terrified*.

One of the nurses took Dannerman's arm and led him away to the recovery room. Once outside the operating theater he pulled his mask off, gazing at Dannerman in wonder. But all he said was, "Holy shit."

The recovery room wasn't actually much of a recovery room, but then it didn't have to be. As far as Dannerman could tell, he didn't really have anything to recover from. What the room was in the normal course of events was an upper-floor solarium for the use of ambulatory patients. On this day the ambulatory patients were out of luck, because the deputy director had preempted the space.

Dannerman was surprised to see that there were two people in it already: the other Dannerman and the Pat from space—not the Patrice or the Pat who had just come from the Bureau's cells, who were still in the operating room; and not the pregnant Pat Five. It took Dannerman a moment to figure out that this had to be the one called Pat One; he was still having trouble keeping them all straight.

The nurse gazed from one to another of them unbelievingly, then shook his head. "We'll want you for tests and X rays," he said, "but you can just wait here now." And he left, still shaking his head, as Pat said:

"Are you all right?"

"I guess so," Dannerman said, rubbing the back of his neck. "Don't ask me what happened. I was asleep."

"Let me see," she ordered. Dannerman bowed his neck while the others studied the place where there should have been a wad of surgical packing, but wasn't.

They were still doing it when Patrice came in, rubbing the back of her own neck in the same way. She did have some answers, though. She had been watching while the Doc removed Dannerman's bug. "But I couldn't see much," she apologized. "It looked like the Doc used a couple of the scalpels to open up the back of your neck, Dannerman, but then he just reached in with the fingers of one of his little arms and fiddled around for a while. It didn't take long. Then he pulled this little metal thing out of you and handed it to Dr. Evergood. I didn't even see how he closed the incision up."

"Let me look," Dannerman pleaded. Obediently the Pat bent her head, but there was nothing much to see. A pair of faint pink lines surrounded her spinal cord just below the hairline. That was all there was, and even those were fading as he looked at them.

The door opened again. Dannerman looked up, but the Pat who came in wasn't the remaining one with the bug. It was the pregnant one, Pat Five, just back from an examination by the hospital's obstetrical staff and looking hostile.

The thought of Pat Adcock, any Pat Adcock, being pregnant was almost as bizarre for Dannerman as his own bug, or the freaks who had implanted it. It didn't seem to strike the other Pats that way. They were quick to find her a chair and perch on either side of it. "Tell," one of them demanded.

Pat Five shrugged. "They said I'm a healthy middle-aged primapara," she said. "They wanted to do ultra-sound and all that stuff, but I wouldn't let them; I want to get back to my—our—own doctor."

"Right on," agreed Patrice. "But what about—" She glanced at the Dannermans, and lowered her voice before she asked her question.

Federal Reserve Inflation Bulletin

The morning recommended price adjustment for inflation is set at 0.74%, reflecting an annualized rate of 532%. Federal Reserve Chairman Walter C. Boettger expressed alarm at the increase, which, he said in a prepared statement, "is entirely due to public hysteria at recent events, does not fairly represent the nation's economic realities and which, if continued, will necessitate adjustments in the interest rate."

They had, Dannerman supposed, got into some of the more intimate aspects of pregnancy. He didn't listen in. What he did, though, was put on a pretense of eaves-dropping, not because he particularly wanted to hear how the pregnant one was doing with such matters as morning sickness and bladder control, but so that he

would not have to make conversation with that other Dan
Dannerman sitting there, as uncomfortable as himself.

When he glanced at the other Dannerman he found
the man looking at him in the same rueful and perplexed way. "Oh, hell, Dan," the other one said, coming over and sitting beside him, "I guess sooner or later
you and I are going to have to talk."

"I guess so," Dannerman said stiffly. The question
was what to talk about. He chose an innocuous subject
to start: "Have they said anything to you about
money?"

"Oh, sure. They said they had never had a situation
like this before and they didn't know who was entitled
to what."

"Same here." The bearded one was glancing at one
of the Pats—*his* Pat—so Dannerman tried something a
little more personal. "Are you two going to get married?"

That Dannerman looked resentful in his turn, but
then he shrugged. "We never said so, but—yeah, I think
we might. Funny, isn't it?"

It wasn't, exactly. Not really funny, but certainly,
considering Dannerman's own experiences with Pat
Adcock, pretty odd. There had been nothing like that
between the two of them before they went to Starlab.
Quite the opposite, in fact.

Jim Daniel was now looking a little bit embarrassed.
"The thing is," he said diffidently, "Anita. The girl I, uh,
we were dating. I thought about her a lot at first, when
Pat and I were getting interested in each other, back in
captivity. I think I had a kind of a guilty conscience,
maybe; Anita deserved better than an occasional roll in
the hay, and— Well, you know what I'm talking about.
Have you seen her lately?"

It was a perfectly reasonable question, but
Dannerman felt a sudden flash of warmth in his face,
and knew it was anger. He was—yes, damn it, he was

jealous. The unpleasant fact was that this other man who was not himself—never mind the fact that in some sense he actually was—had taken his very own Anita Berman to bed. Often. Knew all of her scents and habits as intimately as Dannerman himself. Nothing that had passed between them was secret from him, at least not up until the moment they had left for the Starlab . . . and there had been little enough happening since then.

Dannerman knew it was not a reasonable rage.

But what was there about the things that had been going on for all of them that was really reasonable? "Not lately," he said stiffly, and turned away. He knew perfectly well that sooner or later he and this other Dan would have to try to come to terms. Maybe they could. Maybe sometime they could be as close and amiable as the Pats. . . .

But not yet.

When Dr. Evergood arrived, looking baffled, she had two nurses in tow. It took them a while to sort out which three of the six persons involved had just come out of surgery, but after they did they got busy. The nurses began taking pulses and blood pressures and sticking tiny gadgets in the patients' ears to check their temperatures, while the doctor peered unbelievingly at the backs of the patients' necks. She didn't speak until she was quite through. Then she sighed in resignation. *"Nobody,"* she said, "heals from an incision that fast." She touched the back of Patrice's neck again wonderingly, then shook her head. "Anyway, they're waiting for you three in X ray, but Deputy Director Pell wants to show you something first."

She looked inquiringly at the nurse standing by the door, who nodded. A moment later Deputy Director

Pell arrived. Not alone. Right behind him as he came in the door was Hilda Morrisey, carrying—Dannerman noted with surprise—a lethal-looking carbine. She nodded impartially to the two Dannermans and stepped out of the way to let in four additional armed and uniformed Police Corps guards, two of them pushing what looked like an office safe on wheels.

"I thought you'd like to see what we took out of you," the deputy director said genially, nodding to Hilda. She took a pair of key-tabs out of her pocket, unlocked the safe and stood back as one of the guards lifted out a transparent box. Inside it was an almond-shaped coppery object not much bigger than the end of Dannerman's thumb.

"It's more complicated than it looks," the deputy director said happily, "and now we've got three of them. According to Dr. Evergood here, while it was in place in your heads it extruded little filaments that penetrated large sections of your brains, but your many-armed friend managed to get it to withdraw them again so it could be removed. Seen enough? All right, Hilda, take it away." And when Hilda had relocked the safe and the guards were rolling it away, he looked around at the Pats and added, "One thing. Which of you is the one that's pregnant?"

Pat Five raised her hand. "Me. Is something wrong?"

"You mean medically? No, nothing like that. You're fine, but I got a call from the State Department. The ambassador of the People's Republic paid them a call last night. They didn't waste much time; what he was there for was to serve them with a summons. The complainant is Commander James Peng-tsu Lin, and he's suing you and the government of the United States for custody of the child."

CHAPTER TWELVE

Unsurprisingly, Hilda Morrisey hadn't forgiven the deputy director. She wasn't very good at forgiving. She hadn't had much practice.

What she was good at was facing facts. In the present situation the deputy director held all the cards. She was stuck here with all these Headquarters cruds for the foreseeable future; therefore, she might as well make herself comfortable. For openers, that meant getting a place of her own—not too far away, but definitely not so near that she was under somebody's eye twenty-four hours a day.

Rank helped. The Bureau's housing office was eager to serve a brigadier. They quickly pulled three possible apartments for her out of the databank, and she signed herself out on personal time to look them over. The first was good. The second was better. The third was perfect. They called it a "studio," but it had a Jacuzzi and a balcony and, if you stood just right, even a view of the distant Potomac River. And it had a fine, strong bed, easily large enough for two persons who were on friendly terms. And, of course, when and if some other person might occasionally share it with her they would definitely be friendly indeed.

When she slipped in to take her seat at the team meeting the man from the Naval Observatory was talking about the comet-like object from space that might, or might not, have been the mother ship that delivered the pod that contained the equipment that let the Scarecrows take over Starlab. Hilda didn't listen very attentively. She was thinking of where one might best look for that suitable other person, and of whether the doorman would remember all the instructions she had given him about the personal stuff that would be coming from her New York pad by Bureau courier. She nudged the man next to her and pointed to the coffee pitcher. It wasn't until he had passed it to her with a wry look that she realized he was a new face on the team.

His name was Harold Ott. He was the Bureau's number two electronics nerd, and no friend of Hilda Morrisey's. It was Ott's disdainful opinion that flesh-and-blood agents were the hard way to obtain intelligence that could be got a lot more easily with one of his surveillance tools. Though wrong-headed, of course, the man did know his stuff. But what did his stuff have to do with the Ananias team?

He didn't seem any more interested in what the astronomer was saying than Hilda herself. Ott had his screen up and was idly playing with it. Doing what Hilda could not tell, because he had the privacy flaps up. He seemed to be waiting for something.

So was Daisy Fennell, in the chair. She was nodding absently as the astronomer complained that, although they had identified the object on its approach, no one had been paying much attention to it. Therefore, they had a very incomplete orbit and had not succeeded in tracking its subsequent course. Which would in any case be difficult, since it seemed to have been a powered, rather than a ballistic, flight. "Yes, well, thank you," Fennell said. "Now let's hear from Dr. ben Jayya—" And there was another new face at the table.

It might have been better, Hilda thought, to have done her apartment hunting on a different morning, since she'd missed all the introductions. As unobtrusively as she could she popped her own screen and did some hunting. Then she raised her eyebrows and looked at the doctor with more interest. Dr. Sidoni ben Jayya was a biochemist, and he had just been coopted to the team from his regular base of operations.

Which was Camp Smolley.

That made Hilda sit up. She had never visited Camp Smolley, but she knew what it was about. So did everybody in the Bureau, though not too many civilians did. Camp Smolley was biowar! And what the hell did *that* have to do with the Ananias team?

> Camp Smolley began its existence as a top-secret research facility for the development of biological weapons. When the United States signed on to the treaty banning these, it continued its activities as a top-secret laboratory for developing defenses against biowar. When some busybodies in the Congress thought that was too close to actually making the things, it switched its efforts over to general biochemical research—most of them, anyway. In the change it was administratively reassigned to the NBI, and the Bureau found some uses for its skills it did not think necessary to report to Congress.

As it turned out, plenty. All three of the weird space cratures had been moved there. "For maximum security," he explained, "and for convenience in research. Our primary concern at the moment is feeding them, and so we have been analyzing some of the food canisters that they brought from Starlab."

That made sense to Hilda. There weren't many biolaboratories better equipped than Camp Smolley's, and certainly none that was easier to keep private from the outside world. However, the problem of extraterrestrial nutrition was not a subject that interested Hilda a lot, and her attention began to wander again.

So did Daisy Fennell's. She was paying more attention to her own screen than to the speaker. Hilda studied the woman thoughtfully, because there was a lesson there for her. Time was when Fennell had been a field manager like herself. She had even once run Junior Agent Hilda Morrisey, when they were trying to infiltrate the religious-right groups that had been setting fire to schoolbook warehouses around the country. Daisy had been good at the work, too, until she had made the mistake of letting herself get promoted. As Hilda just had. And now here she was, stuck in administration, trying to keep people like this biochemist from telling the team more than it had any desire to know about the significance of chirality in organic molecules.

Across the table the man from the State Department did seem interested. He frowned and lifted one finger to signal he wanted to say something—it was as close as he ever came to raising his hand. "There would be serious international repercussions if we let them die," he pointed out. "Are you saying there isn't anything you can do?"

Dr. ben Jayya gave him a frosty look. "Of course I am not saying this. We have begun many lines of research. For instance, Dr. Appley has taken cell samples from each of the extraterrestrials. If we could grow the cells in sufficient quantity in a nutrient solution we might be able to feed these—creatures—on cells from their own bodies. There is, after all, one thing every animal can digest, and that is its own flesh. But we're having a difficult time finding the proper nutrients."

"And if that fails?"

Ben Jayya frowned. "But that is only one line of research, as I have just said! In addition we are making genetic studies. There is the possibility that we can immunize certain kinds of food animals against proteins from the aliens themselves, in which case the aliens might be capable of assimilating the meat from, let us say, a hamster or rabbit which has been made compatible—"

Statement of the Central Presidium.

The Central Presidium of the People's Republic of China has released this statement:

"Ever mindful of the vital concerns of its many people, the Central Presidium shares their just wrath at the latest provocation of the snarling dogs of global monopoly capitalism. They presume to kidnap the unborn child of our heroic People's Republic of China astronaut Commander James Peng-tsu Lin. Let these slavish tools of the multinationals keep their bloodstained claws off this heroic unborn Chinese citizen, or the consequences will strike terror to their hearts."
—*South China Morning Post,* Hong Kong, PRC

"I don't think," the State Department man said severely, "that that's good enough, Dr., ah, ben Jayya. They *must* be kept alive."

The biochemist shrugged. "Of course," he said, looking at Daisy Fennell, "there is also the fact that there are additional stores of food on the Starlab orbiter. The subject called Dopey has urged that a spacecraft be launched to obtain them—"

"That's being looked into," Daisy said quickly.

"—but even that, you must understand, is only an interim solution, while our researches must ultimately—"

But he didn't get a chance to finish saying what his researches must ultimately do. The door opened and the deputy director came in, quietly, but changing the climate of the room.

Everyone perked up. "Sorry I'm late. Hope I'm not interrupting," he apologized, knowing that he was, "but I think now it's time we gave everybody a look at the gadget we took out of our friends."

So that was what Harold Ott was doing in the room. The man was already on his feet, politely elbowing Daisy Fennell out of the way to get at the master controls. As he touched the keypad the room lights darkened and the projectors of a 3-D system arose from the tabletop. There was a brief polychromatic haze over the middle of the table, then it cleared and turned into an image of something that looked like a copper-covered almond, slowly rotating as they watched.

"I thought of bringing one of the actual gadgets in for you to look at," Marcus Pell said chattily, "but we're really not supposed to take them out of the secure lab."

One of the men raised a hand. "That's pretty big to go in somebody's head," he said doubtfully.

"It's enlarged so we can see it better," Pell explained. "The actual object is only a little over two centimeters long. It's a bug, all right, and we've got three of them, That's half the world's supply."

"Where's the other half?" the man asked.

"Scattered, I'm afraid. There's one in General Delasquez's head, and he's back in Florida. There's another in the Chinese pilot—not the one that just came back, the other one. We don't know where he is—somewhere in China, anyway. And there's the one the Ukrainians took out of the dead Dr. Artzybachova and they let get stolen. That one we're trying to locate; we have some leads."

The general said testily, "The people who stole it, they're terrorists, right? I don't like having that kind of thing in their hands. What if they take it apart and see what's inside?"

Pell looked courteously at the electronics man. "Harold?"

Ott pursed his lips. "It's not that easy. Here in the lab we've done about all the noninvasive studies we can, and they don't tell us much. Next step would be to use a can opener on one of them, but there's a considerable risk of destroying it if we do."

"Tissue and hair samples from the extraterrestrials give us clues as to the basic proteins, fats and other molecules that make up their bodies, but they are not enough; without invasive surgery we can't tell what less common compounds are required by their glands, nervous systems, etc. However, we have succeeded in isolating a number of their basic chemicals, and, through polymerase chain reaction and other techniques, are capable of manufacturing them in dietary quantities. The proteins are the most difficult. Proteins are basically composed of two parts, an alpha helix and a number of beta sheets. We have synthesized quantities of these. However, it isn't enough to put the right ingredients in a kettle and cook them up; the planar beta sheets, for example, must be folded in just the right way. Still, we have produced basic ration packs for each species, which should sustain life for a period. Whether it contains all the required vitamins and minerals is another question; we cannot guarantee that the ETs will not start developing something like scurvy or kwashiorkor over time."

—The Biowar Report

"So you're stymied?"

"Maybe not." He gave the deputy director an inquiring look and got a nod of permission. "It seems that one of the Doc creatures—the one that isn't a brain surgeon—is supposed to be an expert on that sort of thing. We think probably he could disassemble one for us, and then we could get a better look at it. It's a pretty impressive little gadget. Apparently it monitors full five-sense inputs and transmits them to at least orbital distance. We don't have any idea, really, what its range is. It uses some frequency that we haven't been able to detect. It isn't in any of the conventional radio bands. And it requires no external power source."

One of the men said thoughtfully, "I can see why you'd like to take it apart. If the alien can do it, what's holding you up?"

"Trouble is, we can't communicate with the Doc directly. He never speaks. The Dopey talks for him."

"But if he doesn't speak at all—"

"Well, that's another thing we'd like to know more about. Somehow the Dopey creature communicates with them."

Daisy turned to the neurosurgeon from Walter Reed: "Dr. Evergood?"

"Are you asking if the extraterrestrials are bugged, too? It doesn't look that way. Nothing shows up on X rays."

"Well, they've got something," Ott said stubbornly. "What about this little muff thing that the Dopey creature wears all the time? He won't let us investigate it. Of course, we could simply *take* it—" he added, looking at Marcus Pell.

"Not yet, anyway," the deputy director said. "Go on, Daisy."

The vice deputy turned to the State Department man, whose one finger was again elevated. Hilda resigned herself to five minutes of hearing about all the turmoil that was building up all around the world, but what he said was, "The Canadians are asking for one of those things, since we've got three now. They claim they're entitled to it under the Ottawa Agreement in return for letting us use the base at Calgary to get the people down. The President promised—"

Marcus Pell waved a hand negligently. "We know what the President promised. We'll certainly keep them informed, in due course. Is that all?"

"Well, no. There's also this Chinese custody suit."

Pell looked tolerantly amused. "Wouldn't you say

that's a bit premature? The damn kid hasn't even been born yet."

"That's their point. They say the baby has a right to be born on the territory of the People's Republic so that he may enjoy full citizenship. What they want is for the mother to come to Beijing, not later than ninety days from now, and stay there for the delivery."

"Hmm." The deputy director considered for a moment, then shrugged. "Next time you see the ambassador, why don't you point out to him that unfortunately our domestic-relations courts are pretty well backed up with cases, so their suit might not get heard until the baby's getting ready for college." He gazed benevolently at the man from State, then said, "Now, I'm afraid, I've got some other matters to deal with. Brigadier Morrisey? If you can come to my office for a moment—"

Pell didn't speak to Hilda all the way to his private suite; he was listening intently to the messages coming from his earpiece, and she didn't interrupt.

When they got to the office a man was sitting there. He got up as they entered, and Hilda recognized him. Solly Garand. A field manager like herself—like she used to be, anyway. The deputy director said, "Colonel Garand, Brigadier Morrisey—you know each other."

"Sure do," said Garand, grinning and extending his hand to Hilda. "Congratulations on your promotion, Hilda."

Pell didn't give her time to respond. "Solly's been running some of our ethnics, including the Ukrainian group that's financing the irredentists. The ones that stole the bug from the authorities. You want to tell her where you stand now, Solly?"

"Right. I guess you know we've got assets in the expat

group here in America, and now we've got one in
Ukraine, too. That's courtesy of the Russians, because
they don't want the Ukrainians getting anything they
don't have—"

Doktor-nauk Artzybachova Recovering

Administration officials at Hospital No. 14 confirm that Doktor-nauk R. V. Artzybachova has left
the hospital for rest and recovery. Officials declined
to speculate on her whereabouts or how long she
would remain in seclusion, citing her advanced age
and the exhausting experiences she has undergone.
State Information Agency, Ukraine

"Background her later, Solly. Cut to the chase."

"Well, we haven't located the device yet, but now we
have a problem, It's this Dr. Artzybachova. The irredentists have tried to kidnap her. So she's left the hospital and now she's holed up in her dacha with a few
bodyguards she trusts because they're from old zek
families—"

Hilda interrupted. "From what?"

"Families of old concentration-camp people. From
the Gulag. People who served time with Artzybachova's
grandfather; she knows the irredentists are after her, and
the zek children are the only ones she trusts. Only we
think one of her guards is actually a terrorist."

Hilda mulled that over for a moment. Then she
turned to the deputy director. "That's tough for the old
lady, but why do we care? The woman looked pretty
much past it in Calgary."

"Fooled me, too," Pell said sourly. "That's why I let
the Canadians have her, but it looks like what was
wrong with her was mostly missing her medications for
a few months. Anyway, we can't let the mob have her.
Do you happen to remember what her specialty was?"

"Instrumentation—oh."

"Exactly. Oh. She knows more about the freaks' instruments than anybody else who's human. Does she know enough to get some use out of that bug? I don't know, but I can't afford to find out the hard way. That's where you come in, Hilda. I'm putting you in charge."

She blinked at him. "Back in the field?"

"In the field? Hell, no, Hilda. Solly'll be the field manager, but I want you right here supervising, and— Hold it a minute."

His screen was flashing urgency. He turned it away from his guests and took a message. Then he looked up, furious. "The goddam French!" he snarled. "That was a flash from State. That mission Eurospace was planning to Starlab—they're going through with it. The French sent this note"—he glanced at the screen— "blah-blah, Freedom of the Skies treaty, blah-blah, is an abandoned satellite, blah-blah-blah. So they intend to launch within ten days."

CHAPTER THIRTEEN

With the space freaks gone—gone somewhere or other, no one seemed to be willing to say where—the safe house changed character. The uniformed guards disappeared. So did most of the interrogators, a fact which carried an attractive fringe benefit: Now there was less back-and-forth calling between the safe house and the Bureau headquarters, and so the Starlab people had a chance at the one secure line.

Dannerman lucked out. He got the first crack at the phone, and the person he was calling answered on the first ring. "Hello, honey," he said. "Looks like they're going to let us out of here pretty soon. Any chance of dinner tonight, maybe—tomorrow at the latest?"

There turned out to be a very good chance. Anita Berman was a forgiving soul, and besides she had been watching the news like everybody else. "I've really missed you, Dan," she said, sounding as loving as ever.

"And I've missed you—I can't tell you how much," he said. Meaning it literally, too; because he was reluctant to say all the things he wanted to say to her with two of the Pats waiting impatiently for their turn at the phone.

Anita was saying, "Your voice sounds funny. Is everything all right?" Well, it undoubtedly did, and so did hers, but he couldn't tell her that it was because the secure line was chaos-encoded, and then decoded at the Bureau before being redirected to the open lines to New York. "Look, I have to get off the phone, but—" He looked over his shoulder, swallowed, said it anyway: "I love you."

He gave the nearest Pat a belligerent look as he hung up. She didn't return it. She had clearly been eavesdropping and the look she gave back to him was actually, well, affectionate; but as she took the phone all she said was, "Dan-Dan was calling you. It's about this French thing; he's in the library."

So he was, irritably switching channels. He looked up as Dannerman entered. "What French thing is Pat talking about?" Dannerman asked.

The President: "The presiding officer of the United Nations Council recognizes the honorable representative of Democratic Agrarian Albania."

Mr. T. Gabo: "Mr. Presiding Officer, what is the hurry? Why are we rushing to a judgment in this matter? The so-called Starlab satellite has remained in orbit for many years now. It will remain for many years more. Why must we proceed with such reckless haste to authorize a United Nations flight to secure and exploit this wonderful technological machinery which, we are told, will revolutionize our science?

"I will answer that question. The haste is due to the desperate hunger a few large powers have to secure these secrets for their own use, a gain from which most of our great 188 independent nations will be excluded. I say, go slow! I say, wait until the vast majority of the world's nations have time to catch up, so that we may all benefit from this treasure trove. My little country of Democratic Agrarian Albania is not rich, but we have our pride! And we do not choose to be excluded from our rightful participation in this endeavor."

—*Proceedings of the General Assembly,* Vol. XXVII, p 1122

His duplicate jerked a thumb at the screen. "See for yourself."

That was how Dannerman learned about the Eurospace intention. He peered at the news story, read the French communiqué and then shrugged. "I guess the Bureau isn't going to like that."

Dannerman-with-a-Beard looked at him. "The Bureau? Is that all you think?"

"Is there something more to think?"

"You just don't get it, do you? You haven't seen the kind of stuff they've got on Starlab. What if the French let the Scarecrows in again?"

Dannerman objected, "I thought you smashed the whatever-it-is."

"Sure I did, as much as I could. But what if the French luck out and get it going again?"

Dannerman confronted his copy amiably. "Too many ifs to worry about right now," he said. "Anyway, there's nothing you and I can do about it, is there? And I've got other things on my mind, like getting home."

The other Dannerman sighed, then shrugged. "Which brings us to another problem," he said. "Whose home are we talking about? Yours or mine?"

That was a stopper. "Oh, right. I didn't think of that. Rita's room isn't really big enough for the two of us, is it?" Then he brightened. "Anyway," he said, "I don't think we have to worry about that right now, either, because for the next couple of nights I hope to be sleeping somewhere else."

"Uh-huh," the other said, and Dannerman was pleased to see that he looked faintly jealous.

From the door a tentative voice—Pat's voice—said, "Dan-Dan?"

Dannerman turned around, but it was the other one she was talking to. She looked perturbed. "Rosaleen's left the hospital in Kiev and they won't tell us where we can call her. Can you find out?"

"I'll give it a try," he said, and left them together. It took Dannerman a moment to figure out which Pat it was. They had settled on different-colored outfits from the safe house's stores to tell them apart: blue for the "real" Pat, a red shorts suit for Pat One, a sparkly golden sweater for pregnant Pat Five. This one was wearing a gray tailored jacket—therefore Patrice—and she was lingering. She seemed to want to say something that embarrassed her.

"What?" he asked encouragingly.

She cleared her throat. "It's just— Dan, listen. If you thought I was coming on to you— Well, hell, I *was* coming on to you. Can I explain?"

"You don't have to. He told me."

She bristled. "Oh, really? So what did he tell you exactly? —Well, never mind, what he said was the truth. When we were all in the deep stuff up there and he was the only decent human male around—all right, I admit I got a kind of a crush on him. Well, on you, if you know what I mean, because when I came off the lander and saw you there I figured, hey, here's my chance to have a Dan-Dan of my own. But then I heard you talking to your girl—"

It was his turn to look embarrassed.

"Oh, don't get uptight. You sounded sweet. And it's okay. There's a whole world of men out there; I won't bother you again."

"Listen," he said gruffly, "it wasn't a bother. I was kind of flattered."

She looked him over approvingly. "You said the right thing, Dan. She's a lucky girl."

Surprisingly, she leaned forward and kissed him on the cheek just as the other Dan came back. He gave them both a surprised look, but what he said was, "I got a number in Ukraine, but there's something wrong with the line; I couldn't get through. But I got some news. Hilda's here! We're going home. She's got a van waiting outside to take us to the plane."

And right behind him was Hilda herself, in full

uniform, with the brigadier's golden stars on her collar points. "Some of you," she corrected. "Not you, Danno. The deputy director wants to talk to you."

Hilda wasn't answering questions, either. Not while they were on their way to her little two-seat electro, not while she climbed in to the driver's side while she waved Dannerman to the other, not as she circled around the group loading themselves happily into the van and scooted past the saluting guards at the checkpoint. Only as they were turning into the road Dannerman caught sight of a determined little group of people, no more than half a dozen, waving hand-printed placards: *The Devils Are Among Us!* and *They Are the Antichrist!* and, succinctly, *Send Them Back!*

"Hey!" he said. "Those people are in the wrong place, aren't they? But how'd they even know about the safe house?"

"I wish I could tell you," she said grimly, out of the side of her mouth, and that was all she did say. She was driving fast and silent, with the car on manual so she could exceed the speed limit, and she wasn't talking. Dannerman squirmed around in the bucket seat to look at her face. It wasn't telling much; she was driving manually, and concentrating on it. He tried his luck. "Do you want to tell me what Pell wants with me?"

She obviously didn't. She didn't even look at him. "Come on, Hilda. This is a Bureau car, isn't it? So nobody's listening in. Is it about the damn European launch?"

She gave him a sidelong look. "He'll have to tell you himself."

"Well, if it's a job, don't you think I ought to get a little time off first? I want to go to New York!"

She didn't respond to that, either. He was silent for a

moment, watching her. Her eyes were on the road and her face told nothing. Which told Dannerman a lot. She knew exactly what the deputy director wanted him for, and she didn't think he would like it.

Pacific States Ready to Share Defense Burden.

At an emergency meeting of SOPACTO heads in Papeete, Tahiti, all the states of the Pacific region re-iterated their demand for complete sharing of all in-formation received from the Starlab orbiter, and urged that the flight take place as soon as possible. Prime Minister Gribforth declared, "Australia will place all of its scientific and technical facilities at the disposal of the United Nations in the analysis of Scarecrow technology, but it must not be a European-American monopoly. The states of the Pa-cific region will not be excluded from this venture."
—*The Bulletin,* Sydney

He decided that it had to be the European space launch. He tried a different tack. "What I don't under-stand," he said chattily, "is how the French have the balls to try to take Starlab when they know we've got muscle up there. Do they think we're bluffing?"

Hilda sighed. "We just might be," she said moodily. "The D.D. checked it out. The Pentagon guys admitted that their best estimate for any of our military satellites was that it had a ten percent chance of still being oper-ational. And we only have two that can be maneuvered into position."

"Hell," Dannerman said, startled.

"Exactly, Danno. That's not all of it, either. Ours aren't the only birds up there. The Russians have two. So do the Chinese. And NASA thinks theirs may be a little more reliable."

"Hell and damnation! What are you telling me,

Hilda? Did those people build better war satellites than we did?"

"Better, no," she said judiciously. "The way I understand it, ours were a lot more sophisticated. They could deal with four or five more targets at once, and do it a lot faster. But that made them a lot more complicated, and those crude old Soviet jobs just had fewer things to go wrong with them as they aged."

She slowed down at the entrance to the Bureau's complex. While the guard was checking their vehicle for possible explosives someone might have planted in it, she said, "So we're trying a different tack. We're trying to get the UN in on the embargo; that would mean getting the Russians and the Chinese to join in."

She waved to the guard, who was signaling the all clear. As she started up again, Dannerman asked: "Are they doing it?"

"Well," she said, "not really. They're bargaining."

"So what you really need is time. Like having someone go to Kourou and kind of slow them down," he guessed. "Maybe someone like me?"

She didn't answer that. Unless a faint smile was an answer; but in Dannerman's opinion it was all the answer he needed.

But it turned out to be the wrong answer. When the deputy director at last saw Dannerman—half an hour after Hilda had gone in ahead, leaving Dannerman to sit in a tiny conference room to think about how he might handle the problem in Kourou—he discovered that Pell wasn't at all interested in discussing the French threat. "The Eurospace launch? No, that's being handled, Dannerman. You're not involved. What I want to talk to you about is Rosaleen Artzybachova."

Dannerman was actually startled. "But she's no problem, is she?"

"I'm afraid she is." Pell paused, looking at his screen, making a few changes. "I understand you want some time off, but that's all right. It'll take a day or two to get our ducks in order. Hilda will brief you, and then, Dannerman," he said, smiling pleasantly, "that's where you come in. You're going to Ukraine."

CHAPTER FOURTEEN

Back in her own familiar environment, and especially with that hideous spidery thing out of the base of her skull, the recently debugged Pat Adcock felt kilograms lighter and kilometers happier. If there was any little fly in the ointment, it was simply that there were too many of her.

That was a major management problem for the Dannerman Astrophysical Observatory. When the four of them finally presented themselves to the staff Pat expected an exciting time. The whole situation was totally bizarre even to herself, and at least she had had the time to try to get used to it. What the innocents at the Observatory might make of it she could not imagine, but certainly they would be baffled and confused and excited and—

They weren't. Well, they'd been glued to their screens, like everybody else in the world, and they knew all about how the bunch of them had been abducted to some galactically distant penal colony and what happened there. When Pat explained the dress code that they could use to tell them apart Janice, the receptionist, giggled. ("It's just that I never thought yellow was your color, uh, Patrice," she explained.) And Pete Schneyman, who had been in charge of the Observatory during her enforced absence, asked stiffly, "Which one is going to be the director?"

All four of them opened their mouths, but Pat was the first to speak. "We all are," she said. "We're going to take turns being physically present here, but there'll only be one of us at a time. We drew lots, and Pat One will go first."

"It sounds like a pretty lousy arrangement to me," the ex–temporary director observed.

It sounded that way to Pat, too. She thought about it all the way home—alone, for a change; Pat Five had an appointment with her doctor, and Patrice with a beauty parlor. Then, when she arrived in front of her apartment house and got out of her Bureau-supplied limo with its Bureau-supplied armed driver and its Bureau-supplied personal guard, she found two men waiting on the sidewalk, bundled up against the snow.

They didn't look to her as though they were there by accident. They didn't look that way to the bodyguard, either. "Wait a minute, please," the bodyguard said to her, even before the men moved toward the car.

The driver leaped out to join her, his hands on his gun. For a moment Pat thought there was going to be a firefight right before her eyes, but the shorter of the men was holding up some sort of document. The two Bureau agents studied it, asked a few questions and muttered among themselves. Then the bodyguard turned to Pat. "He's a diplomat," she said. "From China. He says he just needs to talk to you for a minute."

Pat hesitated, but the two Bureau operatives had their guns in their hands now, and the waiting men showed no signs of hostility. Indeed, they had no violent intentions. "Dr. Patrice Adcock?" the smaller one said. "My associate has a summons for you. Thank you. That's all."

They turned and walked away, leaving Pat holding a thick sheaf of folded paper. The man was a simple process server. And when Pat looked at the paper she discovered that she had been served with a suit. Commander James Peng-tsu Lin, plaintiff, was demanding of Dr. Patrice Adcock, defendant, that she proceed forthwith to the People's Republic of China so that the child she was carrying could be born as a citizen of his father's country.

She thought of telling them they had served the wrong, i.e., the nonpregnant, Dr. Pat Adcock, but what was the point? She sighed. "Thank you," she said politely to the Chinese. And to her bodyguards, "It's all right. Let's go upstairs."

There were too many of her for the apartment on the upper East Side, too. It had been comfortably roomy for Dr. Patrice Adcock, but with four Dr. Patrice Adcocks living there it was pretty damn cramped.

The Pats had done the best they could to resolve the difficulties. They'd drawn lots for sleeping quarters, and Pat considered she had done well on that draw. She hadn't got her "own" bedroom, no. That was the one with the canopied bed and the hot tub, and it had gone to Pat Five as a courtesy to approaching motherhood. The two guest rooms had gone to Patrice and Pat One. Pat herself had the never-used maid's room. Small, yes; remote from the rest of the apartment, sure; but the maid's room not only had its own private little bath, it had a full-function screen monitor. The original purpose of that, Pat supposed, was so that the maid could do her meal planning and record-keeping without interfering with her employers.

But it worked.

So the fact that Pat couldn't be in the Observatory didn't mean that she couldn't do astronomy. As soon as she was out of the boots and heavy cold-weather slacks she made herself a cup of mint tea, sat down at her workspace and began digging into this crazy eschaton thing.

The Bureau had exerted pressure where it was needed. As a result some university library had messengered her its file copy of the Frank Tipler book, *The Physics of Immortality.* She opened it gingerly, for the book was packed in its own custom-built casing, with a note pasted to the front cover that said it was in delicate condition and should be handled with extreme care.

That was true enough. The old wood-pulp pages threatened to crack as she turned them, but she was able to read enough to remember the general argument of the book as prissy little Dr. Mukarjee had described it for his class in that ancient graduate-school seminar at Caltech. What Tipler called the "Omega Point" Dopey's people seemed to call the "eschaton." But it was the same thing.

And, of course, it was unbelievable. The only thing going for it was that some pretty powerful beings, somewhere in space, seemed to believe it very much.

On Earth there was still a lot of disbelief around, even about the reality of Dopey and the Docs. For Pat, who had seen—and touched, and even smelled—the aliens from Starlab, there was no question. These were real extraterrestrials, all right. But most of the world had seen only the news broadcasts the Bureau had allowed, and a considerable fraction of that audience skeptically supposed they were nothing but another set of TV morphs.

That didn't bother Pat. What bothered her was the skepticism from her colleagues, notably the fiercely combative arguments that were coming from the Max-Planck Institut für Extraterristriche Physik. The Germans weren't just skeptical. They were downright libelous.

Part of that particular fountain of hostility, Pat knew, was an old score being settled. The Germans had supplied some useful information which had helped to figure out what was going on on Starlab. They'd asked for information about her mission in return; she had refused to give it to them. Naturally they were going to piss all over anything connected with the Dannerman Astrophysical Observatory; whoever said that scientists were never motivated by petty angers?

Invasion Near? What We Must Do!

This latest alarming communiqué from the space aliens emphasizes the need for immediate and affirmative action on the proposals of the Albanians in the United Nations. As the Nigerian representative to the UN, Mr. Albert Ngoro, said this morning in New York, "The flight to the Starlab satellite must take place immediately so that we can begin to protect ourselves from a challenge that is sure to come." Mr. Ngoro also added that the flight must be multinational, and that one of our fine Nigerian weapons specialists should be a major member of the crew.

—*Daily Times,* Lagos, Nigeria

But they had, or seemed to have, a point. What the Germans claimed was that there couldn't possibly be any eschaton, or Omega Point, or grand resurrection, because there wasn't ever going to be a Big Crunch. Everyone knew, they said loftily, that the universe was never going to recollapse, but would simply go on expanding forever.

Well, there was no doubt about it. They did have a point.

Thinking of forever reminded Pat to look at her watch, and what she saw surprised her. It was midafternoon. She had forgotten to eat lunch.

While she was microwaving the handiest thing in the freezer Pat Five came in, looking harried. "Lunch? Yes, maybe so; what've you got there, meatballs? But I'll have to eat fast, because"—pausing to catch a glimpse of herself in the kitchen mirror and frowning—"I've got to go out again as soon as I change. Janice was right, damn her; this isn't my color, is it? I think I'll see what else we've got that might fit me now. Anyway, I've got an appointment with the lawyer the Bureau got me to respond to this suit—"

Tardily Pat remembered the summons. "Wait a minute," she said, in the middle of putting another carton into the microwave for herself. But when she displayed the document Pat Five shrugged it off. "We all got one. I guess they wanted to make sure it got to the right person. Aren't you going to ask me what the doctor said?"

"Of course I am," Pat said remorsefully.

"Well, brace yourself," Pat Five said, spooning Swedish meatballs into her mouth. "What she said was I'm going to have triplets."

"Triplets?"

Pat Five nodded. "That's right. Three of them. All girls, she thinks, but she wants to do another amniocentesis in a couple of weeks. And what've you been doing with your day?"

It took Pat a while to get back to her screen, because long after Pat Five had left she was still thinking about triplets. Three little girls. Genetically her own daughters!—although with the unfortunate genetic contribution of their presumed father, Jimmy Lin. But definitely her own flesh and blood. . . .

She couldn't handle that. It was a relief to turn back to the eschaton file.

If the Ugly Space Aliens were right, one of the Germans had posted, then the quantity astronomers called "omega"—the measure of how much mass the universe contained—had to be more than one. Okay, Pat thought. There was no argument about that; if the universe didn't contain enough mass, the force of gravity would not be strong enough to pull it all back together again. Of course.

Also of course, no one had any good way of measuring omega; you couldn't weigh every star and galaxy, not to mention all the dark and undetectable particles that might add vast amounts of mass to the total; so you had to try to estimate it from other values—values that you *could* measure. Sort of. Though with considerable difficulty, and with huge error bars. Values like analyzing the ratio between distance and rate of recession, to see if there was any evidence of slowing expansion.

For that investigations in a great many areas were under way—though what a pity it was, Pat thought, that they were so prone to giving contradictory results.

Taking one consideration with another, the consensus among Earthly astronomers was that the results that gave an omega of less than 1 were probably more trustworthy than the ones that didn't. That was what the Germans were contending, and for all of her professional career Pat had shared that view.

But not everyone did. And among those who did not were, apparently, those fantastic creatures whose images had appeared on the world's TV screens two years before: the monstrous "Horch," with their snaky long dinosaur necks and their brutal faces, and the even uglier scarecrow-bodied "Beloved Leaders." They could be wrong, too, Pat told herself. But they were obviously a lot more technically advanced than human beings. So maybe they knew. . . .

And maybe it was true that, at some unimaginable time in the future, she and everyone else she knew—and everyone she hadn't ever known or even heard of, as well—would be reborn in this improbable (but possibly real) eschatological Heaven.

Medical report
Gross morphology of extraterrestrials:
   "Docs."
Classified.

The physical measurements of "Doc A" are:
Height, 246 cm, weight 185 kg, resting pulse 27,
resting respiration 16.

For "Doc B:" Height 233 cm, weight 181 kg,
resting pulse 25, resting respiration 16.

Both specimens are vertebrates and apparently
mammalian. They possess the arms-legs-head pri-
mate architecture, except that they have two additional, smaller "arms" on each side. Instead of hair
they possess a chitinous white growth on face, ax-
illae and genitals. It has not been possible to obtain X rays or blood samples. However, stool,
urine and saliva samples have been obtained
which are currently under study. Curiously, few
microorganisms have been observed even in the
excreta.

It is desirable that additional studies be carried
out, but the subjects do not respond to our efforts to
secure their cooperation.

When the doorbell rang it
was the live-in guard who responded, peered through
the spyhole, opened the door. It was a permitted visitor.
In fact, it was Dan Dannerman, escorted there by his
own guard.

As the guards retired to wherever the guards went
when they stayed out of the way, Pat looked him over.
"Which one are you?" she asked.

He grinned wryly. "I'm the stay-at-home one. And
you?"

"The same. That is," she added, "the one that still thinks you're a shit, Dan."

He didn't protest, and Pat felt quick sting of remorse. She tried to be more friendly. "I thought you were off with your girlfriend," she said, more sociably.

"I was, but now I've got a job to do. That's what I want to talk to you about." He hesitated, and then said without preamble, "It's about Rosaleen Artzybachova. She's in trouble. Her life is in danger." Then he noticed the expression on her face. "What's the matter?" he demanded.

"We buried Rosaleen months ago," she said.

"Christ, Pat, pay attention. I'm talking about the *other* Rosaleen."

"I know who you're talking about. But when you tell me her life is in danger it's just kind of funny."

He looked at her with disapproval. "I thought you and Artzybachova were friends."

Medical report
Gross morphology of extraterrestrial:
  "Dopey."
Classified.

The physical measurements of "Dopey" are: Height, 54 cm, weight (including clothing and metallic pouch, which he refused to remove), 17.6 kg, pulse ranging from 33 to 70, respiration ranging from 22 to 40. The cause of the variations in pulse and respiration are not known, and do not seem to relate to changes in stress or emotional state.

The subject, which speaks English, is extremely recalcitrant and states that it will not cooperate in further studies unless demands are met, which, it says, it has already communicated to relevant authorities.

Stool samples have been obtained and are currently under analysis. Preliminary reports have not yet been received.

"We were. Are. What about it?"

"She needs help. There are terrorists who are trying to kidnap her, for what she knows about that alien technology you were so hot for. Do you want to help her or not?"

"Help her how?"

He looked uneasy, but said, "I've been ordered to go to Kiev to take care of things there. It'd make it a lot easier if you came along."

"Why?"

"She's scared, Pat. She knows the terrorists want her, and she's not letting anybody near her that she doesn't know."

"She knows you," Pat said, stalling for time.

"Actually," Dannerman said, "she doesn't, or at least not very well. It's the other Dannerman she really knows, not me. But she and you have been friends for years. What's the matter? Are you afraid?"

And she naturally had to assure him that she certainly wasn't *afraid,* and in the process didn't notice that he hadn't said what "things" he was going to take care of.

CHAPTER FIFTEEN

When Hilda Morrisey met with the woman from the FZB, as the Russians had taken to calling their current successor to the Cheka, it wasn't in the gloomy old Russian embassy, and it certainly wasn't at Bureau headquarters. They met on neutral ground, a Steak 'n' Shake a few blocks from the embassy. When Hilda protested that they shouldn't be talking about secret matters in a public place the woman laughed at her. Her name, she said, was Grace. She was a lot younger than Hilda, and a lot prettier and better dressed, too: iridescent tanktop that made the most of her brassiereless breasts, and as mini a miniskirt as Hilda had ever seen—the latest thing from the ateliers on Nevsky Prospekt, no doubt. "Don't worry, dear colleague Hilda," she said. "It is quite safe here. All the busboys are friends. We call this place our commissary, since the food in the embassy is not great." And indeed there was never a moment in the whole time they sat there when a busboy or two wasn't nearby, rattling dishes at the tables of any other diners who might have overhead anything, dawdling over clearing the nearest tables so that no one could be seated too close.

The two of them confirmed their recognition signals with no problems. Only when they came to the specifics of the pickup Grace demurred. "You would prefer to use an American aircraft? Out of the question, dear colleague. It would certainly attract attention. No, we will supply a brand-new Russian MIG-90 VTOL; it is the same model we sell to the Ukrainians themselves, and it will have appropriate markings. I have already chosen the pilot, a very good man. He will whisk your people to Moscow—"

In the old Soviet days the country of Ukraine did not get the respect it deserved. Most of the world called it "the" Ukraine, as though it were some mere backwater province, while the country's Russian masters did worse. They *made* it a province. To patriotic Ukrainians this was an infamy. Wasn't Ukraine, as early as the tenth century, the first Christian kingdom in the area? Wasn't it, under the princes of the Rurik dynasty, an empire of its own, with the Russian hinterlands no more than a province itself? And wasn't it about time that glorious epoch was restored?

"Not Moscow. Vienna."

Grace put down her chiliburger. "But why Vienna? We can supply perfect security for you in Moscow. Your plane can be waiting at the airport to take them home, a quick transfer, no problem—"

"Vienna," Hilda said firmly.

Grace sulked for a moment, then gave in, and they spent the rest of the meal discussing why Moscow's Dynamo team could beat any Western footballers. And then, back in the Bureau headquarters, Hilda changed back into her uniform while talking on the secure lines to Frankfurt, going over the arrangements Solly had made with the assets in Ukraine. Everything was set for the mission.

But it was *wrong*. It was the first time one of Hilda's chicks had gone off on a mission without Hilda herself lurking somewhere near. Was there any chance that, even now, the deputy director could be persuaded to dump Solly and let Hilda go where she properly should go, near to the scene of action.

There wasn't. When she reported to the deputy director he scoffed at her. "Take field command? You? Not a chance, Hilda. I've got a job for you here; you're going to take over from Daisy Fennell."

Alarm bells went off in Hilda's head. "Running the damn team meetings?"

"Among other things, yes," Pell said, his tone suddenly frosty. "Things are heating up. I'm locked into all the negotiations with the UN, and that's turning into a full-time job. So I'm turning all the operational stuff over to Daisy for the time being, and you're the best choice to take over her assignments. I don't mean just the team meetings. I mean handling the freaks and keeping an eye on the Starlab bunch. You're the one who knows them best— What? Well, certainly you'll still be in charge of the Ukraine thing, too. If you need help, requisition it. Now, go talk to Daisy; she's got her hands full."

Daisy had her hands full, all right; she was in the middle of some problem with the Catalans and the Basques, and a field manager from Bangladesh was waiting to talk to her about Asian drug gangs. She waved Hilda to a seat while she finished dictating a note to the Spanish police, then leaned back and regarded her. "Congratulations, Hilda," she said. "Let's see, where do we start? You'll need to go out to Camp Smolley today, the freaks are bitching about their food and—well, everything; anyway, the one that looks like a parrot is. But the other two are having troubles, too."

"What kinds of troubles?"

Daisy waved a hand. "They'll tell you all about it when you get there. Then there's the team. Marcus doesn't want to lose momentum with the experts, so he wants a meeting every day—"

"All those people? *Every* day?"

"You can choose the participants yourself. You probably don't need the astronomer anymore—or do you? It's your call. And probably you can skip today if you have to; there won't be much time before you get back from Smolley. Then—wait a minute."

She frowned as her screen buzzed at her, listened for a moment, then said, "Apologize to him; I'll be with him in five minutes. Ten at the most."

She turned back to Hilda. "Sorry, where was I? Oh. The Starlab people in New York. Guards and surveillance are being handled by your old office; I've instructed them to report to you, but there haven't been any problems. The Chinese are still trying to get their hands on the pregnant one, and the damn Floridians are pissing and moaning about letting their General Delasquez get killed. Or abandoned. Or whatever happened to him up there."

She thought for a moment, then leaned back and smiled. "So what about it, Hilda? How do you like life in the fast track?"

The answer was "very little"; but all Hilda said was, "I'd rather be out in the field."

Daisy said sympathetically, "I felt that way, too, at first, but you get used to it. And there's a time to settle down, isn't there? Listen, while I think of it, my husband and I were wondering if you'd like to come over for dinner—"

Hilda goggled at her. Husband? When had that happened? And what did Daisy want one of those things for?

"—maybe tonight? You've never seen our house, have you? So, about eight? And there's somebody Frank and I would like you to meet."

All the way out to Camp Smolley Hilda was fuming to herself. Time to settle down? Time to turn into another Daisy Fennell? The worst part of it was that she hadn't ducked fast enough. Now she was committed to dinner with Daisy and Frank and Frank's really nice partner in the real-estate business, Richard, who had lost his wife to a mugger two years before and was just the kind of man Hilda ought to get to know.

She swore under her breath. Then, as she drove up to the entrance of the old biowar establishment, it got worse. There was a Police Corps lieutenant directing traffic at the turnoff, impatiently waving Hilda away with the other commuters until he saw her uniform. Then he saluted and allowed her to enter the public road that led to Smolley's access. But when she reached the gated drive to the labs there was half a company of police lining the far side of the road, across from the two-meter berm that surrounded Camp Smolley itself. Nearly a hundred picketers stood behind the police line, shouting and waving banners: *Beware the Antichrist from Space! God Is Not Mocked! There Is Only One True Word!* And one other small group, shooed away from the other by the police, who had a different crusade on their minds. Their placard read: *Free Dopey and the Docs!*

---

10 a.m. Traffic Advisory

No bomb or free-fire zones have been declared in the District or immediate environs.

There is unusual crowd activity at the White House and in the vicinity of the National Bureau of Investigation headquarters in Arlington. At present the situation is orderly, but alternate routes are advisable.

(Consult Maryland and Virginia notices for other areas involved.)

Damn these people! How did they know? The aliens had been moved here under the tightest security the Bureau could provide . . . but here were the protesters.

Naturally the protesters had no hope of getting into the biowar plant itself. Even Brigadier Hilda Morrisey couldn't pass until she parked her car and went through a metal detector, a patdown and a Bureau cadet with a sniffer like a portable vacuum cleaner to make sure there were no traces of banned chemicals on her person. Then they wouldn't let her take her car the remaining half kilometer to the building proper. "There'll be a shuttle van here in a moment, ma'am," the guard officer said. "You can wait inside if you like. Welcome to Camp Smelly."

She didn't like. She did it anyway, sitting with an unwatched news screen for entertainment. It wasn't entertaining; what was on at the moment was an interview with that Colonel What's-his-name Du-something, the French astronaut—or would-be astronaut, because as far as Hilda could tell he had never actually been in space. The interview was in French, but after the first few seconds an English voice-over translated his words. "We will be ready to launch to the so-called Starlab within the next few days," he said. "The American threat? It is pure braggadocio. I am not afraid. They dare not shoot us down; there are no national boundaries in space, and we have as much right to go there as they do."

"Son of a bitch," Hilda said out loud, startling the lieutenant, who had come in to get out of the damp chill. "Oh, not you," she said, waving at the screen. "That son of a bitch. And those sons of bitches across the road, too."

"Oh, don't worry about those people, ma'am," the lieutenant said earnestly. "Do you see that berm out there? Surrounds the whole base, and there isn't only full electronic surveillance, it's mined. Antipersonnel mines. Squirrels and birds won't trigger them—though we got a deer once—but I guarantee none of those creeps will get through. And here comes your van."

She never got a chance to tell the man that what she was worrying about wasn't the protestors breaking into Camp Smolley, it was how they had known enough to be there in the first place. When she got out of the van she was searched again before she was allowed to go through the ostensibly simple wooden door of the ostensible ancient mansion—neither of which had ever fooled anyone—and then had to be searched one more time before she was allowed to pass through the real door, bank-vault thick, ponderously opening on its huge hinges with a hiss of air being admitted to the lowered-pressure anteroom behind it.

None of that was really necessary, of course. No one thought there was any real need for Category Five containment for Dopey and the two Docs. If the things had brought any horrible alien plagues to Earth with them there had been plenty of opportunities to spread the disease before they ever saw Camp Smolley. But the director had decreed Category Five containment.

Hilda would have done the same. Not for any epidemiological need, but just to cover your butt for the congressional inquiry that sooner or later was sure to come.

Hilda's heavy uniform coat was taken away from her and then she was allowed into the wing where the aliens were housed. The warmth was wonderful, after the damp cold of outdoors, but suddenly Camp Smelly began to deserve its old nickname. The stench of alien metabolism was startling. In one room the two Docs were kept, one characteristically standing immobile, the other very uncharacteristically lying on a pallet on the floor, with two or three medics hovering around.

The cadet who was guiding her explained, "It's diarrhea, Brigadier Morrisey. They were trying to get some minerals into their diet. They think it was the soluble calcium and iron that did it. Now Captain Terman's waiting for you in the laboratory."

There were two more armed guards in front of the laboratory door, but they stepped aside to let Hilda and the cadet enter. The stink of the laboratory was different from the one that came from the sick Doc, but not a lot more pleasant; it seemed to come from an opened canister. Captain Terman stood there, watching a medic carefully measure out spoonsful of what looked like lavender slime. The stuff had orange-and-black lumps in it, and it smelled like a brewery.

Charity—at a Price!

When the High Governor's office announced that our brothers to the North were graciously willing to remove the "device" that was implanted in the brain of our brave astronaut, General Martín Delasquez, they were polite about it. They did not mention that the Yankee authorities have presented a rather large bill for the "costs" of these services.

If our information is correct, the only "services" the Washington government will contribute is the provision of a room for the operation to take place in. The actual surgery will not be done, in fact cannot be done, by any North American. It will be performed by the very "Doc" creature which General Delasquez himself did so much to bring to us. So once again we Floridians learn that "gifts" from the North are never without a price.

—*El Diario,* Miami

The captain was an elderly man, even more past his proper age-in-grade than Hilda had been, and he waited until the canister had been capped before he turned to

greet her. "Sorry I couldn't meet you myself, ma'am,"
he said, not really sounding very sorry at all, "but
they're very strict about how much of this we can give
them at a serving. Has the cadet told you what we do
here?"

"I can see what you do here," Hilda said, looking
around. "Show me what else you do, then I want to talk
to Dopey."

What they were doing was a lot. Through a plate-
glass window she got a look at a sterile-environment
biology lab. Everyone inside wore clean suits and face
masks; one woman was starting a centrifuge, two men
were titrating drops of something into Petri dishes of
something else; three other people, including Dr. ben
Jayya, were clustered around a screen with dancing
curves of red and blue and green—doing what Hilda
could not guess. (But didn't think she needed to, since
this was the sort of thing Camp Smolley was supposed
to be best at.) In another room there was a long table
that contained half a dozen objects, mostly metal. They
were not any kind of objects Hilda had ever seen
before; with a shock, she realized these were some of
the things the rocket had brought back from Starlab.
Inside a containment hood two technicians were carefully dismantling a six-sided gold-colored object the
size of a hatbox. "Dopey says it's a recording unit,"
Captain Terman told her. "Wait a minute, I'll give you
a better look."

He turned on a wall screen, and she was looking
down into something that didn't look like any recording unit she had ever seen. No revolving spool, no drive
heads; what was coming out of the machine, layer by
layer, was a succession of flat, thin hexagonal things
that looked more like filter paper than any mechanical
device, but in half a dozen different colors, some of
them faintly glowing. "We have three of these,"
Captain Terman said with satisfaction, "so we figured

we could try to take one apart. That other stuff? Junk, mostly. That long green thing looks like a crowbar. If you ask me, that's what it is. There's no internal mechanism at all. Do you want to see Dopey now?"

"Probably. What's he doing?"

"Being debriefed, of course. Wait a minute, I'll show you." The captain touched the controls again, and Dopey appeared. The little alien was perched glumly on a chair, surrounded by his debriefers. His cat whiskers were drooping and his fan had turned leaden gray. He was talking in a low monotone, and when Hilda tried to make out what he was saying she frowned. "Is that Spanish he's talking? Why?"

The captain looked unhappy. "He said he was tired of speaking English, and both Herrera and Ortiz are bilingual. He was quite insistent. He's not easy to get along with, ma'am." He looked aggrieved. "You know that belly bag of his?"

It wasn't the most sensible question anyone could ask; Hilda was looking right at the thing. "What about it?"

"Well, the lab people want it for study. Only he won't let us take it."

"The last man to try that," Hilda said, remembering the flight back from Calgary, "nearly got electrocuted."

"Yes, ma'am. They know that, but they think they could use insulated tongs or something. Funny thing is, it doesn't seem to shock him, you know? I can't figure that part out. Anyway, he complains that our tests— they've been going over it with radiation counters and things—the tests are depleting its power reserve, and he can't live without it."

"Do we have any idea whether that's true?"

"No, ma'am. Only one way to find out, though— take it away from him and see if he dies. But I can't do that without orders."

Hilda nodded, eyeing the man. She wasn't going to be the one to get him off the hook; if someone ever gave that order, it wouldn't be Hilda Morrisey. "We'll let that go for a while. Let's go see him."

As soon as Dopey saw Hilda he pushed his way past his debriefers and scurried over to her. "Brigadier Morrisey, you must help me!—what?" He paused to listen to something one of the debriefers said in Spanish. "Please make these people understand that we are starving! We must return to the Starlab and get more of our food."

"You have food," Captain Terman said quickly, glancing at Hilda.

"It is not food! It is certainly not *our* food—a teaspoon of that at a time, that's all you give us—and that other stuff will kill us. You see what happened to my poor bearer!"

"It is only diarrhea," the captain said. "The medics say he'll be better as soon as he gets it out of his system."

"And what if I get it, too?" Dopey bristled his whiskers at them. "I do not like to complain, Brigadier Morrisey, but these people simply do not know me. Can you not have one of the Dr. Adcocks come here? Or even an Agent Dannerman? Someone with whom I have been through adversity, who appreciates the sacrifices I have made? Who would surely not allow these people to give us such foul food?"

Hilda was losing patience. "Shut up about the food for a while," she commanded.

"But I cannot! It is not as though I am asking you for something on my own behalf alone, Brigadier Morrisey! If you go to the Starlab orbiter, there is more than food there, there are wonderful things. Things that will be of great value to you! I have given Captain Terman a complete inventory—"

She turned to the captain, who looked defensive.

"He gave us some kind of a list, sure, but it's gibberish. I didn't bother passing it along, because who can make sense out of 'quantum pseudo-rationalizer' and things like that?"

"It is not my fault that your language does not contain terms for truly advanced technology," Dopey said.

"I want that list," Hilda ordered crisply. "Do we at least know what the things look like? When we do go back to Starlab, we'll want to know what's what."

"I could ask him to describe them all," the captain said doubtfully.

"Describe? But why do I not have my bearer simply draw pictures of them for you?" Dopey said eagerly.

"I thought he was sick."

"It is the medical one who is sick. Do you see what your diet is doing to us? Oh, please, Brigadier Morrisey! Give us proper food! And arrange a flight to Starlab so that we can get more!" And added as an afterthought, "And, please, please, do instruct one of the Dr. Adcocks to come here so I will have the company of at least one person who understands me!"

Before Hilda left Camp Smolley the captain had managed to turn up drawing materials and she had the satisfaction of seeing the uninfected golem begin to turn out meticulous sketches of strange-looking machines. "I want these copied and couriered to me every day," she ordered. "This isn't satisfactory performance, Captain! Why haven't you done this before?"

He looked hangdog. "There's been so much to do," he complained. "You didn't even hear about the war stories he was telling—"

"War stories?"

"Stories you wouldn't believe, ma'am. We've got them all recorded if you want to hear them—"

> Mr. Sanjit Rao: "Will the delegate from the Estonian Republic yield?"
>
> Mme. P. T. Padrylys: "No, I will not yield to the delegate from Sri Lanka. The Estonian Republic cannot allow this inquiry by a few large powers to the exclusion of the smaller nations, whose right to the fruits of any technology arising from interplanetary activities is clearly delineated in General Assembly Resolutions 2357, 3102 and 3103, and on this subject I have a right to be heard."
>
> The President: "The delegate from the Estonian Republic has indeed a right to be heard. However, her time has expired, and if we don't get on with this hearing, we will be here all day."
>
> —*Proceedings of the General Assembly*

She did want to hear them. She was running late, would have to go directly home to change for Daisy's damn dinner party, but she waited an extra ten minutes while one of the techs produced the chip with the interrogation records on it, and then she got out of there. There would certainly have to be a lot of changes at Camp Smolley, she thought as she drove back onto the road.

When she could switch the car to automatic she popped the chip into the car's player. . . .

The man had been right. The stories were hard to believe. They weren't war as Hilda Morrisey knew war. They were stories of annihilation, of whole planets destroyed by dropping asteroids onto them, even of whole solar systems wiped out by making a sun go nova. The people of those planets weren't human, of course. But they were, so Dopey had said, quite intelligent, quite civilized, quite advanced cultures which had simply refused to accept the Scarecrows as their masters.

So there was an actual war going on, and it was universe wide.

She sighed and turned off the player. Not one word of it sounded plausible to her. It was the kind of children's fantasy you came across on the television when you were idly hunting for something worth watching . . . and immediately moved to the next channel. It couldn't be true. The astronomers had been definite about that. The universe was not going to recollapse in the first place. And if it did, it surely would not bring about the miraculous rebirth of everyone who had ever lived . . . a category which, for Hilda, included a fair number of people whose deaths she had personally helped to bring about, and certainly did not wish ever to meet again.

But if it *were* true . . .

Hilda Morrisey didn't spend much time thinking about her own death, and certainly not about some possible afterlife. If anything, she hoped there wouldn't be one. When Hilda thought about dying at all she thought of it as a sort of grant of executive clemency. Being dead meant you didn't have to face any more consequences of things you had done that someone, sometime, might want to hold you accountable for. She didn't want to think that she could have been quite wrong about that.

The next morning she woke early and with a great desire to get the taste of Daisy Fennell's quiche and ratatouille dinner and the chocolate-raspberry dessert that followed it out of her mouth. Her little apartment had a fully stocked kitchen, so Hilda was able to make herself some real oatmeal and pour herself some honest coffee, not flavored with Mexican chocolate or Florida limes. She had not expected so much domesticity from Daisy (though actually it had been Frank who did the cooking), and she especially had not expected the two teenage girls that Frank had brought to the marriage. *Jesus,* she thought, and put the dinner, and Frank's partner Richard, out of her mind.

Forintel sitrep
NBI Eyes Only

The Spanish police have asked us to investigate possible Stateside activities by members or sympathizers of the Basque nationalist organization, the Euskadi ta Askatasuna. It is thought that such persons, particularly in Southern California, are active in supplying funds and possible weapons to the Basque separatists in the Atlantic seaport towns of northern Spain.

No other new alerts are reported at this time. All current surveillance operations will continue.

The first thing she did in the office was recheck all the arrangements for Dannerman's mission. He was in Kiev, he hadn't yet made contact, it was now up to the locals to get him to Artzybachova's hideaway. The second thing was to report to the deputy director, who scowled ferociously at what she had to say. "Pickets? Around Camp Smelly? Now how the hell did they know where to go?" And it wasn't a rhetorical question, either: "Find out," he ordered. "And why haven't you convened a team meeting today? Don't give me you didn't have time, you have to make time, Hilda. And your man Dannerman—the other one—is being a real pain in the ass. Deal with him."

He did not say just how the Dannerman who wasn't in Ukraine was being a pain, but Hilda had a pretty good idea. When she got back to her little office she half expected to find him waiting there. He wasn't but there were five messages from him in her mail, increasingly hostile in tone, demanding she call him back.

She didn't. She was perfectly sure there would be a sixth call, and she would decide how to deal with him then. Meanwhile she had other things on her mind. She dialed the locator service and instructed it to find Junior Agent Merla Tepp and have her report.

Then she gritted her teeth and dropped in on Daisy Fennell to thank her for the perfectly lovely time. Fortunately Daisy was busy. They had at last located the last of the gang that had kidnaped and killed the President's press secretary and she was assembling a team to bring the man in. "Don't go away," she ordered Hilda, and finished giving orders on her screen. Then she turned and smiled. "How did you like Richard? Frank says he was really interested in you. He'll probably call you."

"That would be nice," Hilda said dismally. "Daisy, can't we do better than this Captain Terman who's running Camp Smolley?"

"Oh, Terman," Daisy said. "Yes, I suppose you're right. He lost a leg in the field and the director gave him that job himself—knew the family, I think. I guess he thought it didn't matter, because Terman was basically just a caretaker—who needed Camp Smolley? But if he can't hack it— Anyway, what I wanted to say about Richard—"

But Hilda was reprieved when Daisy's screen buzzed at her again. It only took a moment, then she turned and looked blankly at Hilda.

"Funny thing," she said. "It's that Spanish business. The police got an anonymous phone tip, and when they checked it out they found a munitions dump—all kinds of stuff. Even mininukes. The funny part is, our assets in the Basque community in California? They think it was the Basques themselves that phoned it in." She shook her head. "Listen, Hilda, it's crazy around here today, but how about you and I having lunch one of these days? You know, girl talk. I want to tell you more about dear Richard. . . ."

There wasn't going to be any way of avoiding a lunch and girl talk, but Hilda was firmly determined to avoid dear Richard. No friend of Daisy Fennell's would do, even for an occasional bed partner. But it would be nice to have *somebody,* Hilda thought. . . .

Back in her office, Cadet Merla Tepp was waiting. She stood up as Hilda came in. "You called for me, Brigadier. If it's about my application to be your aide—"

Hilda waved that aside. "What it's about," she said, "is the fact that there were born-again pickets at Camp Smolley yesterday. Looks like they came from the kind of groups you were investigating. How did they know?"

Tepp said promptly, "There was a rumor when I was investigating them that they had a lead into the Bureau."

"Did they?"

"I don't think so, Brigadier. I think they were just bragging. The woman who claimed to have it was picked up in the raids, and I'm pretty sure she's still serving time—that was for the arsons in the California schoolbook warehouses. I didn't interrogate her myself, but I've seen the transcripts. What the inter-rogators concluded was that she was lying. There probably wasn't a real body in place here, but there might have been a leak in the electronics."

"Thanks," Hilda said. "You can go."

The woman tarried. "Ma'am? About being your aide—"

"Go," Hilda ordered. "We'll talk about it later."

And perhaps they would, she thought; she was certainly going to need more help here. But there were things that had to be done first. She put through a call to the electronics man, to tell him that someone seemed to be able to tap into Bureau business. She called Personnel to produce a list of candidates to replace Captain Terman. What she needed, she thought, was a field-grade officer who knew enough about biology and technology to shake up the teams at Camp Smolley—or at least knew enough to know who to requisition as his operations officers. She was studying the personnel files of the first three candidates when Agent Dannerman appeared at her door.

She turned to scowl at him, and he was scowling back at her. "What's happening with the other one?" he demanded.

She elected not to bother with reprimanding him for walking uninvited into her office. "He's on a classified mission, out of the country."

"I know it's a classified mission, and I know it's out of the country. It's in goddam Ukraine, where Rosaleen Artzybachova is."

"And it's none of your business, Danno. How'd you even know about it?"

"Christ. Hilda, the Pats talk to each other, you know. He took one of them with him!"

She sighed and shook her head. "It's not your operation, and it's classified."

"Tell me one thing," he insisted. "What's he supposed to do with her when he finds her. Rescue her? Or cut her head off?"

CHAPTER SIXTEEN

It was the first time Pat Adcock had ever traveled on a passport—actually, on two different passports—that were not her own, and it was certainly the first time she had had to do any of that cloak-and-dagger *hsst!-here-are-the-papers!* stuff. It made her nervous. On the way to Frankfurt she slept as much as she could. She knew that, with the wig and a lot more makeup than she had ever worn before, she didn't really look a lot like herself; but she didn't want to test it by talking too much to her seatmates. She worried about making her connections, but when she walked into the lobby of the airport hotel there was Dannerman, smoking a large cigar and studying a German paper, just as he was supposed to be. *"Liebchen!"* he cried. *"Ma chérie!"* And as he flung his arms around her and gave her a surely unnecessarily big kiss—his stiff German beard scratched her cheek, and the son of a bitch tasted horribly of cigar smoke—he whispered in her ear, "Give me the passport and tickets."

She did—quite openly, because the Bureau spooks who briefed her had had no confidence in her ability to be surreptitious, and, although she watched carefully, she didn't see what he did with them. All she saw was that he picked up his briefcase from the armchair, tossed his newspaper down, put out his cigar and offered his arm. And as they left the lobby she looked back and saw that, yes, just as had been planned, somebody was casually picking up the paper, along with whatever Dannerman had slipped into it, as though simply to see what the day's soccer results were like.

On the Aeroflot flight to Kiev she hoped to feign sleep again, but Dannerman was having none of it. Probably it was the suppressed actor in the man, she thought irritably. He was playing his part to the hilt. Then it was champagne for the two of them, because the honey-blonde flight attendants were glad to make the flight as comfortable as possible for Herr Doktor Heinrich Sholtz, the statistician from the Gesellschaft für Mathematik und Datenverarbeitung mbH, who was combining business and honeymooning with his pretty (though surely a bit long in the tooth?) French bride, Yvette; and how charming it was that neither of them spoke the other's language, and so they could converse only in English. The second bottle of champagne (Georgian, of course, but still) came with the compliments of the captain, with his best wishes for the newlyweds. It went well with the pale pink caviar.

It wasn't such an awful assignment after all, Pat conceded to herself. In fact, the whole thing was turning into an adventure. Flushed with the wine, enjoying playing her cloak-and-dagger part, she thought of the three other Pats who had been passed over. She admitted to herself that she had been a little jealous of them. Sure, they had suffered privation and fear and even pain, but they were the ones who had had the *excitement,* too, had been to places where no other human had ever gone, had met alien creatures—all that— while all she herself had had to talk about was boredom and aggravation in the Bureau's jail. It was only fair that she get some of the thrilling stuff now, while they were condemned to stay at home because the Bureau didn't want to risk—

Didn't want to risk—

Abruptly Pat set the champagne glass down. Dannerman turned solicitously to her. "Is something wrong, Yvette?"

"Not really, Heinrich," she managed to say, but it

was untrue. What was wrong was that she had suddenly realized what it was that the Bureau didn't want to risk. It was what the other Pats and the other Dannerman knew, those little facts about their captivity somewhere in space that the Bureau was not prepared to share, just yet, with the rest of the world. If these terrorists should capture them, they would surely find ways to make them tell everything they knew.

While if she and Dan were captured, even the most painful interrogation was bound to fail, because there wasn't anything of that sort that those two could tell. But that would not keep the terrorists from trying.

Pat had never been in Eastern Europe before. For that matter, she hadn't been in any part of Europe frequently enough to know it; her overseas traveling had been limited to the usual Grand Tour—Singapore, Japan, the PRC—that had been Uncle Cubby's graduation present, plus an occasional weekend seminar. For the seminars you flew in and you flew out, and there wasn't much sightseeing in between. You spent your time in colloquia and cocktail parties with your astronomical colleagues. If you found an hour or two for a quick peek at whatever the local attraction happened to be in whatever otherwise indistinguishable city that particular meeting chanced to be held in, you counted yourself a lucky tourist.

In Kiev she was a *very* lucky tourist. As long as she was able to keep the thought of what might happen if they were discovered out of her mind, there was a lot to enjoy. The Great Gate Hotel was surprisingly comfortable (Great Gate, Great Gate—oh, right, she tardily recalled. Mussorgsky. *Pictures at an Exhibition.* "The Great Gate at Kiev." Which explained the continuing low murmur of music in the elevators.) The food was good—well, interesting, at least; there seemed to be more garlic in the borscht than she had expected. The service was uneven, but always friendly, with a lot of, "What a pity you come in winter! Kiev is so beautiful in spring, the chestnut trees in bloom, everything fresh and lovely." The only thing that troubled her (not counting that one big worry at the back of her mind) was the bed.

What was wrong with the bed in their room was that there was only one of it. It was a big bed, with a comfortable mattress and a giant-sized duvet to keep them warm. But there was only the one. The Ukrainians evidently felt that a married couple, particularly a honeymooning married couple, had no need of separate-but-equal accommodations.

For a moment Pat had actually tried demanding that Dannerman sleep on the floor, but all that had got her was a warning finger to the lips and being dragged to the bathroom. There, with the shower running full tilt to cover his whispers, he pointed out that Slavs had a notorious habit of bugging foreigners and they were, after all, supposed to be newlyweds.

It wasn't until they were actually retiring that night that it occurred to Pat to wonder just how newlywed they were supposed to act. But he got chastely into his side of the bed, and, decorously pajamaed, she got into hers, and that night, at least, the unseen observers, if any, didn't have anything interesting to watch.

Meanwhile, there was sightseeing.

What they had to do (Dannerman had explained to her) was to wait until they were contacted. By whom? By the "zek children" who were supposed to be Rosaleen's bodyguards, but who, he explained, might also be members of the Ukrainian nationalist terror group, who were planning to kidnap Dr. Rosaleen Artzybachova for purposes of their own. Meanwhile they were to conduct themselves just as the newlyweds (but combining business with their honeymoon) Herr Doktor and Frau Doktor Heinrich Sholtz would.

And once they were contacted? What were they supposed to do then?

That was where Dannerman's explanations became vague and unsatisfying. Rescue Dr. Artzybachova, of course, he said; but when she asked him why they didn't simply turn the matter over to the local police all he could say was that some of the police were probably also members of the terrorist group themselves. The two of them would have to thwart the terrorists' plan on their own.

He didn't say how.

Meanwhile they acted their parts. Dannerman conscientiously reserved for their third day in Kiev a car with a German-speaking driver to take them into the evacuated zone around the ruined Chernobyl nuclear power plant. When Pat said plaintively that it was dangerous there he said, for the benefit of any possible eavesdroppers, "But we must, *ma pauvre petite,* otherwise how can I explain our visit here to the people who pay expense accounts?" (And then, in the bathroom that night with the shower going, "But maybe we'll be lucky. We won't have to go if they contact us first.") They visited the Ryemarket and the ancient catacombs by the banks of the Dnieper River— less extensive than the more famous ones in Rome, but ghoulish enough to give Pat pause. It wasn't that she found those narrow underground passages frightening. It was just that she found it obscene to stare at the mummified remains of ancient monks; when you were dead you were certainly entitled, at least, to privacy. They attended a folk-dance recital one evening (much leaping and parading, but the costumes were certainly beautiful) and an opera on another (*Boris Godounov,* of course). They told everyone they happened to meet just what the Herr Doktor Sholtz and his Parisian bride were doing in Kiev—engaged in a lengthy statistical analysis of health problems resulting from the Chernobyl disaster, and therefore desirous of getting a look at the territory to make the numbers come alive. And they looked at every cathedral and museum the city had to offer.

The area which suffered the worst fallout from the old Chernobyl nuclear explosion is called the "Zone of Alienation," and it was evacuated immediately after the accident. It didn't stay evacuated. Old people came back because they didn't want to change their ways, and they died there. Their families came to bury them. Some stayed. So did their descendants, some of them hunting mushrooms in the forests and selling them in Kiev, some simply scrabbling out a living for themselves on the old farms. Over time they were joined by hermit types and a few people hiding from the police. In all, a few hundred people still live in this area of nearly 20,000 square kilometers.

Pat found that she was enjoying herself. She was amused when a woman with a notepad in her hand urged them to sign a recall petition for the Ukrainian UN delegate—until the woman found out they didn't speak Ukrainian and obviously weren't eligible to sign. She was surprised to see how much Kiev resembled any American city—cops patrolling in pairs against possible urban violence; hawkers selling their inflation-proof merchandise just as though they were in New York (though in Kiev the knickknacks were heavily weighted toward old Soviet-style medals and decorations). It was, actually, kind of fun—provided you were careful not to think too much about what might go wrong.

Surprisingly, Dannerman turned out to be an easy traveling companion. Well, she shouldn't have been surprised, Pat thought, remembering the long-ago days when they played together as children on Uncle Cubby's estate; but that had been years past and a world away. The two of them had changed. She had become a rather respectable astronomer, and he, damn him, had turned into a lousy gumshoe for the National Bureau of Investigation. What astonished her was how easily, living their roles as carefree sightseers, they had both turned back. They were even playing house again, just as they had when they were nine or ten years old— though, she reflected with an interior grin, without any of those you-show-me-yours-and-I'll-show-you-mine games they had graduated to a little later.

Of course, that sort of thing wasn't out of the question even now. Might actually enhance their cover as honeymooners, if indeed they were being watched.

Amused at herself, Pat brushed her teeth, and even picked up Dannerman's clothes where he had dropped them over the edge of the tub as he changed into his pajamas. As she was folding his pants she discovered something odd: there was an unexpected sort of interior pocket at the waistband, and what was in it was a peculiar little glass pistol. She sniffed it. There was a faint odor of vinegar. . . .

It was one of those strange little chemical steam guns they called bomb-buggers.

Hell, she thought glumly.

They were not children anymore, of course. And they weren't playing a game here in Ukraine.

So when they climbed into the big, welcoming bed, Pat turned away and stayed virtuously on her own side. So did Dannerman, and those unseen observers, if any, got nothing interesting to look at that night.

The next morning it was snowing again. Pat viewed it with mixed emotions. Maybe they wouldn't go into the evacuated zone after all?

But Dannerman was firm. The car was hired, the snow was only a light dusting, he was definitely going, she could stay in the hotel if she was that frightened of a little residual radiation, but that would make her whole presence here pointless, wouldn't it?

All through breakfast she considered that option, but who was Dannerman to tell her she was frightened?

Then, when they arrived in the lobby, complete with parkas and boots, the concierge was apologetic. Yes, he had arranged their picnic baskets, which the doorman would put in their car—there were no restaurant facilities in the evacuated zone—but it would be a different car. The German-speaking Stefan had had an unfortunate accident. He would not be able to take them after all. However, the concierge had arranged for another man, Vassili, very good, spoke little German but his English was excellent and he knew the zone very well. Besides, he was already committed to go to Chernobyl that morning, in order to drive an engineer who worked with the monitoring crew back from leave; he would drop the woman off at Far Rainbow, the town where the workers lived, and then simply take them on to the reactor itself. She would not be in the way. She would have her own food, as would the driver. Also, she knew the zone well, and perhaps could tell them things even Vassili didn't know.

At least the car was bigger than Pat had feared—the woman engineer sat in front with Vassili, and Dannerman and Pat had the fairly spacious backseat to themselves—and it had a good heater. Pat dozed on Dannerman's shoulder for the hour it took to get to the zone proper, and only woke when she heard the driver talking to him. They were passing a structure like a toll plaza on an American superhighway that sat on the other side of the road. The road wasn't any superhighway. It was paved, but it had a hard and potholed life. There were two or three cars going through the structure on the other side, and the driver explained: "Check wheels, cars, people for radioactivity, do you see? Us also when we come out." The woman rattled something, and the driver grinned and translated: "She says easy to get in, not so easy to get out. You step in wrong place, you pick up radioactive mud, then you have to take shower and wash clothes before you leave. No hot water, either. So please be careful where you step."

What Is Being Concealed?

Are there indeed intelligent creatures living on other stars in our universe? Yes, we are told there are, and some representatives of them are currently being held incommunicado in the chambers of the American spy agency. Do they possess priceless information which is being withheld from the great mass of peoples of the world? There can be no question of that, either. What must be done to rectify this wrong? There can be only one response. The General Assembly of the United Nations must convene its emergency session and seek, yea, demand, answers to all these questions.

—*El Ahram,* Cairo

Behind them was a little village of small houses; it was one of the purpose-built places where the people of the town of Pripyat had been rehoused, after the great explosion. Ahead was nothing. The dead zone didn't look particularly dead in its coating of snow, and when Pat said something the driver spoke briefly to the engineer and reported, "No, is not dead. She say you come back in two months in spring and you see everything wonderful green. Trees, meadows. Even crops still coming up in places, only nobody eat them. Too much cesium-137, you know what that is? You eat them, your children have two heads, unless you die first."

It seemed that the engineer did have a little English after all, because she wasn't letting Vassili get away with any of that. For the next twenty minutes, all the way to Far Rainbow, she spouted facts and statistics to the driver, who dutifully translated the flow of Ukrainian to Dannerman, who, in his incarnation as visiting research scientist, dutifully made notes. When they had dropped her in the company town the driver turned and made a face at Dannerman and Pat. "How she talks! Amazing!" he said, and said nothing more until they were well clear of the town.

Then he stopped the car. He peered up and down the deserted road, then turned to his passengers. "You get out now. I must search you for weapons. Then we will meet a friend, and he will take us to Dr. Artzybachova."

CHAPTER SEVENTEEN

Rosaleen Artzybachova stood as much as she could of the solicitous yammering from the three of them. Then she retired to the bathroom. She did not actually have to move her bowels, and when she did have to she managed the feat expeditiously enough. Still there she was, perched morosely on the pot for half an hour and more, because where else in her little dacha could she be alone?

Even so, she could hear them muttering to each other outside the bathroom door. They were getting impatient. They wanted decisions made and actions taken. Soon enough Marisa would be knocking in polite inquiry, or Yuri would, to ask if she were quite all right in there. Soon enough she would have to come out. Then she would have to face their tender, bossy concern again.

She didn't want to.

What Rosaleen Artzybachova wanted was to be left in the sort of peaceful solitude that had seemed so boring to her just a few months before all this began, and now seemed like heaven. She sighed, gloomily yearning for the tedium of those endless games of chess-by-fax. She stood up and flushed the toilet—not that there was anything there to flush apart from the sparkling (if faintly radioactive) water from the Dnieper River two kilometers away. She ran some more of that water in the sink and looked at herself in the mirror.

In just a few years she would be—God's sake!—a hundred. She observed herself critically. She was definitely more hunched over than she had been a few

months before. That was osteoporosis, one of the side
effects of those months in the captivity of the Beloved
Leaders without her medications, and it would be with
her for the rest of her life. Once the calcium was gone
it didn't come back. But at least she had stopped losing
it, and, taken all in all she looked no more than, well,
perhaps seventy-five, eighty at the most.

But ninety-and-some was how old she truly was, and
wasn't that enough of an age to content any reasonable
human being? Was it worth the trouble to try to prolong
it?

The zek children wanted her to prolong it. They
wanted to save her from all the threats that were building up around her, and it would be impolite to refuse
their kind, if unwanted, solicitude. When she opened
the door Marisa was standing there. The girl had a couple of towels in her hand, not because she was carrying
them anywhere but to provide an excuse for being in
that place at that moment. "All right," Rosaleen
Artzybachova said, roughly but fondly, "you see for
yourself that I did not die in there. So please put those
silly towels down and sit somewhere."

The dacha of Doktor-nauk
Rosaleen Artzybachova had only four rooms, but that
was because she only wanted four. It wasn't her father's
dacha, though it was built on the same tenth of a
hectare, on the same hillside fifty-two kilometers from
Kiev, with the same pretty—if distant—view of the
Dnieper River. Her father's dacha had also been four
rooms, but those rooms were slapped together of
rough-sawn boards from the trees at the top of the hill.
It had not been anything like a luxurious country home.
It was hardly heated at all, apart from one fireplace and
the jawboned-together tangle of copper water pipes
that was meant to, but seldom did, conduct some of the

fireplace heat to the bedroom. Of course it was lacking electricity and running water. And, of course, it had been taken away from the family when the GehBehs carried her grandfather off to the camps.

When Rosaleen began to be distinguished in her field it had given her some satisfaction to buy the dacha back—cheaply enough, after that whole area had been contaminated by the explosion in the Chernobyl power plant—and then to tear it down and have the new one built in its place. Which had been not at all cheap, since the workmen demanded, and got, triple pay for the risks of working in the Zone of Alienation.

In the dacha's spacious living room Tamara and Yuri were somberly watching a news channel; the pictures on the wall screen were of Dopey and the two Docs, caught as they were being escorted from one place to another somewhere in America, but Rosaleen could not tell where because the sound was off. "Where's Bogdan?" she asked.

"He has gone to find an untapped phone," Tamara said. "He will be back very soon, I think. He says we may have to move tonight, tomorrow morning at the latest. Also there is another legal notice in the incoming."

"All right, fine," Rosaleen said, and gestured toward the samovar. While Marisa was getting her a glass of tea she sat down on the comfortable chaise, warmed to body temperature and thankfully free of the bedding her guests used, since there was no actual bed on the premises for anyone but Rosaleen herself. She didn't ask what the legal notice was about. She knew. Somebody somehow had persuaded the village clerk to make a fuss about her ownership of the dacha again. It was pure—pure—pure "chickenshit," she thought to herself, her America-acquired vocabulary always useful for such matters. No one contested that Dr. Rosaleen Artzybachova had owned the dacha in fee simple. What they were making trouble about was that it was clearly established in the official records that Dr. Rosaleen Artzybachova had unfortunately died, having left no will and therefore with her estate reverting to the government. Although this new Dr. Rosaleen Artzybachova certainly *seemed* to be in some sense the same person, there would have to be a hearing, and a court determination, and—

And, yes, it was chickenshit, all right. Rosaleen knew that the only thing those powerful unseen someones really wanted to accomplish was to get her out of the safety of her house. For what precise reason Rosaleen did not know, but was sure it was an unpleasant one.

She took a lump of sugar from the tray Tamara offered and placed it in her mouth. As she sucked the first scalding sip of the tea through it Tamara waved shyly to the picture on the wall screen. "Doctor? What was it like, to be a captive of those horrible creatures? Were you frightened?"

Mr. L. Korovy: "And in our own country of Ukraine, what do we see? Our inflation rate has trebled, for no other reason than apprehension in our financial circles over the impact of these new technologies from space. And whose efforts are largely responsible for wresting these precious articles from their source and bringing them back to us? Why, none other than our own dear Doktor-nauk emeritus R. V. Artzybachova. Yet the Americans have usurped them from us and all the world!

"This is clearly unsupportable. It is the evident duty of the United Nations General Assembly to, with immediate effect, begin a formal investigation into this matter, and then to ensure that the fruits of these discoveries are shared with all the world's people, particularly those who, like Ukraine, have done so much to obtain them."

—*Proceedings of the General Assembly*

Yuri clucked angrily at her impudence, but Rosaleen shook her head at the man. She was grateful to all her companions in this new captivity, but small, young Tamara was the one who touched her heart. She expertly tucked the sugar in the corner of her mouth and said, "Yes, I was frightened, my dear. What was it like? Very much like it is here. Crowded. Frustrating. Worrying. Like being imprisoned anywhere, although you all smell better than the extraterrestrials did. Indeed," she said, smiling fondly at her three protectors, "no doubt better than I will in just a moment, since, as long as Bogdan is not here yet, I think I will do my exercises."

Tamara nodded, and began to set up the exercise machines. Marisa said fretfully, "But where is Bogdan?"

Where was he? Tugging at the weights of her exercise machine before the great picture window, Rosaleen asked herself the same question. It was curious that a short time ago she had been trying to postpone the discussion as long as she could, and now she was impatient to get it over with. All down the slope of the mountain the snow was still thick. The picture window's layered thicknesses of thermal glass and inert gases shut the outside cold away from the people in the dacha. But Rosaleen knew exactly how bitterly cold it would be out there if they had to leave. She did not look forward to being cold.

She didn't look forward to leaving her dacha at all, as a matter of fact, but Bogdan was firm. She could not stay here, he declared.

Well, she knew that. Apart from anything else, she could not allow her companions to remain in this place, where the ground was soaked with cesium-137 and all the residual radiation permeated even the house they were in. True, there was very little radiation left now. Not enough to kill. Not even enough to make one sick—had she not lived in it herself for the years of her "retirement," before Pat Adcock called her to the adventure of visiting Starlab? But in those pre-Starlab days no one had lived in the house but Rosaleen herself and her do-it-all housekeeper and companion, both too old to worry about the real dangers of the radiation. Those dangers were primarily to unborn children. So many had been born with incomplete hearts or brainless heads, with quick-growing cancers, with every sort of damage. Rosaleen would certainly never bear a child, but what about these young people who were protecting her?

Bogdan, of course, said that he was well aware of the problem and was monitoring their exposure. And he was the one who gave orders.

He was the doctor, in fact. That had been useful in getting her out of the Kiev hospital, where she had not been safe—Bogdan had said so himself. That was useful still, because he was the one who kept reporting to those who wanted to come and "interview" her that she simply was even now not well enough for that kind of stress. She trusted Bogdan. His grandfather had been the one who had tried to keep her own grandfather alive, in the camps of dreary memory. He had found the other zek children to guard her and wait on her—all descendants of men and women from the Gulag—Tamara, who was Bogdan's own niece, Yuri and Marisa from families his family and her own had known for generations. In the final analysis it was family that was important to Ukrainians—even to cosmopolitan Ukrainians like Rosaleen Artzybachova herself.

Except that to certain Ukrainians, the ones who wanted to regain for Ukraine the imperial status it had had under the Grand Duke Cyril, it was the nation that was important.

> When, in April of 1986, the controllers at the
> Chernobyl nuclear power plant managed to blow the
> thing up the resulting explosion spread a dusting of
> radioiodine, cesium-137 and hundreds of other ra-
> dioactive isotopes over many thousands of square
> kilometers of the Ukraine and adjacent Belorussia.
> In much of that territory the human inhabitants
> stayed where they were, in spite of growing num-
> bers of childhood cancers and shortened lives, be-
> cause they had nowhere else to go. In the worst of
> it—the so-called "evacuated zone"—the people
> were moved out, but their livestock, and the wild
> creatures who shared the space, remained. The ani-
> mals didn't disappear. They suffered their own can-
> cers and mutations, but, without a human population
> to hunt or exterminate them, they multiplied.

Rosaleen could not understand those people. To be
Ukrainian, yes, that was a good thing; she felt that herself. To have lasting angers against the Russians, yes,
that, too. From Soviet times, from czarist times before
that, the Russians had shown contempt for Ukrainian
customs, language—and people. (Who but the Russians
would have sited that terrible Chernobyl plant where it
could do so much harm?) But to want to make Russia a
mere province of a greater Ukraine, as in the long-
forgotten (but evidently not by everyone) day of Cyril,
that was simply insane.

Which did not mean that it wasn't real. If there
was one thing about human nature that Rosaleen
Artzybachova had learned in more than ninety years of
life, it was that people frequently acted quite insane.

Rosaleen was just getting
out of her after-exercise shower when she heard the
excited voices from outside. She grabbed for a robe and
was still tying the sash, dripping wet under the towel-

cloth, when she saw what was going on. Little Tamara was already in her fleece jacket, assault rifle in her hand, going out the door to take her post commanding the road; Yuri had turned the enabling switch for the mines buried under the pavement and had his hand hovering over the button.

What they were looking at, out the great picture window, was a little electric car whining up the grade. It was Bogdan's car, but there were more people than Bogdan in it. He had, Rosaleen observed without surprise, found more than an untapped phone. Marisa was scrutinizing it through her glasses. "It's Bogdan driving," she reported, "but there are two other men and a woman in it. I know one of the men: Vassili. I don't know the others."

"He's stopping," Yuri said.

Marisa took the glasses away from her eyes to give him a nervous look. "You're not detonating the mines, are you?"

Yuri didn't even look at her. He picked up the desk phone. "Tamara? They're supposed to get out of the car there. Keep them covered."

If Tamara answered, Rosaleen couldn't hear her; but what Yuri said was happening. The little car's doors opened and Bogdan and a woman got out, followed a moment later by the other two men, squeezing their way over the front seats to exit through the only doors the car had.

"I don't know them," Marisa reported, and Rosaleen clenched her teeth.

"Give me the damn binoculars," she ordered; and, when she had them to her eyes, studied the people carefully. Then she set the glasses down.

"I do," she said. "Two of them, anyway. Pat Adcock and Dan Dannerman. They were with me in captivity."

CHAPTER EIGHTEEN

He was waiting for Hilda in her office when she got back from her five minutes with the deputy director: Lieutenant Colonel Priam Makalanos, fifty-five years old but looking no more than mid-thirties, tall, solid, reliable, pulled in from a dirty job in Hanford, Washington, (but one he had been doing well) to become Hilda's new chief at Camp Smolley. Makalanos hadn't been in the top three of the candidates Personnel had offered her, but he had one big advantage over the others. As a brand-new agent he had been part of the team that Hilda had run in El Paso, cleaning up some smugglers of fake antibiotics.

Although Makalanos had had no more sleep than you could catch on a red-eye across the continent, he had already been out to Smolley on his own initiative and was bright-eyed and bushy-tailed as he sat across from her. He'd done more than just visit, too. He'd brought back some samples. "I understand there's a team meeting this morning," he said, "so I thought you might like to show these around." He opened a duffel bag on the floor and pulled out a purplish metal object, hexagonal, the size of a hatbox, to put on Hilda's desk.

"It's one of the food containers," she said.

"Yes, ma'am. This one's empty, and it's been cleaned and sterilized. And these are some of the drawings the Doc made. The things that are on the Starlab orbiter," he added, pulling out a sheaf of papers.

Well, damn the man, Hilda thought, half-annoyed, half-proud of her choice; there was such a thing as almost *too* much initiative. But as she glanced through the papers pride won out over annoyance. They were wonderfully clear sketches of objects she didn't recognize but were clearly strange. "Do we know what the things are?" she asked.

Medical report
Food supplies of extraterrestrials
Classified

The food supplies consist of four items: a leafy vegetable, greenish yellow in color; a compressed bar, dark gray in appearance and with a high water content, apparently manufactured; another bar, greenish in color, circular in cross section and gelatinous in texture, also apparently manufactured; and a small quantity of brown powdery substance, perhaps used as a condiment. The two species of extraterrestrials apparently eat the same foods, though the "Docs" are not observed to consume the brown powdery substance and only infrequently the gelatinous bar.

Biochemical assays are under way, but are hampered by the fact that we have received only a gram or smaller quantities of each. Preliminary examination, following indications from the "Doc," show that the leafy vegetable and the gelatinous bar do contain several sugars, including small amounts of sucrose. More detailed analysis awaits further study. Elemental ash content of each substance, derived from mass-spectrometer analysis, is attached. This does not provide information as to the compounds contained, nor, of course, to the biochemistry. Data on these will be provided as available.

"Sort of, yes. I had the Dopey identify them, as much as he could."

"Well done," she said. "Now you'll need to familiarize yourself with the situation. When you get a chance, pull up the backgrounders on Camp Smolley and the whole Starlab business—"

"Already did, ma'am. I played them over on the flight."

"Well," she said, "good for you. All right. The team people should be getting together already, so you can take this stuff up there. I'll be there in a minute."

She gazed after him thoughtfully as he left. Makalanos was definitely a good man. A good *man,* as a matter of fact; and what a pity it was that he was working for her and thus off-limits for any other kind of relationship. She wondered absently what Wilbur was doing these days—would he maybe like to fly down to Washington one of these evenings?—and then turned to her screen. What she wanted those few minutes for was to try to check up on Danno's progress in Ukraine. There wasn't much to hear: contact had been made, there was no subsequent report.

And then, as she got up to leave, there was an annoying phone call. "Hilda? This is Wretched. I was wondering if you were doing anything for dinner tonight."

It took a while for her to realize that "Wretched" was just the man's Virginia Shore way of pronouncing Richard, and a while longer for her to figure out how he got her number at headquarters (Daisy. Had to be.), and even longer for her to get rid of the man without either making a date or hurting his feelings. So she was five minutes late for the meeting she herself had called.

But no one complained, because they were passing around the food container Makalanos had brought. They hardly even noticed her entrance. Senator Alicia Piombero was there in person today. She had the thing in her hand, and she was asking Makalanos, "What holds the lid on, magnets?"

"That's what I would have thought myself, ma'am, but it isn't. The two rims are so precisely flat that they stick to each other; you can't open it without pressing that little tab on the side. Now if you'll just look at your screens—"

And one by one he fed the Doc's sketches into the scanner, identifying them as he did. A stark white pillar—six-sided again—with vents like a fish's gills along the side: "According to Dopey that one's an environment modifier—like an air conditioner." An oddly shaped coppery object: "He says that has something to do with maintaining the orbiter's orientation in space; he didn't seem to know how. Maybe there's a kind of gyroscope inside?" Multichannel radio receivers, used for monitoring Earth's broadcasts. A different kind of receiver for the bugs they had implanted in the crew that was sent back to Earth. A large object with a door like a refrigerator. "Dopey says this is the transit terminal. Of course, this is the way it looks when it's in working condition. As I understand it, the actual one on Starlab was destroyed by Agent Dannerman as a precautionary measure. We do have some fragments from it in the lab, pieces that were knocked off."

"I've seen the pictures," Senator Piombero said testily. "Pieces of junk, a crowbar, two or three things we're told are recording devices, but we don't know how to make them work—and, what was it, twenty-three cans of food. How come we didn't get anything like the stuff you're showing us now?"

Makalanos glanced at Hilda Morrisey, throwing the ball to her. Alicia Piombero wasn't one of the senators Hilda actively disliked, like Eric Wintczak from Illinois, your damn archetypal liberal, not to mention old Tom Dixon from New Jersey and half a dozen others who were always a lot too curious about just what the Bureau was doing. All the same Hilda took her time to answer. "We got what we got, Senator. They tell me it was Dopey who picked the items to take back. I suppose he was naturally more interested in food for himself." She looked around the room. "I'm sure Colonel Makalanos wants to get back to Camp Smolley. Any more questions for him before he goes?"

"The question I have," the Senator said testily, "is when we're going to go up there and get those things."

"For that," Hilda said gratefully, "we need to hear from Delegate Krieg's associate here, Mr. Downey."

And while the staffer from the American delegation to the United Nations was telling them what complications the UN was giving them she nodded to Makalanos, who quietly departed. She'd have to get out to the biowar camp herself and see what he was doing, she told herself; maybe after lunch? Provided she could get this damn meeting over with.

It was about time, Hilda thought, that she got some personal help.

MOST SECRET
From Brig. Gen. Justin T. Carpenhow
To Joint Chiefs of Staff
Subject: Extraterrestrial weaponry

The full text of National Bureau of Investigation meetings on statements made by the extraterrestrial, "Dopey," in regard to weaponry employed by the so-called "Scarecrows" in subjugating or annihilating other extraterrestrial species, is submitted herewith.

Particular attention may be given to the weapons of mass destruction. These included destroying a planet by diverting a large asteroid or comet to strike it and triggering a release of bound underwater volumes of carbon dioxide from its sea bottoms. An even larger-scale effect is claimed by causing a star to go nova, this apparently in cases where the enemy species has bases on several planets or in orbiting habitats within a system.

Submit copies of this text be forwarded to Pentagon Long-Range Planning Section for analysis and determination of possible inclusion in research efforts.

MOST SECRET

She thought about the person who had volunteered for the job, Merla Tepp. Would she do? While the speaker was droning on Hilda furtively accessed Tepp's file.

It didn't take long to scan through it; there wasn't much to scan. High school grades, not startling but good. The same in college, with a degree in, of all things, agronomy. (But it was a state college and she'd said she came from farm folks.) No near relatives; "person to notify in case" was a widowed aunt by marriage who lived near Frederick, Maryland, also on a farm. Good scores in basic training, with special commendations in marksmanship and martial arts. Good efficiency rating in cadet school; and, in the field, two more commendations for the job with the radical-right godder groups. Her request for transfer to Arlington listed "to be near family" as the reason, and Hilda smiled at that. The reason was because Arlington was where the promotions were, of course, but Tepp knew enough not to say so. Tepp was, Hilda thought, an awful lot like the young Cadet Captain Hilda Morrisey herself, right out of the training corps and as determined as this one was to make a reputation for herself.

Which meant that Merla Tepp probably had a good chance of going a long way in the Bureau . . . and also that she would bear watching.

That was all right. Hilda had no doubt she could take care of herself against any ambitious junior. Quietly she put through a call to have Merla Tepp join her on the afternoon trip to Camp Smelly.

Hilda liked driving the little two-seater, but this time she let Tepp drive so she could both observe her and chat her up. There was no doubt in Hilda's mind that Tepp understood this was a kind of audition for the part. She was doing well. She drove competently and fast; stayed on manual even on the highway and expertly passed the vehicles

on automatic, keeping up her end of the conversation
civilly, respectfully, but not deferentially. Boyfriend?
No, no boyfriend, at least not around here—though
Aunt Billie was always wanting her to meet some of
the young men from her church. What kind of church?
Oh, Presbyterian; no, Aunt Billie wasn't from the fundamentalist part of the family. Friends? Yes, some; she
was getting along well with the others in the general
scutwork pool; one of the women had suggested the
two of them take an apartment together, but she really
liked being by herself. And when they pulled into the
access road for Camp Smolley Tepp glared at the pickets, defying the chill and damp as they waved their
posters, and shook her head. "They're everywhere,
aren't they, ma'am? They're really good people, but
it's about time they got a life."

And Tepp was clearly impressed, as she should have
been, by Camp Smolley itself.

Smolley hadn't been quite mothballed once the
United States signed the convention against biological
warfare. It still did a little contract research—on
phages, for the National Institutes of Health; on diseases that were affecting the Atlantic cod population,
what was left of it, and the Nebraska cornfields. But it
had kept its tradition of total security. If anything, it
was even tighter since Colonel Makalanos had come
aboard. He met them at the inner door, looking not at
all like a man who had had essentially no sleep for
more than twenty-four hours. "You're a tribute to the
Bureau's wakeup pills," Hilda told him, "but I want you
to get a night's sleep tonight. This is Cadet Tepp."

He shook hands, then said, "There's something I'd
like you to look at before we go in to see Dopey. Him?
He's fine. I let him sleep for a while, and now he's busy
telling the debriefers about this universal war that's
going on. Wait, I'll show you."

As they entered the workshop room he snapped on a

screen, and there was Dopey, speaking in English again. Hilda paused to listen for a moment: "Yes, the Horch managed to penetrate our channel for that broadcast. Fortunately I was able to jam most of their message. What else was in the message? Nothing of importance. Only more of their vile libels against the Beloved Leaders. No, the Horch didn't come to Starlab in person; that is a foolish question. If they had, I wouldn't be alive to talk to you. They are utterly ruthless—"

Ruthless, Hilda thought. This from the creature who had cheerfully told them how his own people wiped out whole planets! She noticed a faint smile on Colonel Makalanos's face, and saw that he was looking at Tepp. The woman's expression was pure horror as she stared at Dopey.

Makalanos cleared his throat. "Over here, Brigadier," he said, pointing at a workbench. "You remember the recording device they were disassembling? Well, there was a problem."

There certainly was. The device was in a sealed cubicle now, glass-faced, with attached sleeves so that the workers could work on it from outside. "Dry pure nitrogen," Maklanos remarked. "Seems it was taking up moisture from the air—"

And that hadn't helped it a bit. Two of the dissected parts were on the table next to it, and they looked, well, *moldy.* Where mold had been scraped off so that the original material was visible the parts that had once looked like cardboard were now gelatinous and splotchy.

Whatever the gadget had done, it was clear that it would never do it again. "I've ordered a hold on opening the others," Makalanos reported. "The bio team has taken samples and they're working on them in their own lab; I haven't had Dr. ben Jayya's report yet. I was about to talk to Dopey about it, but perhaps you'd like to question him yourself?"

She would. She did. The creature gave her a lofty look. "But surely you understand that your primitive technology can't hope to deal with truly advanced devices."

"Can you deal with them for us?"

"No, of course not, not me personally." Dopey looked surprised at the question. "That is what bearers are for."

"Are you saying that one of your Docs could have taken the recorder apart without damaging it? Could he tell us how? He can't talk—"

"Yes, he can; and no, of course he does not talk. That is not necessary. He can draw schematics if that is necessary—that is, provided he hasn't been so starved on the inadequate diet you give us that his faculties have been impaired."

"I don't want to hear any more about your diet. We're doing the best we can," Hilda said grimly.

"But it is simply not good enough, Brigadier Morrisey. If you will go to Starlab—"

"I don't want to hear about that, either. I'm asking you about these gadgets."

Dopey's fan turned a sulky pale yellow. "And I am telling you that they are beyond your understanding. Why do you treat me this way? I have befriended your people at great risk to myself! I want you to bring one of my companions down here—one of the Dr. Adcocks, or even an Agent Dannerman. They can tell you—"

"You can tell us everything we need to know, Dopey," she said persuasively. "Now listen to me for a moment."

"I am listening, Brigadier Morrisey. What choice do I have?"

"No," she corrected, "you aren't listening. You're talking. What I want to say is that we have two sets of programs here. Your program is for us to send a flight to Starlab to get you more food. Our program is also to go to Starlab, because we want to learn from your people's machines. So we have a lot in common, do you see? But something prevents us from doing that."

"Yes, Brigadier Morrisey, something does: your bickering among yourselves."

Time for Change!

Although our delegate to the United Nations has continued his wise policy of restraint, the patience of the People's Republic of China is not inexhaustible. His call for an emergency meeting of the Security Council must be heeded. This newest provocation of the Americans in reassessing their inflation indices is the direct cause of the recent large losses in the Shanghai Stock Exchange. Their preposterous claim to "custodianship" of the artifacts from space is without justification, and we do not even mention their high-handed actions in regard to the child of our brave astronaut, Cdr. J. P. Lin.

—Editorial, *New China Journal,*
Taipei, Taiwan, PRC

"No, that's not it. We'll straighten out the bickering, trust me on that. What really prevents us is that we don't know what to do when we get there. How do we take the machines apart to bring them back for study? What's inside them? We don't want our people cutting into some piece of equipment the wrong way and ruining it, the way we did with your recorder. We particularly don't want one of our people touching the wrong thing and getting killed—or accidentally blowing up the whole Starlab. You don't want that either, do you? That would be no good for either of us. So what we need, you see, is for us to have really good, solid, detailed information about the machines before we leave—"

On the way to the room where the Docs were held, Dopey waddling sullenly ahead, Hilda reflected complacently that the skills of interrogation didn't change no matter who you were interrogating, eyewitness, felon, bizarre freak from interstellar space—all the same. Dopey had achieved a small concession from her: she had undertaken to get one of the Pat Adcocks drafted to keep him company. And now she had gained his cooperation in something that really mattered.

She hoped Merla Tepp had learned something from the exchange. The woman was clearly nervous, but that was not surprising in the presence of one of those bizarre freaks. Anyway, she controlled it well, at least until they reached the Docs' room. The great, pale golems were standing statuelike as usual, a medic attendant sitting quietly in a corner of the room taking notes on their behavior—not that there was any behavior to note, Hilda thought. Then, as Tepp got her first good look at them, a flash of pure horror escaped her control for a moment.

Even Dopey noticed it, as he was trying to get up on his platform. Panting; he piped up, "Do not fear, Cadet Tepp. They will not harm you. The bearers are—were—a highly civilized, intelligent race. It is a pity that it was necessary to modify them, but now they can do nothing without orders. Please, will you help me up there? I am very fatigued."

Tepp hesitated. Annoyed, Hilda picked the little turkey up herself. She was surprised to find how light he was, and how hot his body.

He didn't speak, merely gazed at the nearest Doc. Who touched his white-foam "beard" ruminatively for a moment, then moved swiftly to the side of the attendant. Gently, but irresistibly, he took the notepad from the man and began to draw.

Tepp made a small, worried sound, then said tightly, "Excuse me, please, Brigadier." She fled. Hilda was annoyed. The smell was getting to her, of course, but she was not going to let it interfere with her job. And neither should Tepp. Hilda crowded over beside the Doc, watching in satisfaction as the creature swiftly began to draw a recognizable diagram of the recorder.

Twenty minutes later Hilda, clutching the first batch of drawings, found Merla Tepp waiting for her in the cold outside air.

Hilda gave her a curious look. "Are you all right?"

"Certainly, Brigadier. I'm sorry. It's just I thought I was starting my period."

Hilda looked her over more carefully, with dawning suspicion. She leaned forward and sniffed Tepp's lips. The odor was definite. "Do you always vomit when you're having your period?"

"No, Brigadier. I'm in excellent health. I think I may have eaten something—"

"I think," Hilda said sharply, "that you just can't stand touching the little freak. Is that it?"

Tepp was clearly shamefaced. "I'm uncomfortable, yes. I'm sorry."

"Sorry isn't good enough," Hilda said, meditating.

"Oh, please, ma'am, no!" Tepp begged, fully aware of what might be coming next. "I do dislike them, yes, but it doesn't interfere with my duties."

"What do you call what just happened?"

"I give you my word it won't happen again. Please, Brigadier! It means so much to me to have the chance to work with you—"

"Get in and drive," Hilda said, cutting the conversation short.

In a way she wasn't displeased. It wasn't entirely a bad thing for an American to loathe and despise aliens of any kind. But to take this one on as her aide?

That was going to take further thought. On the way

back to the Bureau Hilda devoted herself to catching up on the news on the car's screen. The UN was making trouble again; a speaker at a convention of police chiefs noted an encouraging drop in the number of terrorist actions in the past few weeks; nothing important, really. But she stayed with it, and did not speak again to Cadet Tepp.

CHAPTER NINETEEN

"Come on," Dannerman said to Pat Adcock, half-pulling her out of the car. They stood silent in the packed snow, while the hooded figure in the parka kept them covered with an assault rifle. It was a weapon Dannerman knew well—well enough to suppress any thought of resistance. "Just stand still," Vassili was whispering nervously. "Do not startle her; she is quite young, and may do something foolish."

Her? She? But when the person with the rifle stood up and waved them forward Dannerman saw that it was a woman, all right, in fact no more than a girl, long hair spilling out from beneath the hood of her parka. And suddenly she was not alone. A larger figure, definitely a man, definitely also carrying a rifle, came out of the door to join her. He said something peremptory in Ukrainian. Beside Dannerman the man named Vassili groaned, objected, surrendered. "He says to you must immediately take off your outer garments."

"Here?" Pat cried in surprise. "We'll freeze!"

"But," said Bogdan, his English worsening with strain, "must do it, get weapons of you." And suddenly he had them covered with a gun of his own.

They didn't freeze, though Dannerman's teeth were chattering by the time he had been patted down and his carry gun and radio transmitter removed. Then they were allowed into the house that stood all by itself on the desolate hill.

It was warm there. In fact, the house was a pleasant

and wholly unanticipated oasis of comfort. They came
in through a kitchen, complete with every device modern domestic technology had to offer; they entered a
living room with a huge picture window and a wall
screen, as well as two or three expensive exercise
machines scattered among the pieces of also expensive
furniture. The furniture was not in the least modern. It
was the sort of thing one might have found in a home
of nobility in czarist times, with a huge samovar on a
table and an icon of some tortured saint hanging above
it. Another man and another woman were there, chattering worriedly in Ukrainian to Bogdan and Vassili.
There also was Dr. Rosaleen Artzybachova, looking not
a bit different than the way she had appeared when
Dannerman first saw her, in the office of the T.
Cuthbert Dannerman Astrophysical Observatory in
New York City. She was smiling. She clapped her
hands and spoke sharply in Ukrainian. Then she
advanced on Pat and Dannerman, hands outstretched.
"This is a pleasure I had not expected," she said, kissing Pat, hesitating only a moment, then kissing
Dannerman as well. "This is better than our cell on that
planet, isn't it? Wait—" as Pat opened her mouth to
speak. "Before we talk, there is a custom I want to
observe—when I am in my home, you see," she added,
half-apologetically, "I become very Ukrainian."

She beamed at the woman who had resignedly hurried into the kitchen, and was returning with a tray.
Which contained—

"Bread and salt," Rosaleen said proudly. "It is what
we do to welcome friends. And who could be closer
friends than we, who lived in such proximity for so
long? Eat a little, please. Then we can talk."

"No," Pat said suddenly.

Rosaleen paused with the tray in her hand to look at
her. "No?" she repeated.

"No, we are not the ones who were in captivity with

you, Rosaleen. We're the ones who were returned to Earth. And Dan is still a spook for the Bureau."

"Yes," Rosaleen said placidly. "I am aware of that." She set the tray down before them and retired to sit down. "Excuse, please, the fact that I am quite old and still a bit tired."

"You don't understand!" Pat said. "We aren't here just because we're your friends! We're here because this man has been ordered—"

Prison Cells from Space?

A source close to Sen. Eric Wintczak (D-IL) reports that the National Bureau of Investigation has identified a number of extraterrestrial technologies which it proposes to adapt for use in its own system. One is a sort of energy-field containment device to hold prisoners in an escape-proof cell while jailers and others can pass freely in and out, another is a way of using devices similar to the implants taken from the returnees to tap into the actual thoughts of the subject—a sort of mind control with unimaginable consequences for civil liberties.

—*Washington (DC) Times-Post*

But Rosaleen raised her hand to stop her. "My friends have told me about his orders, Pat, dear. They were given to him by some higher-up spook by the name of Brigadier Hilda Morrisey in the National Bureau of Investigations headquarters in Arlington, Virginia. This Brigadier Morrisey is afraid that I will give information away that the United States wishes to keep for itself, and so she has ordered young Dannerman here to come to my home and kill me." She sighed, shaking her ancient head. "I was going to ask you about that. But won't you for God's sake please sit down and eat some of the damn bread and salt first?"

Pat Adcock did as she was told. She didn't do it right away. She had expected a lot more to happen after what she had said—something drastic, maybe. Certainly *something*. At least some kind of startled outburst from Rosaleen, perhaps some violent action from one of the zek children. What she had not expected was to discover that everyone present knew more about Dannerman's mission than she had.

"Eat," Rosaleen repeated testily, and so she ate. The bread was heavy, dark chunks cut from a round loaf; the salt wasn't the sort of thing you shook onto your french fries in America, but coarse crystals. It occurred to Pat that maybe there was something in the salt or the bread, some mood-altering chemical, maybe something like the date-rape stuff she had been warned against in college, something that would turn them into mere putty in the hands of these young Ukrainian zealots. But Dannerman seemed to have no such fears. He was chewing doggedly away on the tough bread, and she could read nothing from his expression. Nor did Rosaleen's guards reveal anything, except perhaps mild annoyance at the ritual. Then Rosaleen sighed.

"All right," she said, "now that we've all had a chance to settle down, would you like to explain yourself, Dan?"

He swallowed the last chunk of the bread. Then he said, "Sure. But I want you to do something first. Will you ask your friends to put their guns down? Better still, give them all to you—you do know how to use them, don't you?"

"Why should we do that?" the one named Vassili demanded suspiciously.

Dannerman shrugged. Rosaleen studied him for a moment, then spoke. "Let's do as he says, Vass. Give me yours and pile the rest of them in front of me."

Vassili looked rebellious, then complied. Pat, trying

to guess what Dannerman had in mind, had a sudden thought. "Be careful! He's got a bomb-bugger, too!"

Dannerman gave her a curious look, but slowly, carefully, tugged at the waistband of his trousers, revealing the little holster. "That's right. I want you to take this one, too, and give it to Rosaleen. Then we should all back away and give her a clear field of fire."

"And at whom should I fire, Dan?" Rosaleen asked, sounding amused.

"Why, that's up to you. You see, you're right. I did get orders from Hilda Morrisey, and they were to keep whatever information you have about Scarecrow technology from falling into the hands of the Greater Ukraine terrorists. The guys," he amplified, "who already stole the bug that was in the other Rosaleen. They think you can help them take it apart."

"Me? I can't."

Dannerman nodded. "I don't think you could, either. But they don't know that."

"So you were going to shoot me with that thing?"

"That was one of Hilda's options," Dannerman admitted. "It wasn't mine. I was pretty sure you'd agree to be rescued. That radio you took away from me? It's to call a plane to pick us up. Then the three of us, you and me and Pat, will fly to Vienna and then to the States. The Bureau can keep you safe there."

"Safer than I am here with my friends?" Rosaleen asked skeptically.

"Well, yes. A lot safer. You see, at least one of your friends is a terrorist."

Of course, that really hit the fan. All four of the zek children were shouting at once—mostly in Ukrainian, but Pat didn't need a translator to get the gist. The big one, Vassili, was standing up and pleading with Rosaleen.

But Rosaleen was shaking her head. "Stay where you are, Vass, please," she said. "I see now why Dan wanted me to have all the guns—assuming, of course, that he's telling the truth."

"Afraid so," Dannerman said. "Figure it out for yourself, Rosaleen. How did they know what my orders were?"

Steam gun. This hand weapon, colloquially known as the "bomb-bugger," contains reservoirs for two hypergolic liquids which, when mixed, produce a rapid evolution of steam, propelling a droplet of liquid at a muzzle velocity high enough to wound or kill an opponent. Since the weapon contains no nitrogenous chemicals and no metal parts, it is a favored handgun for concealment. The colloquial name derives from the bombardier beetle, an Asian insect which uses a similar system to stun and capture its prey.

"You tell me."

"Because the damn terrorists have managed to get inside information from the Bureau. I don't know how. But they have, and that's how the Greater Ukraine guys knew."

"But these are my friends!" Rosaleen protested. "I trust them, and anyway that doesn't make sense. They've had all the time they need to kidnap me if they're terrorists."

"Oh, not all of them," Dannerman said. "I think only one. Which one? I don't know that, but probably you do. Which is the one who told you about my orders?"

And every eye in the room turned on little Marisa, who began to cry. "But we never would have *hurt* you," she managed to get out between sobs, and Rosaleen put down the gun to take the young woman in her arms.

"My dear," she said, patting her back. "I am sure that is what you intended, but can you speak for all the others? You must tell us all you know."

"They were coming for you tonight," Marisa said. "They waited until now because they wanted to take gospodin Dannerman as well, as a hostage. I was supposed to—well, I wouldn't actually have *shot* any of you, I swear that. But I was to make sure no one resisted."

CHAPTER TWENTY

Hilda Morrisey put the team meeting off as late as possible, because it had been one of those days. It wasn't just trying to deal with that temperamental freak, Dopey, or getting rid of the battalion of time-wasters who managed to track her down with one damn request or another. (The worst was the psychologist from Harvard who demanded—damn well *demanded*—that she give him access to the four Pats, or at least to the two Dannermans, because they were absolutely essential to his ongoing twin studies—and had both the Massachusetts senators insisting that she help the man any way she could.) There was still no word from Danno in Ukraine, either. And the deputy director was in a towering rage . . . and now each last member of the Ananias team was insisting on making demands of their own. Marsha Evergood: "You *must* let me borrow the medical Doc to see what he can do with some of our terminal cases." The astronomer: "If you want me to find the Scarecrow comet-thing you *must* make every large optical telescope in the country concentrate on checking for possible objects." The man from State: "We *must* know how to respond to this note from the Albanians by tonight—"

They all had one "must" after another, and, of course, they all had to take time to explain why their particular urgency was more urgent than anybody else's. Even the ones whose problems Hilda could do nothing about. The Albanian note was the deputy director's concern, not hers, but it wound up in her lap because the man from State hadn't been able to reach Marcus Pell.

**Medical Report
For Bureau Eyes Only**

Agents assigned to Walter Reed Hospital report that the "medical Doc" has effected a number of apparent remissions in terminally ill patients. (Copies of charts are appended.) Some patients resisted receiving this "therapy" as an apparent "laying on of hands," but blood work and gross physical studies indicate real changes. It is suggested that the "Doc" secretes some form of metabolically active biochemicals, administered through small penetrations from the talons in his smaller arms. Attempts to secure samples of these chemicals, if any, have been unsuccessful. The cure rate, however, is significant, especially in intractable cases of immune deficiency, carcinomas and most antibiotic-resistant infectious diseases. His major failures have been on patients who already have had surgical intervention, for example cardiac-bypass procedures.

That wasn't surprising. The note from Albania was one of the two things that were making Pell crazy because it was clearly the tip of the iceberg; every damn pip-squeak country in the United Nations was demanding a share in whatever came out of Starlab, under threat of using their collective veto to make sure none of the big nations got any either.

Well, some good, old-fashioned political horse-trading would eventually settle that. It could probably be handled with a bunch of promises, which might or might not have to be kept. But what about the other thing that fed the deputy director's fury? It wasn't a thing, exactly; it was Senator Alicia Piombero, who had most injudiciously spoken off the record to somebody who had turned around and put it on the record; and so the day's crop of news stories. *NBI's New Spy*

Machine. Tomorrow's Prisons in the Bureau. How Scarecrow Machines Threaten American Liberties.

` It didn't surprise Hilda that Senator Piombero chose to miss that afternoon's meeting of the team. She wished they all had; and when at last she was able to adjourn it she breathed a sigh of relief. She checked herself out and headed for home; because this was the evening she had resolved to take for herself, in order to deal with something quite personal and not very far from urgent.

Brigadier Morrisey was not really off duty very often—she generally kept herself on call, and certainly kept informed of what was happening in her personal turf in the Bureau. But when she was off duty, she was all the way off. When she got out of her swirl tub she stood before the full-length mirror in her bath and studied herself critically for several minutes before beginning to dress. First came the underthings that no one in the Bureau would ever have imagined her wearing, the negligible panty-belt and the pushup half-bra that didn't really need to do much pushing. (But, at Hilda Morrisey's well-concealed age, she took all the help she could get.) The blouse was windowed silk, the kind that opened its mesh revealingly when the wearer was warm, as she had every hope she would be in the bar she had chosen for the evening. The skirt was mid-thigh length, not a practical choice for a Washington winter, but she had a long thermal coat to get her to and from her car.

The pickup bar she had selected was more than twenty kilometers from her little apartment. It was over the Maryland line, but conveniently close to the Outer Belt. Hilda was as careful about choosing a territory for hunting purposes as about dressing for the occasion. Most important, it had to be a place where she had never, or almost never, been before and where she thus was not known. And it had to have, in the background files of the local police, a reputation as a law-abiding and reasonably orderly singles bar. It didn't have to be fancy. Hilda had no prejudices about the economic status of her sexual partners. But it had to be fight-free and clean.

This one was at the fancy end of the spectrum. She parked and locked her car herself, ignoring the hostile looks of the valet parkers; she didn't begrudge them their tip, but she was not having any stranger poking around in her vehicle. She programmed her carryphone to store all messages lower in priority than Director-Urgent. At that point she was truly off duty; and she allowed herself to feel pleasingly expectant as she entered the bar.

It was a good feeling, and she liked what she saw. The bar possessed a two-person "band," an elderly woman on strings, a younger one on synthesizer. They were pumping out familiar tunes with a decent beat, and four or five couples were actually dancing on the tiny patch of hardwood. Hilda Morrisey was encouraged. The evening might well turn out successful, because she had almost always had good luck in bars where the customers actually danced. It was in just that sort of a place, for instance, that she had met Wilbur, the gentle (but not too gentle) and entertaining stockbroker assistant who was her most recent about-to-be ex-lover. Wilbur was a man she was going to miss. (But they'd had sex five times, and, under Hilda's self-imposed rules, that meant it was pretty near time to move on. If you carried on a relationship much longer than that you risked the kind of unacceptable complications that came along with habit.)

When she checked her coat the attendant made her check her carry gun and pass through a detector array. That, too, was a good thing, though no commercial detector was going to pick up her two emergency weapons.

Singles were three deep at the bar, busily hitting on each other. Hilda made no attempt to join any of them. Her practice was to check out the available talent before committing herself, so she walked slowly toward the ladies' room, inconspicuously noting which interesting-looking men seemed to be getting close to moving to one of the booths with the women they were talking to, and which were still searching. There were at least four possibilities, she thought, and her good luck was that three of them were fairly close together near the service corner of the bar. One of them was large, fair and amused as he chatted with the little blonde who was not getting anywhere with him. Hilda noted that he was also a good fifteen years younger than Hilda herself, but that wasn't really a problem, could even be an asset. Another was an older man—but not too old—and the third she hadn't really had a good look at, but the size of his shoulders was promising. In the ladies' room mirror she checked her hair—okay—and the little bleached-out circle around the ring finger of her left hand. (That was one of her best devices. When a man asked if she were married she could say, "Not now," and then when it was time to break it off she could confess that the husband was still around, and getting suspicious.) She esteemed herself ready for the encounter as she left the powder room—

But that was when she saw a familiar face gazing around the bar. It was that cadet agent—what was her name?—yes, Merla Tepp.

That spoiled things. Hilda didn't like to have Bureau people anywhere in sight on occasions of this sort. Reluctantly she decided it was time to cut her losses and try again on another night. Or perhaps simply in another place, she thought as she reclaimed her coat and gun; the night was still young, and there were other spots on her list.

Fortunately Tepp didn't seem to have seen her. But then, as she was heading for the parking lot her carryphone beeped.

That was bad news, too. It could only be something serious enough to get past her message block, and that meant that maybe there would be no prowling for her that night. She heard a car door gently close somewhere nearby, but paid no attention as she stepped into the shelter of a large van to take her call.

She never got the call, though. Just then someone hit her over the head from behind.

Hilda was knocked to the ground, half-stunned and cursing to herself. It was an unpleasant reminder of the fact that not all violence was political. Quite a lot was generated by people who wanted to own things without the trouble of working for them; and it was just her bad luck that a couple of them had chanced on her. She struggled to get at her gun, but one of the two attackers kicked her arm, sending the weapon flying, while the other had pulled out a knife. It was suddenly looking like a very bad evening indeed for Brigadier Hilda Morrisey.

And then there was rescue. She heard two muffled shots. The kicking stopped. The men fell away. She rolled over, getting to her knees, ready for whatever was going to happen; and when she looked up there was a figure with a gun standing there, and it was Junior Agent Merla Tepp.

Brigadier Morrisey tried to get up, got as far as a sitting position and thought better of it. She was woozy. Her arm hurt like hell where one of the bastards had kicked her, and her long coat was a filthy mess from the slush in the parking lot. She was vaguely aware of sirens coming into the lot and of Cadet Tepp standing over the prone figures of the attackers. Then Tepp let the cops take over and came back to Hilda, holstering her gun. "I called for backup," she said apologetically.

And she had got it, more than anyone could need for a simple mugging: there were three police cars there, and two ambulances. "One of perps is dead," Tepp added. "And the other looks pretty bad." She didn't sound upset about having just killed another human being. She sounded as though she were making a routine report.

Hilda rubbed a hand over her face. "Good shooting," she said. "What— How—"

Mr. Shigasimu Yana: "I speak in support of the remarks of the gentleman from the Czech Republic. It is certainly essential to the well-being of our planet that we make maximum use of whatever technologies we may learn from extraterrestrial sources, but I would go beyond that. For many years Japan has urged the resumption of a full-scale international space program on scientific and humanitarian grounds. Now it is more urgent than ever. As the distinguished members of this body are aware, my country has languished in the grip of a great economic depression for some years. We have the skills and knowledge to participate in this needed space program; what we do not have is the capital. I submit that it is the duty of the countries which can afford it to provide funding for an enlarged space program, in which Japan stands ready to play a major role."

—*Proceedings of the General Assembly*

"I saw you going out," the cadet explained. "And I thought I better, uh, tell you what I was doing here. So I followed you and—"

Hilda said grudgingly, "A good thing you did. Thanks." Then she eyed Tepp more carefully. "You're pretty handy to have in a dustup. Didn't I see you got commendations in martial arts?"

"Yes, ma'am. Also in marksmanship."

Hilda sighed. Probably she owed the woman something, and in any case she did need an assistant. "All right. Do you still want to be my aide? Fine. You've got it. Report to my office by oh-seven-thirty in the morning; I'll be in by eight. And I'll clear it with the deputy director."

"Thank you, ma'am," Tepp said eagerly; and would have said more, but one of the medics had left the wounded mugger to the others and insisted on checking Hilda out.

The arm didn't seem to be broken, but Hilda was aware she was going to have a hell of a bruise. The blow to the head was something else. She really ought to let them take her to the emergency room, the medic was telling her; and while they were arguing the police sergeant was strolling thoughtfully toward them, rolling a little metal object in his fingers. He looked at Hilda with more interest than the incident seemed to warrant. "You the NBI woman who called it in?" he demanded.

"She's Brigadier—" Junior Agent Tepp began, but Hilda shushed her. She stood up shakily and let her ID holo do the talking for both of them.

"Oh," the cop said. He didn't sound impressed. He didn't sound particularly happy, either, but then local police hardly ever were really friendly to Bureau personnel. "Well, maybe that explains it."

"Explains what?"

"We searched their car," he said, "and found a locator radio. So we checked yours, Brigadier. This was stuck under your right front fender. You were bugged."

"Oh, shit," Hilda said. And didn't have to say what that meant: this was no simple mugging, these people had followed her from her apartment and what they were after was Brigadier Hilda Morrisey herself.

She would have none of the medic's desire to take her to the emergency room for a checkup, nor of Agent Tepp's to escort her home. She was perfectly capable of driving, and annoyed besides. This damn business would have to be reported. Which meant that people would know that Brigadier Hilda Morrisey was known to frequent make-out bars.

She was aware, as she was leaving the parking lot, that there was suddenly a lot of shouting going on from inside the bar—something on the news screen, odd enough to have distracted the clientele from the pursuits that had brought them there. But it wasn't her business and she had other things on her mind.

She was halfway around the Outer Belt when she remembered two things. The first was that Junior Agent Tepp hadn't finished explaining what she was doing in the place. The second was that she hadn't finished taking the call on her carryphone when the thugs attacked.

"Radio intercept received 2248 hours. Transmission follows."

And then, as she listened to the message, she learned what the commotion at the bar had been all about. She sat bolt upright behind the wheel. "Jesus," she said out loud. *"Now* we've got troubles."

CHAPTER TWENTY-ONE

Pat Adcock was the first to reach the old car, flinging the doors open, but Dannerman came slipping and sliding down the snowy hill after her, half-tugging old Rosaleen Artzybachova. "You drive," he ordered, hustling the old lady into the backseat, before trotting around the car to get in beside Pat. "Do you know how to drive this thing?" he asked as an afterthought, but she already had the motor going and was turning the car around. The car's screen had lighted up as soon as Pat turned the key, displaying some weird kind of creature that Dannerman didn't have time for. He slapped it off. "Hurry up," he ordered. "We have to get to the rendezvous before sundown, and we don't know if they have friends nearby— What?"

Artzybachova was pounding on his shoulder. "Turn that back on!" she demanded.

Dannerman craned his neck around in honest puzzlement. "What for? We can watch TV once we're in the VTOL—"

"Do it *now!* Didn't you see who was speaking?"

Pat resolved the dispute; as soon as she had the car heading downhill she reached forward and snapped the screen on again. "Oh, hell," Dannerman said sulkily. "What's the matter with you? What can be so important that we have to see it this minute?"

But then the picture showed an agitated-looking woman, with a sheet of fax flimsy in her hand. "—was received just minutes ago," she said. "We will repeat it now, and then we will go to the White House for comments on this astonishing new development. Stand by, please—"

She disappeared. There was a moment of white-screen silence. Then a picture appeared. It showed a bizarre creature with a pumpkin head and a spindly body and a mouthful of teeth, and Dannerman did not ask again what it was that was so important.

The Scarecrow didn't seem to be speaking; it stood stolid before the camera—whatever kind of camera it used—with its spindly arms crossed over its spindly chest, but there was a voice, and it spoke in English. "People of Earth, your difficulties are at an end. We have succeeded in establishing communication with you once again. Soon we will provide you with further information as to how you may join the legions of sentients who are proud to call us their Beloved Leaders."

The picture faded. "Oh, Christ," said Pat Adcock, almost going off the road. "It's starting all over again."

CHAPTER TWENTY-TWO

The Scarecrow message changed many things for Hilda Morrisey. Not just for her. For the whole damn world, of course . . . but all that she would have to think about later, when she found time. What it meant for her right now was another all-nighter, still wearing her makeout dress with no time to go home and change, up to her unsatisfied loins in things that had to be attended to *this instant,* if not before, loaded on wakeup pills, frazzled, harassed, overtaxed . . . and, yes, loving it, because it sure-hell beat doing nothing at all.

Lacking a specified job description, Hilda took a hand wherever she was needed. The entire Bureau headquarters staff had to be found and wakened and called in. The team had to be convened. Situation estimates had to be prepared. Current Bureau missions had to be prioritized. Some would go forward unchanged— the "clear and present danger" ones like imminent bombings, ongoing hijack plans, missions that involved serious loss of life or major property damage—though probably even some of them would be starved of manpower. Everything else had to go on hold. By 2 A.M. the headquarters was fully staffed and buzzing like a wasp nest, and Hilda had her own most urgent jobs under control. She had time, finally, to stop in at the clinic and get a pill for the head that was still pounding from the assault in the roadhouse parking lot.

That turned out to be a mistake. "About time you got here," said the duty doctor. "We buzzed you hours ago."

"For what?"

"For your post-trauma checkup, of course," the doctor

said, picking up the phone to call in supporting staff. Then there was nearly three-quarters of an hour gone out of Hilda's life, just when she wanted the time most: X rays, blood tests, peeing into a bottle, having one or more medics stare, in relays, into the pupils of her eyes. Not to mention the infuriating business of having to count how many fingers were being held up before her.

It could not be helped. She'd hoped that no one would have reported the incident. That hope was doomed; Tepp, of course, had quite properly ratted her out.

At least no one was having quite enough gall to ask her what she had been doing in a pickup bar. Probably didn't have to, she thought gloomily as she finally made her escape. By now the rumors about Hilda Morrisey's sexual habits were no doubt already flying around the Bureau.

Just before she went through the door the head medic at last gave her the pill she'd asked for. "You really should get some sleep," the medic warned. "And you've been taking a lot of those wakeup pills; they're not advisable for more than seventy-two hours."

"Thanks for your concern," Hilda said, swallowing the pill and walking out on him. Sleep! Who wanted to sleep when the world was going insane? It wasn't just the Bureau, it was all of government. The President would be getting in an emergency meeting with his immediate staff, maybe the whole Cabinet; the Pentagon War Room would be filling up; all over the world, in every country, people in high places would be doing just what they were doing here.

Hilda reflected that headquarters duty might not be so bad, if it could always be like this. It was almost like one of those triumphantly glorious nights in the field when the net was spread and the evidence collected and it was time to spring the trap on the unsuspecting malefactors and open the celebratory bottle of champagne.

And then, as soon as convenient thereafter, to perform that other rite of celebration and get laid.

Unfortunately, neither one of those was going to happen very fast this time . . . but then, Hilda reminded herself philosophically, you couldn't have everything. For now, the rush was enough.

When Hilda entered the conference room Marcus Pell was already in the chair, conducting the meeting that, for a change, was unexpectedly dealing with matters of actual importance. He wasn't fooling around, either. The man the deputy director had in his sights was the astronomer from the Naval Observatory, and the man was sweating. "Yes, they did get a line on the broadcast, but it was too short for a real fix. The source is somewhere within about a five-degree area, but that's a lot of space to examine—"

"Examine it!" Pell snapped. "That message came from some kind of a spaceship, and I want to know exactly where it is. I thought you already had plates of the whole damn solar system."

"Not quite that much," the man said stubbornly. "And nobody was looking for this particular emission source. Unless it turns up serendipitously we're out of luck. So we'll need to organize a search—"

"Fine," said the deputy director. "See to it. What about you, General?"—looking at the man from the space agency. "If we find this thing, can we bring any of the space-based weaponry to bear on it?"

"Maybe yes, maybe no," the man said, and went into a lengthy explanation of why that would depend on where it was and, also, on whether or not the damn things would still fire after decades of neglect. "But the warsats aren't in optimum position for that purpose.

You ordered us to redeploy them to protect Starlab, if you recall."

The Lessons of History

Our nation, which successively endured the tyranny of Spain, the United States, Japan and then the United States again for many years, is now said to be a free and equal state, with all the rights of every other member of the General Assembly. But do we have them? We have been denied a seat on the Security Council. We have been refused our request to make Tagalog one of the official languages of the United Nations. Our delegate has been given posts on only the most menial committees of the General Assembly, and no Filipino has ever been appointed to high office in the UN bureaucracy. And now we are told that our delegate will not even be permitted to take part in questioning the witnesses in the present emergency session.

It is time to make a stand. The forthcoming summit meetings on trade and human rights issues with the United States, Japan and the People's Republic will be the place to do this. If we are not to be given the status we deserve, we can retaliate. It is our right to do so, and it is our duty.

—*Manila Herald*

"And what position would be optimum?" the D.D. said fretfully—he too was paying the price for all those wakeup pills.

"Again, that depends on where it is. Those weapons were meant to be used primarily against other-nation assets and ground-launched missiles, not for targets that can be millions of kilometers away." The general coughed. "Excuse me, but I have to ask you this. Are you sure you're going to want us to fire on this extraterrestrial vessel?"

"That decision will be made when we have to make it; what I want now is to know what our options are." Pell checked the notes on his popup. "Let's talk about security," he said. "We assume the Scarecrows are monitoring all our broadcasts again, so we want to make sure nothing goes out to the public about using the orbital weaponry. God knows what kinds of armaments these people might have, so if it does come to pulling the trigger, we want to shoot first and we don't want them warned in advance." He paused, looking at Hilda, who had her hand up.

"It's the bugs, Deputy Director," she said. "I've been talking to Colonel Makalanos. There's another security problem there. Remember what the returned people told us? They said they knew everything the people on Earth wearing bugs knew."

The D.D. turned to the electronics man. He was calm. "We haven't detected any transmissions from them. Besides which, what would they be going to transmit anyway? The bugs don't have a chance to pick up much information while they're on a shelf in the lab."

"Then make damn sure nobody accidentally gives them any," the deputy director ordered. "No conversation inside the lab, especially gossiping about what goes on here. Is that what you wanted, Hilda?"

"Up to a point, sir. Colonel Makalanos called my attention to another possible problem. The one they call Dopey may be bugged, too—so as to communicate with the ones that don't talk, if nothing else."

"Ah," said Deputy Director Pell, sinking back in his chair. "Now, that's a problem." He looked around the table. "Recommendations?"

"Yank the damn things out of 'em," growled the man from the Pentagon.

Hilda spoke up. "I think not. If we did that, then

Dopey couldn't communicate with the other two things. Besides, who would take the bug out of the one who knows how? If we have to make sure he isn't transmitting, it would be easier to kill him outright."

Pell stared at her. "Is that your recommendation?"

"No, sir! Only to take precautions. We can just keep them ignorant. But there are two bugs still in place—General Martín Delasquez in Florida and Commander James Lin in China."

The man from the State Department came alive. "Right! Can I pass this along to their embassies?"

"Just the fact that they may be broadcasting to the Scarecrows, yes. Make them an offer: if they bring the subjects here we'll have the bugs taken out; if not, they should at least take maximum precautions to keep either of them from knowing anything that might be useful to the Scarecrows."

The man from State made a note, and then looked up. "One other thing. Your agent in Ukraine has caused us a bit of trouble by—"

"I know what our agent in Ukraine did," Pell said irritably. "Can't we just apologize?"

"We already have, of course. They may want more."

"More what?"

The man from State looked ill at ease. "Well, they've suggested informally that we return him and the woman to Kiev for possible trial. . . ."

Hilda caught her breath, but before she could speak, Pell answered for her. "Not a chance."

"Well," said the man from State, "we may want to keep that option open, you know. There's all this trouble from the little countries in the UN. They're even talking about conducting hearings in the General Assembly."

"Since when do we give a damn what they do in the UN?" Hilda demanded, but the deputy director shook his head.

"Since we want them to support an exclusively American flight to Starlab," he said. "He's right. Let's keep our options open."

Turning her own agent over to some hanging judge in Kiev was not an option Brigadier Hilda Morrisey intended to keep open. If Dannerman had screwed up, he would get his lumps. But those lumps would be delivered by Hilda herself, not by some damn Ukrainian.

What she needed to do was to talk to him herself before anyone else did. Which meant she would have to arrange to see him first. She needed to find out when and where he would be arriving, and the place to do that was in her office. When she got there she found Lieutenant Colonel Makalanos waiting, and Merla Tepp sitting at a desk in the anteroom. "About those people from Kiev—" Hilda began, and Tepp nodded.

"Yes, ma'am. I checked. They'll be arriving in New York in two hours," she said. "I assumed you would want to interview Agent Dannerman, so I've booked you a place on the courier flight at 1400 hours."

"Hmm," Hilda said, eyeing her. Apart from her difficulties with the extraterrestrials, the woman wasn't bad at her job. Which reminded her to ask the question that had been on her mind. "Did you report what happened last night?"

"Yes, ma'am. As required by regulations. I—ah—I mentioned that the reason you and I were there was that we were looking into the question of electronic security leaks."

Was that a little presumptuous? But it wasn't a bad way to handle the present problem, so Hilda just said, "Fine. Get me a car to the courier plane, and send Colonel Makalanos in."

A doctor showed up uninvited to check her over

again, and she allowed him to do it while she talked to the colonel. "Dopey's all right," he reassured her, pulling a sheaf of papers out of his bag. "When that message from space came in I didn't know if you'd want Dopey to know about it. So I told the people at Smolley to keep it under their hats until they got further orders from you."

Well. She hadn't lost her touch at picking good staff. She didn't comment, only asked, "What have you got there?"

"More of the Doc's drawings. According to Dopey, he's now given us pictures of everything on Starlab."

She nodded. "Give them to Tepp, tell her to make one copy for me and pass the others on to the deputy director. I'll look them over on the plane."

And she rose to shake his hand as he got up to leave. Priam Makalanos had a nice, firm grip, and a nice male aroma. What's more, he was damn good at his job. As she turned to collect her messages she reflected what a pity it was that he wasn't eligible for anything more personal.

A Father's Rights

Everyone is familiar with the high-handed actions of the Americans in the case of Commander J. P. Lin of the People's Republic of China and his solicitude for the welfare of his unborn child or children. The Delegate of the Mongolian People's Republic should support the demand of the People's Republic for the custody of this infant or infants, as well as the PRC's rights, and our own, to share in whatever benefits these space persons may bring.

—*Steppes Times*, Ulaanbaatar, MPR.

But the first message on her screen was a note from the Maryland police, and it took her mind off Makalanos.

They had interrogated the survivor of the two who had attacked her. Apparently they had been told that she had been carrying big bucks, in *cash*, of all things. Why? Because she was planning to run off with somebody. Who had told them this crock of crap? The vindictive wife of the man she was supposed to be planning to run off with. But the only description they had of this woman was that she was kind of elderly and pleasant-faced, and how many thousand women like that were there in the District?

Hilda scowled at the screen. Was it remotely possible, she wondered, that maybe Wilbur's ex-wife had suddenly taken an interest in who her former husband was seeing, and decided to do something about it?

No. Not possible at all. The whole thing was nonsense. There was no ex-wife, only somebody who had wanted to get Hilda herself attacked or maimed. Very possibly somebody she had put away, sometime in the long course of her work for the Bureau.

So who was this individual who had gone to so much trouble to get her attacked? Hilda didn't know. She didn't care, either. She only cared that, regretfully, she would have to be somewhat more cautious the next time she went to a singles bar.

CHAPTER TWENTY-THREE

All the way from Vienna across the Atlantic, Pat Adcock was glued to the plane's passenger screen, trying to understand just what the message from space meant. She didn't get much satisfaction. From wherever on Earth the broadcasts came they were all the same: hysteria, everyone startled and frightened, everyone demanding reassurance and action. But there wasn't much of either to be had. News of any kind from the Scarecrows could not be good news. She was glad when the aircraft was settling down toward the airport in New York City and she could get back to the complications of her own personal life.

Which wasn't all that much better. The last thing Pat wanted was to be back in the clutches of the National Bureau of Investigation, but she wasn't given the choice. There they were, three of them. Two of the men had stunsticks in their hands; the other, standing by their waiting van, was an officer with a carbine slung over his shoulder. And that was not counting the two agents who had accompanied them across the Atlantic, now hustling them toward the exit.

Their jet hadn't gone to one of the passenger terminals. It had rolled to a stop on a bypass, far from the public parts of the airport, and there weren't even any steps for them to get down to the ground on. Instead someone had brought up one of the extensible gadgets ground crews used to lift the racks of packaged meals to the stewards' galley, accordion struts raising a wobbly platform up to the aircraft door. "Go," said one of the guards behind them, and Pat, Dannerman and

Rosaleen Artzybachova stepped cautiously out onto the shuddery flat.

It was cold and wet outside, though nothing like the chill of Ukraine, and the interior of the van that was waiting for them was overheated. "Sit down, please," the officer said, the "please" contrasting with the hostile tone of his voice.

That was all he said. When Pat asked where he was taking them he didn't reply. She looked at Dannerman for support, but he was tugging absently at his false beard, his expression weary but resigned. Rosaleen Artzybachova, who had slept placidly through most of the flight, patted her arm.

"They're policemen," she explained. "It is their nature. Pay no attention. You did nothing wrong."

That was true enough, in Pat's own opinion, but whether the police were seeing it that way was an unresolved question. The van stopped in front of a doorway marked AIRPORT SECURITY, which did not seem like a good sign. As they were getting out another car raced up and parked a few meters away. Pat recognized the woman who got out of it: Hilda Morrisey, the Bureau agent who was Dannerman's boss. She was looking almost as tired as Pat herself was, and the dress she was wearing seemed to have been borrowed, for the way it failed to fit her.

Morrisey took charge. She shepherded the three of them into a conference room, vacated for her by the airport security people, and sat them down. "The Ukrainian government," she said, looking at Rosaleen Artzybachova, "is raising hell about all this, so I have to ask you a formal question. Do you want to go back to Kiev, Dr. Artzybachova?"

Rosaleen shrugged. "Not particularly, but I'd like to get out of this room. Am I under arrest?"

Hilda shook her head. "Of course not. Once you are debriefed you're free to go anywhere you like. You, too, Dr. Adcock."

Dannerman spoke up. "And me?"

Hilda gave him a chilly look. "You know better than that, Dannerman. The deputy director wants to talk to you himself."

"Well," Dannerman said in a placating tone, "I kind of thought he would. But there's someone I'd like to see here in New York, so how about if I come down tomorrow?"

"Not tomorrow. You'll go to Arlington with me on the return flight."

"Why?" Dannerman asked reasonably. "I did my mission; here's Dr. Artzybachova, where the Ukrainian terrorists can't get at her. I think I'm entitled—"

"*No.* Today. That's an order."

"But Hilda—" Dannerman began, his tone no longer reasonable; but Rosaleen interrupted him. She was smiling.

"Speaking of orders, I have a question. Do you know what I think? I think that the reporters will be after Pat and me to ask questions. Would you like to give me an idea of what we ought to tell them?"

Hilda transferred her chill gaze to Rosaleen. "Tell them nothing at all."

"But I don't think that would be possible," Rosaleen said reasonably. "They already know I was, ah, rescued—I do not use the word 'kidnapped,' as I believe my government does. So tell me what I should say about Dan's orders. Should I say that you instructed him to save my life? Or should I mention—as my friends told me—that that was only a secondary option, and in fact you authorized him to kill me to keep me from giving information to those foolish children?"

"Artzybachova," Hilda said harshly, "you're screwing around in places where you can get punished."

"Punished? But why do you speak of punishment, when we are all friends here? Friends do not say things that can cause their friends embarrassment. Just," she added, "as friends would not deny a friend a harmless few hours on his own. Would they?"

Hilda eyed her for a long, cold moment. Then she spoke to Dannerman. "First thing tomorrow morning, in my office, or your ass is chopped meat. Now. Let's start talking about just what happened in Ukraine."

CHAPTER TWENTY-FOUR

Pat didn't mind the joyous clamor with which Pat Five and Patrice welcomed Rosaleen. Well, didn't really *mind* it. After all, the three of them had shared a whole harrowing existence as captives of the Scarecrows that she herself had missed. She didn't even mind that Patrice hospitably insisted that Rosaleen come and live with them—"There's plenty of room, now that Pat One isn't here, and I'm afraid the place where you used to live must be long gone by now." That was the first Pat heard that Pat One had been drafted to Camp Smolley to keep Dopey company, along with her own personal Dannerman. There wasn't really what you would call *plenty* of room, either. In fact, Pat gave up her own little bedroom to Rosaleen; old bones needed a real bed, and so Pat found that she would be sharing a bed with Patrice.

That wasn't the end of the housing problem. There also were the guards. When this Brigadier Morrissey said they would be set free she hadn't mentioned that they would have a Bureau agent keeping them company, three shifts of agents for each of the Pats and for Rosaleen as well, night and day. The agents did their best to stay out of the way, slept each night on futons in the dining room. But there were so *many* of them.

"On the other hand," Pat Five said, looking at the bright side, "now we don't have to pay a personal bodyguard anymore, do we?"

"Besides," Patrice added, "they're pretty good about lending a hand for the scut work in the Observatory. And we can use all the help we can get."

Pat blinked at her. "For what?"

"For the search for the Scarecrow ship, of course."

"But," Pat said reasonably, "now they know where it is, don't they? I mean, they got a line on it from the transmission, so that's not our job anymore. The need is real telescopes and we don't have any—"

Patrice looked at Pat Five, then shook her head. "Oh, you don't know, do you? There's nothing there. The Scarecrows must've used some kind of relay to send their message, maybe a little drone too small to be picked up. The ship itself is somewhere else, so we're back to square one."

So, like every other observatory in the world, the Dannerman was officially commandeered for the Scarecrow hunt. The whole staff was put to work searching old plates—every plate every telescope in the world had taken, ever since that first observation of the comet-like object that was surely no comet, but the ship that had brought the Scarecrows to Earth's solar system.

Not all of the staff was happy about the new assignments. Gwen Morisaki didn't want to be taken off her Cepheid count, Christo Papathanassiou was, he said, on the very point of a breakthrough in his quantal approach to cosmology, and he absolutely must have computer time *now*. Pete Schneyman was worse. He was already glum about Pat coming back—about so *many* Pats coming back—and reducing him once more to second-in-command (or fifth!), which was probably why he was so irritable when he complained that checking stock images for some serendipitous observation of possible comet-like objects was the kind of thing you turned over to a machine, or, if you didn't want to waste valuable machine time on it, then to some two-for-a-nickel postdoc. The only one who didn't seem to mind was their planetary astronomer, Harry Chesweiler. The solar system was his turf anyway; his only request was that he be allowed to confine his own searching to the plane of the ecliptic, where he might get some useful data for his own studies. Even Janice DuPage, the receptionist, was drawing lines in the sand. She was willing to do what the Pats told her to, especially because it was what the government wanted, but she warned that it better not last longer than a week or so because her vacation was coming up and she wasn't going to miss out on her cruise to the Amazon and Rio de Janeiro . . . not to mention that it didn't make any sense to treat her like some irreplaceable astronomical expert when, geez, Dr. Adcock, she wasn't really any kind of a real scientist anyway, was she?

To all of them the Pats turned a deaf ear. There would be no exceptions. Everybody, and every computer, was to be totally immersed in the hunt for the Scarecrow scout ship. They even impressed into service the Bureau agents, because even an untrained cop could lend a hand now and then.

In principle, the hunt was simple enough. You looked at a recent picture of a section of the sky—recent being defined as anything in the past couple of years, since the Scarecrow scout had dropped its probe off to leech onto Starlab. You compared it with an older frame of the same area, and what you looked for was to see if there was a dot in the new frame that hadn't been there before. There was nothing to it. . . .

Except that there were some tens of millions of images that needed to be pulled up out of the world's astronomical archives and examined. Except that there were thousands and thousands of those little dots to be considered, since the space around Earth's Sun was crawling with comets and asteroids and bits of cosmic debris of every sort that were *not* the Scarecrow scout ship. Except that most of the plates had no precise equivalent and one had to be reconstructed.

Notes and Comment

Since the time of the Babylonians at least, probably since the days of the Neanderthals, human beings have scanned the night skies for points of light unaccountably moving among the fixed stars. The first of the wanderers—they were called *"planeten,"* in Greek—were the naked-eye planets, from Mercury to Saturn, as well as the brightest "hairy stars" or comets. With the invention of the telescope the number of wanderers multiplied beyond counting: new planets, from Uranus to Pluto; the myriad smaller rocks of the asteroid belt; comets by the thousand that never reached naked-eye brightness. The tally of bits and pieces of rock and snow that swing though space as part of the Sun's gravitational domain grew so huge that professional astronomers hardly bothered to count them anymore, much less give them names . . . until it became a matter of urgency to find the one faint dot among the anonymous millions that was neither asteroid nor comet, but something quite different, and far more worrying.

—*The New Yorker*

The computers did the bulk of the work. They were quite good at taking one image of a quarter-degree square section of, say, the constellation Virgo and manipulating it to an exact match with another plate that included most, but not all, of the same stars. The computers were also quite able to identify a point of light in one that didn't exist in the other. The computers were even then able to sort through the infrared and radio images of the same area, if any existed, to see if there were spectrograms or other data that could identify its composition well enough to reject it as normal or flag it for further investigation.

But then it took a human being to decide about that identification, or to order new observations by some available telescope to clarify the point, and to try to figure out an orbit.

All this effort was bearing fruit—of a sort. Previously unidentified comets were being discovered every few minutes. So were new asteroids, if you could call some of those pebbly car-sized things real asteroids . . . but the Scarecrow scout ship remained elusive.

Pat Adcock did her best to wake early in the morning. The advantage of that was that you got the chance to jump right into the shower without waiting in line. Time was when one real bathroom and a closet-sized half bath for guests seemed perfectly adequate in the apartment, but that was before the new Pats and the Ukrainian visitor had come to share it.

On the third morning of the regime she missed her turn. Rosaleen had wakened earlier still, and was first in the shower—and the old lady did like to take long, long showers. While Pat Five had already preempted the half bath and showed no sign of coming out of it, either.

Grumpily Pat joined Patrice in the kitchen, putting together coffee and some sort of breakfast. Patrice inclined her head toward the half bath where Pat Five remained closeted. "Morning sickness again, I guess," she said. "Poor baby."

"Yeah, poor baby," Pat said, pouring herself a cup of coffee and taking it into the living room to drink in solitude.

But that was denied her, too, because there was a knock on the door. It was the Bureau guard who had remained outside all night long, and he was letting in a pair of uniformed people Pat couldn't identify.

"They're from the United Nations. They claim they have official business with all of you," he said, but keeping one hand on his gun anyway.

The taller of the two pulled out a sheaf of blue folders. "Subpoenas from the United Nations," he said.

Pat giggled. "We already have them," she informed the man, but he shook his head.

"Not these. There's going to be a special committee-of-the-whole session of the General Assembly to look into the Starlab mission, and you're all ordered to testify."

Patrice looked incredulous. "All of us?"

"All of you and about twenty others," the UN man said. "They're even subpoenaing the space people. So brace yourselves for a long day."

CHAPTER TWENTY-FIVE

Hilda did her best to argue, so did the deputy director, but the director herself was adamant. "Forget the legal crap," she ordered. "It doesn't matter if they aren't human beings. It doesn't matter if you think you can get a tame judge to void the subpoenas. The General Assembly wants those freaks there to testify, so they will. Or the one who talks will, anyway. We don't want to piss the UN off any more than they already are."

"But—" Hilda began, and didn't finish. The director firmly overruled her.

"That's what the President says, and that's what we're going to do."

Outside, Hilda complained to Marcus Pell, "This screws everything up. We've been keeping the ETs closed up and ignorant. Dopey doesn't even know anything about the Scarecrow message yet. So how are we going to keep it that way if he's up in New York and the damn General Assembly people start asking him questions?"

"You can't," the deputy director said flatly, and held up a hand to preempt argument. "Go get the damn things and take them up there. I'll order a plane for you. Get."

She got, seething. They had gone to a lot of trouble to isolate Dopey and the Docs. There had been plenty of argument about that, too. That doctor from Walter Reed, Marsha Evergood, had been bitter in opposition to Hilda's decree. She wanted the medical Doc to keep up with his faith healing or laying on of hands or whatever it was that he did, and wasn't content that she was to be allowed to bring a few of the transportable cases to Camp Smolley for his ministrations. But Hilda had the authority, and what she said was what happened. The technical Doc kept on pouring out his meticulous scale drawings and Dopey continued to complain, and everything was going fine. Until now.

Colonel Makalanos wasn't pleased, either, but he didn't have the rank to complain. "Yes, Brigadier," he said, "I can get them ready in ten minutes. But that means—"

"Yes," she said, "that means we're going to have to tell Dopey some of the things we've kept from him. I'll do that now. You get the van ready."

Although the Bureau had provided Hilda Morrisey with a plane to get her parade of freaks up to the UN hearings, it wasn't one of the Bureau's deluxe jets. It was a damn courier aircraft. It had few amenities, not even coffee, and it wasn't big enough for the sixteen of them.

The problem wasn't the human passengers—Hilda herself, Pat One, and her semiattached Dannerman, along with Colonel Makalanos and Hilda's new aide, Merla Tepp. It was the aliens—Dopey and the two Docs—and the eight, count 'em, eight guards the Bureau had deemed necessary to keep them in order. And the aircraft really stank, because just after takeoff one of the Docs had had to move his bowels. The creature wouldn't fit in the tiny airplane toilets so he had blandly relieved himself on the box of shredded paper included for his use.

Hilda averted her gaze. She wondered absently where the shredded paper had come from. Some Bureau big shot, somewhere, who was addicted to making hard copies of things he shouldn't? And was it possible that those unnecessary documents, or something like them, had fallen into the wrong hands, so that half the crazies in the world seemed to be able to find out everything that was going on in the Bureau? The Ukrainians had known about Dannerman's mission. Most of the wilder religious groups seemed to have detailed information about the whereabouts of the aliens—there had been a knot of men and women and even little children, all carrying the usual placards and shouting the usual demands, where they boarded the courier plane. Which no one should have known; and the pilot had warned her that there were more of the same waiting for them in New York. Bureau security had definitely gone to hell.

But, Hilda decided, the notion that someone was smuggling hard copies of Bureau plans out of the headquarters wouldn't really fly. The logistics were too tough. There had to be another explanation.

She turned around to peer at Dopey. The little turkey had taken the news that he was summoned to appear before the United Nations with equanimity—"It is about time, Brigadier Morrisey, that I had the opportunity to speak to the people of your world entirely, not just one department of one of your 'nations.' " And then when she told him the other bit of news he took it without surprise. "That is good to hear, yes, but who knows when the Beloved Leaders can get here in person? And meanwhile there is the problem of our food—"

What had crossed her mind at the time was that maybe the security leak had a different explanation. Maybe this damn freak had been in communication with the Scarecrows all along. But that didn't make sense. She couldn't believe that Dopey had somehow listened in on every conversation in the Bureau, and passed them on to the Scarecrows, who in turn had relayed them to all Earth's terrorist nut groups. And anyway, he certainly had not known where they would meet this plane.

No. The leak couldn't come from Dopey. It was almost as if—

"Oh, *shit,*" Hilda said out loud, causing Dannerman to look up from Pat One's head as it was nestling cozily on his shoulder.

"Is something wrong?" he asked.

"No. Yes. Stay out of it," she ordered, and crooked a finger to Colonel Makalanos. When he had left his charges to come up beside her she pulled his head down and whispered: "I just had a bad thought. It may be possible that some Bureau personnel have bugs in their heads. Go up and use the pilot's radio, secure channel: I want every son of a bitch in Arlington X-rayed, and I want it right away."

He didn't answer, only nodded and headed for the pilot's cubicle.

But, she thought dismally, even if that were the explanation, her idea might not solve the problem. It wasn't just the headquarters staff that needed to be checked for some damn Scarecrow thing. It was everybody. It could be someone on this plane. It could be— that was the worst thought—it could be Hilda herself who had somehow been bugged. And, as with the Dannermans and the Pats, she would never know it had happened.

When the VTOL landed it was at a helipad along the East River. Then they were all hustled into two armored vans—happily enough in two shifts, with the two Docs and their guards filling one of the vans by themselves so that Hilda was spared their aroma for a while. They headed north to the UN Building at high speed, with four motorbike outriders to clear the way and a half-track chewing up First Avenue's already potholed pavement behind them.

Along the way they passed a dozen knots of protesters of one kind or another, most of them apparently religious. "Damn them," Makalano remarked to Hilda. "What do you suppose they want?"

Hilda nodded to her aide, busily making notes about the protesters as they drove. "You're our expert, Tepp."

Merla Tepp looked up. "I've identified three groups so far. The Inerrants—that was my own old bunch—and the Radical Southern Methodists are two of them, plus the Christian League Against Blasphemy. They think the aliens are the Antichrist, or at least agents of the Devil, and they want them to be fired back into space right away. But there's another bunch, too. All I know about them is what I see on their posters, but they look like charismatics to me."

"They want to get rid of the aliens, too?"

"Oh, no. Quite the contrary, if I understand their posters. They think they're angels direct from God. All they want is to be allowed to worship them."

Makalanos laughed out loud. "I know how we can straighten them out on that. Just let them get close enough to get a good smell."

CHAPTER TWENTY-SIX

Traffic was unbelievable. Dannerman's taxi inch-wormed along Forty-sixth Street, lunging forward a meter or two and then stopping dead, with the driver angrily slapping the wheel and muttering obscenities to himself. When at last they reached Second Avenue there was a solid line of cops to keep everybody from entering the last block. "Street's closed," the nearest one bawled, waving her stunstick. "Move it on!"

Dannerman had to walk the rest of the way. At the United Nations Plaza there wasn't any traffic moving at all, not vehicular at least. The whole street in front of the UN Building was choked with thousands of human beings, chanting, shouting, milling around in defiance of the police squadrons trying to move them along. And when he had zigzagged his way through the pack he found a long line waiting at the gate to the UN complex. Most of them appeared to be would-be spectators hoping to get in for the show. Most of them weren't succeeding.

Tolerantly Dannerman took his place at the end of it. He was in no particular hurry, and a few thousand brawling religious fanatics weren't going to spoil his day. Dannerman considered that his world was definitely improving itself. He had accomplished his mission in Ukraine without bloodshed. He no longer had a guard tailing him every moment. . . .

And then there was Anita Berman, who had been the biggest improvement of all.

Anita had always been a sweet and forgiving woman, with plenty to forgive: any number of broken dates and long absences when he could not tell her what was going on because it was Bureau business. Now that she knew he was a Bureau agent all the lapses were explained. No, better than just explained. Anita was thrilled. She had been as swept up in the Scarecrow turmoil as anyone else on Earth, and here he was, her lover, astonishingly at the very heart of it! "I was always pretty crazy about you, Dan," she had whispered in his ear the night before, "but, wow, now it's really *special!*"

He was grinning reminiscently to himself, when someone tapped his shoulder. It was a cop, pointing at the beginning of the line. There a woman inside the gate was beckoning peremptorily to Dannerman. He recognized her as Senator Alicia Piombero, and she was gesturing for him to come in.

Even at the UN, a United States senator could smooth all ways. When he had run the gauntlet of catcalls from the waiting line and was at the gate, she looked him over, and said, "You're Dannerman, right? You were summoned to appear at this thing?" And, when he nodded: "That's what I told the guard. Just show him the summons and he'll let you in."

The guard did. As they walked toward the actual doorway he thanked the woman, and she said, "You're welcome. Maybe we can do each other a favor."

"What's that?" he asked, but she shook her head, pointing at the other guard post just inside the door. When they had finished with the metal detectors and the patdowns and the sniffers she took him aside.

"Listen," she said, "I only have a minute because I have to get up to the Security Council, but you've been having trouble collecting your pay, haven't you? I mean, because now there are two of you?"

It was a sore point. "The damn payroll people are taking forever to figure out what to do, yes," he said.

"Well, Representative Collerton—I don't know if

you know her? She's willing to get a special members' bill through to pay both you Dannermans in full. You're entitled, after all, and that would cut right through the red tape."

Dannerman perked up, then his guard went up. "That would be good," he said cautiously, waiting for it.

"Glad to do it, Dannerman, but you can do something for me, too, if you want to. You know Marcus is a little annoyed with me?"

Mr. L. Koga: "Whatever may or may not be going on in the Security Council at this time, it is our undoubted duty to learn the facts in this matter to the satisfaction of each and every delegate, not just those who represent the so-called Great Powers, so that we may take appropriate action."

Mr. V. Puunamunda: "Will the gentleman from Kenya please yield?"

Mr. L. Koga: "I will yield to the gentleman from the Marshall Islands for thirty seconds."

Mr. V. Puunamunda: "I thank the gentleman. I wish only to call to the attention of this body that our islands may be endangered, owing to the severe tropical storms of recent years, but they are still voting members of this General Assembly, and we, too, should be allowed to participate in the questioning of the witnesses."

—*Proceedings of the General Assembly*

"I know about Senator Wintczak's stories that he thinks came from you, yes."

She clearly didn't want to discuss the stories. She just said, "So he's doing a lot of stuff that I'm not kept informed on. I can't let that happen. You can understand that. We aren't going to go back to those old CIA days, with you spooks going off on all sorts of tear-ass mystery missions and the Senate kept fat, dumb and ignorant."

"No, ma'am," Dannerman said, because she seemed to expect it.

"So we can do each other some good. If you could just keep me posted on what's happening that isn't talked about in the team meetings—"

Dannerman did his best not to laugh; the woman wanted him to spy on the spymaster!

"I'm not asking you for anything I don't have a right to know," she went on persuasively. "Give me a call when you can, and I'll get Susie Collerton started on the bill. Right now I've got to get up to the Council."

That made him frown. "You're going to the Security Council? But I thought it was the General Assembly that was meeting."

She looked at him with faint pity. "That's where the circus is. The Council is where the work will be done. Think about it. We'll talk later."

Once inside the building a uniformed woman in a blue UN beret escorted Dannerman to a waiting room. Dannerman, still mulling over his conversation with the senator, paid little attention to where they were going until she stopped at a doorway, saluted smartly, and said, with an accent Dannerman couldn't identify, "In here, please, until you are called."

The place was marked "VISITORS' LOUNGE" on the door, in all five of the official languages of the UN, but the only visitors in it that day were the ones with subpoenas from the General Assembly. Some of them were there already. Dannerman saw Rosaleen Artzbachova and Pat Adcock sitting near the door and, at the far end of the large room and not sitting at all, four people in the uniform of the People's Republic of China.

Dannerman recognized one of them—no, Dannerman corrected himself, he recognized *two* of them, and they both were the pilot who had taken them to Starlab in the first place, Commander James Peng-tsu Lin. He nodded toward the Lins, but, standing stony-faced and silent, they didn't meet his eye. He shrugged and turned to the others. "Morning," he said. "You look like you're all recovered from our trip."

Rosaleen corrected him. "This one wasn't in Ukraine. She's Patrice. Pat's in the ladies' with Pat Five, but, yes, we're fully recovered. How did things go in Arlington?"

"Oh," he said, recollecting himself, "no problem. The D.D. ate me out a little, but then they sent me right home, because they had other things on their minds. They did have orders for me, so you'll be seeing a lot of me for a while. They've put me in charge of your guard details at the Observatory."

The door opened again. When Dannerman turned he saw the two Pats, returned from the washroom, but they didn't enter right away. They were peering curiously down the hall, and so was their escort.

Dannerman had no trouble recognizing which was Pat Five. In just the few days since he had seen her last she seemed to have become much more pregnant. She was definitely heavier than the Pat beside her, and a lot of the gained weight appeared to be in her face, which looked almost bloated. Dannerman had had very little experience of pregnant women, but he remembered hearing that they were supposed to be at their prettiest when pregnant. It hadn't worked that way for Pat Five. The guard in the blue beret spoke to them, and they hastily got out of the way to make room for the next arrivals.

Of which there were a lot. First came Hilda Morrisey and her new aide, along with a uniformed Bureau lieutenant colonel Dannerman didn't recognize; then a

couple of Bureau guards, curiously lugging large, flat
boxes of torn-up paper. Then there was another clutch
of guards surrounding the aliens: the two huge, pale
Docs, one of them carrying the little turkey thing,
Dopey. Finally the other Dannerman and his Pat One
strolled in, keeping their distance from the space freaks;
and suddenly the large room didn't seem very large
anymore.

Hilda Morrisey glanced around, then nodded to the
lieutenant colonel, who began issuing orders. The two
guards with the paper boxes set them down near a window, while the others shepherded the aliens to the same
area, Dopey looking on interestedly but silent.

The Chinese officers looked up, first startled and
uneasy as they found themselves in the presence of the
weird beings from space, then in revulsion as they
caught the scent of them. The senior officer spoke
sharply. They began to move farther away, but the two
Jimmy Lins didn't follow. They were speaking agitatedly to each other, then one of them hurried across the
room to Pat Five, wearing a broad and suspiciously
fake smile. "How nice to see you, my dear!" he cried.
"And my unborn child, how is he doing?"

Pat Five gave him nothing but a hostile look, but
Patrice answered for her. "He isn't yours, he's ours, and
he isn't him. He's them. Three of them. She's having
triplets."

"Triplets! How very wonderful!"

"Oh, cut it out," Patrice said in disgust. "Really,
Jimmy, you don't want these kids, do you?"

He glanced over his shoulder at the PRC officers.
"Certainly I want my children! And I want them
brought up in their homeland!"

The senior PRC officer snapped a command as
Patrice was saying, "Come off it, Jimmy."

He looked at her, then turned to obey his keeper's
order. But as he left he whispered, "I can't."

Hilda Morrisey, standing by the door, watched curiously for a moment, then turned and rapped on the door. When the UN guard opened they spoke briefly, then Hilda conferred for a moment with her lieutenant colonel before waving Dan over. "I don't think you've met. Dan, this is Priam Makalanos, who's helping me with the freaks; Priam, Dan Dannerman. You'll take orders from Colonel Makalanos while I'm up at the Security Council chamber, Dan," she finished, and rapped again on the door.

Warily Dannerman shook the lieutenant colonel's hand, expecting, but wincing from, the punishing grip. "What orders are those, Colonel?" he asked.

"None, I hope. These guys aren't giving us any trouble now, for a change."

He was gesturing at the aliens. They not only weren't causing trouble, they weren't doing anything at all. The two Docs stood silent and impassive while Dopey, curled in the arm of one of them, appeared to be asleep, his great fantail overspreading his body.

Dannerman had expected that as soon as they arrived they'd be conducted into the General Assembly auditorium, but that wasn't the way it was. Colonel Makalanos explained to him that the reason Hilda had left was that some sort of procedural fight was going on. The Security Council was meeting independently of the General Assembly in its own wing of the building, and a fierce battle was going on in the General Assembly itself over who was to be summoned before them for questioning, and who was to be allowed to ask the questions.

Meanwhile, they waited. Dannerman restlessly prowled the lounge, taking note of the pictures on the wall (Trygve Lie, Boutros Boutros-Ghali, half a dozen other figures prominent in the history of the UN), the little barlike cubicle, which contained a coffee machine (unfortunately not in use), the rack of ancient magazines. He became aware of the eyes of the other Dannerman on him, and gave his twin a guardedly friendly hello—another personal problem that he couldn't see a good way of dealing with. The other Dannerman returned it in the same tone.

He was spared the necessity of making conversation when two men in the uniforms of the Free State of Florida entered. One of them was General Martín Delasquez, who had been one of the pilots Pat Adcock persuaded to fly them to Starlab in the first place.

Rosaleen caught sight of General Delasquez coming in and hurried over to him. "Martín!" she cried affectionately. "I thought you were dead! It's so wonderful to see you again—"

And then, when the general gave her a frosty look, her expression clouded. "Oh, hell, you're the *other* one, aren't you?" Shaking her head, she went over to sit before a low table and began tearing up bits of paper. "Anyone for a game of chess?" she asked.

When at last they were brought into the General Assembly Hall Dannerman blinked at the size of the audience.

Dannerman had had the experience of being debriefed, or made to testify, often enough before. At least the Bureau's interrogations had been more or less private. Even in the Pit of Pain there had seldom been more than a few dozen watchers, but this was on a whole other scale. The General Assembly Hall was packed, all 194 nations fully represented in their individual stations, and the visitors' gallery solidly filled as well. There were easily two thousand people in the auditorium, muttering and whispering to each other as the thirteen "witnesses" trudged to the raised dais and took their seats on spindly-legged gilt chairs.

Dannerman counted heads: there were four Patrice Adcocks, two Dan Dannermans, two Jimmy Lins, one each of Rosaleen Artzybachova, Martín Delasquez and Dopey, now alert and looking curiously around the room. That wasn't even counting the guards in dress uniform and riot guns, standing behind each chair to "protect" them. The guards wore UN blue helmets, but their uniforms were of the U.S. Marines.

And then, to complete the roster, the pair of Docs, their moss-bearded faces impassive, their half dozen arms moving placidly. Those things weren't real witnesses, of course. They couldn't be, in any practical sense, since they never spoke. Nor, also of course, were they seated on the frail gilt chairs. They weren't seated at all. They stood remote and still at one end of the row of witnesses, and each one of the Docs had not one but three Marine guards standing tensely over it.

Dannerman did not think the Marines were there to protect the Docs. They weren't watching the audience at all. They were all precisely focused on the immense, multiarmed creatures from space, and that was the way their weapons were pointing.

Still, Dannerman thought, maybe the Docs did need protection after all. The word was that some of the demonstrators had briefly broken through the massed police battalions around the UN Building complex, before reinforcements managed to get to that point to drive them back. He had seen half a dozen people turned away as they failed the screening for unchecked weapons. Whether the weapons were on their persons from absentmindedness or malicious intent wasn't stated. It didn't matter. Either way, those people would be watching the televised proceedings, if at all, from their cells in one of New York's city jails.

The delegates to the General Assembly were still earnestly wrangling—in several languages, few of which Dannerman understood. Though Dopey, with his total command of nearly all Earthly tongues, was alertly following it all.

But then the presiding delegate gaveled everyone to silence. "Gentlemen and ladies," he said—in English—"let us begin the questioning. Ask the witness known as 'Dopey' to take the stand."

When the little alien hopped onto the witness stand two thousand people sighed in unison. The interrogator rapped for order, looking pleased as he motioned to the clerk to swear the witness in.

Federal Reserve Inflation Bulletin

The morning recommended price adjustment for inflation is set at 1.06%. Federal Reserve Chairman Walter C. Boettger declined to set an annualized rate, stating, "This unprecedented increase in the rate of inflation is a purely temporary phenomenon which cannot be tolerated. If it continues, a third increase in interest rates must be considered, but I have confidence that the good sense of the American people will assert itself."

When the clerk approached with the Bible he got a curious look from Dopey. The look got curiouser as the clerk rattled off his formula: "Please put your hand on the Bible. Do you promise to tell the truth, the whole truth and nothing but the truth, so help you God?"

"I beg your pardon," Dopey said. "Which God are you referring to?"

So naturally there was another ten minutes of off-mike whispering before one of the interrogator's aides had the intelligence to have his principal ask Dopey just what it was he did believe in. Dopey considered that for a moment, then said doubtfully that one could say, yes, he believed in the Beloved Leaders. Then it took another five minutes before he was allowed to swear himself in in their name, without the Bible; and then the interrogator made the mistake of courteously asking him if he were being well cared for.

When she managed to turn off Dopey's lengthy and even more than usually repetitious reply, things went better. Yes, he had occupied Starlab for the purpose of eavesdropping on Earth for the Beloved Leaders. And, the interrogator asked, what was the information to be used for? Was Mr. Dopey preparing the way for an invasion?

Mr. Dopey took offense. "Invasion? Certainly not! They merely wished to protect you from the tyrannical rule of the Horch—not only now, but in the eternity of the eschaton to come."

"Ah, the eschaton," the interrogator repeated, smiling. "Would you tell us, please, about this 'eschaton' of yours?"

Dopey would. He did. He kept on doing so until a restive delegate, on a point of order, reminded the presiding officer that, after all, what they were here to do was to discuss the *benefits* the world might hope to gain from these extraterrestrials and their technology, not some philosophical question of an afterlife.

Which, of course, produced another free-for-all. Dannerman wasn't listening. He was watching one of the Docs, who was showing signs of being restive. The creature wasn't going to hold out forever, Dannerman thought. . . .

He didn't. The inevitable happened. A titter and gasp from the audience turned everyone's eyes to the Doc, who had blandly relieved himself, with his paper boxes still left in the lounge room.

Startled, then amused—and a little belatedly—the

president declared a recess; and all the witnesses
trooped back to their holding room.

To Dannerman's surprise,
he saw the deputy director just leaving the room as they
arrived. Hilda Morrisey was inside, looking strangely
thoughtful.

"Is something wrong?" Dannerman asked.

She considered the question. "Wrong? No. The
Security Council has taken a vote, though, so what you
guys were doing in the G.A. doesn't matter much anymore. They've okayed the Eurospace launch, only it's a
UN thing now and one American and one Chinese is
going along. So I'll be seeing you people at your
Observatory."

"Why?" Pat demanded, suddenly suspicious.

"Why? So you can give me a crash course on what
Starlab is like. See, I'm going to be the American."

CHAPTER TWENTY-SEVEN

While Pat was trying to get dressed for work the next morning the atmosphere in the apartment was grouchy. Patrice was complaining about the wasted hours at the UN and Pat Five was grousing about, well, everything: she hadn't slept well, she didn't feel well, she wished the damn kids would get themselves born and get it over with . . . and, she added, the smell of the damn bowl of chili Rosaleen was placidly spooning into herself in the kitchen was making her physically ill. Rosaleen was apologetic. "I'm afraid I got a taste for the stuff while we were captives. Do you know, there isn't a decent bowl of chili to be had anywhere in Ukraine. I won't do it again."

"Oh, it's not just that," Pat Five said, cross but repentant. "It was the smell of the Docs yesterday that started me off, probably. Or just being so damn pregnant and miserable." She looked it, too; Pat and Patrice exchanged glances. "Anyway, I think I'm going to stay home today, if it's all right with everybody."

"I'll stay with you for a while," Patrice decided. "You two go on ahead; I can work from my screen here."

On the way downtown Pat and Rosaleen took a cab—paid for by their Bureau guards, because they didn't want to risk their charges in the subway. For that much Pat was grateful; money was an increasingly urgent problem, with four Pat Adcocks to share what really hadn't been quite enough capital for one. Something was going to have to be done about that.

Then, as they arrived at the midtown office building

that housed the Dannerman Astrophysical Observatory, she saw Dan Dannerman strolling toward them, arm in arm with a tall, redheaded woman, and inspiration struck. Abruptly Pat knew what that "something" might be. Suddenly more cheerful, she sent Rosaleen up ahead of her and waited for them at the door.

Dannerman saw her, nodded amiably and paused to whisper to the woman. She giggled, kissed him, waved to Pat and turned away. Dannerman joined Pat. "Am I late again, boss lady?" he asked cheerfully.

Full of her new idea, she shrugged the remark off. "Dan, you know a lot of lawyers, don't you?"

His expresson sobered. "Have you got a problem, Pat?"

"You bet I have. A lot of them, but the one I'm thinking about is money. Starlab belongs to us! Well, to the Observatory, but that's close enough. We should have some claim to whatever the UN flight finds there, shouldn't we? So I need to talk to a lawyer. I don't want to use Dixler—"

"Right," Dannerman said immediately; they both knew the old family lawyer who had handled Uncle Cubby's estate.

"—and the Observatory's lawyer is real good on leases and employment contracts, but I think I need somebody with a little more shark blood in his veins for this."

Dannerman pondered for a moment. "Let me see what I can do," he said at last. "I'll make a couple of calls."

Upstairs, Brigadier Hilda Morrisey was already closeted with Rosaleen Artzybachova, studying the blueprints of the Starlab orbiter. She wasn't in sight, but her mere presence had made a change in the climate of the Observatory. The

Bureau agents were sitting up straighter and moving faster, and they had infected everyone else. Pete Schneyman was demanding Pat's attention to the previous day's harvest of observations, Janice DuPage, sulky because she had had to cancel out on the vacation cruise she had planned, was snapping at Dan Dannerman for preempting a corner of the waiting room as his command post. Even mild old Christo Papathanassiou waylaid Pat on her way in, bristling. "I do not protest sharing my office with the policewoman, Merla Tepp. I understand the urgency of the situation. But must she use my terminal so very much of the time?"

By the time Pat had run that gauntlet she was glad to retire to her own office and close the door.

In a physical sense, the only thing that had changed in Pat Adcock's office was the pictures on her wall. In the old days, before the Scarecrows and the Horch, what the wall pictures usually displayed was the familiar Horsehead Nebula, or Saturn's rings or even the looming shape of Starlab. She kept such pictures on the wall because they were pretty to look at, and even for a more practical reason. They were a reminder of the glamour of astronomy. When prospective donors visited the Observatory the pictures helped get them in the right mood to endow some particular search, or even to kick in with a handsome gift or legacy that would help pay the Observatory's bills.

Those bills still had to be paid, no matter what. Figuring out how to do it was still part of the director's job—the boring part, but what could you do? She settled down to it but, as she worked over the numbers on her desk screen she couldn't help looking up from time to time at the wall display. The pretty pictures were gone; what the wall showed now was all alphanumeric, the constantly changing, always growing, list of new discoveries from the world's telescopes. Each time a new dot was discovered—they were coming less than a minute apart now—its coordinates flashed on the screen. As one of the great telescopes accepted the task of checking it out, the name of the instrument appeared. When the same dot was found nearby in that instrument's search, the coordinates changed color. If there was a third sighting the computers took over; and then, with luck, the first approximation of its orbital elements were displayed in their turn.

Then the object went on the waiting list for instruments operating in other frequencies: gamma rays, infrared, ultraviolet, radio telescopes—even the ancient pair of orbital X-ray telescopes that were still, sometimes, creakily operational. What all those instruments were looking for was the chemical and physical composition of that point of light. The ones that showed a coma of gases, however tenuous, were dropped from the screen. They were nothing but ordinary comets. Their elements went into the cometary databank for any future astronomer who might take an interest, but they were of no importance in the present search. . . .

And, for that matter, dawdling over the search wasn't getting the bills paid. She gritted her teeth and worked doggedly away until hunger reminded her she hadn't had any breakfast.

On her way to an early lunch Dannerman stopped her. He looked amused. "I think I've got a lawyer for you," he said. "He's a shark, all right. He worked for the Carpezzios—they were big druggers; I was working on them before, uh—"

"Before you decided to come and spy on us," Pat said helpfully.

"Well, yes. The only thing is, he's expensive. First thing he said was that he wanted a fifty-thousand-current-dollar retainer before he'd even talk to you."

"I haven't got fifty thousand—" Pat began, but Dannerman was shaking his head.

"Wait a minute. When I told him what it was all

about he said he'd waive the retainer, only he wanted half of whatever he collected for you."

Pat was scandalized. "That might be millions!"

"More than that. So we went round and round for a while, and he finally came down to twenty-five percent. You're not going to do any better, Pat."

"I'm not?" She thought for a moment, then sighed. "He's really good?" she asked.

"He's really *bad*. He got the Carpezzios off with two years in a country-club jail, when I figured they'd be away for life. And he's handled big suits against the government before. Anyway, he'll be here this afternoon."

At the elevator Rosaleen Artzybachova came hurrying out of her office. "Take me along," she pleaded. "I have to get away from that truly exhausting woman for a while."

In the elevator Rosaleen described her morning with the Bureau brigadier. Hilda Morrisey had all but sucked Rosaleen's brains out to get the data she wanted, which amounted to a complete plan of the Starlab orbiter as it had been abandoned, with every bit of equipment marked and identified, and then the whole thing compared with the sketches the instrument-Doc had been ceaselessly turning out at Camp Smolley. "I left her transmitting the plans to the Doc back at the biowar plant, so he could mark the positions of all the Beloved Leaders material—oh, sorry. I mean the Scarecrow material, of course; it's just that we called them Beloved Leaders for so long, I got in the habit. But, Pat, do you have any idea how much stuff is there? God knows what it will do to our lives when we get it sorted out. If indeed we ever can do that. It's like—it's like giving some Renaissance genius like Leonardo da Vinci a brand-new pocket screen to play with. Or a fusion bomb. Or like all of current technology, all at once, to see what he could make of it. And we're not Leonardos."

In the restaurant Pat toyed with her Caesar salad while the old lady devoured a huge platter of fajitas, washing it down with a bottle of Mexican beer, talking the whole time. It had been an active morning for Rosaleen, with Brigadier Morrisey setting an unflagging pace—"She's trying to get it all in today because she's leaving for the Eurospace base at Kourou tomorrow morning. And I don't think she'd had any sleep last night, either." She chewed in faintly envious silence for a moment. "Makes me wish I was fifty again."

But those labors had been productive. From the Doc's sketches they had identified four separate power generators of different types—though without a clue as to how any of them worked—plus the gadget that transported people across galactic distances faster than light—plus several dozen other bits of equipment which did God knew what, and God knew how.

Pat glanced at their Bureau guard, alertly nursing a cup of coffee two tables away, and wondered if she would try to stop Rosaleen's chatter if she knew what the woman was saying in this very public place. But of course there wasn't any real hope of secrecy anymore, anyway. Once the UN mission came back with whatever samples of Scarecrow technology they could carry the whole world would be looking on and it would all be common property. . . .

But not if she and this lawyer could prevent it. "Come on," she said, signaling for the check. "Let's get back to work."

As soon as she was at her desk she turned on the screen and instituted a search for all the morning's transmissions from Rosaleen

Artzybachova's terminal. Most of what she found was gibberish—the damn woman had encoded all the traffic to Camp Smolley—but among the remaining messages there were the twenty or thirty of the Doc's admirably precise sketches that could be salvaged.

What the sketches might represent, Pat could not say, but they certainly looked potentially valuable. When the lawyer arrived she had a display of them ready for him. He glanced at it, then frowned and said, "Turn off that machine, please. Let's just talk for a bit."

His name was T. Lawrence Hecksher, and he didn't look like Pat's idea of a mob mouthpiece. Hecksher didn't look like a hotshot, jury-befuddling lawyer from some video serial, either. What he looked like more than anything else was somebody's grandfather—white, muttonchop whiskers, twinkly sky-blue eyes under feather white eyebrows, apple red cheeks. He would have made a fine department-store Santa Claus, Pat thought, if his talents hadn't been more in demand for helping tax evaders and mob assassins stay out jail.

He acted grandfatherly, too. When he had settled himself across from the desk the first thing he said was, "If you have recording systems going, my dear, please turn them off." He had no recorders of his own, either. As Pat began to describe what she hoped he could do for her he made notes. With a *pen.* On *paper.*

"Why can't we use the screens?" Pat asked suspiciously.

He waggled his head at her. "Records we don't have can't be subpoenaed. I don't want to have anything on the record that can be construed as any sort of admission, or anything that represents privileged information we aren't supposed to have. That's why I didn't want to look at your screen. Don't forget, this is not a small matter. In order to protect your interests we will need to prevail against some of the best lawyers in the world. All *over* the world."

Pat gave him a dismayed look, but he smiled reassuringly. "Don't worry. I have dealt with government attorneys for many years. I'll eat them alive. And I'll get all the information we need in disclosures, but I'll do it legally. Now. The first thing I'm going to want from you is documents. . . ."

And so, documents he got: documents, documents and more documents. By the time T. Lawrence Hecksher left the office he had the registry numbers of every document that could have any bearing on the case: Uncle Cubby's will and the probate records; the instrument creating the trust for the T. Cuthbert Dannerman Astrophysical Observatory; the records of the building of Starlab and all the disbursements made from Uncle Cubby's estate to pay for it; Pat's own contract of employment, to show that she had authority to institute a suit on the Observatory's behalf—"We'll need all your, ah, sisters to sign the complaint as well, of course." When Pat suggested that most of this could be obtained with less trouble from Dixler, the lawyer for Uncle Cubby's estate, or from the Observatory's own attorney, he gave her a forgiving smile. "I don't think we'll trouble them, my dear. I find I work best when I don't involve any other attorneys if I can help it. I'll have the complaints and summonses ready to sign and serve by tomorrow morning. Serve on whom? Why, on everybody, Dr. Adcock: the President of the United States, the secretary general of the United Nations, the director of the National Bureau of Intelligence—that's because they have custody of the aliens. For that matter, on the aliens themselves, but I'll have to do a little research on that. Trial? My dear Dr. Adcock, there won't be any *trial*. All we want is money, and they'll throw that at us to get rid of us. What you have to do is decide how much you want. I'm thinking of, let's see, giving them a quit claim for whatever the cost of manufacturing, outfitting and launching

Starlab was when it was built, adjusted for inflation, with interest, and perhaps a one hundred percent penalty . . . yes, quite a large sum, I think. But we can discuss all those details later. Good afternoon."

When he was gone Pat spent a few dizzying minutes calculating just how many hundreds of millions of inflation-adjusted dollars all that might come to. It would definitely be a *lot*. It was certainly enough to relieve all four Pats from financial worries forever, and for Pat Five's unborn triplets and all their descendants as well.

She leaned back, studying the numbers on the wall to take her mind off these giddy visions of prosperity. A flash of color showed that another object had been identified and an orbit plotted, but the flashing red showed that this one was special. The funny thing about it was that it seemed to be heading in the general direction of the Earth.

That explained the flashing signal. It also caused Pat a moment's shock, but when she checked its orbital elements she relaxed a bit; its trajectory seemed to bring it within a couple hundred thousand kilometers of the planet, but that was not particularly worrisome. Every few years an object was detected at ranges like that, some of them coming closer than Earth's Moon. It would bear watching, of course. But—

Her phone rang. Annoyed, Pat touched the screen control. "What is it?" she demanded, expecting to see Janice DuPage with some new urgency to make demands on her time.

But the face wasn't Janice's. It was her own face— well, Patrice's face, at least—and she looked scared. "Pat? It's Pat Five. She's hemorrhaging. I've got the medics here and they're taking her to the hospital. You'd better come."

CHAPTER TWENTY-EIGHT

Hilda Morrisey got a few hours sleep on the plane to Guyana, needing it. The night with Wilbur Carmichael had been really pleasant, but it might have been a mistake. Was she getting too fond of the man? Should she have promised to see him again as soon as she got back? It had certainly cost her sleep that she could have used. But it was a mistake she would have been glad to repeat, because Wilbur had been *fine*.

She woke at dawn, just as the aircraft was circling the town of Kourou. All she could see from the air was the giant new Holiday Inn between the lights of the Pizza Hut and the all-night casino, but with the dark solid green of the jungle just outside the town limits. The plane swooped out to sea to come in for a landing from the east, and there, a kilometer or so from the town itself, was the starkly floodlighted launch area, ancient gantries still standing in spite of rust and time, the liquid fuel plants steaming away, the hideous barracks blocks where most of the base's personnel lived.

When she got out of the aircraft the heat hit her. Kourou was hot and wet, and there were bugs. The zappers electrocuted a few thousand of them every hour, but there were always thousands more coming up out of the rain forest, thirsty for Hilda Morrisey's blood.

It was not, it seemed, going to be a comfortable assignment. Hilda wondered if it was going to be a safe one; she had never signed on to be an astronaut. It wasn't just that people got killed in space. She had long come to terms with the possibility of early death, because in Hilda's line of work people got killed from time to time just about everywhere she'd ever been. The hard part was the thought that in a few days she would be climbing into that ancient and ugly-looking LuftBuran space vehicle that was squatting on its hardstand at the end of the runway and then she would be departing in it from the planet she belonged on. When was the last time the damn Europeans had fired one of the things? Would it still work? Her skin crawled in ways she had never experienced before as she thought about all the questions.

On the other hand, Kourou had one very great advantage for Hilda Morrisey. It wasn't the Bureau's hated Arlington madhouse.

Here in Kourou she was the senior American officer present, at least until the deputy director got there for the actual launch. So she had no boss at all. She certainly didn't take orders from Colonel duValier—although, in spite of the fact that she clearly outranked him, he did his best to give them.

If Hilda put up with the colonel at all it wasn't because he was chief pilot and commander of the expedition to Starlab. He had something more interesting going for him. He was not only a well-built man but a *French*man, and something in Hilda's brain was telling her that, satisfactory though Wilbur was, it was about time to change her luck. Although Hilda's few experiments with French males had not been very encouraging, there was that old rumor that they were the ultimate in lovers. Well, sure, they went to a lot of trouble to foster the rumor themselves. But still.

As a matter of fact, it was apparent that the personnel roster at Kourou was heavily weighted with rather good-looking men. Not only that, but men who were either single or—just as good—married to someone who was thousands of kilometers away. There were the Belgian, Bulgarian and Danish astronauts, for instance.

They weren't in a very good mood, because they'd been bounced from the launch to make room for Hilda, the Chinese commander Lin and most of all that great, silent, smelly creature, the Doc. Hilda sympathized with the rejects. They might well need a little consolation, and, if things happened to go that way, Hilda had an open mind about supplying it for them.

She had plenty of time to think about such matters, because the preflight "training" she was supposed to be going through was a clear waste of time. They were not going to have to wear spacesuits. She wasn't going to be allowed anywhere near the controls of the giant LuftBuran spaceship that would carry them into orbit. All Hilda was really going to have to do was make sure American interests were protected when at last they did dock with Starlab, and when it came to the protection of American interests Brigadier Hilda Morrisey had received all the training she needed long before.

Hilda's first day was spent listening to briefings she didn't really care about. The launch controller, a dour Welshman who hated Kourou's jungly heat, kept talking about launch windows and trip times; pointless, in Hilda's view. Starlab sailed around the Earth in its Low Earth Orbit every eighty-eight minutes; it hugged Earth's equator, and so the windows that were best for rendezvousing with it, allowing for the Earth's own rotation, occurred just about every eighty-eight minutes as well. When that boring lecture was done the Portuguese who was their combat instructor went over and over the weaponry they were to take along against the outside chance that some Scarecrow troops had somehow managed to sneak back in. But what had some Portuguese to tell Brigadier Hilda Morrisey of the National Bureau of Investigation about weaponry?

More interesting were her colleagues. It was the first time the entire crew of the LuftBuran had been in one place. Hilda looked around and chose to sit between the two most interesting of them. One was Jimmy Lin—the formerly captive Jimmy Lin, along because he had firsthand knowledge of what the Scarecrow matériel on Starlab looked like; the other was the Floridian General Delasquez, along because he knew it from its unaltered state. Both had been recently debugged for the purpose of the launch, but if Hilda had hoped for any interesting tidbits from either of them she was disappointed. When she tried to strike up a conversation with the Chinese astronaut, he shot an agonized glance at his PRC guard, standing stiffly at the back of the room, and shrank away. The Floridian merely ignored her.

Stop the Spaceflight!

Save our planet! Save our country! Every launch produces tons of hydrochloric acid which destroys living things! We, the people of Guyana, well remember the effects of the poisonous Ariane 5 rocket which killed or damaged plants and animals as far as ten kilometers from Kourou. We will not tolerate a resumption of these deadly launches. Our priceless natural resources must be protected! This project must be abandoned!

(Signed) Pou d'Agouti

Besides themselves and, of course, the Doc—stolidly waiting in his little holding cage on the outskirts of the base, and not invited to the briefings—there were four others: the two Germans, the female French lieutenant whose main duty was to be to remain in the shuttle in case of disaster and Colonel duValier, who listened irritably to the briefings, grumpy because he knew it all and because the briefings were being given in English.

It took the Portuguese weapons man nearly half an hour to explain why the handguns they would be issued were to carry a reduced charge—"Because there is much danger of ricochet if fired"—while the carbines would be loaded with armor-penetrating rounds in case of dire necessity. Judging by the expressions on her crewmates' faces, none of them was learning anything more than Hilda herself. She cast a sidelong glance at General Delasquez, who appeared unaware of her existence, and another at Commander Lin on her right. Hilda was not unaware of Lin's reputation. According to gossip of the Pats he had harped incessantly on the sexual wisdom of his great ancient ancestor, some two-thousand-year-old sage named Peng-tsu, though none of them would admit to having experienced any of Lin's expertise for themselves. There might be an additional possibility there, she thought, and allowed her forearm to slip onto his side of the armrest between them.

That produced nothing but a sudden jerk away from her, the man's attention doggedly fixed on the speaker. She sighed and did her best to pay attention to the lecture on the sheath knife and crowbar.

All things ended in time; even this lecture. When they got up to go Hilda's fleeting notion of trying to get Lin aside for a little chat evaporated when the Chinese officer whisked him firmly away. Evidently Commander Lin was not in the good graces of his government.

Her second choice was General Delasquez, but the chance of that diminished when Hilda saw that her aide was waiting for her outside the briefing room. Tepp saluted smartly. "Three messages from headquarters, ma'am. First, Colonel Makalanos reports that the X-ray screening is complete and no bugs were found. Second, Agent Dannerman thought you might want to know that Dr. Adcock—the pregnant one, ma'am—is having some sort of emergency. She's in the hospital, but they give her condition as fair, not critical. Third, Vice Deputy Fennell advises that the deputy director is making arrangements to come here in person as soon as your mission is on its way back from the orbiter."

To oversee the distribution of the spoils, of course, Hilda thought. "Thank you. How's our Doc?"

Tepp's expression didn't change, but there was a touch of strain in her voice. "Apparently doing just fine, ma'am. Do you want me to look in on him?"

"No," Hilda decided; no reason to push the woman to do something she hated. "I've got time before lunch to do it myself. What I'd like you to do is make friends among the permanent-party junior officers here, see what sort of gossip you can pick up. And meet me again after the afternoon briefing."

"Ma'am," Merla Tepp acknowledged as she saluted. She looked relieved. As Hilda turned toward the Doc's pen she wondered if she were being too indulgent. Not really, she thought. For now, at least, Tepp could be more useful functioning as an extra ear than making herself sick in the presence of the space freak. Whether that meant she might need to be replaced sometime in the future was another question. *Maybe not,* Hilda thought. Maybe things would go so well on the mission to Starlab that they might once and for all be relieved of the burden of caring for the aliens.

She glanced up at the tall, rusting shape of an old Ariane 5 rocket, memento of Kourou's early pioneering days, and then caught sight of the man who was studying it.

General Martín Delasquez. Sometimes your luck was good, Hilda thought, and turned to join him. "How did you like the briefing, General?" she asked chattily.

He gave her an unwelcoming look. "It was certainly

a complete waste of time for me. I was stationed here at Kourou for months, and there is nothing they can tell me that they haven't already told many times."

She gave him an apologetic chuckle. "Our fault, I'm afraid; they want to make sure we new guys get all the dope. I know being stuck with us is an inconvenience, but I hope you won't hold it against me personally. . . . General? Since you have actually been on Starlab and I haven't, I was hoping you could tell me something about what to expect when we get there."

"And how could I do that, when those creatures tampered with my memory?" he demanded.

It seemed like a good time to offer sympathy. "That must be awful for you," she said.

He glared at her, then shrugged. "What I remember is an abandoned astronomical observatory. There was no gravity, so it was difficult to move about, and the air smelled stale—because, I thought, it had been unused for so long, but perhaps it was the natural aroma of these creatures from space. But I didn't see any sign of them."

"Haven't you seen the Doc?"

He looked at her with what might have been amusement—at last, a human sign! "This one, no. I did see quite a bit of its—brother?—when it removed that device from my brain. But I was not in a position to study it carefully."

"Well, General," she said sunnily, "I'm on my way there now. It isn't time for lunch yet, so you have the opportunity if you want it. Would you care to look in on the damn thing?"

Hilda's interest in the Floridian was not particularly sexual. She certainly did not exclude that possibility. However, General Delasquez represented a force in the world with which she had little personal experience, that is, the kind of semipatriotism which marked the people of the breakaway State of Florida: adamant on running their own state as though it were a sovereign nation, yet unwilling to, or perhaps too sensible to, provoke the military retaliation that would come with any attempt at outright secession. The Floridians were not ignorant of history, and they were well aware of the outcome of the War Between the States.

Outside the Doc's shed an armed guard was crouched over a news screen, but he was alert enough to forbid them to enter. "What's so interesting?" Hilda asked the man in a friendly way. He shrugged.

"There's an object coming pretty close to the Earth. For a while they thought it might hit, but it's going to miss us by about fifty thousand klicks." Then, more obligingly: "I can't let you go in, but you can look at the damn beast through the door if you want to. It won't disturb him."

The Doc looked as though nothing at all would disturb him, as a matter of fact. The creature was standing motionless, half-turned away from them, not bothering to look around to see who had come to look at him. Delasquez looked at the Doc in silence for a moment, then said wonderingly, "Excuse me, but is this the one that made the pictures of the interior of Starlab?"

"The very one."

"It doesn't look capable of that kind of work."

"I know," Hilda agreed. "The story is that they come from a very high type of civilization, but the Scarecrows conquered them and planted some sort of controls in their brains. It doesn't affect their intelligence, but now they can't make any decisions on their own—especially to rebel against the Scarecrows."

He gave her a sardonic look. "How useful that would be for your country, for dealing with people like myself."

"Oh, but we would never do anything like that, General," Hilda protested—as a matter of form; knowing that that wasn't true, knowing that the General was well aware it wasn't.

"Of course not," he agreed, as duplicitous as herself. "Shall we go to lunch now, Brigadier? I've seen all I need, and the creature does smell unpleasant."

"Of course," Hilda said, cozily slipping her arm into his as they turned away; thinking about how the general was going to feel when they were stuck in the confined space of the LuftBuran with the Doc. "You know," she said, "I've always thought of Florida as a good experiment in cooperation: you have all the advantages of being part of the United States, but the freedom to follow your own principles."

He looked at her in amusement, but without removing her arm. "Yes, that is true. I wonder, though, how well the experiment would work if we Floridians did not have our own National Guard and Air Force."

Brigadier Morrisey would have preferred a quiet table for two, but there weren't any tables like that in the Kourou officers' mess. They wound up at a table for six, sharing it with Colonel duValier and some people on the launch controller's staff. They seemed to be old friends of General Delasquez, though there was something in their gently mocking tone that Hilda did not quite understand. Then Colonel duValier explained: "When our friend Martín was here before it was under something of a cloud, Brigadier. We borrowed him from the Floridians to brief us on what we could expect when we visited your Starlab, since he had been there himself. Of course, then we discovered that there was not much truth in what he told us."

Delasquez said stiffly, "I told you what I thought was so. I did not know that my mind had been tampered with."

"But of a certainty," the colonel agreed. "We did not know that you were transmitting information to our enemies, either. We did not even know that we had enemies! Or else we would have put you in a cage like the one this malodorous Doc we are taking with us is in."

"Dr. Artzybachova says the only way to be sure the Docs aren't transmitting information is to make sure they don't get any," Hilda put in. "Of course, that policy got blown when they were at the UN."

General Delasquez sniffed. "Dr. Artzybachova," he said in a dismissing tone.

"You don't like her?"

"I have no opinion at all about the woman. I saw her briefly on the launch, and then she died."

"That one died, right," Hilda said, nodding. "But the one that's here now, she says you—the other you—and she were great friends as captives of the Scarecrows."

Delasquez looked uneasy. "I have thought about that," he admitted. "But since that other copy of myself is not here, I am not bound by any relationships he may have assumed. She is a type of woman I do not care for."

"What type is that?" Hilda asked. He shrugged without answering, but she didn't really need an answer. She had already diagnosed General Delasquez's own type: authoritarian male, which meant sexist pig. It was a type that she had always enjoyed encountering, on official business or in the boudoir.

The woman from the controller's staff diplomatically changed the subject. "So, Brigadier Morrisey, are you ready to explore outer space?"

"Of course," Hilda said, politely enough. "In fact, I wish it would happen. How long are we going to have to wait here?"

"That's not my decision. The LuftBuran is nearly fueled, and all the supplies are already stowed. As soon as the crew is ready we can go."

Interoffice Memo:
The Eurospace rocket.
Classified.

The "LuftBuran" was built from a German design with German money, but using Russian facilities and labor. The French didn't like the name. They wanted to call it the "Ariane 9," but when that was turned down they settled for naming a French astronaut as chief pilot.

"I'm ready now," Hilda declared, digging into the fish course that one of the waiters had placed before her. She didn't recognize the fish. There were two of them, quite tiny, but delicious; evidently Colonel duValier had made his wishes known to the kitchen staff.

They had reached the cheese course when carry-phones began beeping all over the mess hall. "What is happening?" Delasquez asked irritably.

The woman from the controller's staff was already answering hers, and when she turned to look at them her face was pale. "That object that was approaching Earth? It is a spacecraft. It has been observed to make a burn, and its new course will impact the Earth."

The cheese boards sat abandoned on every table, rounds of perfect Camembert, slabs of *bleu* and Brie. There was no one left in the room to eat them. Everyone had flown to the briefing room, where Colonel duValier had a phone to his ear and an eye on the wall screen.

Hilda stared at the pictures. After all the searching, not one of Earth's giant telescopes had had its instruments bearing on the incoming object. That was left to the smaller ones, and so they had been the ones that were dazzled when the object emitted a stream of fire. Beside her Martín Delasquez muttered something in

Spanish, but when she asked he said it in English for her benefit. "It is a braking burn," he said. "They are preparing for reentry."

"But what *is* it?" someone asked. No one tried to answer. Everyone was thinking the same thoughts, though, for they had all heard the stories the captives brought back of Scarecrow vengeance that dropped KT-type asteroids on the planets of their enemies, wiping them out as thoroughly as the sixty-five-million-year-old impact not far from where they were standing had wiped out the dinosaurs.

Hilda could not help a small shudder. Then someone cried, "Look at the other screen!"

It was displaying a series of numbers—orbital elements, Hilda supposed, though the digits meant nothing to her. Then the screen provided a graphic, a globe of the Earth, with a great oval of pink light overspreading a west-to-east area from Baja California almost to the African coast.

"That is its landing footprint," Delasquez said tautly. "When it makes final course corrections it can strike anywhere in that area. If you notice, we are inside it here in Kourou."

Everyone in the room had noticed that. Colonel duValier was gabbling with the controllers. Then, grimfaced, he seized the microphone.

"It is my belief," he said, his voice taut and his accent thickening, "that these Scarecrows are aiming this missile directly at us in order to keep us from accomplishing our launch to the Starlab orbiter. I do not intend to let them do that. Our next launch window is in eighteen minutes; we can't make that one, but we can make the one after that. I order refueling topped off and the alien creature to be brought aboard. It is now a little after thirteen hundred hours local time; the remainder of the crew will board the spacecraft by fourteen ten, for possible liftoff at fourteen fifty-seven."

CHAPTER TWENTY-NINE

Even a Bureau agent was entitled to an afternoon off now and then. Once Dannerman had supervised the changing of shifts for the guards at the Observatory and the apartment, and the other guard at the hospital where poor Pat Five was flat on her back in the ob-gyn wing, he was free for personal business.

Which, of course, was Anita Berman. He met her for a pleasant, if inexpensive, lunch not far from his room in Rita Gammidge's condo, and when he suggested they go up to his place afterward she was not surprised.

The landlady popped out of her own room to see who was coming into her condo in the middle of the day, but when she saw Anita she smiled and closed the door. Then Dannerman and Anita did what they had come there to do; and that went well, too. Then, satisfied, they lay spooned in the bed, Dannerman's arm over her, his face in the sweet, red hair at the nape of her neck. He was quite content. When she spoke he didn't hear her at first, she spoke so softly. "I said," she repeated, "what happens next?"

"Oh," he said. He stretched, yawned and tried to collect his thoughts. "Well, I guess I kind of get back to my life. I'm still waiting for the damn payroll people to clear my status, now that there are two of me. The big problem is—"

But it wasn't Dannerman's file and pension account she wanted to talk about. She said, "That isn't what I meant. I meant, what happens next with us?"

"Oh," he said again, suddenly thoughtful. He readjusted his mind. He had been asked that "what about us?" question more than once before, by more than one other young woman. When you decoded it, it usually turned out to mean, "Are we going to get married?"

All the other times he had been asked that question the answer had been pretty much out of his control, often enough because the woman who asked it happened to be a suspect in his ongoing mission. But now . . .

She wasn't waiting for his answer. She had something else on her mind. "Listen," she said tentatively, "there's something I didn't tell you."

Oh, hell, he thought, because he could decode that one, too; it meant a lot of things, and one of them might be that another man had suddenly appeared in her life.

But not this time. "Dan," she said, "have you ever thought of leaving the Bureau?"

He propped himself up to look at her, honestly puzzled. "And do what?"

"Well, I always had the idea that you really wanted to be an actor. Am I wrong?"

That came right out of left field. Be an actor? He'd certainly thought about it, especially while he was taking all those drama courses in college. It had been a sort of dream-time thought, the way he'd also now and then thought about how nice it would be to win the Olympic decathlon or run for President. It was a daydream and not at all realistic. . . .

> Uncle Cubby financed Dan Dannerman's education right through graduate school, whence he emerged with a doctorate in theater arts—just in time to be called up for active duty from the Police Reserve Officers Training Corps he had ill-advisedly joined as an undergraduate. Working for the Bureau didn't end his interest in theater, it just made it hard to do anything about it . . . until he was assigned to a drug case in New York City, and found the Off-Off-Off Broadway Theater Aristophanes Two, and the girl named Anita Berman who acted in it.

No, that wasn't true anymore. It hadn't been realistic before because of his job. The Bureau wouldn't let him go public as an actor. By definition actors were there to be seen, while a Bureau agent's chief asset was his invisibility.

But he wasn't invisible anymore. That had been taken care of by the Scarecrows.

"If I quit," he said thoughtfully, "I'd be able to collect all my back pay. I guess I'd have to split with the other guy, but there should be enough there to live on, maybe."

"What are you talking about?"

"Well, they don't pay much at Theater Aristophanes Two—"

"Oh, Dan! Who said anything about Theater Aristophanes Two? Do you know who Ron Zigler is?"

"The producer?"

"Yes, the producer. He came backstage at the theater the other night and he wanted to talk to me. Did you ever hear of *Star Trek*?"

"*Star Trek?*" Dannerman tracked down an old memory. "Oh, sure. Back in—what was it, the 1980s? Uncle Cubby was a Trekkie when he was a kid; that's what got him into the astronomy business."

Anita frowned. "Trekkie? What's that? Never mind; the thing is, Zigler wants to do a remake of *Star Trek*. He's got a script, with the Scarecrows in it and everything, and he's casting. The thing is," she said, clearing her throat, "Zigler's been trying to get in touch with you, either of you, but the Bureau won't pass his messages on. He wants you for Captain Kirk. That's the lead part, in case you didn't know." Dannerman stared at her. She stood up, beginning to dress. "He said there'd be a part in it for me, too, if he could get you for the Kirk role," she finished, sounding embarrassed and defensive, "but that's my problem, not yours. Think about it, will you? Now, which way is that bathroom of yours?"

When Anita was gone Dannerman pulled his own clothes on, thinking.

Too much was happening. Never mind the fact that there were two of him, never mind the Scarecrows, never mind any of those great events that were screwing up the lives of everybody in the world. The things that were happening in his own personal world were already more than he knew how to handle. *Acting?* A starring part?—and with one of Broadway's most famous producers? And what about Anita Berman herself: what a chance this was for her, if only he'd agree to do the thing that any would-be actor in the world would kill to do?

When the hammering began at his door Dannerman was deep in fantasies of stardom, married life with Anita, the stage, the life of a Lunt and Fontanne, fame, riches—

"Here I come, Anita," he called, reaching for the doorknob.

It wasn't Anita, though he saw her standing farther down the hall, looking like a woman in a state of shock. The one doing the hammering was his landlady, and she looked terrified. "Dan!" she cried. "Turn on your screen! Those space people are shooting rockets at us!"

CHAPTER THIRTY

Back in New York, Pat dithered for some time before reluctantly leaving Patrice in sole charge at the Observatory. That was where all the excitement was, but sisterly duty was compelling. At the hospital entrance Pat didn't have to go through the weapons search. The Bureau guard spoke to the hospital security man at the door, who listened, then reluctantly waved them through. He didn't even make the Bureau guard check her weapon, though Pat's own little derringer was taken away.

Pat Five was in a private room—really a suite—and paid for, the funny thing was, by the government of the People's Republic of China on behalf of the triplets' putative father. Pat Five's own guard was sitting on a straight-backed chair outside the door; alerted to their coming, she clapped her hands and the door opened.

Pat didn't see her semisister at first, because Pat Five's bed had pull-up sides to keep her from falling out, and they were hung with sheets to keep out drafts. Pat had to step right up to the bed and look down in order to show Pat Five the flowers she'd brought. "How are you doing?" she asked.

Pat Five opened her eyes to peer up at her. She looked like hell. Her face was blotchier than ever, and her auburn hair was sweated into clumps. She was not going to be able to take advantage of the comfortable sitting room next door, with its picture-window view of the city, or even the fully equipped bathroom that came with the suite. One of her arms was strapped down because of the IVs that were taped in place; pulse monitors were mounted on her throat and a respiration microphone on her right side. From under the light blanket that covered the lower half of her body inconspicuous tubes led to plastic waste bags, showing that she was still catheterized. "How am I doing?" she asked. "I'm doing lousy. Do you know they want me to stay flat on my back for the next six weeks?"

"Ah, honey," Pat clucked. The words weren't meant to convey information. It was only what you said when you had nothing better to offer. She thought of reminding Pat that this was all for the benefit of her unborn babies, but the last time she'd tried that Pat had talked fretfully of the attractions of a midterm abortion.

"Anyway," Pat said brightly, "I've got some news. Mr. Hecksher served all the papers, and he has an appointment to talk to the people at the UN this afternoon. He has a new paper for you to sign—something for the Chinese government, to say that you are accepting their financial assistance *ex gratia*, whatever that is, but without admitting any claim to the children. Can you actually sign?"

"Legibly, no. But the nurses help me, so just leave it. What's this about an object approaching the Earth? Is it the goddam Beloved Leaders?"

Pat's strictest order from the doctors was not to excite the patient, so she said reassuringly, "People say it might be, but it's not coming anywhere near the Earth."

"I don't trust the bastards," Pat Five said glumly.

"Well, no one does." Pat cast around for a more cheerful subject. "You wouldn't believe the get-well messages that have been coming for you. From people all over the world. Everybody we've ever known, even our ex-husbands—and relatives we haven't heard from for years."

"Sure, they think we might be coming into a lot of money."

"Oh, not all of them," Pat protested. "There are a lot of people that just like you—us. And—wait a minute."

It was her carryphone. She frowned as she answered it; she wasn't supposed to be called on the private line except in emergency. It was Patrice on the line. She said, "Pat? Get your ass back here. Don't say anything to Pat Five—but the damn thing has changed course, and it looks like it's going to impact the Earth."

When Pat Adcock got back to the Observatory she saw the whole thing, from that first chance-caught burn on, because the news channels kept rerunning every sighting. At twenty-five Earth radii the object—no, damn it, Pat said fretfully to herself; call it a spacecraft, because there wasn't any more doubt that that was what it was—the *spacecraft* produced another great display of fireworks. When the burn was over and they calculated the new orbit—a stretched-out ellipse, with the spacecraft now on the descending leg—there wasn't any doubt. It was definitely going to impact the Earth. "Right on top of us," Patrice groaned as she inspected the oval of the expected footprint, swallowing up half of the western Atlantic and a lot of the bulge of South America. "They know we're all here, and they're after us."

"If it's big enough," Rosaleen offered, "it doesn't much matter where it hits. Remember how the Scarecrows offed their enemies by dumping asteroids on them?"

But it wasn't that big. Pat was sure of that much. *What* it was was another question entirely: supernuclear bomb? Bioweapons? Patrice, thinking along the same lines, said tightly, "I wonder if the government's going to try to evacuate the Eastern Seaboard."

But if they did, where would they evacuate the people to? And how could they move a hundred million men and women out of the way, when they weren't sure just where the way was?

> The Earth is a sitting duck for all the floating bird shot that orbits the Sun. Thousands of meteorites strike its outer atmosphere every day, most of them so tiny that they burn up quickly and are not even noticed by Earth's people. Once in a while a slightly larger one— perhaps the size of a grain of sand—burns brightly enough to be seen as a "shooting star." More rarely one is large enough to reach the ground as a hot lump of pitted rock. Very seldom does one make a crater, and only a few times in a million years will one be large enough to do serious damage. But *never* before has one been seen to change its course by a rocket burn to make sure of hitting its target.
>
> —*Newsweek*

The big telescopes were no use now; the thing was too close and moving too fast for them. But telescopes weren't necessary. Every news camera on Earth was scanning the skies, for there wasn't any other news that mattered at that moment. The lucky ones zoomed in on the Scarecrow spacecraft, and for a few minutes each was able to hold it—sometimes long enough to catch it as the thing plooped out a minor course-correction jet. On the dozen screens in the Observatory's conference room there were sometimes as many as eight or nine different shots of the spacecraft, flickering in and out as the harried operators in the network control rooms tried to keep abreast of the rapidly changing feeds.

Then, abruptly, one screen switched to a wholly different scene: Eurospace's LuftBuran caught in its liftoff from Kourou. "Hell," Dannerman snapped. "They've launched ahead of schedule! Why would they do that?"

No one answered; they were all too full of questions of their own.

And then the spacecraft made a final burn, and turned into a sun-bright meteor as it entered Earth's atmosphere, plunging down.

"It's going to miss us," Patrice breathed.

"It's going to miss the land entirely," Pat corrected, as the footprint on one of the screens wobbled, shrank, finally turned into a point in the ocean.

Then all the ground-based scenes blacked out at once, and one by one each screen came on again, all of them showing a single picture. It came from a traffic-spotter plane belonging to a Puerto Rican TV station, urgently redirected by its control room as the Scarecrow ship's splashdown became predictable. The pilot was quick and the cameraman was good. They caught the fireball of the descending spacecraft from a distance, even saw the immense splash and clouds of steam when it struck. The pilot had piled on the coal, and they were closing in on it before the steam had dissipated, while Pat—and everyone else in the world—held their breath, awaiting the explosion. . . .

It didn't come. When at last the steam blew away a metal object, the size and shape of an old naval torpedo, was floating placidly in the ocean swell, and it wasn't exploding at all.

Within half an hour there were a dozen other planes circling above the floating Scarecrow ship; within an hour, the first surface vessels began to arrive.

There wasn't much to see, but no one in the Dannerman Observatory turned away from the screens. The ships were an oddly assorted lot: fishing vessels, fast cigarette speedboats, even a cruise ship that happened to be nearby and altered course to give its passengers an unanticipated thrill.

When a Navy tug approached, flank speed ahead, a mustache of white foam curling away from its bow, the first thing it did was to put an officer on the loud-hailers and warn everybody else away. Then it slowly approached the floating hulk, circled it suspiciously a time or two, then stopped. A moment later a pair of frogmen went over the side.

Then the tempo of events slowed down to a crawl. One of the frogmen paddled over to the floating object and gingerly touched it with some sort of metallic probe, while the other trod water a few meters away. They jabbered to each other, then one of them waved to the tug. A moment later deckhands flopped an inflatable raft overboard and a couple of others climbed down a rope ladder to get into it. Nothing happened for a moment, then some sort of metallic-gleaming equipment was lowered into the raft and its crew began to row it toward the Scarecrow object.

"They're being pretty damn cautious," Pat grumbled. Rosaleen gave her an amused look.

"Wouldn't you be?" she asked. And yes, Pat admitted to herself, she would. They still didn't know whether the thing was a bomb or not . . . or whether it might suddenly give anyone nearby one of those devastating electrical shocks . . . or even whether it might pop open and a horde of Scarecrows would come charging out, weapons blasting.

But nothing like that happened. Nothing much was happening at all, except that the sailors in the raft were gingerly touching the Scarecrow object with probes, frowning over their instrument readings, talking on their headsets to the command personnel on the tug about what they found . . . who in turn were, no doubt, talking to higher authority somewhere ashore at every step while someone decided what to do next.

Pat grinned to herself. It was actually getting pretty boring, but neither she nor anyone else in the

Observatory could tear herself away from the dozen identical displays on the screens. . . .

Until the display on some of them changed. A human face appeared, looking agitated. "A transmission has been received," it began to say, and then it froze; whatever it was saying was no longer heard as the audio portion of that transmission was replaced by the very transmission it had announced.

How the Object Was Found

The "Scarecrow" missile happened to be in Earth's daylight skies when it emitted the burn that changed its course. It was almost directly overhead, as seen from the islands of Hawaii, where a BBC crew was interviewing a group of astronomers at the Canada-France-Hawaii dome. A script girl, glancing up at the sky, saw the flare. When she yelped in surprise the BBC cameraman caught the object in his finder, and that was how the world first saw it.

Within ten minutes every telescope in the world that could bear on the object was searching for it. Cerro Toledo was the first to locate it, once the burn was over. It was moving very rapidly, but the Chileans were able to hold it long enough to project a track, moving east by northeast. Using the Chilean data, telescopes in the little observatory in the hills over Rio de Janeiro picked it up and refined the orbit before it vanished over the Atlantic.

Twenty minutes later telescopes in the Azores, and moments later on the European continent, had it, and since then it has been under constant watch.

—*Sky & Telescope*

"Do not be afraid," a mellow, reassuring voice said. "Our intentions are friendly. The lander you are approaching is not dangerous. It simply carried a cargo of food to supply the needs of our loyal associates presently on your planet. As you see, the Beloved

Leaders care for those who cooperate with them. We will care for you, too, if you wish it. And most of all, we will help you defend yourselves against the forces of the evil Horch. We suggest that you examine our lander and its contents to reassure yourself we mean no harm, and when you have had an opportunity to do so we will speak to you again. . . ."

"Just *food?*" Pat said incredulously. "They scare the pee out of us just to give Dopey some *food?*"

"Hold it," Dannerman said, listening, because the voice was going on—not quite as mellow, now; almost sounding agitated:

"But we must warn you against your foolish attempt to visit your Starlab! The mechanisms it contains are highly dangerous! Recall your spacecraft at once! Do not enter the Starlab! The consequences will be very grave!"

CHAPTER THIRTY-ONE

Long before Starlab was in sight the word had come over the LuftBuran's radio that the "missile" was a dud. That did not appear to make Colonel duValier feel any safer. When they came within docking range of Starlab he brought the old rocket to relative rest for half an hour while he studied the exterior of the orbiter centimeter by centimeter. The French female astronaut had unbuckled herself and swum up to confer with him—endlessly; in French, and pitched too low for anyone else to hear.

She was the only one allowed freedom of movement. Everybody else was ordered to remain strapped in their seats in case the colonel decided to get out of there in a hurry. Hilda did her best to be patient, though little twinges in her belly reminded her that a lot of people got spacesick in this kind of microgravity . . . even without the odor of the Doc that filled the vessel.

Then the colonel reached a decision. "Check your weapons, everybody," he ordered. "I am going to dock."

That was a little better, though the odd, slippery-slidey motion of the LuftBuran as duValier twitched it to mate with the Starlab port caused Hilda to swallow nervously. But then he announced the docking secured. Everyone unstrapped and took their places by the door—well, almost everyone. The great pale alien remained lashed to the cradle that had been built for him, of course, and one of the Germans remained by him to release him when Colonel duValier gave the order.

Which the colonel was taking his time about doing. He was obviously mulling something over in his mind—perhaps trying to find the proper historic words to speak before ordering his crew to enter, Hilda thought sourly. But what he said at last was, "You all know your orders. I will be the first person to board Starlab. You will then follow in the order assigned, except for Capitaine des Esseintes. She will remain in the LuftBuran, in constant radio contact with those of us in the boarding party. This will be done as a precaution. If anything goes wrong, she will undock at once, until the problem is cleared up."

And if the problem weren't cleared up? Hilda tried to imagine what it would be like if the Frenchwoman took it into her head to decide they had all been taken over by the Scarecrows, and then pulled the LuftBuran away for a return to Earth. It was not an attractive prospect. If it were a false alarm, they would all be marooned there for an indefinite period. And if it weren't a false alarm. . . . No, Hilda didn't want to think about that at all.

The colonel was speaking to his controllers on Earth, presumably to announce that he was ready for his historic task. But he suddenly frowned and lost his composure. He spat rapid-fire French into the microphone, too fast for Hilda to follow, listened again, then looked up. "There has been a development. There is a message from these Scarecrows, and they warn that we must not enter Starlab. This is— This causes—" Then he shook his head and was silent.

He was the only one silent. Everybody else was shouting at once—"Warning of what? What do they mean?"—everyone but Hilda. She had a different concern. It wasn't so much what the Scarecrows had said as the fact that they had said anything about entering Starlab at all. For that meant that they weren't thousands of light-years away. They were close enough to see what was going on. And that meant—

That was another thing Hilda didn't want to think about.

Another hour went by while everyone jabbered to everyone else, with many more exchanges between Colonel duValier and the ground controllers. Then the colonel shrugged and pulled the lock door open with a crash. *"Allons!"* he said hollowly; and the troops stormed the citadel.

In Hilda Morrisey's eighteen years with the Bureau she had stormed into enemy territory often enough, guns blazing, people getting killed. This wasn't like that. For one thing, rushing a target when your feet were firmly on the ground and things dropped to the floor when you let go of them was one thing. This microgravity business was something else entirely. They didn't storm the Starlab. They damn well *floated* in through the lock, one after another, as easy a collection of big, slow targets as ever graced any church-carnival shooting gallery. If there had been actual enemies inside, they would have had no problem picking the invaders off, one at a time, as they floundered and soared.

Well, there weren't any waiting sharpshooters. There was nobody in sight at all. Hilda caught a confused glimpse of rows and clusters of odd colors and bizarre objects, looking like some mad interior decorator's going-out-of-business sale; but then Martín Delasquez thumped into her from behind, propelling her into one of Colonel duValier's flying feet; and all her attention was taken up with the job of trying to grab on to something solid. Her interior ear canals were complaining about it, too; her queasiness got worse, to the point where she seriously thought she was going to toss her cookies right into the lap of the Chinese guy, Lin. And it was not helped by the smell of the place: something like spice, something like decay, a lot like a nastily rasping kind of chemical smoke.

The chemical part at least had an explanation. "It's the transporter," Jimmy Lin gasped, hauling himself up Martín Delasquez's leg to clutch a wall bracket. "Dannerman shot it up to keep the Scarecrows from following us. Outside of that, the place is just the way we left it."

Federal Reserve Inflation Bulletin

The morning recommended price adjustment for inflation is set at 3.21%. Acting Federal Reserve Chairman L. Dwight Gorman, replacing the late Walter C. Boettger, issued a prepared statement demanding that all banks immediately adhere to the recent eighth increase in interest rates. "Dr. Boettger's suicide should be a warning to us all," he said in the statement. "If we do not pull together, we can expect financial anarchy, which will cause great harm to our democratic institutions in this time of public unrest."

Maybe so, Hilda thought, but she hadn't forgotten what had happened when this same Jimmy Lin and the others made their first landing on Starlab. It had looked innocent enough then, too; and then, without any foreplay, they'd found themselves captives of the Scarecrows.

The colonel evidently had the same thoughts. He ordered a thorough search of the orbiter, and so the landing party dragged itself through the corridors of the orbiter, looking for—looking for what, exactly? Hilda asked herself. God knew there was a lot to see, for the satellite was full of inexplicable machines and gadgets. The things came in all colors and textures. Some looked like lime Jell-O, some were silver-bright. There was one huge copper-colored thing, like a huge, metal, six-sided pillar, that seemed to be emitting a sullen heat. Some of the objects clicked and whispered to themselves, some glowed, some were silent and dark, and what any of them were for Hilda could not guess.

Still, it could have been worse. The one thing that they feared to find was not there: no living creature, no Docs or Dopeys nor anything else out of the Scarecrows' menagerie of oddities. And when Colonel duValier was quite sure of that, he got on the radio and commanded, "Bring the beast in," and the expedition began to earn its pay.

At that point most of the people aboard Starlab became extraneous, which meant that they were free to follow their private agendas, whatever those were. General Delasquez pulled out a camera and, without a word to anyone else, methodically began to photograph everything in sight. Hilda herself retraced her steps around the Starlab, looking for those particle-beam weapons the Scarecrow troops were supposed to have. There weren't any visible. The Chinese astronaut, Commander Lin, had a priority project of his own; he had stationed himself by the charred wreck of the machine that had brought them there, with his weapon still in his hand. When Hilda came near he pointed the gun at her face. "Back off. Nobody comes near this thing," he announced. "I'm not taking any chances on letting it get fixed."

Hilda looked at him curiously. "How would I know how to fix it?"

"I don't know," he admitted, "and I don't care. Maybe the Scarecrows have some way of making you do it—same as they made us forget all this stuff?"

"Then they could just as well do it to you, Lin," she pointed out.

He scowled. "Stay away. And keep the Doc away from here. I swear, if he tries to touch this thing, I'll blow his damn head off."

The Doc showed no such intention. He, too, had his own program. As soon as he was inside the Starlab he headed down one of the corridors at high speed— startling Hilda; the creature was making faint mewing sounds, the first she had ever heard from him. Clearly he was practiced at getting around in the microgravity environment. Equally clearly he knew just where he wanted to go.

Which wasn't where the colonel wanted him. "Halt!" Colonel duValier commanded, flailing after him with his gun drawn. The alien paid no attention. He didn't stop until he reached a green-glowing panel. He clutched it for support with one huge arm, reached out with a smaller one to touch on its surface. The panel sprang open, revealing a cubicle filled with racks of what looked like plant matter and smelled faintly peppery. Mewing in excitement, the Doc pulled out a clutch of the stuff and thrust it into his great mouth.

General Delasquez was amused. "The creature is hungry, of course," he reminded the colonel. The colonel was not amused at all. He took a moment to scowl blackly at Delasquez, then returned to muttering angrily at the Doc in a mixture of English and French.

If the Doc understood either, he showed no sign. He chewed energetically, cramming new fistfuls of the stuff into his mouth before the last batch was quite processed. He was a messy eater, too, for little sprigs of greenery fell off the clumps he was shoving in; some clung to the froth of white around his mouth.

He seemed to be more than merely hungry. Hilda had never thought she could detect any emotion on the face of either of the Docs, but now there were signs that had to be some kind of strain. He was actually sweating, and the great eyes were darting about as though in distress.

Then he pulled a couple of additional clumps of food from the locker and, clutching them in two of his extra arms, abruptly gathered his stubby legs under him and kicked himself down the hall for a dozen meters.

Colonel duValier was taken by surprise. He barely got out of the Doc's way in time, then clumsily followed after. "Wait!" he ordered. "Come back!" The Doc paid no attention. Munching as he went, he paused in front of a blue-green mirror. Whatever he did Hilda could not quite see, but the mirror vanished, and where it had been was a sort of tool rack. The Doc selected a couple of items, then, still ignoring Colonel duValier, hurried agitatedly back along the corridor until it came to a luminous golden hemisphere. The mewing noises were louder now; they sounded distressed. Agitatedly the Doc slid one of the tools under the edge of the dome. The glow winked out. The dome retracted silently, and a jumble of incomprehensible alien objects appeared behind it.

Alarm bells went off in Hilda's mind. Were these things weapons? DuValier was having the same thoughts, because he was flailing around, trying to get his body in position to aim his gun at the Doc.

If the Doc knew he was in danger he showed no sign. All his attention was concentrated on his task. He thumbed through the gadgets agitatedly, large arms holding him in place, smaller ones sorting feverishly through the array, until he found a length of what looked like woven cloth of gold. Hurriedly he wrapped it around his head, as though in pain.

Colonel duValier slowly lowered his gun and began talking on his radio to the LuftBuran, watching suspiciously as the Doc relaxed.

The eyes closed. The expression on the broad, pale face turned peaceful. He hung there in silence for a moment, then opened his eyes, turned to Colonel duValier and touched him on the shoulder—was it meant as a pat of reassurance? The Doc tugged at the shawl over his head, awkwardly twisting the ends of it to secure them under his chin. Then he found another square of the brassy fabric, tucked it under one of his smaller arms and stepped back.

Joining the Hundred-Mile-High Club?

Private Eye's gaze is on the LuftBuran that's on its way to the Starlab orbiter. Who have we got here? There's the American spook, Hilda ("Hot Pants") Morrisey, who has never explained what she was doing in a makeout bar not long ago. There's the Chinese James ("My-Grandfather-Could-Do-It-Better") Lin, with his little ancestral book of positions and procedures—will he be adding new chapters in zero-G? There are the two French pilots, Il and Elle, and you know the French, not to mention the big zombie from space. Sounds like a first-rate rave to us!

—*Private Eye,* London

He gestured encouragingly at the collection of objects and pantomimed carrying them into the LuftBuran. Hilda began to breathe again; whatever had been on the creature's mind, it seemed he was now finally ready to go to work.

The Doc looked consideringly at a brightly gleaming trapezoid and a pale blue rhombus, but finally began to dissect a purplish pyramid. When he had loosened it from its attachment to the wall he gestured to the colonel to take it away, and immediately began doing the same to a grapefruit-sized blister of orange nearby.

Colonel duValier whispered to himself in words that might have been French or may have been English, but were certainly profane. Then he turned to the others.

"The beast is at last doing as he was ordered," he said. "We can start loading these things into the spacecraft."

Although the machineries of the Scarecrows weighed nothing at all in the orbiting Starlab, they still had mass; it was sweaty work to try to maneuver them down the narrow corridors of the satellite and through the port—careful not to smash them into the walls, the other machines, the fixtures of the LuftBuran.

That kind of grunt labor was primarily reserved to the humans aboard. The Doc was the specialist now, fully occupied in dismantling bits of machinery, pausing only to collect another fistful of the aromatic food. It wasn't light labor, either. Hilda had not done this much physical work in a long time; in her normal existence that sort of thing was what she directed others to do. Even after the machines were inside the lander the work wasn't over. The things had to be stowed with care—with very great care, Hilda thought, imagining one of those bulky objects breaking loose in the shuddery violence of reentry and crashing down on her unprotected head.

The exertion and the well-used air inside Starlab were having their effect on her, too. She wasn't at the point of throwing up, quite. But the queasiness did not go away, and at last she was forced to make her way to the ancient microgravity toilet.

The training she had received at Kourou was not adequate to her present needs. It took her forever to close the lid on her wastes and then manage the stiff levers that noisily disposed of it. And when she came out the Doc had declared a halt. He was demonstrating to Colonel duValier that the other machines of any interest were simply too big to fit through the docking port.

The colonel surrendered. He ordered everyone inside

and grouchily sealed the ports. While the French female astronaut checked the stowage of the goods, the colonel himself strapped down the unprotesting Doc, who still had the one scrap of metal cloth bound oddly around his head, the other clutched firmly in one minor arm. Hilda, busy with her own seat fastenings, was paying little attention until a yelp from the colonel made her turn swiftly.

But General Delasquez was laughing. "You should not attempt to take that thing away from him," he said. "Naturally he resisted."

Colonel duValier sucked his wrist, where the Doc had thrust him away—not violently, but enough to hurt. "We will see," he snarled, "if the creature continues to resist when we are back at Kourou." But he left the Doc alone and pulled himself back to the control deck. A moment later he called, "Check your restraints. Are we all secured?"

When the crew, one by one, reported themselves strapped in, he said crisply: "Disengage."

The copilot touched something; there was a gentle lurch. The nausea that Hilda had quelled came back. She inhaled deeply and managed to repress it once again, bracing herself for the thrust that would start them back to Earth.

It didn't come. They weren't moving, except to drift slowly away from Starlab. Craning her neck, Hilda saw that the colonel was speaking into a microphone while the copilot was scanning the interior of the LuftBuran with a handheld camera. He was speaking softly and in French; Hilda could catch only a few words, but it sounded as though he was complaining about the Doc and demanding armed guards to meet them on landing.

Stupid, she thought . . . but then something new caught Hilda's attention. She wrinkled her nose and craned her neck to look back at the Doc.

All that food had had its inevitable result. The Doc

had relieved himself again, and the stench was one thing too many for Hilda Morrisey to bear. She barely got the spacesick bag to her face before everything came up at once.

CHAPTER THIRTY-TWO

When the new orders came in over the command channel Lieutenant Colonel Priam Makalanos saw no particular problem. *Immediately* on off-loading the object will be airlifted to Camp Smolley for study and biological analysis. If suitable, limited amounts of the contents may be included in rations for the extraterrestrials.

Curiously it was signed *D. S. Fennell, Vice Deputy Director,* rather than by the deputy director himself, but that was only a small puzzle that undoubtedly would be clarified in time. Makalanos glanced up at the wall screen, which for some time had been displaying the object in question. The thing from space was lashed to the deck of a Navy tug steaming toward Hampton Roads. Two destroyers, three Coast Guard corvettes and half a dozen smaller vessels were patrolling the perimeter around the tug, keeping the ships of other nationals away from what, after all, was something that had been found in American territorial waters. Makalanos grinned at the thought of all the indignant diplomatic protests that would be storming on the American State Department over this episode, but that wasn't his problem. All Makalanos had to do was to get Camp Smelly ready to receive the cargo.

Actually, he thought, Dr. ben Jayya and his old biowar staff would be glad for something to do that was more along their lines of expertises; but while he was alerting the laboratory chiefs a breathless corporal rapped on his office door. "There's some kind of trouble with the turkey, sir," he panted. "Dr. Adcock thinks you ought to come."

Even before Makalanos got to the isolation room he could hear Dopey's excited yammering. Pat One was waiting for him at the door. "He's been like this," she managed to get out before the little creature turned to him, great fan almost glowing with passion.

"Lieutenant Colonel Makalanos! What have you done with my bearer? Is he dead?"

Makalanos glanced at Pat One for help, but she only shook her head worriedly. He tried his best. He said, trying to be placating, "If you mean the one at Walter Reed—"

"I do not mean the one at Walter Reed! I mean the one I agreed to let you take to your Starlab for the purpose of obtaining food, which it appears we no longer need, and devices for your study, which I now believe I should never have permitted. What have you allowed to happen to him?"

Puzzled, Makalanos did his best. "As far as I know, nothing has happened to him."

"As far as you know!" Dopey sneered.

"Which is pretty far, actually," Makalanos said levelly, "but it's always possible something has happened I don't know about. If you'll try to calm down, I'll go to my office and check." Turning, he gave Dannerman a curt nod. "You come with me."

In his office, he turned on the agent. "All right. What happened?"

Dannerman shook his head. "Beats the hell out of me, Colonel. We told him about his food package coming—your order, Colonel."

"I know what my order was. What did he do?"

"He seemed pleased, that's all."

"Pleased? Not surprised?"

"Just pleased. Then he complained for a while about the food he's been getting, as usual, and then, all of a sudden, he went ape. He said we'd killed his bearer."

Makalanos scowled. "Just like that?"

"Just like that. There wasn't any warning, just one minute he was pissing and moaning as usual, then all of a sudden he was having fits. I tried to tell him that killing the Doc was the last thing we wanted to do, because we needed him, but he wasn't listening. Shaking all over. Screeching. As close to hysterical as I've ever seen him. We couldn't calm him down, even though we kept telling him the Doc was all right." He paused there, and then asked, "He is all right, isn't he?"

Was the creature all right? The obvious way to find out was to query headquarters. What was wrong with that was that Makalanos felt a little foolish about asking that sort of question on nothing more substantial than the unsubstantiated conjecture—or hunch, or suspicion—of the bizarre little beast from space. Colonel Makalanos didn't like to feel foolish.

He liked it even less when the Bureau duty officer assured him that of course the Doc was all right, the Starlab party was busily loading Scarecrow matériel into the LuftBuran at that very moment. "Anyway," she added, "when they're through there'll be a report, so why don't you just watch your news screen?"

Nettled, Makalanos sent Dannerman back to give Dopey the word and do his best to keep him quiet. Then he considered what he should do next. Was it worth reporting Dopey's hysterics to the deputy director?

It probably was, he thought—but when he tried to get through he found the D.D. was not taking calls— was getting ready to head for Kourou himself, to be there when the LuftBuran landed with its cargo.

He swore to himself. Colonel Makalanos was as good at following orders as he was at giving them, but what orders was he to give to deal with Dopey? And who was to tell him what to do, with Brigadier Morrisey off somewhere in orbit and the deputy director too busy even to answer his phone?

D. S. Fennell, that was who; the one who had signed his latest orders. Makalanos put in a call to her on the coded line, and found her impatient, harried, annoyed at being bothered—but willing to talk. She listened briefly, then shook her head. "Did you tell him the Bundles for Beasties were on the way? And that didn't cheer him up? Well, just do the best you can, Priam."

"I wish I knew more of what was going on," he complained.

"Don't we all? But what's to tell? There was a Chinese submarine shadowing the tug with the capsule, but we warned them off from territorial waters and now they're headed south. To Kourou, I guess. And there were a couple of Mexican frigates that got too close and had to be chased away—and, naturally, a lot of diplomatic complaints, but screw them. So everything's under control . . . I hope. Now can I get back to dealing with all this crap, please?"

Unwarranted Exclusion of Peaceful Shipping

Federal officials in the Costa Rican Naval Department have announced that Costa Rican fishing and pleasure vessels have been driven out of international waters in the vicinity of the recent landing of the spacecraft from the "Scarecrows." Our ambassador in Washington has asked for an appointment with the American State Department in order to file a protest against this high-handed act.

—*Tico Times,* San Juan, Costa Rica

"I guess," Makalanos said reluctantly. "Daisy? What are you doing with this Starlab stuff? I thought you were assigned to head up all the rest of the Bureau's business?"

She gave him a wry look. "What other business? Haven't you been paying attention? There isn't any. It looks like all the subversives are pulling their heads in. Right now this Scarecrow stuff is about the only action around."

Agent Dannerman knocked and came in while Makalanos was channel-surfing the civilian news. "Dopey wants to talk to you, so Pat's going to bring him along," he reported.

"Talk about what?" Makalanos asked, glancing away from a late-breaking story about the English Prime Minister's hurried visit to Cardiff, in Wales.

"About this idea he has that something's happened to his Doc. He's quieted down some, so it ought to be all right." He was looking past Makalanos, at the news screen. "I guess that's part of this Welsh thing," he offered. And, when Makalanos looked perplexed, he added: "It was scuttlebutt going around in Arlington. The way I heard it, the Welsh nationalists were negotiating with MI5 for a truce, and this Dawid ap Llewellyn guy? He was supposed to be surrendering to the police in Brownsville."

"I hadn't heard," Makalanos admitted.

"It's getting to be an epidemic. The Ukrainians, the Tamils in Sri Lanka, the Shining Path in, where is it, Peru? Even the Cambodian rebels and the Irish. I haven't heard anything like that about our own nut groups, but all over the world there are these revolutionaries packing it in. Makes you wonder—ah, there he is."

Dopey had waddled in, Pat One right behind him, as they were talking. The little alien seemed subdued—worried, Makalanos thought, although he had not learned how to read Dopey's feelings from any expression on the cat face or hues of the great fantail. As Pat One lifted him onto a chair and began to work the controls of the screen, Dopey commented, "It is a common thing."

Makalanos looked at him. "What is?"

"This submerging of differences. Many affiliated races have behaved so, in that time of fear and confusion before they came to accept the Beloved Leaders."

"Or didn't," Dannerman said sharply.

"Oh, yes, Agent Dannerman, that is true. Some did not. With inevitably tragic results." The thought seemed to cheer him up. He added politely, "One hopes your species will not necessitate extreme measures, but your actions must not give provocation. It is my bearer I am concerned with!"

From her position crouched beside the screen, Pat One interrupted. "Fight later, guys. I've got something."

The news screen she had been working over now showed the face of Colonel Hugues duValier, clutching a bracket to keep himself from floating around, and proudly informing the world that he, Colonel duValier, had successfully completed his mission and they were preparing to return to the Kourou base as soon as they were in position for the reentry.

Then the camera panned around the ship. Makalanos saw Hilda's face, peering into the camera, and the German astronauts, and the baffling bits and pieces of alien technology, and the giant, silent figure of the Doc, curiously wearing a sort of metal babushka, but obviously alive and well.

There was a startled shriek from Dopey.

Makalanos turned to him. "What's the matter? He isn't dead, is he? He's all right—"

The little alien seemed stunned. He mewed to himself for a moment, seeming at a loss for words. Then he said: "He is not at all all right, Lieutenant Colonel

Makalanos. It is worse than I feared! Something must be done at once!"

Pat One, perched on the arm of Dopey's chair, tried to soothe him. "Take it easy, will you? Look, they'll be back soon, then you can see him yourself, so if you're worried—"

"I am worried, Dr. Adcock! I am extremely worried! Can't you see, the bearer has cut himself off from contact? It is an extremely dangerous situation, and—and—and there is no alternative. He must be destroyed. Please order him shot at once!"

CHAPTER THIRTY-THREE

Back on the ground, Hilda Morrisey discovered that Kourou had changed. While she and her shipmates were looting the old Starlab the population of the Eurospace complex had exploded. Planes were landing every hour, bringing in more and more people. The planes weren't just any old commercial jobs, either; these were official government aircraft, from forty or fifty different governments, and every one of them was packed with lawyers and high officials and whatever that government could scare up in the way of scientists and engineers to squabble over the loot as it came off the LuftBuran.

That wasn't Hilda's worry. She had done everything she was supposed to do on the orbiter—had prevented any of the others from pocketing any odd little bits of alien technology, had kept a sharp eye for dirty tricks. She had done her job, and now all she wanted was a bath and some clean clothes and a fast plane back to Arlington . . . but Marcus Pell turned out to have other ideas for her.

The deputy director's plane had deposited him and fifteen others on Kourou's landing strip before the LuftBuran touched down. It seemed to Hilda that he had brought enough manpower with him to do everything that still needed to be done, but Pell didn't agree. "You're one of our best agents, Hilda," he told her benignly. "You've had a chance to get to know some of these people. You can talk to them. So talk. Circulate. Find out whatever you can. Leave the bargaining to us.

Rest? You can rest later." He paused, his nose wrinkling. "You'd better clean your teeth first, though."

So Brigadier Morrisey did clean her teeth—again; and rinsed her mouth four or five more times, too, until she was certain that her breath no longer showed any trace of her unfortunate spacesickness. Then she bathed the rest of her as well.

That, however, she was not able to do in the little room the base housing officer had assigned her during training, because that was now occupied by a pair of high-ranking diplomats from Sierra Leone. At that point Merla Tepp earned her pay. She had made friends among members of the spaceport's permanent party while her brigadier was away and had been able to borrow a key to their barracks. Which had showers.

Cleaner, "So where do I sleep?" Hilda asked her aide, putting on a little of Tepp's makeup before a mirror in the washroom.

Tepp seemed preoccupied with something. "Sleep?" she repeated. "Oh, sleep. On the deputy director's plane. I've staked out a couch in the lounge for you; I'll have to sleep on the floor right next to it, if you don't mind." No surprise there. Kourou had run out of facilities for the influx. Now the LuftBuran's longest landing strip, having served its main purpose when the spacecraft came down, was packed nose to tail with aircraft that had been kept on as emergency housing. The Argentinians were the best off, Tepp explained. They didn't need an aircraft to sleep in. They had the luxury of a battle cruiser steaming in circles offshore, with their people helicoptering back and forth. Other countries had ships on their way to join the bedroom fleet. Some of the more important newcomers had rooms or even suites in the hotels of the old town of Kourou itself, a few kilometers down the coast. They commuted. Most of the influx were less fortunate. They were doubling and tripling up in rooms that didn't have air-conditioning against the steamy equatorial heat, and might not even have windows, because they hadn't ever been intended for sleeping in the first place.

It was nearly dark now, the Sun gone over the hills to the west with a sliver of a Moon following its descent. Out over the ocean there were quick illuminations of lightning, though too far away for the thunder to be heard. Over the spaceport itself there were patches of stars. They were obscured by the lights beating down on the little mounds of goods removed from the lander, but Hilda made out the familiar outline of Orion, queerly lying on his side because of their latitude. There was a constant *bzzt-bzzt* of insects frying themselves on the electrified mesh over the lights. Even so, people were slapping at bugs on their necks and arms.

That didn't stop any of them from doing what they were here to do. The bickering was intense and Marcus Pell was in the thick of it, backing up the President's personal representative. Starlab was American property, the President's man was announcing, and so everything on it was American property as well. Nonsense, said everyone else. The goods were treasure trove, belonging to whoever found them and, besides, the United Nations had declared them the common property of all.

Of course, there was no real chance that the lander's cargo was going to be delivered to the UN Building. It would be divided among the world's powers. The bickering here was over how many pieces it would be divided into, and who would get the pieces. Hilda eavesdropped on a group of Germans and Poles arguing about whether the Slavic countries of Europe were entitled to any consideration at all, but really ought to consider themselves part of Eurospace—"We have had enough experience of being part of your space," one of the Poles was saying in German rudimentary enough for Hilda to follow. A few minutes later some Australians and New Zealanders were complaining that the damn Pommies still thought they were a major power, for God's sake. She wandered past the Canadian delegation, speaking urgently among themselves until they caught a glimpse of her uniform. Then they became freezingly silent—still no doubt pissed off because their country hadn't got anything out of letting the U.S. use their landing strip in the first place.

Then she caught a glimpse of Merla Tepp, standing by herself and gazing somberly at something Hilda couldn't quite see. When she got closer she saw that it was the Doc, placidly silent and still wearing his incongruous, metallic old-lady head shawl, with another like it held in one of its lesser arms—*stolid and stunned, brother to the ox,* some old words came to Hilda's mind. If the Doc was at all aware of the ferocious arguments going on all around, he gave no sign.

Tepp held half a sandwich in one hand, and that reminded Hilda that her recently emptied stomach was ready for refilling. "Where'd you get it, Tepp?" she demanded.

Tepp blinked at her, then came back to alertness. "There's a chow line giving them out, ma'am, but it's only this kind of thing. You're entitled to get a decent meal in the deputy director's aircraft."

"I don't want a decent meal. I want one of those. Where's this chow line?"

"Right outside the general mess. But you've got to queue up."

For a moment Hilda considered requisitioning Tepps's remaining half sandwich away from her, but decided against it—not out of any particular consideration for Tepp, but because a chow line was as good a place as any to listen in on talk.

The trouble with doing that was that some of the people at the end of the line were talking to each other in Japanese, others in what seemed to be Pakistani. Hilda wished for the presence of that ugly, but gifted, little turkey, Dopey, as a translator, then caught sight of Jimmy Lin and his two minders coming along to join the line. "Here!" she called, waving. "I've saved you a place!"

That got them all dirty looks from the Pakistanis just behind her, but they didn't push it any farther than that. The minders paid no attention, since there was an irritated-sounding discussion going on between them—in Chinese. They weren't paying much attention to their charge, either, and, after one searching glance, none at all to Hilda Morrisey.

Low-voiced and with one eye on the minders, Hilda asked Lin cordially, "How's it going?"

Lin looked weary and tired. "How would I know? All I know is I want to go home."

"You'll feel better after you get something to eat."

"Eat this slop? Christ, Morrisey, I used to feed my gardener better than this. We were supposed to have our own meals on a submarine, and sleep there, too, but the damn thing never showed up."

That was interesting. "What submarine are you talking about?" she asked, keeping her voice idly conversational.

But that was more than the minders were willing to put up with. One of them broke off their discussion to say something sharp to Lin, who hung his head. "He says I shouldn't be talking to you, so leave me alone," he told Hilda; and that was the end of conversation on the chow line.

It was pretty nearly the end of arguing, too. Everything that could profitably be said in Kourou had been said already. The next step depended on what happened at the United Nations, and only God knew when there would be any decisions there. Gossip said the General Assembly was pulling an all-nighter. Most of the people in Kourou were drifting away toward whatever beds they had been able to find. And Hilda, she abruptly realized, was bone-tired.

The deputy director's airplane was performing a function it had never been designed for. It was meant as luxury transportation for a privileged few, not as a boardinghouse. The overextended galley stewards did their best. They managed to provide a hot meal for everybody, but it was a long way from epicurean. Sleeping on the plane was no pleasure, either. There just weren't enough blankets to go around. Hilda's rank earned her one for her very own, though it wasn't much of a blanket. The thing had started life as a lap robe and covered very little of Hilda herself. Merla Tepp didn't have that much rank. On the floor beside Hilda's couch she made do with somebody's abandoned trench coat thrown over her.

It didn't keep Tepp awake, though. It didn't even keep her from snoring.

At first Hilda almost enjoyed the sound, which was associated in her mind with enjoyable nights of male bedmates, but it quickly got stale. Tepp wasn't male. They hadn't been making love. The noise was only noise, after all, and it was keeping her awake. She reached over to poke Tepp. The woman muttered something incomprehensible without waking, then turned over on her side. The snoring stopped.

Hilda, however, did not go immediately to sleep. Too much had been happening; her mind was racing with the memories of her first venture into space, and the way her familiar world was being remade, without her consent, by these bizarre creatures from other worlds.

Now that they had actual samples of extraterrestrial

machines, and the expertise of the Doc to dissect them, the reverse engineering could start. And what then?

It was one thing to contemplate the possible uses of adding Scarecrow technology to the Bureau's already formidable capacities. That could be very fine. Capturing and bugging terrorists and dopers and turning them loose to be unwitting spies; new weapons; instant transportation anywhere by means of these portals . . . why, the Bureau would have more power than any organization before in the world's history. . . .

Except that the damn UN had forced itself into the act, and those same abilities would be given to their enemies.

That thought made her scowl up at the dimly lit ceiling. There had to be some way of keeping a competitive advantage for the Bureau. Well, and for the rest of the United States, too, but the important thing was to keep the NBI several steps ahead of everybody else in the world. Was old man Krieg, the UN American delegate, skillful enough to make that happen? Probably not. Probably the Bureau would have to protect itself, as it always had. . . .

A new sound from Merla Tepp made her turn her head and look down. It wasn't a snore this time. It was more like a sob. Astonished, she saw that Tepp's face was damp with tears.

Now, what was that all about? Was Tepp, too, worrying about the future? But then Tepp turned restlessly, still asleep, and the snoring started again.

That was insupportable. Hilda was confident there was no way she could ever get to sleep with that racket going on half a meter from her ears . . . but then she did.

What woke her was the deputy director's voice snapping through the aircraft's PA system. "Wake up and get going, everybody! The

UN has agreed upon a plan and distribution of the items will start in thirty minutes."

For an old hand like Hilda thirty minutes was all the time in the world. She was down the wheeled steps of the plane in less than twenty, and she had even managed to browbeat the sleepy stewards into coffee and a couple of sweet rolls. Of course, that meant she was still wearing the slept-in clothes of the day before and she hadn't even attempted a turn at the aircraft's inadequate showers, but she was awake and ready. It was still dark in Kourou, though there was a faint early glow on the eastern horizon, and it was not yet unbearably hot.

The UN's decision had been to divide the objects from Starlab into four packets. One would go to the United States, on behalf of the whole Western Hemisphere, one to China for the mainland Asian powers, one to the Europeans, one to Australia to be shared with Japan, New Zealand, the island nations of the South Pacific and the countries of Indochina. Possession did not, however, confer ownership. So the UN's edict said firmly; research would be done under multinational supervision, with the resulting data to be made public as soon as obtained.

It was a tribute to the histrionic abilities of the experts and diplomats on the scene that not one of them was laughing out loud. Data to be made public! Hilda had no doubt that when the Bureau's technicians produced data the part that would be made public would be strictly limited, and the most valuable data would stay within the Bureau forever.

The best part was that the UN resolution clearly said the Doc was to be in charge of any real investigation . . . and, Hilda thought comfortably, she knew who was in charge of the Doc. She made her way to where he was being peacefully led out from the shelter in which he had spent the night by his armed guards. Had anyone bothered to tell him what he was supposed to be doing? That did not seem likely. The creature did not even seem curious as, under everyone's watchful eyes, the lucky nationals began removing the bits they had been awarded. He simply stood immobile in rest mode, still wearing the one coppery babushka with the other still held firmly in his lowest-left hand.

United Nations Security Council
Resolution 4408

Under the powers vested in the Security Council by the Charter of the United Nations, as amended, the Secretary General is ordered to execute the following instructions:

1. The artifacts of alien origin are to be divided into four parts, in a manner to be chosen by the Secretary General, each part to be deposited in an appropriate research facility in one of the four specified regions of the world.

2. All investigations into the nature and functions of these artifacts are to be conducted in the presence of a representative of the United Nations and of each of the nations party to said region.

3. Investigations are to be limited to noninvasive procedures until further notice. It is contemplated that the individual identified as "Doc" is to be present when any dismantling is undertaken, provided the individual is physically able to undertake supervision of said artifacts.

—By Order of the Security Council

But that caused a minor fracas, as one of the Indians announced that the extra babushka was definite Scarecrow technology and, as no one else had claimed it, it should be awarded to China for India to share.

Colonel duValier laughed at that. "You want to try to take it away from him?" he sneered.

"Of course it must be taken from him," the Indian

replied indignantly. And, when no one volunteered for the job, she reached for it herself.

Well, Hilda could have told the woman that that was a mistake, but by the time Hilda opened her mouth to warn her it was too late. The Doc's eyes sprang open; one of his great upper limbs pushed the Indian delegate out of the way—not violently, but not gently, either. The woman went flying. The Doc didn't look after her. He turned and plodded away in the direction of the parked American aircraft. His armed guards raised their weapons in bafflement, but someone shouted, "For Christ's sake, don't shoot the thing!" The Doc paid no attention to that threat, either, simply strode along with the one metal scarf on his head and the other still clutched in one arm.

"So," the deputy director said pleasantly, to no one in particular, "I guess that settles that."

It did, of course—though, of course, everyone around began arguing vociferously. Hilda didn't wait to take part in the renewed bickering. She hurried after the Doc, now stolidly climbing the steps into the deputy director's jet.

By the time she got inside the Doc was in the lounge, and he was no longer in standby mode. He had commandeered some of the aircraft's monogrammed notepaper and was busily filling pages of it with his meticulous drawings. The crew was passing them around interestedly until one of them caught sight of Hilda, with the deputy director behind her. Then they passed them over to higher authority.

Hilda puzzled over them. The first sketch showed the two Docs together, both wearing shawls over their heads. The second one showed both Docs in what was recognizably a hospital room, one of them doing something surgical to the head of the other. A human woman, actually a quite good likeness of Dr. Marsha Evergood, was standing by. And in the last drawing the former surgeon Doc was himself being operated on, and Dr. Evergood was doing the surgery.

The deputy director looked up at Hilda. "I think," he said judiciously, "that he's trying to tell us he wants to go back to Walter Reed Hospital."

"Well, yes," she said, suddenly thoughtful. "But what's this one here?"

She was pointing to a drawing that showed a human being next to a very peculiar creature. It wasn't a Scarecrow, nor was it any of the Seven Ugly Space Dwarfs. It looked a little bit like some ancient dinosaur, one of the long-necked, long-tailed ones that they called apatosaurus, but it was standing on two legs, and its rubbery neck was hovering menacingly over the human.

"Yes, well," Marcus Pell said, sounding unhappy, "I was wondering about that myself. The man looks kind of like Dan Dannerman, doesn't he?"

"He does. And that other thing—could it one of those things Dopey calls a Horch?"

CHAPTER THIRTY-FOUR

All the way down on the early flight to Arlington Dannerman was pondering the question: Should he tell Hilda Morrisey that he and Anita Berman were getting married? Or maybe he should just lay the ultimatum on her: either she got his back pay for him, so he could have some kind of decent life, or he quit the Bureau.

Well, she wasn't at the headquarters. She was off at Walter Reed Hospital, and when he tracked her down there she was standing on the loading dock, giving urgent orders to a flock of serious-looking junior agents, and she wasn't interested in his problems. "Resign? Bullshit, Danno. State of emergency; nobody's quitting; I tried the same thing myself. But as long as you're here you might as well be useful."

So five minutes later Dannerman, borrowed stunstick in hand, was marching with five others down a hospital corridor toward the Doc whom, according to Hilda's orders, he was supposed to "restrain." Although the creature was facing them, he didn't seem aware of their presence. He was simply standing there, pale, ugly and immense, in that next-to-dead trance state the things assumed when they had no orders.

But, damn it, the creature was *big*. The stunstick wasn't much comfort to Dannerman. He would have preferred a riot gun, but they weren't supposed to hurt the Doc, only tackle him if he gave any resistance. Even the stunsticks were to be used only as a last resort, because Hilda had warned them that they didn't know enough about a Doc's metabolism to know if the damn thing might kill him.

Dannerman hadn't been that close to a Doc since the
flight home from Calgary. He had almost forgotten the
spicy-sour stink of the thing, or how preposterous he
looked with his foamy "beard" and six ill-assorted
arms. The topmost right arm was the one Hilda had
assigned for Dannerman to deal with, and naturally it
was one of the big, muscular ones. He was just trying
to figure out where to grab it when the other Doc
appeared, moving quickly and silently toward his twin
from behind. He wore that dumb-looking metal-mesh
babushka Dannerman had seen on TV and he wasn't
alone; just behind him were Hilda and half a dozen
more of the Bureau guards, all trying to be as quiet as
they could—

Not quiet enough. Or maybe it was that the immobile
Doc had caught the scent of his fellow at the last
moment; but just as the one with the babushka was
reaching out to wrap another length of the material
around the target's head the creature sprang into action.
And then it got noisy. It didn't matter where Dannerman
tried to grab that gorilla-strong upper arm, either. He
didn't get the chance. As he was reaching out for it the
flailing arm caught him and slammed him straight
across the corridor and into a wall.

A dozen human beings turned out to be no match at
all for a fighting Doc; but the one with the babushka
was another matter. He had one of those great arms
around the throat of his twin from behind, and all of the
other arms frantically trying to stretch the metal mesh
around his head. It didn't happen right away, because
the captive Doc was doing everything he could to avoid
it; but when the shawl was in place everything stopped.
The attacking Doc mewed, a sharp, high-pitched cat's
yowl, to the other, who abruptly let go of the unfortunate guard who had managed to grab him. He stood up,
shedding guards, mewing back excitedly to the other,
adjusting the shawl for himself.

That seemed to be it, and wonderfully no one appeared to be seriously hurt.

Linguistics Team report
NBI Eyes Only

The task of providing a translation methodology for the language employed by the "Docs" is without precedent in our discipline. There are of course no loan words or cognates, nor any evident grammatical morphology relevant to any Earthly language or dialect. Lacking linguistic markers, our present line of investigation relies on attempts to identify the "words" (or lexically unitary parts of speech) by analyzing such traits as time depth and sound diversity, and to categorize them in the Bu"hlerian three-modality functional model (expression, arousal and description). So far, however, none have been identified.

"Let him go!" Hilda gasped, triumphant. "That does it. Is everybody all right? Fine, now we get them down to the operating room."

The operating room didn't look like an operating room anymore; all the usual equipment had been pushed out of the way and something that looked like a torture rack had been constructed on the floor—ten huge metal manacles of varying sizes, bolted to the cement, looking capable of holding an elephant.

Whether they were capable of holding a Doc was another question, and the two of them, yowling those high-pitched feline sounds at each other, were testing them with all their strength. As Dannerman and the others took their gallery seats Hilda was jubilantly explaining what was going on. "See, as long as they've got those things on their heads they're out of Dopey's control, but they've still got some kind of bugs inside them. So what we do now is we operate, only in order to get them they might have to remove the shields, and then— Well, then see for yourself." She pointed proudly at what was going on in the operating room before them. One of the Docs was lying down, while the other fixed the clamps around arms, legs, neck. "So now we're going to do it," Hilda finished with satisfaction, and then looked at Dannerman in a different way. "Come here a minute while they're getting organized," she said. And, when they had moved out of anybody else's earshot: "Listen. Are there any more of you Dannermans around?"

He looked startled. "Jeez, I hope not. Why are you asking?"

She sighed. "I don't really know. It's just that that other Doc's been drawing pictures again, and one of them showed one of you guys along with what looked like a Horch. Any idea what that means?"

"With a *Horch?* No. I never saw any of those."

She looked pensive for a moment. Then she shrugged, and added in a friendlier tone, "Oh, and by the way, Danno, congratulations. Can I be your best man?"

CHAPTER THIRTY-FIVE

Pat Adcock could have counted on the fingers of her two hands the number of times she'd visited anyone in a hospital. If you left out the visits to Pat Five, she probably could have done it on her thumbs; it was not one of her favorite ways of spending an hour.

Pat Five didn't make it any more appealing, either. She was thoroughly sick of her incarceration, and she let everybody know it. "I want some water," she informed Pat at once. "You'll have to hold it for me; I'm not supposed to lift anything."

Pat did as requested, holding the bottle with the flexible straw while Pat Five sipped. Then, thirst quenched, she spent five minutes explaining how she felt, which was weak and bored and wishing the whole damn business was over. Then she wanted to know how things were going at the Observatory, which was a gratifying change of subject. So Pat told her how hard it was to track the actual Scarecrow ship, and how Rosaleen seemed healthier and stronger than ever, thanks, it seemed, to whatever the medical Doc had done to her metabolism back when they were in the Scarecrow captivity, and how the two Docs seemed to have liberated themselves from Scarecrow control and were now helping with the reverse engineering of the things from Starlab.

"Yes, they're very good at taking things apart," Pat Five said bitterly.

Pat said—humbly, because she hadn't experienced what that taking apart was like for herself—"Well, it's not all their fault. They were under Scarecrow control; now they're not."

"I suppose so," Pat Five said, unconvinced. And then there didn't seem to be anything else to talk about.

When Pat finally got out of the sickroom there was still one other chore to take care of. She tracked Pat Five's doctor down as she stood at the nurses' desk, chatting with somebody who seemed to be a dietician.

When Pat asked after Pat Five's condition the doctor said, "Why don't you come into my office?" She was a slim, Oriental-looking woman, perhaps Bengali, but she spoke without an accent. Her office looked like a smaller, less expensive version of Pat's own. Instead of astronomical pictures the doctor's wall screen was running looped views of some kind of surgery—startlingly, not *human* surgery. The doctor noticed where Pat was looking and, slightly embarrassed, flipped the screen off. "It is the removal of the instrument from the Doc," she apologized. "Not my specialty, of course, but it is simply interesting to see that much of alien anatomy, even if only around the neck and skull. Would you like some tea? No?" Then she got down to business. "As to your—ah, sister," she said, for lack of a better word, "her condition is somewhat improved. The fetal heartbeats are good, but we may have to deliver early. It seems she evidently had some pretty rough-and-ready surgery before she became pregnant, as well as malnutrition and a bad time in general early in the pregnancy."

"That she did," said Pat One.

"Yes. It's a great pity. She's a little older than we usually see for a primapara, but if she'd had decent food and care, she could have a dozen babies without any trouble. She's built for it." Her expression was resentful, as though she were angry at Pat Five for not having taken better care of herself. "Well, as it is, there are some problems. We may have to do a C-section, when it comes to that, but the babies will be better off the longer the pregnancy continues. In any case, the prognosis is reasonably good, but we're watching her carefully. Did you have any specific questions?"

And when Pat couldn't think of any the doctor looked embarrassed again. She pulled a copy of Pat Five's chart out of her desk and displayed it hesitantly. On the margins were two signatures, both in Pat's own hand: *Dr. Pat Adcock (Pat Five)* and *Dr. Pat Adcock (Patrice).* "If you wouldn't mind—just for a souvenir— do you think I could have your autograph as well?"

In the taxi on the way back to the Observatory, her guard mercifully quiet beside her, Pat meditated on her sudden vicarious fame. Was it going to last? How would it affect her life—would she ever be able to have dates again like any normal human being? For that matter, shouldn't she be getting out more now? And—big question!—what was that the doctor had said about having been built to deliver a dozen babies? And if that was true for Pat Five, after all the things the Scarecrows had done to her, how about Pat herself, who shared the identical physiology?

It was a queer, scary-attractive thought. It made something inside her twitch, and she was glad when the cab ride was over and she had to attend to current reality. At the Observatory's reception desk, Janice DuPage was talking to a woman who looked vaguely familiar, and turned out to be Maureen Capobianco, the cruise companion Janice hadn't had. The cruise, however, hadn't been a total success. Capobianco told her they'd had some sort of accident as the ship approached Rio de Janeiro—engine trouble of some kind; they'd lain dead in the water for most of one night, with the antiroll pumps that shifted ballast around not working and the ship heaving uncomfortably in the Atlantic swell and everybody getting sea-sick. They finally limped into Rio twelve hours late. "So we had a day in Rio," Maureen told her, "but then they canceled the rest of the cruise and flew us home."

"And they're all getting some kind of a refund," Janice said bitterly, "but I got stuck for the whole thing, and I didn't even get to go. Pat? Is it all right if I go out to lunch a little early?"

Whether it was all right or not, Pat felt, she had to say it was—having made Janice miss her cruise because of the "emergency." Once in her own office it didn't take long to find that that emergency search for the Scarecrow scout ship had still produced nothing. On the other hand, it had pretty well ruled out any new spacecraft heading in toward Earth at any immediately worrisome distance, too.

She flipped on the news screen to see if anything else was happening, but the only fresh items that came up had mostly to do with things like the thousands of religious fanatics at that moment demonstrating before the White House, demanding that the President do something—which particular something they wanted done varying from group to group, who were, as usual, fighting among themselves.

She was checking the latest summaries from the "Scarecrow Search" site when, belatedly, she remembered to make an announcement in everybody's mail about Pat Five's condition. A moment later Rosaleen peered in.

"But she's all right?" she asked.

"Hope so. What've you got there?"

The old lady was carrying a hard-copy printout. "Nothing useful," she said. "I've been going over what's been published about the artifacts from Starlab. The people at Camp Smolley have started disassembling the green object."

"Disassembling? But I thought they weren't supposed to do that yet."

"Yes, of course," Rosaleen said impatiently. "You thought they would wait until observers could be present, or some such thing. You have always been quite naive, dear Pat. In any case, I'm damned if I can figure out what that thing is supposed to be doing, much less how it does it. I'd love to get my hands on it—"

"Talk to Dan. Maybe he can arrange it," Pat suggested. "You're one of the best instrument people in the world."

"I'm one of the best instrument people in the world who unfortunately also happens to be a Ukrainian national," Rosaleen pointed out.

Technology Analysis, NBI
Agency Eyes Only
Subject: Tachyon transfer

The so-called "matter transporter" which is used for communications and travel at speeds faster than light does not transport any matter. The device analyzes whatever is to be transported and transmits a sort of "blueprint" by means of the radiation called "tachyons" by some American scientists. (Until the arrival of the aliens, tachyons were known only in theory; none had ever been detected.) There at the receiving station an exact copy is made. Even living creatures may be transported in this way.

There are two unanswered questions about this device. 1, how is the object or person to be transmitted analyzed and encoded? 2, what is the copy made from? It was at first conjectured that the receiver took all the necessary elements from its surroundings and used them to construct the copy. But that does not seem to be the case. According to statements of the human and extraterrestrial witnesses, there does not appear to be any depletion of matter in the vicinity of the receiver, no matter how much mass is transmitted.

"You could at least ask."

Rosaleen grunted. "Maybe. Listen, I've been thinking about how that transporter works."

Pat looked puzzled. "I thought we knew that. It doesn't transmit anything material, only a kind of blueprint of whatever's involved—people, machines, whatever, and then the thing gets constructed at the receiver."

"Right. Out of what?"

"What do you mean, out of what?"

"I mean," Rosaleen said patiently, "suppose you want to transmit a human being. The raw materials in the human body are carbon, nitrogen, oxygen, hydrogen, calcium and about fifty other elements. What if some of those elements don't exist at the receiving station?"

"Um," Pat said, seeing the difficulty.

"Right. So I was talking to Pete Schneyman about it. Do you know what a virtual particle is?"

"Sure. Well," Pat qualified, "sort of."

"Yes, well, I don't remember that quantum stuff all that well, either, and it's been a lot longer for me than for you. So I asked Pete, and he began talking about the Big Bang. First there was nothing, then particles began to be generated spontaneously—"

"I do know about the Big Bang," Pat said.

"Of course you do. But that spontaneous generation of particles goes on all the time, only they don't last: they appear and disappear in tiny fractions of picoseconds. But sometimes they don't. Sometimes they last for a long time—like our universe."

Pat frowned, trying to remember those long-ago graduate-school classes. "You think that's how the Scarecrows do it? Making things out of virtual particles?"

"Pete does. Well, at least he thinks that's *possibly* how they do it."

"But the virtual particles always come in pairs,

particles and antiparticles, and they annihilate each other. What would they do with the antiparticles?"

Rosaleen sighed. "Yes," she admitted, "Pete said that was where the problem was. But Pat—I *wish* I could be there and help them figure it all out."

"Um," Pat said, just as the phone rang. She pushed the phone button. "All right, what is it?"

But what it was was a woman in a nurse's uniform. For one scary second Pat thought it was the hospital she had just left, with something terribly wrong with Pat Five.

But it wasn't. Different nurse, different hospital, and the person she was calling about was Janice DuPage. Who had got herself in the way of a drive-by shooters' car—

"Janice has been *shot?*" Pat asked, uncomprehending.

"No, no. She was hit by the car; it was being chased by police and it seems to have run onto the sidewalk where she was walking." The nurse was peering in bewilderment into her own screen, no doubt catching sight of Pat One in the background, and realizing, for the first time, who she was talking to. "She asked us to call."

"Is she—?"

The nurse shook her head. "She'll be all right. She's got, let me see, a fractured right tibia and a good many lacerations and abrasions. She had head injuries, but the skull is intact and it seems to be only a minor concussion. But the woman she was with"—the nurse consulted her screen—"Maureen Capobianco, that is. She's still in surgery. I'm afraid the prognosis for her isn't as good."

CHAPTER THIRTY-SIX

By the time the Docs were successfully debugged—and by the longer time it took for Dr. Marsha Evergood to be convinced that they were fit to travel—it was too late for Dannerman to catch the night courier flight home. When he called Anita Berman to tell her he'd be late the tracker found her waiting for him at the Observatory. She sounded excited. She didn't complain when he told her his resignation hadn't been accepted. "No, I guess it wouldn't be, would it? We've been watching the news— I even caught a glimpse of you, hon. I think. Anyway, I talked to Zigler again and he's got a new idea. He's thinking about doing your life story."

Dannerman grunted in surprise. "*My* life story?"

"And with you and me playing our own parts, if the Bureau will let you. And the Pats, too. Which reminds me, Patrice wants to talk to you."

What Patrice wanted to talk about was some papers she needed to get Pat One to sign, and as long as he was staying over, would he mind picking them up from the morning courier plane and taking them out to Camp Smelly? "Just as a favor from one movie star to another," she coaxed. And Dannerman was too dazzled to refuse.

He was still dazzled when he woke the next morning. But the place where he woke was in one of the VIP suites in the deep-down headquarters of the National Bureau of Investigation, where he had cadged a room from the duty officer. A quick breakfast in the canteen sobered him up: Having his life story made into a major production was an intoxicating fantasy. Now he faced reality. The Bureau would never allow it. And besides—

Well, something seemed to have changed between Anita Berman and himself. He couldn't blame the woman for wanting to be a star, even if it was happening only because she was riding on someone else's coattails. Namely his. It didn't mean that she didn't love him, he told himself. Certainly she'd put up with any number of broken dates and unexplained advances, when there was no advantage at all in it for her except her affection for Dan Dannerman.

But she did seem to be pushing pretty hard for this.

He put it out of his mind and headed for breakfast, where he discovered his luck wasn't all the way out. In the canteen he found an old acquaintance, Sherry Walton, once his contact person when he was with the Scuzzhawks. Over their basically flavorless miso soup and their limp toast Dannerman got a chance to catch up on some of the Bureau gossip. A Chinese submarine had gone lost after being driven off from the Scarecrow landing area, and though it had been found again, the Chinese had shot most of its officers. Activity among the world's terrorist bands seemed to have dwindled to a ten-year low. The deputy director was pressuring the President to denounce the United Nations agreement about sharing the Scarecrow technology. And the Bureau's more sporting staffers were getting up a pool on when the next Scarecrow missile would arrive—a less benign one. "Crap," Dannerman said positively. "If they were going to bomb us, they would have done it already."

"Maybe they didn't have time," Walton offered, pouring herself another cup of weak coffee.

"Of course they had time. They sent the food capsule, and the message with it."

"Ah-ha," she said, nodding, "the message. I was talking to some of the experts about that. Did you notice the second part seemed sort of improvised? Like they'd already sent the capsule and timed the message to arrive when it did, and then they found out we were getting ready to board the Starlab? They could be a really long way away, you know. They can't use that instant-transport gadget of theirs without a terminal, so they probably have to use rockets . . . and what if they've already fired off a rocket, and it just hasn't had time to get here yet?"

A Space Future for India

When India signed Part Three of the Non-Proliferation Treaty it carried out all of its obligations, including scrapping all of its missiles and bases and, like most nations around the world, abandoning its fledgling space program. It now seems that was an error. As recent developments have shown, the conquest of space is now urgent. The nations which have retained some sort of rudimentary space capability—the Europeans, the Americans, the Chinese—are now confronted with unparalleled economic opportunities and, very possibly, grave military responsibilities. As the second most populous nation on Earth, we should join them forthwith.
                        —*Hindustan Times,* New Delhi

There was something new at Camp Smolley. The Bureau guards were still in place, so were the rain-soaked protesters across the road, but now there was also a company of blue-helmeted United Nations troops, fully armed, deployed all around the perimeter, and a detachment of the same at the checkpoints. They were thorough. After they put Dannerman through the electronic search and stripped him of his weapons, *all* his weapons, they had just begun. Two of them opened the little satchel of documents Dannerman had picked up from the courier flight, talking to each other in Spanish—these particular UN troops were Chileans, it seemed. They turned every page, one turning while the other held a lamp that pulsed blue, green, white, orange—looking for some suspicious kind of fluorescence, Dannerman supposed—before they gave them back to him and let him proceed. Two more guards, one Bureau and the other UN, convoyed him to an office and took their posts outside the door.

Pat One was waiting impatiently inside. She wore a quarantine gown and quarantine gloves, and there was a transparent visor hanging loose under her chin. She looked tired. "All this damn *paper,*" she complained when Dannerman handed her the packet. "Couldn't you get us a lawyer that had ever heard about electronics?"

"I got you a lawyer who's going to make you rich," Dannerman pointed out. And while she was signing he looked around. Half a dozen wall screens were displaying interesting things—a news screen by the door, next to it one that showed one of the Docs disassembling a Scarecrow gadget while half a dozen experts stood by, a third screen that showed the other Doc mewing and gesturing as he drew pictures for another group of experts. Pat One looked up. "Those guys are mostly linguists," she said. "We can't talk to the son of a bitch, you know. They're trying to figure out what they call the deep structure of his language, but all he wants to do is draw pictures."

"Can't they get Dopey to help? He's supposed to be a real hotshot with languages."

Pat One shook her head. "He won't help us. He's not even eating, he's so shook up. He won't even tell us what that thing is they're taking apart, he just says the Beloved Leaders are going to punish us all for this."

Dannerman thought uneasily of his breakfast conversation with Sherry Walton. "Did he say how?"

"Not him. Maybe the Doc's trying to tell us something about that, only we can't figure out what. Maybe—" She thought for a moment, then shrugged. "I don't know if I'm supposed to let you see this stuff, but, what the hell, you're a spook yourself, aren't you? Wait a minute. This is Priam Makalanos's office, and I don't know all the systems, but— Here."

She finished playing with the controls on Makalanos's desk, and the pictures on the wall screens changed. They were drawings, done in the Doc's neat draftsmanship. The first one showed the UN Building in New York, then Beijing's Forbidden City, the Arc de Triomphe in Paris, India's Taj Mahal—one after another, the most celebrated sights on Earth. And in all of them there was something that didn't belong there: Scarecrows. Walking around. The pictures weren't photographs, but they were neat and unmistakable drawings of the pumpkin-headed creatures. They were showing Scarecrows present in all the major cities of Earth.

Dannerman frowned at the pictures and shook his head. "It beats me," he said. "It can't mean what it looks like. If there were that many Scarecrows here, we would have seen some trace of them, wouldn't we?"

"It beats me, too," Pat One said somberly. "But I'm sure of one thing. It isn't good."

CHAPTER THIRTY-SEVEN

Lawyer Hecksher got to Pat Adcock's office before Dannerman got there with the signed papers, but he didn't seem to mind waiting. He sat in a corner, carefully rereading his papers and making cryptic pencil-on-pad notes for himself, paying no attention to Pat or his surroundings as she went on with her work.

It wasn't a long wait. Dannerman had made a quick trip from the airport, and as Pat went out to meet him she found him standing at the reception desk, his Anita Berman on his arm, chatting with Janice DuPage, who was standing uncomfortably on her crutches.

Pat frowned. She hadn't expected to see Janice there. Then she remembered why. "I thought you were going to your friend's funeral."

Janice looked put-upon. "It's been postponed. Don't ask me why. Some damn kind of red tape."

"Too bad," Pat said absently, taking the clutch of documents from Dannerman and leaving him there.

Mr. Hecksher took the papers from her courteously and spent a good five minutes checking them over. Then he gave her a cheerful smile. "Looks all right. Signed in all the right places. Now, if you'll excuse me, I'll start getting them served."

"Does that mean somebody will have to fly to China and all?"

"China, no. We'll serve that one on their ambassador here, that's what ambassadors are for. But I think we'd better serve the Europeans in person—oh, I see what's on your mind," he added, beaming at her.

"You're worried about the costs. Don't worry. It'll all be on the bill when we settle."

"And if we don't settle?" Pat asked.

He looked surprised. "But we will. Did you read the texts you signed? Part of the court submission is a request for an estoppal, ordering them to make no changes in the artifacts already on hand because of the risk of damaging the Observatory's property."

Pat frowned. "They're not going to do that, are they?"

"Exactly, my dear! They're going to want this little problem to go away, and the easiest way to do it is to throw money at us. Oh, I think we'll have an offer to settle within a week; the only question is how much we're willing to take. We should discuss that, of course. I was originally thinking of a hundred million dollars, adjusted for current inflation, with an additional royalty on all commercial devices based on the discovered technology, but—" He paused, listening. "What's that?"

Pat had heard it, too, raised voices from outside. She went to the door and looked out. Pete Schneyman was standing there, looking thunderstruck. "We're invaded," he announced. "It's the Feds. They've taken Janice away, and now they want to question all of us."

As soon as Lawyer Heck- sher saw what was going on he patted the nearest Pat on the shoulder, and said benevolently, "I'll take care of this."

But he didn't. He went away with the agent in charge and didn't come back. There were at least a dozen new Bureau agents, tough ones. They were full of questions, though what they were questioning everybody about, exactly, they would not say. The first thing they did was to shuttle everybody in the Observatory up to its top floor, with Bureau agents making sure they stayed there. Phones rang unanswered, computer screens beeped impatiently for inputs that didn't come. The Observatory staff milled in the top-floor file rooms and hallways while they were taken, half a dozen at a time, down to the middle floor for interviews.

When it came Pat's turn she was conducted to her own office, where a middle-aged woman had pre-empted her desk. Now, that was too much! Scowling, she asserted herself: "I protest this unwarranted—"

"Yes, yes," the agent said without patience. "Have a seat. What I want to know is what Janice DuPage has been doing in the last three weeks."

"What happened three weeks ago?" Pat demanded.

"That's when the three weeks I'm asking about began. Just answer the questions, Ms. Adcock. Have you noticed anything unusual about the subject's behavior in that period?"

Pat thought. "You mean, outside of getting run over by a car?"

"Yes."

"Not really. Of course, she was in the hospital for some of that time, and I was away sometimes, too. What do you mean by unusual, anyway?"

"By unusual I mean anything that isn't usual," the agent explained. "Start with Tuesday, the twenty-fourth—"

"Oh, right!" Pat said, enlightenment coming. "That was the day that Scarecrow spacecraft scared us all half to death."

"That day, yes. Well?"

And so it went, day by day. The questions were thorough, but Pat was pretty sure that the agent wasn't getting anything useful—wasn't getting anything from her. that she hadn't already heard from the previous interviewees.

When she was released she was told she could go

home. She didn't, though. She went down to the lower floor, where the people the agents had finished with were congregating in the conference room.

Then Dannerman came in, looking worried. "I came as soon as I got your call," he told Pat One. "And I talked to Jilly Hohman—she's the agent in charge here."

"So what's it all about?" Pat One demanded.

He looked even more worried. "It's that friend of Janice's. They did a routine autopsy on her . . . and they found a bug."

"A bug? In Janice's friend? But—but she was never out in space," said Pat, and Dannerman nodded somberly.

"That's the problem," he said. "She never was."

CHAPTER THIRTY-EIGHT

The news about the bug in the cruise passenger's head caught Hilda Morrisey on the wing. She was halfway to Arlington. For a moment she thought of pulling rank, ordering the pilot to take her back to the scene of this unwelcome new glitch in New York. Reason prevailed. The New York Bureau people were dealing with it, and most of them had recently been her own people. She could leave that to them. Anyway, she could get a better picture at headquarters.

The picture refused to come clear. When all the questioning was done, nobody at the Dannerman Astrophysical Observatory had any useful information about the late Maureen Capobianco. Neither did any of her friends and family once the Bureau had tracked them down. Nor did the X rays find a bug in any of them. It wasn't until they got a passenger list from the operators of her cruise ship that the Bureau struck pay dirt.

That was a break. A checker recognized two of the names on the list as his own neighbors. When the Bureau's people descended on them they were startled but cooperative . . . and the X rays told the story. They, too, were bugged. Both of them. So, when they were tracked down, were the members of a bridge club from Baltimore who had treated themselves to the cruise, all twenty-six of them. So was a barman from the cruise ship, furloughed to his mother's home in the District itself.

So was every last one they could find of the ship's 826 passengers and 651 crew members.

That wasn't all. Hilda Morrisey got the news first and brought it to the deputy director. "There were these six Ecuadorians from a fishing boat that had been near the splash site. They had it, too."

"Shit," Marcus Pell said dismally. "It's an epidemic. We should have anticipated this, Hilda; it's what the Doc was trying to tell us, with those pictures."

"I guess we thought he meant actual Scarecrows were coming."

"I guess we did." He sighed. "All right. Take off for Camp Smelly, Hilda. See if you can get anything out of that damn Dopey."

She stood up to go, then turned. Pell had not seemed all that surprised to hear about the Ecuadorians. "Is there anything else?"

He hesitated, then shrugged. "Keep it under your hat, but yes. We got a report from an asset in Vietnam. The Chinese are rounding up the whole crew of that submarine that went missing. The one where they executed the captain and the engineering officer?" He grimaced. "You know how they execute criminals, one bullet in the back of the neck—so the organs won't be spoiled for transplant. Well, the shot hit a bug."

"Jesus." A thought struck her. "I thought we had our own asset in the Chinese Navy, how come we had to get this from the Viets?"

"They shot our asset, too."

In the back of Brigadier Hilda Morrisey's mind she had been thinking of this as a good time for another recreational evening—a long soak, a light meal, the new dress with the skirt slits that made the best of her still very good legs, the address of a new bar that was highly recommended for good-looking men. It wasn't much to ask. She was fully entitled to it because, for God's sake, she was *human*.

But here she was at Camp Smolley again, and what was in the back of Brigadier Morrisey's mind stayed where it was. The camp was in an uproar. Daisy Fennell was there, giving Colonel Makalanos a hard time for imagined failings at getting more information out of the Docs. All three of the freaks were back at the biowar station, and security precautions were doubled. There was an armed guard at the door of the interrogation room, where the two Docs were vociferously mewing at Dopey. Whatever they were saying, they seemed to think it was urgent, but the little turkey was adamantly refusing to respond, his cat eyes squeezed shut, his little paws thrust firmly into that coppery belly bag. In a corner of the room Dannerman was having an agitated, low-voiced conversation with a woman; it wasn't until Hilda recognized the woman as Anita Berman that she knew which Dannerman it was. The linguistics team was on hand, doing their best to get a clue as to the Docs' language, but if they were making any progress at all, Hilda couldn't see how. It didn't seem that way to her.

Her first target was Dannerman. As she approached, Anita Berman was in the process of jumping up and delivering a final, scathing remark: "I don't care about the money, I don't care about the part, what I care about is getting you out of this crazy life you're leading!" She flounced away, leaving Dannerman peering after her. The funny thing was, he was actually looking pleased.

"What's that all about?" Hilda asked.

He shook his head. "Something I was worried about, that's all. Listen, is it true about all these bugs being found?"

"Damn straight it's true, but that isn't what I wanted to ask you. Have you had a chance to talk to Dopey about that drawing the Doc made?"

The fond smile evaporated from his face. "Uh, yes,"

he said reluctantly. "He said—well, he didn't say anything for *sure,* only maybe—"

"Damn you! Maybe what?"

He swallowed. "He said he didn't know anything
really, but, after all, the Horch captured everything the
Scarecrows had on that planet. Including the transit
machine—the one that made copies of us? So if they
wanted more copies of me, or anything else, there
wouldn't be anything in the world that could stop
them."

There was a goddam *limit,*
Hilda Morrisey told herself, to the number of things she
should have to worry about at one time. How many
crazinesses were going to be thrown at her? She sat
down, trying to collect her thoughts. Merla Tepp
appeared from nowhere, silently bearing a cup of coffee, and when Hilda looked at the woman's face there
was one more annoyance staring at her. The woman
had the expression of someone more put-upon than was
bearable—even more put-upon than Hilda herself,
though perhaps for different reasons. (What was it with
Tepp? It couldn't be just the fact that she loathed the
aliens. Was there some personal problem? And if there
was, who cared?) Hilda put her aide's problems out of
her mind and concentrated on what was going on.

Hilda Morrisey had presided at plenty of interrogations
in her career, but never one like this. This time the subjects were doing their best to spill every last thing they
knew. In fact, they were doing it nonstop, their mewing
voices sometimes plaintive, sometimes yowling mad, but
what they were carrying on about no one could say.

It was the translator who was the problem. Dopey
was not cooperating. Occasionally he mewed irritably
back at the Docs, mostly he merely sat huddled silently
on his perch, eyes closed in suffering, tail plume dull

and dejected. From where the observers sat on the other side of the one-way glass they could see Patrice, in the interrogation room with the subjects, where she had been for the last hour. She was expostulating with Dopey, but he was ignoring her as well.

Patrice sighed and came out. "I need a break," she said, looking at the linguistics team as they hovered over their frequency analyzers and screens. "You guys getting anything?" she asked.

The head of the team shook her head. "Can't tell." *Well,* Hilda thought, *theirs was a pretty forlorn hope to begin with.* A language was not like a cipher, and all the computers in the world were not likely to solve the translation problem.

While, infuriatingly, the finest translation system the world had ever known was sulking on his perch not a dozen meters away, and refusing to help. "If we could just get a few sentences that were in both languages to match up, we might make a start," the woman said pensively. "Like the Rosetta Stone, you know."

"Damn the Rosetta Stone and damn that goddam freak," Daisy Fennell said. "Don't we have any way to make the little bastard cooperate?"

Patrice Adcock looked almost amused. "What would you suggest? Threaten his life, maybe? But he isn't worrying about dying. He thinks he'd get brownie points with the Scarecrows if he died doing something in their service—like refusing to translate for the Docs."

"Who said anything about dying? He can feel pain, can't he?"

"Oh, no," Patrice said, shaking her head. "Put that idea right out of your mind. I've told you. He's too fragile for us to beat it out of him. You know we actually killed a Dopey, back when we were captives. Didn't take much, either. Martín Delasquez fell on him, and he died." She thought for a moment, then added,

"That time it seemed not to have mattered particularly, because another Dopey popped up right away. But now—"

> **Technology Analysis, NBI**
> **Agency Eyes Only**
> **Subject: "Virtual energy" and tachyon**
> **transport**
>
> According to quantum theory there is no such thing as a "vacuum" anywhere in the universe. Everywhere—at the heart of a star, on a planet like the Earth, even in the great "voids" between clusters of galaxies—every volume of space, however tiny, is constantly seething with a boil of "virtual" sub-atomic particles, particles which appear spontaneously, interact with others, are mutually destroyed by canceling each other's charges out and disappear—so rapidly that they are impossible to detect.
>
> But—theory suggests—they don't always disappear. In fact, the birth of the universe in the "Big Bang" can be best understood as a sudden explosion of such particles which somehow are not annihilated, but survive, and increase—and, indeed, become everything we see in the vast universe around us.
>
> Is it possible to reproduce this process artificially? If so, can the generated particles be the ones needed to create particular atoms? And, if this is also so, can this be the way the Scarecrows' tachyon transporter builds the raw materials to make its copies?

Hilda knew the answer to that. Now they had only the one Dopey, with no magical mystery transporter box to create another if they wasted this one. Hilda appreciated the difficulties of the situation. She appreciated, too, the fact that Vice Deputy Director Daisy Fennell was here to carry the can. That was a break. If anyone was going to be associated with a failed enterprise, she didn't want it to be herself.

She became aware that her aide was clutching the back of her chair. "What is it, Tepp?"

The woman looked even more haggard than usual, her face strained, her demeanor peculiar—in fact, Hilda thought, Tepp had been acting even more than ordinarily strange ever since they got there. "Nothing, ma'am," she said thickly.

Hilda glared at her. "Nothing, my ass. Are you going to puke again?"

Tepp seemed frightened. "Oh, no, ma'am, I don't think so. But that smell—"

Hilda sighed, resigned. The time had come. She said crisply, "You're relieved. Get out of here. Go back to Arlington for reassignment."

"Ma'am!"

"Go!" Hilda ordered, and turned her back on her former aide. Not for long. When she heard a pathetic throat-clearing from behind her, she turned back, now angry. "You still here?"

Tepp held her ground. "Yes, ma'am. I'm going, ma'am, but there's one thing—"

"For Christ's sake, what now?"

"It's my aunt. I promised I'd come and see her tonight, and I didn't get a chance to call her before we left the headquarters. She's sick. If I could just have permission to use a phone for a minute—"

Hilda shrugged. It wasn't exactly giving permission, but it wasn't a flat rejection, either. As Tepp hurriedly left the little viewing room Hilda didn't even look after her. Merla Tepp was now a dead issue.

She turned to Patrice Adcock. "Didn't Dopey say anything at all when you told him about all the bugs?"

"He was delighted to hear about it," Patrice said sourly. "He asked me half a dozen times if we were sure it was the same kind of bug I had. The Docs were doing their best to ask him what was going on. He mewed something at them, but then he paid no attention to them at all. Then he said to me, 'You'll see,' and went back to not talking. I took that as a threat. I think—"

"Wait a minute," Makalanos said suddenly. He turned to the linguistics crew. "Did you get that? See if you can check what he said to the Docs right then, the first thing after Dr. Adcock told him about the bug."

"Hey," said the linguist, coming alive. "Good point! It might help."

And indeed it might have, but not right then. That was when the interrogation came to an abrupt halt, and it was Merla Tepp who halted it.

CHAPTER THIRTY-NINE

Outside the zoo cage Merla Tepp took a deep breath, forcing herself to be calm. She wasn't surprised at what had happened. The brigadier had been on the point of firing her often enough before, but she couldn't help wishing it had happened just a little later. She was going to miss the job. She would even miss Hilda Morrisey herself, a wicked woman, certainly, but in some ways an admirable one—

There was no use thinking that way. She knew what she had to do.

She turned her back on the armed guard, who had been looking at her with some concern, and marched to the office of Lieutenant Colonel Makalanos. His assistant, transmitting copies of the Doc's latest drawings to headquarters, looked up in surprise. "Out," Merla ordered. "I have to make a secure call."

The man got up to leave, looking baffled but obedient, and Merla sat before his screen. When she had terminated the assistant's transmission she sat for a moment, moving her lips in silent prayer.

Then she dialed the number in Roanoke, Virginia, and spoke to the placid, gray-haired lady whose face appeared on the screen. "Aunt Billie? I'm really upset. Brigadier Morrisey has fired me as her aide, and I don't know what to do."

The woman looked concerned, though not particularly surprised. She tsk-tsked sympathetically. "That's too bad, dear. I know how you must feel. Is there any chance that she'll change her mind?"

"I don't think so."

"What a pity," the woman said vaguely. She paused, shaking her head in regret. Then she came to a decision. She said, "I'm sorry if I sound a little upset. It's one of my bad days, you see. The left knee and both elbows again—I'm afraid I'll have to have the surgery very soon now."

Tepp caught her breath. "The knee and the two elbows? When?"

"Oh, very soon. As soon as possible, in fact. I wish it weren't necessary, but there's no sense in putting it off any longer, is there?" She was silent for a moment, then, briskly, "I'm afraid I must go now, dear. I'll pray for you."

Tepp terminated the connection and sat for a moment, breathing deeply. Then she stood up and left the office. "Thanks," she said to the assistant, and headed back for the cage. The outside guard had gone back to his daydreaming but he woke up quickly when Tepp ordered: "Give me your weapon."

"Do what? But I can't—"

"It's Brigadier Morrisey's order," she said, taking it from him and checking the safety. "Here, you can ask her yourself." And she pushed the door open.

Inside Hilda Morrisey turned to glare at her. "Now what the hell do you want, Tepp?" she demanded, and then saw the gun.

The guard, suddenly alert, reached for the weapon. Merla Tepp was faster than he was. She stepped back and put a quick round into his right thigh; the man screeched like an owl and collapsed as she set the weapon to full automatic and, sobbing aloud at last, sprayed Hilda and those devil-inspired alien monsters from Hell. She got off half a hundred rounds before she realized that Lieutenant Colonel Makalanos had a gun of his own and he had drawn it.

Too late she turned toward him. When his first shot hit her right in the breastbone it was like being struck with a leaden baseball bat, and that was the last Merla Tepp knew of anything at all in this life.

CHAPTER FORTY

For Daisy Fennell it was the worst night of her long career with the Bureau, and it went on forever. Dr. ben Jayya dithered uselessly over the casualties, protesting that he was a *research* M.D., not a caregiver, but someone had already called the paramedics.

They were there in five minutes, three cars of them, screeching past the startled UN guards with their siren going. It took them a lot longer than that, though, to figure out what to do once they got there. The leg of the wounded guard was all in a day's work for them. So was the lobe of Dannerman's ear, which he had nearly lost to Tepp's spray of fire. For Hilda Morrisey the big problem was stopping the bleeding from her throat, and getting her into one of the ambulances on the very faint chance that she would still be alive when she got to the emergency room.

And there was nothing at all to be done for either Tepp herself or for the one of the Docs who now lay doubled-over on the floor and exuding great amounts of a pinkish fluid, beyond doubt well and truly dead.

It was the other two extraterrestrials that were the problem. Tepp's shot had caught Dopey in his great, colorful fantail. And, though he was complaining bitterly about the agony he was suffering, he had allowed Camp Smolley's medics to dress the wound as best they could. The surviving Doc was another matter. He had taken three of Tepp's rounds. Two were in his left major arm and, though whatever he had for a tibia had been shattered, those wounds didn't seem immediately life-threatening. It was the one that had struck his chest that worried the medics. The bullet was still in there, and he was mewing softly in pain as he lay flat on his back on the floor, with Pat Adcock—Pat One—comfortingly holding one of his lesser paws.

The head medic looked up from where he was bent over the golem's torso, his face grayish. "That bullet has to come out," he informed Daisy Fennell. "Do you authorize us to do it?"

Fennell hesitated, wishing she could buck that question to somebody higher up, like the deputy director. She couldn't. She temporized. "Do you know what you're doing?"

Pat Adcock spoke up. "Of course they don't know what they're doing," she said scornfully. "Why don't you get that Walter Reed doctor out here? She's the only one who knows anything at all about Doc Anatomy."

"Dr. Evergood? But all she did was take a bug out—"

"Do you have any better ideas?"

And, of course, she didn't. When they got Dr. Marsha Evergood she looked tousled and sleepy and pretty damn mad. "Have you stopped the bleeding?" she demanded. "Applied broad-spectrum antibiotics? All right, then get him over to Walter Reed right away; I'll meet you there."

"We thought maybe you might want to come out here," Daisy offered, aware she was sounding uncharacteristically humble.

"Think that one over again, lady. Bring the dead one along, too; I'll use the cadaver for a quick anatomy course. *Now.*"

No matter how much Daisy Fennell tried to hurry him along, Dr. ben Jayya was being a pain in the ass. No laboratory specimen, he was insisting firmly, should ever be transported anywhere until it was stabilized, preferably by soaking it in formaldehyde first, Fennell overfirmed him. "Shut up," she said, and turned her back on the biologist to beckon to Colonel Makalanos.

"Get some ice," she ordered. "Pack him up and let's get the two of them the hell out of here."

The trouble with that was that the medevac chopper was barely able to cope with the weight of the two extraterrestrials, one in his plastic body bag filled with ice cubes, the other with the head medic standing by with spare compresses if needed on the way. Daisy and the Dopey had to wait for another helicopter to be summoned.

Reverend Portman Denies Responsibility

At the headquarters of the Christian League Against Blasphemy, their spokesman, the Reverend Alec Portman, declined to be interviewed but issued this prepared statement:

"We deplore the actions at Camp Smolley. If it is true, as has been alleged, that the woman who committed these vile crimes was associated with some members of our organization, she has done our cause no good. It is our belief that these alleged creatures from space are indeed evil, and may be incarnations of the Devil. However, we are nonviolent. We accept no responsibility for these alleged acts. If these creatures had been returned to the Hell they came from, as has been in our prayers ever since they arrived, none of this need have happened."

—*The New York Times*

When she finally got to Walter Reed the two Docs lay side by side in the operating room. Evergood had already slashed the corpse's torso open and an assistant was severing ribs—what looked like ribs, anyway—with a power bone saw.

It was more than Daisy Fennell wanted to endure. She fled. In the nearest ladies' room she locked herself in a cubicle and sat. She was breathing hard, and most of her thoughts were not about the surgery going on a few dozen meters away.

The subject uppermost in Vice Deputy Fennell's mind was her career, and whether she was still going to have one by this time the next day.

Of course, the whole damn screwup was Hilda Morrisey's fault. Hilda was the one who had taken this Merla Tepp on as her aide and thus given the woman access to biowar.

But Hilda was not in a condition to be put on trial, at least for now, and neither was the Tepp woman. Permanently. That wasn't Fennell's doing; she wasn't the one who shot Tepp dead.

But she was the senior officer present, and so she knew who the responsibility would belong to. She shuddered.

It was bad, but it would get a lot worse if the deputy director arrived and caught her screwing off in the crapper. She stood up, marched to the washstand, splashed water on her face, looked at herself in the mirror, shuddered again and resolutely went back to the operating room.

To her surprise, she was allowed inside, but not before one of the other doctors stopped her with orders to scrub up and put on a surgical mask. When Daisy protested he snapped, "Right, the Docs didn't bother with asepsis, but we're going to do it Dr. Evergood's way. Use that washstand, and plenty of soap."

The Docs hadn't bothered with anesthesia, either, and there wasn't anything Dr. Evergood could do about that; she didn't dare try putting her patient out, or even numbing the immediate vicinity of the wound. The patient seemed to accept that. The mewing stopped. He lay immobile, eyes closed, and the only sign that he might be feeling pain was the trembling of his lesser arms while Evergood cautiously widened the entrance wound and probed for the bullet. It took her a while to navigate through the unfamiliar architecture of the Doc's muscles and blood vessels, but when she finally extracted the round she breathed a sigh of relief. She doused the whole area with broad-spectrum antibiotics and stood up wearily, regarding her patient.

Who opened his eyes and gazed at her for a moment, then turned to Pat One, miming writing something with his lesser arms.

"He wants to draw some more pictures," Pat guessed. "Can I let him?"

Evergood shrugged. "Why not? Make sure you give him clean paper and a clean pen, and don't let him touch the dressing. Fennell? Let's go talk."

Daisy Fennell was glad enough to get out of there; she hadn't been willing to leave while the operation was going on, but the smell of the Doc was getting to her. They found the deputy director outside, snapping orders to his portable screen in Colonel Makalanos's office, but he switched it off when he saw them.

Evergood got right to the point. "The bullet's out, I've stopped the bleeding and now we have to watch for infection. I'm hoping there won't be any. If there are any disease organisms around, they're probably terrestrial ones, and the antibiotics should deal with them. Of course, we'll have to do something about that arm."

"Thanks," he said, and remembered to add, "A fine job, Dr. Evergood."

It was a dismissal, and the surgeon took it that way. Then he turned to Daisy Fennell.

"Jesus, Daisy," he remarked. "You let things go

pretty sour, didn't you? Tepp dead, Morrisey close to it. The Dopey and one of the Docs wounded—and we can't get the other one to care for them, because he's dead, too. Well. Let's get the facts. We'll have to have a court of inquiry, but for now, start talking."

CHAPTER FORTY-ONE

The bodies had been removed and the blood mopped up—carefully sponged up with sterile plastic pads, actually, at least the thin, pink stuff that had come out of the Docs, because Dr. ben Jayya demanded every atom of it for his endless lab work. Dan Dannerman, on his second wakeup pill, finally got a chance to reassure Anita Berman. When she saw his bandaged head she gasped in shock. He did his best to reassure her. "No, no, I'm fine. It's nothing. Just my ear." And had to explain that it was just a little piece that was missing. Reattach it? Well, the Bureau surgeon had talked about that when he got there, he admitted, except that by then they couldn't find enough of it to bother with. Which produced another yelp of horror. "Honestly, it doesn't even hurt," he said, and tried to change the subject. "Have you talked to the people at the Observatory? How are things?"

Things at the Observatory were crazy. Rosaleen Artzybachova was upset; did Dannerman know that the Doc that got killed was the one that had saved her life? And was he sure that Patrice and Pat One were all right? And when—pleadingly—were they going to get out of this lousy place?

"As soon as I can," he promised. "Maybe tomorrow. I don't know. There's doing to be a court of inquiry and they want me to stick around for that. Trouble? No. I'm not in trouble. Nobody thinks I'm to blame; it's Daisy Fennell that's in trouble here. But I have to testify." He cast about for something more cheerful to say, and found it. He grinned at her. "Listen, one good thing. You wanted to know how you could tell us apart? That won't be a problem anymore. I'm Lop-Ear Dannerman now."

She was silent for a moment, thinking about that. Then she sighed. "All right, hon. Tell me one thing. Have they found out why she did it?"

That was what the whole Bureau was working on at that moment, and their investigation had begun to bear fruit. Tepp's phone call was easily traced, and, since it had been made from a Bureau secure phone, it had been recorded. The receiving party was Mrs. Willa Tepp Borglund, widow lady living by herself in a little house near Roanoke, Virginia; and when the recording was played the conversation was brief and agitated. The actual words between Tepp and her Aunt Billie were trivial enough, but the tones were not. There was an undercurrent of strain and excitement that didn't match the words actually spoken. Well, it was obvious enough to Daisy Fennell. They were talking in code, and the old lady had given her niece the order.

Obvious enough—but too late to be much use.

When the Bureau raided the house of Mrs. Willa Tepp Borglund they found an armory of weapons and an iron-haired, iron-willed old lady who spoke not to them but to her God, praying in whispers every waking moment.

They checked her phones, of course, and found calls to places all over the country. Bureau agents in Wichita and Brooklyn and St. Petersburg and Spokane were pulled away from their smugglers and tax evaders and assembled into raiding parties—two dozen of them in all. It was a massive effort, typical of the wonders the Bureau could accomplish when it put its collective mind to a task.

Of course, it, too, came a little late.

> The keys to deciding whether the universe would ever slow down and recollapse were the Hubble constant—the rate at which the universe was presently expanding—and the associated value called "q-zero," or the rate at which that expansion was slowing down.
>
> The best way to measure the Hubble constant was by studying the most distant observable type 1a supernovae, which, like the Cepheids formerly studied in the same way, could all be assumed to have the same intrinsic brightness, so the dimmer they seemed, the farther they were. The big advantage the supernovae had over the Cepheids was that they were about a million times as bright. Which meant they could be seen, and measured, about a million times as far away; and once you used that fact to estimate their intrinsic brightness and thus their distance, and contrasted that distance with what *should* be their distance as indicated by the redshift of their light, why then you could tell what the q-zero function said about whether the universe's expansion was slowing down.
>
> There were other things you could measure as well, but they all seemed to give the same answer. The universe was not going to recollapse at all.... .
>
> So what was it that the Horch and the Scarecrows knew that Earthly astronomers hadn't even guessed?

When Dannerman got to see the deputy director, Pell flicked his screen on and fiddled with the pad until it displayed a picture of a dark-skinned man in a fringed leather jacket, stubbornly silent while he was being questioned by Bureau agents. "I thought you'd like to see," he said grimly. "This guy is one of Willa Borglund's phone chums, runs a souvenir shop in Navajo country. According to his phone records he has been making calls to a Chinese trade commission member at his home. Faxes, mostly, and they're all naturally encoded. But what it looks like to me," he said, sounding somber, "is that the damn nuts are all in touch with each other."

"So there really was a leak in the Bureau," Fennell breathed.

"Right. And her name was Merla Tepp."

If it was true that Merla Tepp was blatting out Bureau secrets to half the world, it explained a lot—the way the Ukrainian nut cult knew exactly what the plans were for Rosaleen Artzybachova, for instance; the way the protesters always knew where to go. But it also meant that almost everything the Bureau had done since Merla Tepp arrived for duty, or at least everything that Hilda Morrissey might have known about and let her aide in on, was now compromised. And that meant—

That meant some long, hard weeks or months of cleanup and damage control. All of the Bureau's encryption programs would have to be changed. Every field operation would have to double-check personnel and contacts to see how far the leak had spread. Some good, hard administrative work was called for—the very thing that Vice Deputy Director Daisy Fennell was good at. As she went looking for Marcus Pell she was planning in her mind the series of orders and directives that would have to go out, this minute. . . .

The deputy director didn't seem to want to hear. He was leaning over an assortment of scraps of paper littering Colonel Makalanos's desk, Adcock and Dannerman by his side. Even Dopey was in the room, waddling triumphantly around with the great bandage on his tail hardly hiding its blazing colors. Pell raised a hand to cut off what Daisy Fennell had to say. "Look at this," he said heavily.

There were a dozen of the sheets of paper, arranged

in some sort of order. The first showed a recognizable drawing of the food ship. The second showed the ship again, but this time it was attached to a larger metal capsule. The third showed the capsule detaching itself, underwater, while the food container floated on the surface..The fourth showed that larger capsule with five or six others just like it all around it. The fifth showed one of the larger capsules drawn tiny in one corner, with a balloon encircling a host of aliens—a Dopey, several Docs, but three or four other species Fennell had never seen before.

She looked up, puzzled. "I *thought* there should have been more to that food ship!" Dannerman was grumbling, while Pat Adcock explained:

"Those other creatures are other races that work for the Scarecrows. The ones that look a little bit like Bashful? I think they're warriors."

"Warriors?" Fennell rocked back on her heels, regarding the deputy director. "Does all this mean what I think it means?"

"What I think it means," Pell said heavily, "is that some of their terminals came to Earth along with the food, and now they're making more of them—underwater, where we're going to have a hard time finding them." He shook his head. "We didn't understand those other drawings he made for us, did we? He wasn't thinking about the bugs in those people from the ships. He was trying to tell us that the Scarecrows had their people on Earth already, all around us."

ABOUT THE AUTHOR

A multiple Hugo and Nebula Award–winning author, Frederik Pohl has done just about everything one can do in the science-fiction field. His most famous work is undoubtedly the novel *Gateway,* which won the Hugo, Nebula, and John W. Campbell Memorial Awards for Best SF novel. *Man Plus* won the Nebula Award. His mature work is marked by a serious intellectual agenda and strongly held sociopolitical beliefs, without sacrificing narrative drive. In addition to his successful solo fiction, Pohl has collaborated successfully with a variety of writers, including C. M. Kornbluth and Jack Williamson. A Pohl/Kornbluth collaboration, *The Space Merchants,* is a longtime classic of satiric science fiction. *The Starchild Trilogy* with Williamson is one of the more notable collaborations in the field. Pohl has been a magazine editor in the field since he was very young, piloting *Worlds of If* to three successive Hugos for Best Magazine. He also has edited original-story anthologies, including the early and notable *Star* series of the early 1950s. He has at various times been a literary agent, an editor of lines of science fiction books, and a president of the Science Fiction Writers of America. For a number of years he has been active in the World SF movement. He and his wife, Elizabeth Anne Hull, a prominent academic active in the Science Fiction Research Association, live outside Chicago, Illinois.